AUTUMN REIGNS

The Autumn Series
Book Two

A novel by E.S. Maria

ISBN-13: 978-0-9924772-0-2

Cover art by Kellie Dennis at Book Cover by Design
www.bookcoverbydesign.co.uk

TABLE OF CONTENTS

Dedication...04
Prologue...05
Chapter 1..09
Chapter 2..12
Chapter 3..17
Chapter 4..23
Chapter 5..31
Chapter 6..34
Chapter 7..47
Chapter 8..57
Chapter 9..65
Chapter 10...67
Chapter 11...79
Chapter 12...91
Chapter 13...98
Chapter 14..110
Chapter 15..120
Chapter 16..122
Chapter 17..130
Chapter 18..141
Chapter 19..167
Chapter 20..201
Chapter 21..224
Chapter 22..240
Chapter 23..268
Chapter 24..285
Chapter 25..322
Chapter 26..336
Epilogue..344
Autumn Reigns Playlist..347
Acknowledgments...348
About the Author..350

DEDICATION

This is round two, and this is for you ...

because I love you greater than the universe.

PROLOGUE

Magnus

> *I fucked up.*
> As I watch the woman I've fallen so hard for walk away from my life, I know how much I royally fucked up. I call out for her, begging her to listen so I can explain the truth, promising anything and everything, just to stop her from walking away, and have her run back in my arms where she belongs. But she refuses to turn around ... not even once. Then I see her hailing a cab.
> *She's really leaving me.*
> I try to give a chase, but she's already getting into the cab before I can reach her. I slam my hand on the door of the cab, calling out for her to come out, not caring about the glares I'm getting from the onlookers. That's when she turns and stares at me ... unblinking, and I am taken aback by the emptiness in her eyes ... the same green eyes that looked up at me adoringly no more than an hour ago are now devoid of any emotion.
> That's when I realize she's gone.
> *My Isabelle is gone.*
> I take a step back, letting the cab drive off, finding it harder to breathe as our distance increases. At this moment, I realize how the autumn air feels colder on my face. So I reach up, and I feel the wetness from the tears I had never expected I'd shed. I shake my head in grief, hoping an impossible hope that this is just a nightmare I should be waking up to. I'm not even an emotional person. Never had been. Yes, I've suffered from losses before. But nothing like this ... *nothing ... like ... this...*
> Isabelle didn't give me a chance to explain. But who can blame her? How much of that conversation did she hear? What she might have heard from that room with Martine, may not even be the whole truth. But it doesn't matter. She heard what she thought she needed to hear.
> *She left me, and I deserve it.*
> It shouldn't have been like this. I should've come clean from the beginning. But I was a coward. I was too fucking afraid for her to find out the real reason why I sought her in the first place, because there was a chance that I would lose her.

And now it's too late. She might never know how *everything* changed, the moment our fingers first touched, or how she improved me in ways that are impossible to explain.

Isabelle feels betrayed, and it's entirely my fault.

But I will make it up with her. I heard what she said, and I understand why she never wants to see me again. But I'm not the type who gives up easily. Never had been. I love Isabelle Morrison. I love Autumn Bridges. Fuck it, I just love *her*. And I won't stop until she realizes how much I do. And when that time comes and she's back in my arms, I will make sure to tell her every single day how much I love her. I will kiss her sweet-tasting lips over and over again, and I will reassure her that everything will be okay from now on, because I will make damned sure of it.

Cooper Thornton.

The motherfucker I knocked out earlier for chasing after Isabelle is *the* Cooper Thornton; the same person I swore to protect her from. He's found her here, in New York ... in Mother's fundraiser, of all places. It doesn't matter if Isabelle kept the identity of her abuser. In her mind, her reason was sound ... she wanted to protect me. And who was I protecting when I didn't even come clean in the first place?

I am a selfish son of a bitch.

I swore to her that I'd keep her safe, and yet I managed to put her and Ethan's life in even more danger. Isabelle must've been looking for me, desperate for help, and all I managed to do was break her heart. How could I fail her so monumentally?

But it's not too late yet. I have to redeem myself in Isabelle's eyes, and I'll start tonight.

I walk with a whole sense of purpose, back to where I left Cooper Thornton unconscious and hopefully bleeding.

I'm going to kill that son of a bitch!

He's still at the same spot where I left him, passed out, with Martine trying to help him get up.

"Martine! Step away from him and leave us," I command in a voice that promises a bad consequence, if not heeded.

Martine stands up, looking stricken. "Magnus, why did you knock this guy out? Who is he?"

"Listen to me because I'm not going to repeat myself. Martine, our business partnership is over. I will help you find another investor, but I am out. Now step away from him and leave us alone. If you don't, our friendship will be thrown out of the window as well. So if you still value our friendship, leave now, and make sure no one comes in here. Do you understand?"

Martine's eyes are almost as wide as her gaping mouth. But she manages to nod in understanding and follows my instructions. Once the hallway is clear, I look down at the piece of shit on the floor and hear him coming to. As soon as I see him moving, I grab him by his coat lapels and forcefully haul him up against the wall.

"What the fuck? Why'd you punch me, you asshole? Do you know who I am? I can ruin you," he groans out, grabbing his now broken nose. It delights me to see him hurt and bleeding like this.

"You're a mouthy piece of shit, aren't you? I know who you are, Cooper Thornton, and I know about what you did to that woman you were chasing." I slam him back on the wall, making him grimace in pain. He tries to break free, but I'm bigger and stronger. I push my forearm against his throat, holding him forcefully until he's struggling to catch his own breath.

"Let ... go ... of ... me! Who ... are ... you?" he gurgles out.

"I'm someone who promises to end your sad life if you don't stay away from that woman. And I will personally make sure that you and your family will regret it for the rest of your lives! Why are you here? Answer me!" I roar out at him, my eyes like razor blades as I stare him down.

I can see the fear emanating from Cooper's eyes, but I also see a glimpse of recognition. "Wait, I know who you are. Okay, okay, just let me go, and I'll tell you everything!" I ease my arm away, and Cooper starts to breathe in deeply while bending down, placing his hands on his knees for support. I watch on with contempt, using all of my self-control not to end him right here.

He raises his head at me. "I'm ... I'm here for her," he says in-between gulps of air, "because her father told us that you reneged on the acquisition. Then one of my friends saw a picture of you and Autumn together in some trashy gossip blog. The blogger didn't know who she was, but I do. Doesn't take a fucking genius to realize she must be here in New York, then ... if she's with you. So ... so I got myself an invitation here since there's a good chance she'll be here. Why do you care about Autumn, anyway? Sure, she is one hot piece of ass, but—"

I didn't let him finish. I force him downwards so my knee can make contact with his chest instead, watching with satisfaction as he slumps back on the floor.

Nobody can talk about Isabelle like that.

And Cooper cannot know that she had changed her name either.

"I will deal with Michael Bridges myself. And as for you," I push Cooper back up against the wall again with my hand gripped around his neck, "if I see you *anywhere* near Autumn, I will not show you the same mercy I'm giving you right now. I know what you did to her, you piece of shit. If it were up to me, you would be locked in jail, being someone else's bitch. *I* can make that happen, you hear me? So play nice and stay away from her. Do. You. Understand?" I hear Cooper groaning, but he doesn't answer. So with my hand still wrapped around his neck, I pull him off the wall and push him against it with enough force to make him cry out.

"Answer me, motherfucker!"

"Yes … yes … I'll stay away." His eyes are glistening, like he has tears in his eyes. It makes the corners of my mouth twitch up, seeing this dog shit cry. I just hope I put the fear of God in him that he'll never seek Isabelle and lay a hand on her ever again.

"Oh, and by the way …" And in one sweeping move, I reintroduce Cooper's head with my fist, leaving him passed out cold on the floor once again.

Placated, I pull out my phone. I have to call Isabelle to tell her I'm taking care of everything, to try to convince her to let me explain. And if she can't be convinced right now, I just need to know that she's safe. It takes a lot out of me not to chase after her. But I know that I need to give her some space, at least for the time being … but not forever. No way. She might not see it now, but she will never be anyone else's but mine. And if it takes me my whole lifetime to convince her, then, so be it.

She doesn't answer my call, nor does she reply to my text message. Exhaling a deep breath, I decide on another approach. I'm not fucking giving up on her. I just need to get Cooper sorted first. I press the Contacts button to search for a specific name. I need to call in a big favor from a very trusted friend. I just hope he'll agree to help me on this one.

—

CHAPTER 1

Isabelle : *Next Day*

> *Life goes on.*
> At least that's what I try to tell myself.
> My stupid, idiotic self.

With puffy eyes too tired from crying, yet wide open and unwilling to succumb to sleep, I stare up at the ceiling for what seems like hours.

What the fuck just happened? What. *The fuck.* Just happened?

I do not know how I came home last night, how I managed to give my home address to the cab driver while in tears, how I managed to stop crying as soon as I got home so I could pay the driver, how I opened the cab door, then the front door of our building. I don't know how I was able to drag my feet up the flight of stairs, how I opened our apartment door, and how I closed it ever so quietly so as not to cause panic from my best friend and my son. I don't remember how I was able to gently take my gown off so I could change into my pajamas, and how I walked to my bathroom to clean off my smudged makeup.

And now, as my head is laid on my pillow, the tears start rolling down again. I want to scream until my throat feels raw. I want to punch something, or someone. I want to hurt myself. I just need a release because as numb as I feel on the outside, in the inside, I feel like I'm being burned alive.

It hurts so damn much. How can someone, in a tiny amount of time we've known each other, manage to break every part of me into shards and splinters?

I slowly feel the deceiving warmth of the morning sun as it touches my skin. I'm still lying in bed, in the same position, my body tucked inside my duvet, and yet I barely moved in God knows how long.

My hand clutches at my chest because it feels too damn tight in there. So I beat on it with that same hand, now fisted, hoping that maybe I can ease the tightness. My teeth are gritted, and the beating I'm giving my chest becomes stronger, more forceful. That's when I start hearing the hallowed out sound, thinking my heart must've been shattered beyond recognition, that all that's left is an empty cavity. And yet, my fist continues beating on it, because right now, I need this physical pain. I welcome it. It's a far lesser evil than the dull ache I'm feeling in the inner recesses of my chest.

I should've seen the clues, because looking back, they were there, staring me in the face. But I was blinded by my lust, by my love for this man who couldn't even say he loved me back until he had to, in an act of desperation.

He didn't really love me. He said he wanted to deserve my love, that he wanted me to be sure.

Those were the words of a guilty man.

Nothing but bullshit.

My phone has been switched off, and it's right next to me on my nightstand. How it got there and when I switched it off, I can hardly recall. I'm surprised I haven't smashed that damn thing.

My hand moving in its own accord, I pick my phone up and switch it back on. So many missed calls, so many voice mails unheard, and so many text messages unread. And I don't need to open each one to know who they are from.

I didn't give Magnus a chance to explain. I was too angry, too hurt … just as I am now. And I don't think there's any chance of this feeling dissipating in the near future. Did he really just pursue me because he wanted to buy my father's company? Surely, he couldn't be that callous ... that heartless? Surely, that passion and that intensity couldn't be faked, right? He might not have said he loved me before, but he must have cared about me one way or the other, because his actions go far and beyond what any man would do for a woman. Or am I still so completely blinded by my feelings for him that I'm not able to see beyond his affections towards me … and towards my son?

Ethan. Oh my God, I don't even know what I'll tell him. My son has grown to love Magnus. But he is young, and eventually, he'll come to know that this is a part of life. That sometimes we love, and at times, we suffer a broken heart.

But, as a parent, I need to be able to protect him from getting too hurt, even if I have to take on the burden myself.

And I will, just as I always have … for Ethan.

Because most men … fucking … suck.

And I will make sure that my son will grow up to be the exception.

———

10

One day, maybe I'll find my happiness too. It might not be soon, it might be for a long while, but it will happen … one day.

Life goes on.

It has to.

CHAPTER 2

It's still too early in the morning, and it surprises me how completely aware I feel, even with little to no sleep. Sure, my head is pounding, and my eyes feel like they're made of lead, but it doesn't sway me from what I need to do.

I get up from my bed and grab a couple of painkilling tablets from my bathroom cabinet. The painkillers take the edge off, but my head is still throbbing. I ignore it, at least I try to, because I need to do something important before I lose my resolve and back out.

I open the e-mail app on my phone, doing my best to concentrate as I type the e-mail address with shaky fingers. Then I inhale deeply, exhaling from my mouth like I'm trying to relieve myself of the nerves.

This needs to be done. It's just the right thing to do.

Dear Mr. Dune:

I am writing to inform you that I am respectfully handing in my

irrevocable resignation, effective immediately. It has been quite

an experience being under your tutelage, and I will miss working

for you. However, because of the recent events, I find that it is in

my and the company's best interest for me to move on to other

endeavors.

Again, thank you. I wish you and your family all the best.

Sincerely,
Isabelle Morrison

After checking my e-mail a couple of times, I hit the Send button, and almost in an instant, I feel a heavy load beginning to lift off my shoulders, though not off of my chest. That burden will take time to heal, if at all. But it's only right for me to leave the company. I don't think I can stand another day working for Grant Corp.

Or I just can't stand the thought of seeing Magnus again.

As soon as my e-mail was sent, I close the app, almost about to lock my phone, when my eyes drift to the numerous messages and missed calls. I stare at the screen for a few moments, in two minds. My pride will not allow me to open each and every message, especially since they all came from the same person. But curiosity wins out, and I let myself open the last message … okay, the last three messages.

I close my eyes for a few seconds. I don't know why I have to psyche myself. Am I this scared to find out what he had to say? I don't give myself a chance to answer that question, pressing the message box so I can read the last three entries.

Message one: *"I can say I'm sorry until I'm out of breath. But I won't stop*
until you've forgiven me."

Message two: *"This can't end like this, Isabelle. I'll wait until you're ready to*
hear me out. I'm not giving up."

Last message: *"I love you. Come back to me. Please give me a chance to deserve you."*

Without any warning, the damn tears are back. Why is he torturing me with those lies? Why does he keep pretending that he still wants me when I heard it loud and clear that I'm merely a pawn in his business acquisition?

It would've been a lot easier if he told me the truth, if he was unapologetic, if he said he was using me to buy my father's business, if he just admitted that he was a gigantic asshole of a person, and I was an idiot for falling hard.

He shouldn't have said he loved me in the end, because then, I can truly hate him, and I can eventually begin my healing, knowing I'm better off without him.

The previous wounds from years ago have scarred over, though I know I'll never be my old self again. But Magnus came into my life, soothing my scars away, only to hack them open with his betrayal.

And now, not only are these wounds back open, but the scars are going to be a lot uglier.

I hear a door open outside my bedroom, and I listen at Michelle and Nathan, talking in muffled tones as they pass by my room. I can hear their footsteps shuffling on the hardwood floors. Then one person stops, just outside my door. I hear Michelle telling Nathan to go start on our breakfast. That's when I hear tapping against my door.

"Billie, baby? You awake?"

I reconsider answering back. Maybe she'll think I'm not inside and just leave my door alone. But I don't hear any footsteps moving away.

"Billie? I heard you came in last night." Pause. "When you're ready to talk, I'm here for you, baby."

Before I can stop myself, I hear my voice calling out to her, "Come in. I'm … I'm awake now."

I see the door opening, and Michelle enters, closing the door softly behind her to avoid waking up the kids. As soon as she sees me and my state, she rushes to me, holding the sides of my head with her two hands.

"Shit, girl, what the hell happened last night?"

I clasp both of her hands, trying to get some sort of support. Lowering my head, I answer, "It's over. Magnus and I … we're over."

I pull away from her and cover my face, feeling so defeated. In an instant, I'm engulfed inside Michelle's arms. I can feel her rocking me, shushing me softly, melodically, like a mother to her child. It brings me comfort, at least temporarily.

"What happened?" she asks.

"He lied to me, Michelle. Everything he did … he's a liar. I just … I just …" I sputter on, unable to speak comprehensively.

"I don't understand. Did he cheat on you? Is it his ex-wife, what's that bitch's name again?"

14

I shake my head as I pull away again. "No, no. He didn't cheat, but it was worse. He … he was only interested in me because he wanted to buy my father's business in Texas. I think he's using me as some sort of leverage."

"What?!" Michelle's voice grows an octave higher, before she corrects her tone, possibly so the kids don't wake up. "How did you find out? Did he tell you? Did that son of a bitch admit to it?"

"I overheard him and Martine talking with each other about it. If that's not bad enough, he never denied it when I confronted him either. All he said was that he needed to explain."

"That motherfu—"

"That's not all," I interrupt. "Last night, it got worse. Cooper found me. I don't know if it was just a coincidence that he was at the fundraiser, but he came for me, Michelle, and he was as vicious as before."

I notice my hands shake, knowing what I'm about to say … and what I've realized I need to do. "Oh my God, I can't stay here, Michelle. Ethan and I have to leave New York."

I bolt out of bed, pacing like a crazy person. "I need to pack lightly, pull Ethan out of school, and figure out where we can go …"

Michelle stands up as well and holds me by the shoulders to stop my frazzled movements. "Hold on, hold on. You don't need to move, Billie. You don't have to displace your son and run away."

I push her hands off me, now feeling indignant and frustrated at my best friend. "I'm protecting my son from that monster, and you can't stop me!"

"Yes, I can't stop you. It's completely your decision. I get it. But in case you haven't realized it, this isn't Texas. Your family, at least those who count, are here in New York. You know my family is your family, Billie. You *know* that. You've seen how massive my family is, and I'm not just talking about the numbers. My cousins alone can crush Cooper Thornton. This is *our* city. We have home court advantage, and all that shit."

"I don't know, Michelle," I whimper, shaking my head stubbornly.

"Baby girl, we got this. If you run away and Cooper finds you again, there won't be anyone to protect you. I think it's safer if you stay put."

"I just don't know … I'm scared for Ethan." Taking a few deep breaths, I try my best to continue in a calm tone.

"I think Cooper found out I was here through Magnus." I throw my hands up as soon as I see her reaction. "Wait, before you react, when Magnus told me he didn't know who Cooper was, I believed him. In fact, before I confronted him, he told me he decked some guy who was chasing after me. I think he knocked Cooper out. But I was so angry at Magnus for me to realize what he'd done … until now."

I grasp my hair with both hands in frustration. "God, I don't know what to do, Michelle. Magnus has been texting and calling me, wanting to explain himself."

"Well, maybe you should let him. Don't get me wrong, I still want to hurt him, like really hurt him badly for what he did to you. But I still don't believe he could be that heartless. I really think he genuinely loves you, Billie."

I shake my head and look away, unable to respond back. After a few moments, I turn back to her, "When I'm good and ready. I just don't know if I'll ever be ready though. It hurts too much. I mean, how can someone do that?"

"I don't know, baby girl. Some people do the stupidest things. But once you're ready, talk to him. Get his side of the story."

I shrug back at her. "He could also spin more lies, and I'll probably believe him. And God, Cooper—" I cover my entire face with my hands.

"Give yourself time. I'm so sorry this happened, Billie. I actually thought Magnus was different too. And as for Cooper, my cousins will be happy to help look out for you and Ethan, especially if you feed 'em. Your fried chicken will do."

"If you're trying to make me laugh, I'm sorry, but I'm not exactly in the mood for it." I walk over to my bed, tucking myself under the sheets.

"You will be … eventually," she says softly.

"Yeah, maybe. But right now, I'm tired," I whisper out, giving in to the urge to close my eyes and sleep as my best friend lays a gentle kiss on my temple.

CHAPTER 3

With all that had happened in the previous night, waking from a dreamless sleep leaves me extremely grateful. I check the clock, and it's close to noon already. Ethan would've been jumping on my bed or knocking at my door by now.

I have a feeling Michelle is the person to thank for this. She knows I need my space. After all, I don't have the luxury of a mourning period after a break-up, where I get to sit around in my pajamas, eating ice cream all day and drinking anything with alcohol at night.

I have a son who needs me, who is sensitive enough that he worries about me.

I need to move on for him.

All of a sudden, I hear a commotion outside the door, with Michelle instructing the kids to stay in their room. Then I hear Nathan's voice saying that he's going outside. He sounds agitated, and I'm hoping that he's not having an argument with Michelle. I open the door and peek out. Michelle sees me and hurriedly comes to my side.

"What's going on? You guys fighting?" I ask with concern.

She shakes her head hurriedly but keeps turning towards the front door. "No, no, we're not. It's nothing. Nathan's taking care of it."

She seems distracted, making me realize it's not 'nothing' at all. I step outside of my bedroom, still barefoot and with my pajamas on.

"Stay here, Billie," Michelle urges, her hand clasping my arm.

"No. I want to know what's going on." I swipe her hand off of me and stride down the hallway. I instantly hear two grown men's voices on the street, and it doesn't sound like they're talking about the weather. The two men are arguing, and by the brashness of their voices, it doesn't sound like it's going to end well.

I recognize both voices, one is Nathan's for sure, while the other voice … the other voice comes from someone who broke my heart.

I find myself standing by the window, confirming my suspicions. In an instant, he looks up, possibly sensing my presence. Our eyes lock, and I can't help but notice that he has tired-looking eyes, much like mine.

Surely, he wasn't up all night like me, unable to sleep, wondering what the hell went wrong and what we did to deserve it.

"Isabelle!" Magnus calls out for me, trying to push past Nathan, who's refusing to let him through.

"Fucking let me go, man!" Magnus barks aloud at Nathan who, with almost the same build as Magnus, is still holding him off. There's no Alex, which means he drove himself here.

What was he thinking?

"Go home, Magnus. I meant what I said last night," I croak out, my throat still feeling raw.

"No. Not until you hear me out … please, Isabelle!"

He calls out for me, but I'm slowly distancing myself from the window, unable to hear anymore … unwilling to see him anymore.

It hurts too much.

Then suddenly, I hear both men shouting again, then there's a grunt, a thud, then silence.

Something's wrong. My heart starts beating faster. Even Michelle looks alarmed. We both rush to the window, and I gasp aloud at the sight of Magnus on the ground, a bouquet of flowers that I didn't realize he was holding a while ago is now on the ground. He tries to get up, clutching his jaw. Nathan is breathing heavily, his hand still formed into a fist.

I don't even have to think about it. My legs start moving, taking me down the stairs and out the building, where I see Magnus already standing, shoulders slumped, and unable to look me in the cycs.

I don't want my heart to break at the sight of him like this, because I want whatever's left of it to stay intact. And yet, I feel pain at the sight of this proud man looking every inch defeated.

"Look, I didn't mean to hit you, man, but you didn't give me a choice. You need to calm the fuck down. You heard Billie—"

"It's okay, it's okay," I interrupt Nathan, holding him back with a hand on his shoulder. That's when I notice Magnus lifts his head, and he gives Nathan a hard stare.

I choose to disregard it. "Just give me a couple of minutes with him."

"Are you sure?" Nathan looks at Magnus warily, then at me. His expression softens as he continues, "If he tries to hurt you …"

"Magnus will never hurt me," I pause, before staring pointedly at Magnus, "at least, not physically."

I can't help but feel an ounce of triumph at the sight of him closing his eyes and looking away in shame.

Nathan nods in understanding and goes back inside. Looking around me, I notice a small crowd has gathered to watch the whole spectacle, with some, blatantly pointing their phone cameras at us.

I quickly grab Magnus's hand, ignoring his stunned expression, and trying not to show the effect his touch still has on me. "Come. Let's just hope no one has filmed that fiasco and posts it on social media sites."

Magnus follows me inside, with the slightly tattered flowers in his other hand. As soon we're in the foyer, I let him go, instantly feeling the loss of warmth in my hand. He leans against the wall, rubbing his jaw slowly.

I hesitantly inch closer, "Are you okay?" I raise my hand to touch his aching jaw, before stopping myself and stepping back once again. He sheepishly offers the flowers to me, and it takes me a few seconds to accept it. "I should probably get you some ice for that." I quickly turn to head up the stairs, when I feel long fingers circle around my wrist, promptly stopping me.

"No, please. Just stay here … with me." The sound of his voice, as he speaks the words that would have melted me just the day before, now only manages to give me a kick in the guts.

Because I want to melt for him again.

But I can't and I won't.

A broken heart can harden up a person so easily.

I look down at his hand on me, before looking him straight in the eyes, raising my brows in silent assertion. But he's meeting my stare head on, and he's refusing to let me go.

I pull my wrist from his grasp again, and with a loud exhale, he succumbs. This gives me the opportunity to take a few steps away from him. I need that distance to compose myself.

"I've seen you knock someone cold before, Magnus. Why didn't you defend yourself with Nathan?"

He pushes himself off the wall and closes in, as he reasons, "Because I deserved it. I should be the one protecting you, not him."

"You, … protecting *me?*" I laugh sarcastically, distancing myself from him once again. "How's that going for you lately?"

"Isabelle …"

"Why are you here, Magnus?" I ask harshly, surprising myself with the bitterness in my voice. "We broke up, remember?"

His blue eyes are still fixed on me, and they are cold and hurt at the same time. "*You* broke up with *me*. You never gave me a chance to explain. Do you really think I'm going to accept that?"

"I don't care whether you accept or not," my voice rises, but I correct myself, not needing to earn any more eavesdroppers. I lean back against the wall, suddenly feeling exhausted. "I'm tired. Just tell me what you want, then, please leave."

I close my eyes for a moment, and even before I open them again, I can sense that he's close … so close, in fact, that I can smell his distinct scent.

The effect on me is instantaneous.

I open my eyes slowly, and the first things I see are his lips, and they're slightly open and inviting. His minty breath, warming my chin, my mouth, my cheeks, and my nose. And then I'm looking into his eyes … his striking blues that can disarm me in the best and the worst kind of ways. And right now, he's holding me captive with them, as are the hands that are firmly planted on the wall, his strong arms merely inches on either side of my head.

"What I want, Isabelle, is right here in front of me." And before I can even sound a protest, his lips are on mine.

Oh, dear God.

It's exquisite and explosive, making me drop the flowers I'm holding. His uncertainty dissipates as my mouth opens on its own accord. I feel his tongue graze my lower lip, making me sigh. One of his hands finds my hip, and it locks me against his lower torso. As his kiss deepens, I feel his hips undulate against me. A moan escapes him, and my core tightens in response.

"This is wrong … I can't …" I mumble, half-heartedly, in-between sucking his lip and meeting his tongue with my own.

"I won't let you leave me," he whispers as his lips travel across my jaw, sending delicious shivers all over my body. "Please let me make things right," he pleads in a low growl.

Why does this have to feel so good?

"Magnus ... please ... I—" We're interrupted by his phone buzzing. It distracts him, thankfully, and with my hands on his hard chest, I push him off.

He exhales roughly, infuriated at the interruption. But as he takes the phone from his pocket, I manage to catch a glimpse of the screen.

It's a missed call ... from none other than Ms. Martine Harper. Or should I say, former Mrs. Martine Grant.

This is such a mistake! Why do I keep letting Magnus do things to me that cloud my judgment?

"Leave!" I yell out with gritted teeth, pushing him backwards with so much force that it takes him by surprise.

"Don't do this, baby." He tries to reach for my shoulders, his expression becoming worried. But I swat his hands away.

"*Baby?* You don't get to call me *baby* anymore. Just be thankful my son is upstairs or I would've called the cops. Or do I need them to escort you out of here? Leave now and don't ever come back!" I try to push him towards the direction of the door. But he grabs hold of my wrists and pulls me against him.

"Let me go!" I cry out, struggling, my teeth still clenched in anger.

"I will, if you give me a second chance. You know that what we just felt when we kissed was real. All I ask for is another chance to—"

"Oh, you want a second chance?" I cut him off with exaggerated sarcasm. "Well, from what I recall, the last time I gave another man a second chance, he reciprocated by violating me, and making me lose everything. My family, my dignity, myself ... everything!"

That shocks Magnus enough to loosen his hold on me, but the expression on his face makes me want to take back what I just said. I stand my ground, nonetheless. The magnitude of hurt I may have inflicted on him, by comparing him with Cooper is a low blow, but I can't have him here anymore.

If I can't push him out with my own hands, then I'll push him out with my words.

And it looks like it's working because he's backing away and turning towards the door. So why are tears welling up in my eyes now? Why am I suddenly feeling like this is a big mistake?

He opens the door, pauses, and turns back to me. He regards me for a long moment, both of us not uttering a word.

He speaks first, albeit quietly, "I took care of Cooper. He will never come near you again."

A cold chill runs down my spine. "What? What do you mean by 'took care' of him? What did you do?"

He chuckles slightly, but his voice sounds menacing, "I didn't kill him, if that's what you're asking, no matter how much I wanted to."

Relief washes over me, not for Cooper being spared of his life, but because Magnus showed restraint. Cooper isn't worth spending jail time for. And as angry as I am with Magnus, I don't know what I'd do if he loses everything because of me.

I'm not worth it either.

Magnus adds, "He's never stepping foot in New York again. And if he does, I will know, and I won't be so forthcoming then. I want you to know that you have no reason to be afraid of him. I'll make sure of that."

I don't want to know this information Magnus is telling me. I don't need to know about the lengths he'd go for me because I need to stay angry with him.

He's doing it again.

He's trying to knock down the walls that I'm trying to rebuild.

I made myself vulnerable to him and look where it got me.

"Good-bye, Magnus," I speak back, keeping my voice from faltering.

His jaw clenches, and his mouth forms into a hard line. It's not what he wants to hear from me, obviously. But there's nothing else for me to say except good-bye.

He doesn't speak a single word at me. He just turns away, and he walks out the door, but not before I catch a glimpse of his eyes. Those same eyes that were once full of mischief during our happier days are now tired and just ... sad.

And I want nothing more than to rid those eyes of sadness.

But I know I can't ... and I won't.

CHAPTER 4

Isabelle: *Three Months Later*

"Seriously, Billie, you're just being paranoid." Michelle shakes her head at me. We're sitting on her couch, in the apartment she now shares with Nathan and Tasha, having an after-dinner coffee while watching the kids play.

"I'm not, Michelle. I really think I'm being followed," I insist, before taking another sip of the warm beverage. "It's either that, or it's an extremely weird coincidence that I see this same person almost everywhere I go!"

"Hold on, didn't you say he's cute? Has he approached you yet? Maybe he's just keen to meet you, but he's too shy." She raises a brow at me teasingly.

I glare back at her. "It doesn't matter if he's cute or not. What if he's *keen* to kill me? What if Cooper hired him to follow me around? Michelle, what if Cooper is having me followed so he can keep track of me?" I feel a panic attack coming on at the thought of Cooper harming me and Ethan.

"Okay, first of all, calm the hell down. Ethan might freak out if he sees *you* freaking out. Secondly, what if this guy is just super shy, and he couldn't approach you because you're sending off negative vibes? Thirdly, could it be possible he's a hired man working for Magnus to keep track of your whereabouts?" Michelle says jokingly.

"That's ridiculous," I scoff.

"Is it? We all know what Magnus is capable of," Michelle replies.

I stop midway from lifting the cup to my lips. Magnus's name still brings a wave of emotions that I can't seem to get rid of, no matter how hard I try. Just the thought of him can still make my heart beat like crazy.

Magnus Grant.

I want to stay angry at him for having betrayed me in the worst kind of way, by using my past against me for his own benefit. I want to blame him for Cooper finding me. To this day, I'm still kicking myself for falling for Magnus so fast, when all this time, he was only using me as a bargaining chip to acquire my father's company.

Time heals all wounds? Yeah, that's bullshit.

The wound is still as fresh as it was three months ago.

So I plan on holding onto this anger. My anger is the only thing that's keeping me from running back to him. Because as much as I want to deny it, the fact remains I'm still in love with him.

I guess he really has ruined me for anyone else.

What a jerk!

"Earth, to Billie! Hello? Earth, to Billie!" I notice Michelle waving her hand in front of my face, so I turn back to her. She shakes her head at me in dismay. "Baby, it's been three months, and you still have that same look on your face from the last time you saw him. Clearly, you need to talk to Magnus or at least find some closure. You may be good at hiding it from Ethan, but I can read you like a book, and I've never seen you this miserable in all the years I've known you. And you've had some doozies, girl. "

I regard her thoughtfully. "But I'm not ready yet. I'm not ready to see him face-to-face again." I swoop my hair over one shoulder, toying with some strands, still conscious about how my locks look.

I decided to change my hair color, albeit reluctantly at first, from my natural auburn to blonde. I've never felt the need to make such a drastic change before, but since I've decided on staying put, I might as well try to remain incognito. I've been told this color suits my skin tone, but I don't really care. I just need to not look like my old self.

"Would it help if we ask one of my cousins to keep you company when you and Ethan are out or something? The offer still holds, you know," she asks.

"Yeah, maybe. We'll see how this plays out," I consider her suggestion with a nod before changing the subject, halting our conversation about my pseudo stalker crisis. I'm still worried about this guy who I think might be stalking me, but for some reason, whenever I discuss this with Michelle, we end up talking about the other man I'm trying my hardest to forget.

After the whole clusterfuck that was my breakup from Magnus three months ago, no matter how much I wanted to, I didn't give myself a chance to grieve … even though my whole being was dying on the inside. Fear won out. All I wanted to do then was to

---

move out and be as far away from New York as possible. Cooper had found me, and I couldn't risk him finding out about Ethan and hurting us both. I was ready to leave soon after I broke things off, but Michelle convinced me not to … at least not yet at that time.

Not until after a month when I considered moving Ethan and myself into Nathan's brownstone at Brooklyn Heights. Apparently, a couple of days prior to *that night*, Nathan told Michelle that the tenant living in the converted apartment on the top floor of his house had moved out. So he offered the apartment to us and nervously asked Michelle if he wanted to move in with him as well. They've been talking about taking their relationship up another level, so I guess my situation was the push they needed. Nathan didn't know the real reason why I panicked, so when he approached me with the idea, I refused it at first. But Michelle made me realize that if Cooper was able to find me, he can find me again. And worse, he might also know about Ethan. I don't think I can protect Ethan on my own should that time comes.

Michelle also made me realize that … well, Magnus and I still have an unfinished business. If I wanted to be perfectly honest with myself, I hated the way we ended things, no matter how I reassured myself that I did the right thing. If I left town at that moment, there would always be a part in me that would regret not seeing him at least that one last time.

So two months ago, we decided to move in at Nathan's house. He had been understanding about our whole situation, and he even made our rent quite affordable, considering the rent on this side of Brooklyn is considerably high.

I must admit, consider me old-fashioned, but I do feel safer, knowing there's a man in the house. And Ethan is beyond ecstatic at having a playmate and a father figure at the same time. He was just as heartbroken as I was when I told him Magnus would no longer be around to see us, but Nathan's presence somehow eases his pain.

Back in our apartment, and after tucking Ethan into bed, I step inside my own room, somehow relieved that this one doesn't hold any lingering memories of my time with Magnus. That is, until my eyes move on to the sealed box containing the gown and the shoes he gave me that night of the charity event. Three months on, and the memory of that night, and the next day, still renders me to tears.

I handed my resignation by e-mail to Charles Dunn in the morning after that fateful night. There was no way in God's green earth would I go back to Grant Corp after what happened. Magnus never stopped hand-delivering flowers every single day, even though I drove him away the day after we broke up. He called my phone, even Michelle's. He did this each consecutive day as well. I didn't give him a chance to explain. I didn't even allow myself to see him, asking Michelle or Nathan to turn him away each time he showed up. He never forced himself inside our old apartment though. Maybe he knew deep down that he had no right to … that he had no stake on me anymore.

He refused to give me back my overnight bag, using it as leverage for me to see him. After all that had happened, he was still as calculating as ever. But I also knew that he was really desperate to explain himself, that he'd even use my small bag of belongings to see me again. I could not understand why he was even wasting his time. He should just cut all ties with me, so he could continue to buy more companies and date whomever he wanted.

I just wished it didn't hurt so much when I thought about it.

Christmas in our new place was a struggle. I had to put up a brave front and showed everyone, especially my son, that I was happy, that I've moved on. I survived it on autopilot and managed to shower Ethan with enough gifts I could afford, so he could happily open them on Christmas morning. I had to hand it to Ethan though, he knew how to make his momma happy.

If Christmas without Magnus was bad enough, New Year's Eve was the worst. On that day, I would always get hyper-paranoid and anxious to the point of nausea. That was the time when Michelle was extra vigilant of me. But over the years, I know I've improved, and my anxiety is gradually decreasing.

Then there was the self-imposed complete ban on any news or media coverage about Magnus. That was the hardest part. If they mentioned his name on TV, I switched channels. I stopped reading newspapers, especially the *Business Section*, and I avoided passing by the Grant Corp building as well. Michelle and the girls tried to open conversations about him, but I put a stop to it every single time. Three months on, and what he did still literally hurts me physically and emotionally. And I thought no one could ever hurt me the way Cooper did back then. But what I truly felt for Magnus in that short amount of time we were together was deep-rooted … fiery at times, but for me, it felt so real. I loved Magnus to my very core.

No, scrap that. I *still* love Magnus to my very core.

But it's too late now. Magnus's attempts at reaching out have stopped completely as soon as we moved neighborhoods. It was what I wanted, or rather at least that was what I thought I wanted. Sometimes I catch myself wishing he never gave up on me.

God, even *I* don't understand me sometimes…

Maybe it's a good thing. I've been putting off returning this box with the gown and the shoes for quite some time now because I want to return it personally. Not that I want to see him. I just want to make sure he receives it back. But I couldn't do it right after we broke up. The wounds were still too fresh.

As if they're any closer to being healed, anyway.

But I'm starting all over again, just like I'm sure he is. What we had could be considered a fling—a very intense fling—but nothing more. And even though he said he loved me that night, I was sure it was a desperate attempt on his part to draw me back because he knew I was waiting for those words to come out of his mouth. He wanted me, sure. He even mentioned many times that he needed me, but they were all said in the heat of the moment, and people say things they don't really mean in the heat of the moment.

His words, not mine.

I've given it more than enough time. I'm sure I can find the courage to walk up to the grand foyer of Grant Corp with this box and leave it at the front desk, so Magnus can pick it up whenever he sees fit. I'm not leaving a note or a letter. Just the box with the gown and the shoes, nothing else.

Maybe that's all the closure I need.

I turn away from the box on the floor, and I switch my lamp off, feeling a little weary about falling asleep. My old nightmares never left me, in fact, they've become worse. Now I get to relive every single moment of *that night* as well, from the moment Cooper found me in the charity event, to the moment I found out that Magnus was using me, and of course, my all-time favorite, the moment I broke up with him.

I wonder what I ever did in my past life to deserve this kind of retribution from the universe. I must have been a killer, or worse, a cruel rapist, or a ruthless businessman. I inwardly chuckle cynically as I pull the covers up to my chest.

I'll get this over with, tomorrow. Tomorrow, I'm returning that box so I can finally close this horrid chapter and move on with my life.

I am ready.

***

Sometimes I question my state of mind during the late hours of the night. I'm walking towards Grant Corp, carrying a box containing an expensive designer gown and shoes, on a cold January day, just after a snowstorm. I already slipped once, having stupidly worn the wrong pair of shoes. Luckily, my ass broke my fall. I wince inwardly, picturing how big my bruise will be on my ass cheeks. I'm just thankful that I sealed the box before leaving, so nothing spilled out. The last thing I want is for Magnus to think I deliberately ruined the gown and the shoes out of spite.

God, why do I even care what he thinks anymore? If I didn't feel the need to personally return the gown and the shoes out of principle and out of propriety, I would have just sent this box by post.

But it's too late now.

Oh well, screw it!

With one deep breath, I take one step through the doors of Grant Corp and into its magnificent foyer.

The first thing I'm thankful for, as I make my way to the front desk is that it's nice and warm inside. Being from Texas, the cold blistering air of winter is something I don't think I'll ever get used to. The second thing I'm thankful for, as I'm looking around me is that I'm not seeing anybody familiar, and no one seems to recognize me either, including the staff at the front desk. It could be because I made sure that I made it here at an odd time when most of the employees are still in their offices, settling into their work. Plus, I only worked in the company for about a month, *and* I changed my hair color. I'm a stranger to these people. The third thing I'm thankful for is that I didn't see Magnus's car in front of the building, which means he's either not inside yet, or he's not leaving his office anytime soon. I think I don't need to explain why I'm grateful about that.

With a wary smile fixed on my face, I place the box on the island separating me from the front desk staff. The woman across from me looks up from her computer screen and gives me a polite, but reserved smile.

"Hello, um, I'm just here to drop this off. It's for Mr. Magnus Grant." My mere mention of his name sends a tingle down my body, which I promptly ignore. The woman's eyes widen in mild surprise, then, she eyes me and the box, skeptically.

"May I ask what's in the box, ma'am?" she asks courteously.

"Just tell him, please, that this box is from Isabelle Morrison. He knows that name." At least I hope he still does.

She cocks a brow. "Ma'am, for security purposes, we can't just hand this box to him without any further information. Do you have the sender's details on the box?"

"No," I answer shaking my head. "Look, he *knows* who Isabelle is. Please, if you can't give this to him, can you please give this to Alex, his driver? He can check what's inside the box if he wants to, before handing it to Mr. Grant."

Why is this woman giving me hell over a box? "Miss, I'm not a bad person, I'm just trying to do the right thing here," I add.

The woman eyes me intently before she speaks again, "Well, here's what I can do for you. I'll call Mr. Grant's assistant, and she can check this box and take it to him if it's safe to do so. I hope you don't mind, but if she refuses to accept this package, we can't keep it here. Therefore, you will have to take it back with you."

"Oh, for crying out loud, of course, it's safe." And then I realize that Denise can verify who I am, and as long as Magnus doesn't show up, I'll be able to make a clean break and shut this door once and for all.

And then I should be able to move on with my life, right?

"Fine, his assistant can check the box," I reply back with a resigned sigh.

The woman nods back at me, "Please take a seat while I call for Mr. Grant's assistant." She waves at the group of leather seats nearest to the front desk, then, she lifts the phone handset next to her. "Hello, is this Denise—"

Not waiting for her to finish the call, I grudgingly sit down on the same seat I sat on my first day at Grant Corp, crossing my arms in defiance, but wincing as soon as my bruised ass touches the padding of the leather seat.

Why did I think this was a good idea again?

CHAPTER 5

I'm tapping my foot, waiting nervously for Denise to come down, still unsure if I should show myself to her or not. I check my watch, which is ridiculous since I don't even know what time I got in here, but the wait is getting worrisome. I grab my phone off my bag, and I start typing a text message to Helen, my new boss, to let her know that I might be a little late in opening the store this morning.

"Mr. Grant! Mr. Grant, excuse me!" The same lady at the front desk calls out, and my breath hitches.

Shit! Shit! Shit!

I look up slightly, trying to cover my face as I see *him* turn from the direction of the building entrance. I failed to see him come out of the elevator on his way out, since my back is turned from his path, and a plant is blocking me off. He walks past me, and I sneak a look to see if he can sense my presence, but he barely flinches.

Oh.

Why would I even be upset if he doesn't notice I'm here? His building would be the last place he'd think I'd be in. I also changed my hair color, I'm wearing layers of clothing, and I have a beanie on to protect my head from the cold.

He also seems distracted, his handsome face wearing a familiar scowl. It makes me wonder what's causing him to appear so foreboding, and it gives me a sudden urge to put my arms around him and tell him it's all going to be okay.

Even if it's not. Even if I don't believe it myself.

Magnus is now standing next to the box, his back facing me. I hasten a quick once over. Big mistake. His hair has grown, and those rebellious locks of his add a playful contrast to his custom-tailored black suit and tie. A thick scarf is wrapped around his neck, and he's carrying a gray coat, most likely to prepare him from the harsh chill of winter outside.

I can't help but think how great he looks. Sure, he's got scruff on his face, like he couldn't be bothered shaving this morning, but even that just adds to his appeal. I hate that because I don't want to feel what I'm feeling right at this minute. That even after months since we've broken up, he still can manage to tighten my core and to make my heart skip a beat, or two, or three.

Damn. It.

I exhale slowly, trying to calm myself down.

Get a grip, Billie.

"What's this about, Ms. Reed? Have Denise take care of this one, please." Magnus speaks curtly to the same woman I spoke with earlier, like he's in a hurry to get to somewhere and cannot be bothered.

Well, I'm not hanging around to find out. While his back is still turned, I hurriedly sneak out, thankful yet again, that my shoes aren't one of those that make squeaking sounds. I breathe a huge sigh of relief as soon as I'm out of the building. I sneak a quick peek inside. Magnus is still standing next to the box, but now he's talking on the phone. With a sigh of relief, I make my way towards the subway on my way to work.

I *cannot* believe how close I was to Magnus catching me in his very own building! He must think I'm stalking him or something, except that I'm not. I'm actually returning something he gave me. That's what exes do. They return things that aren't supposed to be theirs anymore, or items that hold too many bad memories. In this case, the gown and the shoes fit those two categories. Maybe I should have gone to his place in Tribeca. But my feet took me to his office building instead. Could it be my subconscious fear of encountering Martine? She wants him back, and Magnus can't seem to get her off his system … and his life. It would hurt too much to return in a place where Magnus and I shared our most intimate moments … a place where I completely bared my whole self to him, complete with all the broken pieces, only to realize that those memories can be easily replaced by someone who he probably has never gotten over with.

I am navigating through the crowd, trying to make my way towards the subway which is two blocks from here, when all of a sudden, I feel that now familiar, warm, tingling sensation on the tips of my ears, with the hairs on my nape standing upright as well.

It's the feeling of being watched.

I've been feeling this way almost every day since I moved. It's making me paranoid. On several occasions, I caught him watching me … following me. I've tried calling the cops, but every time I reached for my phone, or approached a uniformed officer, that person disappeared from my line of sight. Michelle suggests that my paranoia's just heightened from knowing that Cooper knows where I am based. But she offered to ask her cousins to keep an eye on me, while she and Nathan can keep an eye on Ethan when I'm at work. I agreed about keeping Ethan safe, but declined the offer on my part.

I need to start fighting my own battles.

And it helps that I have pepper spray in my purse.

That awareness is still there. But the feeling is a lot stronger than usual. Does this mean he's close? I turn around, trying to look for *that* face. I know what he looks like, and there is no way in hell that seeing the same face almost everywhere I go, can come close to being serendipitous.

I also know he's good at hiding. I can feel him watching me, but I don't know where he is. What strikes me as completely odd, however, is the fact that I don't feel the least bit scared. Am I frustrated? Yes. Is it making me anxious? Most definitely so. He might be working for Cooper, which means he must be dangerous. But do I feel scared about it? No.

Like I said, odd.

I'm sure it has nothing to do with the fact that he's good-looking, even from afar. He may still be capable of hurting me though, no matter what he looks like. But he doesn't appear like he wants to do me any harm.

And if there's any sign that he'll harm me, I won't hesitate to call the cops on him, whoever the hell he is.

Wow, is this really me? Is my paranoid inner self finally catching up with my inner bravado? The thought makes me smile inwardly. Maybe I'm getting there … finally … one step at a time.

I make it to the end of the block, feeling slightly better. I'm waiting for the pedestrian light to turn green so I can get to the subway entrance across the road. There's a small crowd already gathered around me, and usually, people still give you your personal space. I mean, *hello*, this is New York after all. But as soon as the light turns green, I get a nudge from someone who either doesn't care about personal spaces, or a tourist looking up at the skyscrapers. The force nudges me forward, almost knocking me off-balance.

What the … seriously? Amidst the push of the crowd, I turn around, expecting an apology from whomever it was that almost made me lose my footing.

But I'm not expecting that person to be *him*.

CHAPTER 6

I thought I had a clean break, that I could close this chapter with no problem. Why did I think it was a brilliant idea to personally return the gown and the shoes in his office building, nonetheless? Am I subconsciously masochistic?

The sight of Magnus standing just inches from me—with me looking embarrassed at being caught out, yet still breathtakingly enigmatic at the same time—makes me realize I'm still completely susceptible to him.

I cannot allow that.

So I swiftly turn around in an attempt to avoid any further contact. I try to hurry as I cross the street so I can distance myself from him. But I miscalculate the sidewalk gutter and before I realize it, my ankle bends in a way that it shouldn't. I feel a sharp pain from my ankle up to my knee, and it buckles instantly. And before I can face-plant on the asphalted road, I feel the strong and all too familiar arms around my waist, and those arms are lifting me off the ground.

"I got you," he says as he takes me away from the intersection, heading …

Wait, why am I allowing Magnus to carry me like it's the most natural thing in the world to do?

"Let me go, Magnus!" I start kicking around, but the pain on my ankle makes me cry out in agony.

God, can this get any more humiliating?

"You're hurt, Isabelle, and you're lucky I caught you, or you could've done more damage if you hit your head on the ground," the severity of his words are in sharp contrast to the way he's chuckling softly from behind me. Then he lowers his mouth against my ear and whispers, "I'm not letting you go."

My breath hitches, but I manage to regain my composure.

Stay angry. I remind myself, trying to replace the thrill his words are bringing to me with a well-deserved resentment.

He finds a small alcove at the side of the building, and he gently leans me against the wall but maintaining his hands on my waist to keep me stable. Even through my thick, winter clothing, I can still feel the heat from his touch. And his scent … I hate that his unique scent can still turn me on. That, and the fact that he's so attractive with that scruff on, make me frustrated with myself because every single nerve ending in my body is singing with joy.

"You need to get your ankle checked." Magnus's blue eyes are set on mine, and I feel that same connection as before. And even though we've been apart for longer than we were together, I still yearn for this connection every single day.

"Let me take you to the hospital. I can—"

"No, you need to let me go, Magnus!" I cut him off, surprised at my assertiveness.

I instantly notice the look of hurt on his face, but the hurt is gone as quickly as it appeared. He leans forward, and I'm paralyzed as his mouth stops a mere inch from my own.

"No," he replies, and I feel his warm breath against my now hyperaware lips.

One monosyllabic word, one defiant response, and my whole body awakens from its forced hibernation.

"We're not together anymore, Magnus. You have to accept that," I protest, my voice breathy and unconvincing.

Magnus pulls back ever so slightly, so he can look intently into my eyes. "And *you* have to accept that I will never give up until you take me back."

Shaking my head, I defiantly reply back, "Never."

His scowl deepens as he searches my face. "We'll see about that." He loosens his hold on me, but still keeps me close. "What did you drop off, Isabelle? What's inside the box?"

"I knew that was a bad idea," I answer back, unable to look him in the eyes. I exhale deeply before responding, "I'm returning the gown and the heels you gave me. You can have them back."

"Why did you just drop it off like that?"

I look straight at him with a new fire building within me. "Because I needed a clean break, and I don't really think I needed your presence, or approval, to do so."

"I'm not taking those back. They were my gifts to you, Isabelle."

"No!" I push him away with all my strength, using the wall against me as leverage. I manage to push him off … but only by a foot. "That was a bad memory that I want erased from my head. I don't know why I needed to give them back personally. But that was *my* closure! Mine!" I answer back defiantly as tears begin to well up in my eyes.

Shit, I don't want to cry in front of him!

The hurt in Magnus's face is back, and this time, it stays. "Is that what you think our whole relationship was? A bad memory you want erased?"

"What relationship?" my voice rises and a few people walking past turn their heads at our direction. We must appear like any bickering couple, except that's only half-true. "I don't consider what we had as a relationship, Magnus. How about we call it for what it truly was—a really elaborate prank?" I chuckle cynically. "At least one of us got what we wanted."

Before I know it, he locks me in again, with both hands against the wall, and arms on each side of my head. He leans closer, the intensity in his eyes filling each of my nerve endings with jolts of electricity.

"Say you don't mean that. You loved me at one point, didn't you? Look into my eyes and tell me how you really feel, damn it!"

A bitter laugh escapes me. "Love? Is that what you really think I feel for you?" I match his intense stare with my own. "I *hate* you, Magnus Grant! Do you hear me? I *hate* you!" I cry out with tears poised to fall.

"Good! *Hate* me then!" Magnus roars back. "I'd rather you hate me with a passion, than for you to feel nothing for me at all. Just remember, my dear, that there's only a thin line between love and hate, and so God help me, I'll make you cross that line sooner or later."

He slams the palms of his hands so hard against the wall that it makes me jump. Unable to take anymore, I push his arms away before more tears spill out, trying to walk away from him before I break down completely. But in my anger, I foolishly forget about my hurt ankle. As soon as I put some weight on it, my knee buckles again, and I cry out in pain.

Magnus's quick reflexes break my fall, the second time around. "Okay, that's it. I'm taking you to the hospital to get your ankle checked," he declares with authority, taking his phone out. "Alex? Pick me up at Fifty-fifth and Madison. We're just at the side of the building, near the intersection."

"I can go to the hospital myself, Magnus! I don't need your help, or your pity. Just leave me. The hell. Alone!"

"And if I don't, what are you going to do? Run away? That's right, you're good at that, aren't you?" Magnus snaps back at me.

I turn to him, my face feeling hot with rage. But I manage to answer back in an even tone, "I only run away from people who hurt me."

That leaves an impact, his face a mixture of shock and hurt. His hands fall to his sides, and as angry as I am with him, my whole body reels from the loss of his touch. I lean back on the wall again for support.

He nods, his eyes lowered. "I'm sorry. I'm so … sorry." The sincerity in his voice is clear-cut, and it's tugging at my heart. But I choose to ignore it.

"I'm sure you are," I breathe out.

Magnus turns his head to me, his eyes searching my face, as he asks, "Will you ever give me a chance to explain my side?"

"Will it make a difference if I did?" I reply, but unable to look back at him.

"Yes. Once you hear the whole story, the whole damn truth, it *will* make a difference." He reaches out for my hand, and I naturally hesitate at first. But my body has its own mind when it comes to Magnus, and I let him hold my hand at his second attempt. Even with my gloves on, I can still feel how warm his hand is, and how my body gets tingly in response. I stare at our hands, and so does he, both of us undoubtedly sharing the same feeling.

"Sir?" We both look up to a familiar form standing before us. He regards me with a sympathetic smile, before nodding at Magnus, "The car is ready."

"Thank you, Alex," Magnus replies before turning to me. "Please, Isabelle, just let me help you. You need to see a doctor."

There's a desperation in his eyes that's undeniable, and before I can stop it, I find myself nodding back. "Okay," I answer, reluctantly pulling my hand away from his grasp. Magnus frowns a little, but before I can react, he swoops me in his arms and carries me to his Cayenne. My arms loop around his shoulders involuntarily, and before I can look away, I notice his mouth twitching up with the beginnings of a smile. I have to bite the insides of my cheeks to stop myself from doing the same.

He sits me gently on the backseat, before walking in long strides, towards the other side of the car. I use the time to buckle my seat belt while looking around my immediate surroundings, thinking everything looks the same, with Magnus's scent still lingering like it used to. The familiarity makes my heart flutter with excitement, then it spikes up as soon as he opens the door and sits next to me. He instructs Alex to go to Mt. Sinai, so Alex drives off in that direction.

The drive is quiet, with no one initiating small talk. This is fine by me as I'm finding it increasingly difficult to calm my nerves, knowing that the person I'm still in love with, but trying to move on from is sitting next to me. Magnus is quiet as well, but the heat I feel from the way he keeps looking my way, speaks volumes.

We make it to the hospital, which could not have happened soon enough. The tension inside the car is so palpable you can cut it with a knife. I reach for the door handle so I can hop out, but gasp when I feel his hand on my arm.

"I'll help you out," Magnus's voice is gentle, yet with a touch of authority that forces me to concede. He gets out of the car, motioning for Alex to stay inside. Magnus opens my door and lifts me off the seat. But what surprises me is that he continues to carry me inside the hospital like I'm some severely injured sap who's completely helpless.

It's embarrassing.

"Um, you can put me down now."

"I will, when it's safe to do so," he answers nonchalantly.

"I can walk, Magnus. It doesn't feel as bad as it was earlier, now c'mon ... "

I pat him on the shoulder several times, urging him to heed my request. But he just pauses and looks down at me with a look I give my son when he's not behaving. I instantly pout, and he reacts with a smile.

One never realizes how much he or she misses something, until he or she sees it again for the first time in what feels like eternity. Magnus's smile instantly makes me smile back, and that chip I've started carrying on my shoulder is slowly slipping off. I really do miss that smile.

I miss *him*.

Magnus sits me down on one of the chairs at the waiting area. "I'll get your ankle checked as soon as possible, okay? I'll be back soon," he reassures me in a gentle tone.

"I'm not going anywhere," I reply back.

He regards me a moment longer before giving me another smile, the kind that turns my insides upside down. "Good." Then he turns towards the reception desk.

"God, what am I doing?" I mutter to myself when Magnus is out of range. This is not my idea of a 'closure.' Not by a long shot.

Magnus walks back to the waiting room in a few short minutes with a middle-aged female doctor beside him. "Isabelle, I'd like to introduce you to Dr. Trent. She's our family physician and a trusted friend of the family."

Dr. Trent reaches for my hand and shakes it firmly. "Hello, Isabelle. Let's get you to my office, shall we? I'll get one of the nurses to put you in a wheel—"

"There's no need, Doctor," Magnus interrupts. "I'll gladly carry her."

"Magnus!" But before I can protest further, I am back in his arms, much to Dr. Trent's bemusement.

"Well, this isn't our standard procedure, but I'll make a very small concession since it's you." Dr. Trent walks ahead, with Magnus following closely behind, effortlessly carrying me like it's his business to do so.

Well, it's not. I'm no longer his burden to carry.

"This is getting ridiculous. Why are you even staying back for this? I can manage, for crying out loud. Don't you have an empire to run? People to deceive and to ruin, that sort of thing?"

I promptly regret the words that came out of my unfiltered mouth. Magnus pauses mid-step, letting Dr. Trent move ahead. He looks down at me, and I meet his eyes indignantly, steeling myself from the sea of blue that hits me like a rogue wave. But I'm not prepared for the beginnings of a smirk that appears on that damned handsome face of his. He lowers his face and lifts me up slightly, so his mouth is just grazing the tip of my earlobe.

"You have no idea how much I missed that gutsy temper of yours, Isabelle. I don't even mind that it's directed at me. But know this, I do have means to make your anger dissipate, so just give me an excuse, and I will take pleasure in using every single one of them on you."

I stifle a gasp.

Arrogant bastard!

And as soon as he straightens up, I turn my head away and cross my arms, trying to create a barrier between us. It's an impossible feat, knowing I'm still being carried in his arms. It doesn't help either that what he just said is actually getting me excited. Why can't my body just work with my brain for once when it comes to him?

We step inside the elevator with Dr. Trent and continue to follow her to her office. To my relief, we finally make it inside Dr. Trent's office, and he sits me on the examination table. He moves away, but stops just by the door, leaning on its frame with his arms crossed. I roll my eyes at him, trying not to notice how utterly breathtaking he looks in his suit. I turn my attention to the doctor instead. After removing my sock and shoe on my injured foot, she examines my ankle, all the way up to my knee.

"Well, young lady, it appears you may have sprained your ankle. It's nothing serious, and the slight swelling will go down hopefully by tonight. Just make sure to ice it as soon as possible. Otherwise, if the pain gets too much, I can prescribe some painkillers. Within a week or so, you should be able to walk around with it like normal. But for now, if you do have to walk, I suggest you do it in very short spurts."

"Are you sure Isabelle doesn't need an X-ray? Will she need bed rest, just to be on the safe side?" We both turn towards Magnus, and I can't help but notice the genuine concern on his face as he stares at my affected leg.

But this is my ankle, and it's not really any of his concerns what needs to be done with it. "So I can go to work, Doctor? I'll just sit down most of the time if I have to, or get someone to help me out?"

Dr. Trent nods, "If you can manage the pain, then yes, it should be okay. And to answer your question, Magnus, no, an X-ray isn't necessary. She merely rolled her ankle, and once the swelling is gone, she can put some weight on it, but only for very short periods of time until it's completely healed."

Dr. Trent turns back to me. "So do you have any questions, Isabelle?"

Shaking my head, I answer, "No. Thank you so much for seeing me so quickly, Dr. Trent." I reach for my sock and shoe, but Magnus won't have any of it. He now has both in his hands.

I look up to him questioningly.

40

"Let me," is all he says before gently putting the sock over my foot and tying the laces of my shoe. Magnus's eyes never leaves my face when he starts speaking again, "Doctor, Isabelle can be stubborn and refuses to listen at times, even if it's for her own good. Is there something she can use to assist with her walking while she's in recovery? Knowing her, she'll most likely refuse help in the first place. So if she prefers to do things her way, is there something she can use so she won't suffer in the process?"

Oh my God, he didn't just ...

Ugh, this man is insufferable!

If he wants me to read between the lines, then I won't have any problems doing so. He might as well put them in all caps with blinking lights everywhere!

Dr. Trent eyes us both warily. "Well ... Isabelle, you can use a walking stick if you prefer to, so your ankle won't feel too much pressure, but—"

"We'll get one, Dr. Trent. If you can arrange for that, please, I will be very thankful," Magnus interrupts not so subtly, feeling my ankle once more and leaving a slew of tingles all over in its wake. Then he stands up and straightens himself like what he just did was nothing short of normal.

"No, Dr. Trent, *I'll* get one," I firmly insist.

Dr. Trent sighs and shakes her head before standing up. "You can work it out between you two," she says before turning to me. "I'll have it ready for collection at the reception desk. I would say you're about five feet four or five, right?" she asks.

Nodding, I answer, "Yes, I'm about five feet five, Doctor."

She nods back and enters some details in her computer. I slide myself off the table, so I can be on my feet, not giving Magnus a chance to put his hands on me again. The last thing I want is to have my legs feel like jelly from his touch.

"Thanks again, Dr. Trent. I'll see myself out." I turn to leave, just as Magnus is signing off some papers. But before I can reach the door, he has his arm around me once again.

With gritted teeth, I turn to him and whisper, "If you try to carry me again, I *will* hurt you."

Magnus opens the door for me and leaves enough room so I can make my way out, and just as I'm walking past him, he responds, "You can't hurt me more than you already have, but I'd like to see you try."

His words hit me like a punch in the stomach. How dare he say he's hurt when he's the one who broke my heart?

"Whatever you got, you well and truly deserved," I answer back coldly. Just like that, I am off my feet and in his arms again, making me yelp out in surprise.

"Well, if I'm in for more hurt, I might as well make it worth my while," he replies just as coolly as he makes his way towards the elevator.

"Put me down, you bastard!" I smack my fists against his chest, but he doesn't even flinch. So I act on instinct. I slap him, but only hard enough to get his attention. He clenches his jaw but doesn't react and continues to carry me like nothing happened. As soon as we're inside the elevator, all by ourselves, I consider slapping him again, but before I know it, he puts me on my feet, places one of his arms around my waist and holds me close, while his other hand gathers my wrists. Now I see in plain sight that he is livid, his blue eyes darkening. I should be scared of it because I've never seen him angry like this. But what comes next is something I didn't foresee. He pulls me closer, and he slams his lips against mine. A whimper escapes me from the force of his act. His mouth doesn't open, nor is he forcing my own mouth to open for him. There's no softness to this kiss. His intention is to shock me, to leave me breathless enough to be subdued.

And it's working. As my eyes close involuntarily, I *know* it's definitely working.

But just like that, our contact is lost. Magnus pulls his head away, still holding me close against his body. I don't even realize that the elevator isn't moving until he presses the button going to the ground floor.

I will my brain to form cutting words to throw at him, but all I manage to do is stare in his eyes while trying to keep my heart from beating too fast. The elevator doors finally open, and instead of carrying me, Magnus places my arm around his waist, as he secures me with his arm, finally allowing me to walk, while using him as my crutch. I am still too stunned to protest, my whole body still reeling from that sudden kiss. And that's when I realize he was able to use one of his means to curb my temper … he kissed me to shut me up.

Am I that much of an open book that he can read me so easily? Does Magnus know that in those three months we were apart, my whole body literally ached for his touch? My cheeks feel hot, and I'm sure I'm blushing like an idiot. This can't happen again. I've let him use my attraction for him to control me … *again*. I need to get hold of myself and keep myself from getting this affected by him.

He has taken over on my behalf at the reception desk, signing off more paperwork, and securing my walking stick, while I'm just standing next to him, still trying to gain some of my composure.

"Would you like to try this one?" Magnus hands me my walking stick, and as soon as I have it in my hand, I let go of him. He keeps a hand on my back, but once I feel stable enough with the stick, I push that hand off me as well. He frowns but turns to the paperwork instead. That's when I carefully make my exit out of the hospital, and hopefully out of Magnus's life.

Yes, I'm running away from Magnus. Again.

If I can't be with him, I want to be as far away from him as I can.

The first thing I do is scan the street for a cab, thinking I need to call Helen and let her know I can't go to work today. I have to go home and rest my ankle, and then go back to work tomorrow.

"If you think I'll let you go home on your own in your condition, then you are sadly mistaken." Magnus catches up, and that's when I notice his car is waiting for him nearby.

I turn to him with a scowl, "And if you think I'll let you take me home, then you are sadly delusional. This is where we part ways, Magnus." I take a step forward, before turning back to him. "Oh, and I was going to thank you for taking me to the hospital but then I realized I wouldn't even be in this predicament in the first place if it weren't for you. So good-bye, Magnus."

I attempt to limp away, holding my head up high, but he quickly closes our distance, and he is now standing only inches away from me. "Why do you keep running away from me, Isabelle? What are you so afraid of?"

My eyes widen incredulously. "*I'm* afraid? Well, that's rich! I was the one who opened up to you. I told you my darkest secret. Me! I did that! I wasn't the one who was afraid … you were. You had so many chances to 'fess up but you never did!"

"You told me about what happened to you because you felt you had no choice! Remember, you said you didn't want to tell me?

Or have you forgotten, Isabelle? But I listened … I listened, and I never left your side because I care about you. Fuck that, I listened because I care *and* love you."

He renders me speechless with his statement. *Love…* in the present tense. He still loves me?

Or is this another lie?

God, I'm still as confused as ever.

"Have you read my letters, at least?"

His letters. During that time we were living in the old apartment, Magnus personally came to visit with flowers. But it wasn't just flowers. Every other day, a letter would be tucked inside. Michelle accepted them on my behalf because I refused to see him. If Michelle wasn't around and Magnus came by, he would just leave the flowers by the steps, waiting until Michelle was around to hand his letter.

"No, I threw them away," I answer hastily. But I'm lying. I kept them all, but I couldn't bear to read them, fully convinced they were lies conjured by Magnus, just written on some fancy paper.

I glimpse the hurt in his eyes, and I should be enjoying seeing him squirm, but instead, I only feel guilt at my spiteful words.

"Why can't you just let me explain, Isabelle?" he asks me softly.

Again, that question. I struggle for an answer, biting my lip in the process. Unfortunately, it draws his blue eyes down to it, and now he stares at my lips as he lets out a deep exhale, a small cloud of foggy mist forming between us. He lifts his hand up, his thumb close to touching my mouth, but I move my head, knowing his touch will just break down my defenses.

"I'm still fighting for both of us, Isabelle. But I can't fight for us if you keep fighting *against* us."

"Excuse me, but why? A lost cause is never worth fighting for. This battle was fated to fail from the beginning," I answer stoically.

"Isabelle …" he tries to touch my face again.

"No, stop." I raise my hand up, shaking my head. "This is not the right place, nor the right time."

"Does that mean you're giving me a chance? I need to see you again. If you want closure, then you need to hear my side first." He looks on, with determination in those eyes.

"How do I know if you're going to tell me the truth?"

———

"Because I have never lied to you. I just kept the truth from you. There's a difference. I can tell you everything right now, if you'll let me."

His suggestion is tempting, but I'm not sure myself if my heart is open and willing to accept what he has to say.

"Not now, but soon, maybe ... hopefully." I inch backwards, about to turn away. But he takes hold of my hand, and he places a card or some sort, on my palm.

"Here, I'm not sure if you still have my number, and I wouldn't be surprised if you deleted me from your contacts. But now you have my card, and when you're ready, please do call me."

I actually still have his number. I could never bring myself to delete it, no matter how wounded I am with what he did to me. Somehow, having his name in my phone feels like a necessity to keep me from going insane.

But he doesn't need to know that.

So I just nod back at him, "Okay, thank you."

I try to pull away, but he won't let me go just yet. With his other hand, Magnus tilts my head up so we are face-to-face. It's freezing outside, but his touch makes me feel completely warm all over, so I relent. He grazes his thumb on my cheek, and I suck in my breath as he dips his head. My eyelids begin to lower down, my face tilting up on its own accord. It's as if my whole body is yearning for his kiss. But his lips barely graze my trembling mouth, as he moves slightly over my cheek, and stops a hairs breadth from my ear.

"I'm sorry about your ankle. I'll admit that's my fault. But I'm not sorry for kissing you because deep down, you know you miss my lips as much as I miss yours." Magnus lifts his head and holds my gaze. "Look me in the eyes and tell me you don't want me to kiss you again," he whispers in a tone rich with conviction.

"It doesn't matter what I want," I answer back, looking straight in his eyes as I form my own onslaught of questions.

"How were you able to follow me, and what directions I went to? There were so many people out there, and as you can see, I changed my hair color. How did you do it, and why were you standing so close at the lights? Were you stalking me?"

My barrage of questions catches him off-guard, and he loosens his hold on me. "If you want me to answer all your questions, then go out with me. I'll tell you everything, Isabelle."

I want to say yes so badly, but I'm not willing to risk opening that door again. The wound is still raw, even after all this time has passed.

So instead, I remove myself from his hold.

"Good-bye, Magnus," I manage to say.

I turn around, and I carefully walk to the curb, surprised to see Alex beside a cab he just hailed for me. I turn my head one last time while Alex opens the cab door, for me to get in. Magnus is just standing there with his hands in his pockets, looking forlorn, yet still managing to give me a small smile and a nod. My chest constricts at the sight, so to ease the dull pain, I get inside the cab, thanking Alex before closing the door. After giving the driver directions to my new place, I sit back as he drives on. As I look straight ahead, I'm hoping that I can hold my composure, and not scream out to high heaven.

What. The hell. Just happened???

CHAPTER 7

I'm sitting on the couch with my leg propped up on pillows, an ice pack wrapped around my ankle, while eating a bag of potato chips with a big mug of hot chocolate. The only thing good enough to watch on TV is a sitcom from thirty years ago.

Yet neither the mind-numbing show nor the cholesterol-laden treat succeeds to distract me from what happened this morning.

A while ago, Michelle came up from the apartment she's sharing with Nathan to help me out, but not before asking me how I had the injury in the first place. As soon as I told her everything, she was shocked at Magnus's stalking, then thrilled with his apparent chivalry.

But all her hopes of a possible reconciliation were dashed when I told her that I still refused to hear Magnus out. She called me an idiot, I called her a bitch, we had a stare-off, but then we eventually giggled out aloud. She hugged me, and she stayed on until it was time to pick up Ethan and Tasha from school. I tried to get up so I could come with her, but Michelle ordered me to sit my ass down and have a rest. She told me she would pick up the kids herself.

So now I'm all alone again, waiting for my son to arrive, dipping my salted potato chips in the hot chocolate before popping them in my mouth, trying to ignore the small rectangular piece of cardstock that's burning a hole through my jeans.

Why did I even think that going back to Grant Corp was a good idea? I thought I had timed it right, making sure I would avoid Magnus when I returned the stuff he gave me. Subconsciously, however, I must have known there was an off-chance that I would see him. But when I did, I ran away. And yet, he found me, and so easily at that.

We're like two opposite ends of a magnet; the pull is too great that resisting is virtually impossible. I can't deny it, and no matter how hard I try to resist, I'm still attracted to him. And seeing him today just proves it's not just a chemical reaction, or an effect from the memories of our times together—past tense feelings, spilling over to the present. This is real. This is all happening now.

And yet, I still refuse to listen to him. Why am I afraid to hear him out? I want to know the truth, but on the other hand, I'm reluctant to hear it from him. Am I afraid that I'll believe his explanation, forgive him, and make myself vulnerable to a new world of hurt?

Yeah, that sounds about right.

Seeing him again had awoken emotions I thought were better left buried. He upset me, confused me, made me want to hurt him … and damn it, I did, and it felt awful and gratifying at the same time.

My blood pumped like it hadn't done in months.

My reaction to Magnus was like an adrenalin rush that, I know from experience, could be terribly addictive.

That's when I realize that this is what being alive is all about, and I had another taste of that this morning.

As much as I hate to admit it, I want more.

Why did he have to kiss me?

My fingers drift up to touch my lips, with the memory of Magnus taking them as a consequence for slapping him. I pushed him to his limit, and, if this were Cooper, he would have taken the opposite route and hit me back.

There were times back then when I thought disciplining me that way was justified. But Magnus retaliated with the one thing that could weaken me more than any slap, or punch … his kiss. Granted, there was no ounce of tenderness in that kiss. It was primal—but pure and a little savage.

Damn it, he was right. I do miss his lips … his kiss.

My stomach tightens at the memory, and I know I have to put an end to this ridiculous pining. I'm supposed to be angry with him, not obsessing about him. That's when my focus diverts to how my ass hurts from sitting on it for too long. I drop the ice pack on the table and plop my leg down gently. I reach for my walking stick, and I get up carefully, ambling my way towards the only window with a view of the street. Ethan, Michelle, and Tasha will be returning back shortly, so it would be nice to see them as they come inside the brownstone. Setting the stick against the wall, I open the window and lean my arms forward on the window frame, loving the chilly winter breeze as it hits my face. I smile as I look around me. This part of Brooklyn is so much better than where we used to live because the neighborhood has been gentrified into an area that is

---

safer and cleaner, and more child-friendly. The serenity relaxes me. I exhale deeply as a smile rises from my lips.

That is, until I notice someone leaning by a post across the road from our apartment. I squint my eyes in his direction. He's wearing jeans, a thick bomber jacket, and a beanie, with one hand inside his jacket pocket, and the other holding a phone. He looks familiar. Of course he is, I've seen him before. My initial thought is that he's probably one of my neighbors.

Only, this guy just doesn't *happen* to be in the neighborhood. He appears to be the same guy who's been following me around! That's why he looks familiar. I survey his movements blatantly, making it known that I'm fully aware of who he is and what he's doing. He must've felt my eyes on him because he looks up to me, before walking off, about to turn a corner.

What the hell? Is he meeting my stare with a smile?

And a roguish smile at that?

Well, damn, why does he have to be cute?

Wait.

What was that about? I should be scared of him, not checking him out like he's a piece of eye candy! He may be a thug, hired by Cooper to keep watch of me, and he can assault me at my most vulnerable.

Oh, holy shit, I'm alone!

I start to panic, my heart beating erratically. I'm this close to calling 911, when from the corner of my eyes, I see Michelle, Nathan, and the kids approaching the building from the other end of the street.

Thank goodness!

I close the window and lock it firmly, my heart thumping out of my chest in panic. Michelle told me once that I'm just being paranoid, but this isn't paranoia. This is really happening. This guy is following me, and now he knows where I live. This is going too far!

I consider calling the cops … but if I do, am I ready to expose my past when I've been so careful at protecting it?

Hearing the loud knock on the door makes me jump out of my skin. But I laugh at myself for being ridiculous. Michelle opens the door, as I'm about to make my way to that side of the apartment.

Ethan steps in, hurling his backpack on the floor as usual. He sees my bandaged ankle and walking stick, and he instantly runs to me with a concerned look on his face.

"Mommy, what happened?"

I laugh softly, hugging him as soon as he's within arm's reach. "I'm okay. I just had an accident because I wasn't looking where I'm supposed to."

Because I was running from Magnus, Ethan, that's why I hurt myself.

"You have to be careful next time, alright?" he reminds me in a tone that makes me think that I'm the kid and he's the parent.

"I will, honey. Thank you for your concern," I reply back with a smile on my face, holding his hand while I make my way back to the couch.

"How about we have dinner up here, babe?" Michelle asks Nathan. "I seriously don't think Billie can cook with her condition."

"I have to go back to the clinic 'til late, so I can't help with the cooking tonight, but yeah, sounds good," Nathan nods back.

Michelle looks up to him with a small pout, "Another late night?"

Nathan sighs out aloud, "Yeah, too many animals in need, not enough people to help," he adds with a shrug, "but I'll be back in time for dinner here, okay?"

"Guys, no need to make all the effort on my account. I can manage fine," I interrupt, cringing slightly as I raise my ankle up on the coffee table.

"Oh yeah, I can see that," Michelle replies with a raised brow and eyes soft with concern.

"Mom, you can't cook when you're hurt."

"Ugh, fine! You can even help Michelle out, but only after you finish your homework, alright?"

So I gather Ethan and Tasha beside me so I can be of some use, by helping them with their homework, leaving Michelle to finish up her work, so she can help prepare the dinner later.

By the time dinner and clean-up are finished, my ankle is beginning to feel a little better, although I have a feeling I'll be going to work tomorrow still needing my walking stick. I tuck Ethan to bed after an hour of watching some shows on the kids' channel. I place

---

several pillows near the foot of my bed so when I'm lie down, my ankle will be propped up.

I'm lying in bed with my eyes open, hesitating to let sleep claim me. Sometimes I drink these herbal teas, and they help relax me to some extent. But teas don't take away the nightmares. I can't go back to my therapist. I can't believe I only went to see her again that one time! But my new job isn't as high paying as my previous job, working as a PA to the CFO at Grant Corp. But I'm not complaining about that. I love my new job.

I work as a store manager in this indie bookstore called The Written Word. The store-cum-café is owned by Helen McMillan, a lovely woman who is also a passionate book lover. She's actually from old money, whose father owns one of the leading hedge fund companies in the US. But the investment business was not for her, and when she was old enough to acquire her trust fund, she decided to open a bookstore instead, much to her father's chagrin. I seem to be drawn to people who like to pave their own path, no matter how easier it is to take a path chosen for them. It's probably because I can completely relate to it. Helen's business has been around for over four decades, and still going strong, in the age of mega bookstores and e-books. And in the event that she decides to give up the business, she still has her family's money to fall back on.

Not that she needs to, anyway.

Helen was also a single mother, who cared for her two kids on her own when her husband expired from a heart attack, just after her second baby's first birthday. She never remarried, focusing her time between her kids and her business. Now, because of her age, she can only really be in the shop once in a while. Plus, she wants to spend more time with her grandchildren. So she needs someone to be there to manage full time. I'd been going to her shop regularly, buying books that were usually on sale. Reading is my only vice, if you can even call it that. So when she told me about this new job opening, I jumped at the chance to apply. She knew who I was, and we've had some conversations in her shop before. So she knew that I'm a book lover, just like her. She offered me the job even before I completed the application form. Sure, the pay is far from what I would've earned if I stayed with Grant Corp., but I get the books I like for free, and food and coffee in the café are included as well.

I've been working there for a little more than two months now, and loving every minute of it. Helen is a wonderful boss and extremely understanding of my circumstances.

I grab the book I'm close to finishing, hoping the romantic undertones of the story will inspire better dreams. After a couple of chapters, I let out a big yawn, letting the hazy side-effect overcome me. It doesn't take long before sleep wins over, and I'm finally able to close my eyes.

***

I'm sitting next to the counter by the coffee machine, engrossed with the new novel I just picked up today. Two days after my run-in with Magnus, my leg is still not a hundred percent. I'm balancing the pen I'm holding above my upper lip, pursing my lips to hold the pen between my mouth and my nose. I'm sure I look ridiculous, rocking a pen moustache, but it has been a slow afternoon in the shop, and I'm bored. Not that I'm complaining. I need this quiet period, considering I was teetering on panic mode during the lunch rush. Chris, the barista and waitress, called in sick today at the last minute, so I was spread too thinly. It's a hard task to do when the shop is full … even harder when you only have one fully-functional leg.

I actually welcome the near-empty shop. With my ankle still bothering me, the last thing I want is to lose my balance when I'm serving hot beverages. I prefer customers to be hot and bothered by the books they purchase from the shop and not from the coffee I might potentially spill on their lap.

I don't immediately look up when I hear the chime of the door opening. I inwardly groan in annoyance, when I notice a large figure coming into my peripheral vision. He isn't walking towards the books, but towards me.

I look up with a fixed smile on my face, standing up carefully to greet the customer in. "Welcome to The Written Wo—"

Oh my God, it's him! I barely finish my greeting, and my hand grips on my walking stick a little too tightly, instinctively thinking it's a potential weapon if the need arises.

Shit. I'm gonna die tonight.

My legs refuse to move from their position, and I hold my breath as soon as he's right in front of me. I can't talk either. *This is just great, I'm going to die, and I can't even scream.*

52

"Hello. I'd like a large cappuccino with an extra shot, no sugar, to go please." He, whom shall be called my stalker, speaks to me for the first time.

And he has a British accent, spoken in a slightly rough tone. *Interesting.*

Another thing I note that's interesting? Having him this close doesn't put me on fight or flight mode.

"That'll be three dollars fifty," I finally manage to reply back.

He takes some coins out of his pocket and tries to hand me the money. I hesitate. This is why I prefer to be at the book counter instead of the café. Customers who are buying books usually pay by credit cards or bills. If there are any coins to give, I just lay them on the table and push them in the customer's direction. No touching, no panic attacks, no problem.

It's even more worrying because it's *him*. He raises his brows, waiting for me to take his money, while I'm still unwilling to move. With a slight shrug, he concedes and places his payment on the counter. I quickly slide the money over to me and mumble a quick thanks before I start making the coffee.

Try as I may, I can't help but sneak a look towards him. He's just standing there with his arms crossed, his legs spread a little apart, looking around the shop and outside of it, once in a while. He's intimidating as hell, possibly taller than Magnus, and *large*. Now when I mean large, I mean like built-like-a-tank large. And his shape is even more exacerbated by the bulky winter jacket he's wearing … the same jacket he wore yesterday when I saw him looking up at me in my apartment. I gulp slowly, feeling a nervous prickling all over.

He starts to walk closer as I'm frothing up the milk. The first thing that comes to mind is that I can use the hot milk to throw at him if he gets any ideas. But he stops just next to the benchtop where we hand the to-go coffees to customers.

"That looks like it hurts," he makes me jump with his comment.

"S ... sorry?" I turn my head in his direction. He is leaning forward, nodding at my leg. I follow his eyes before looking back at him. And that's when I notice how long his lashes are … and how gray his eyes appear, gray, with some specks of gold in it. And right now, those eyes appear concerned. The contrast of his eyes and softened expression, against his intimidating frame is quite startling, and I'm lost for words. My mouth opens, and closes, and opens again, but nothing is coming out.

What the fuck is wrong with me?

At least my hands seem to operate singularly, and they manage to finish making his cappuccino.

"Your leg. You probably shouldn't be on your feet like this."

"Oh," I nod, fixing the lid on his cup. "Um, yeah, it's not that bad. I'm perfectly capable of defending myself."

Ugh, seriously, did I just say that out loud?

He actually chuckles as he takes the cup I hastily push towards him, eyeing me still. I meet his stare head-on. I don't know why, but somehow, he doesn't really scare me like he should be.

"Well, that's good to know. Pretty girl like you should be careful in a place like this." He steps back with a crooked smile, the same one I saw yesterday. Then he turns around towards the door before I can even respond back.

Was that a warning? A threat? Or is it just a general observation? Why am I even analyzing his remark?

Thankfully, a young couple enters the premises, and Mr. Big Brit holds the door for them before he leaves himself, but not before looking back at me with that same crooked smile. I follow his movements, feeling my chest tightens until he's finally out of my eyesight. Once he's gone, that's when I realize that I was actually holding my breath.

***

I decide to close the shop an hour earlier than usual. Slow afternoon plus that encounter with the brutish Brit leave me with the need to be in the company of people I love. After arming the shop and double-checking the locks from the outside, I push my beanie down a little further and carefully walk my way down the snowy sidewalk towards the subway. I barely make it a block when I feel eyes on me once again. I know it from the hair at the back of my neck standing up. I look around me, knowing exactly who to look for, but as usual, nothing. Even in the cold, the sidewalks are still filled with people. I walk a few more feet, but the feeling of someone watching me is still there.

Well, I have enough of this shit. He knows I'm injured, and he might use that against me. I have to be one step ahead of him. So, as soon as I see the alley to my right leading to another street, I turn to it immediately and hide behind a large dumpster. I try to peek through the gap between the dumpster and the wall, and I see him stop just at the entrance, looking ahead of him with a frown on his face.

C'mon asshole, I'm right over here. I'm gripping the walking stick with both hands like a makeshift baseball bat, trying to ignore the pain on my ankle because of the way I'm crouching down. Big Brit takes the bait and cautiously walks inside the alley. As soon as he passes me, I stand up and swing the walking stick, aiming for his legs. But before I can make contact, he turns and grabs the walking stick off me, and in one fell swoop, he tucks my arms in front of me, and holds me firmly, with my back against his.

"Let me go! Let me go!" I struggle in a futile attempt to be freed.

"Whoa, lady. You were just about to take a swing at me, a cowardly way at that. But *you* were going to hurt *me*," he answers back calmly, but what I hear is the mirth in his voice.

Oh, so he thinks this is funny? I'll show him funny! "I said, let. Me. Go!" With my free and uninjured leg, I attempt to kick him in his shins. But he must've anticipated it, and he backs his leg away just in time.

Shit!

"Tsk, tsk. I gotta give you credit for your tenacity. But I suggest you calm the hell down before you hurt yourself even more."

"No, I'm going to hurt you!"

"Maybe I shouldn't let you go, until you realize that between us, I'm not the one who's going to get hurt."

"What ... what are you going to do? Please don't hurt me," I cringe at the way I'm pleading with him. This has got be my most idiotic plan to date!

"I'm not intending to hurt you at all, I swear. That's why I'm going to let you go, but only if you promise you won't pull that shit on me again."

I don't know why, but I somehow believe him. After a second or two, I nod my head, "Okay, okay. Now let me go."

He sighs out aloud, "I'm letting you go now." And he slowly frees me from his grip. I turn around to face him, and he steps back with his arms up, trying to prove that he's not going to hurt me like he said. He hands me my walking stick with a sheepish grin on his face. I grab it off of him, but I don't walk away. I'm not leaving without answers.

I speak up, though unable to look at him directly, "I know you've been following me. I want to know why."

"What makes you think I was following you?" he asks like he thinks I'm being ridiculous.

I snap my head up at him, blood rushing up my head in anger. When I see that same crooked smile, my anger goes into boiling point.

He's playing games!

"Don't you dare pretend like you weren't! Who are you, and why do you keep showing up where I am? Who sent you?"

He cups his chin and stares at me in a contemplative manner, like he's weighing the pros and cons of answering my questions.

"Fine! If you're not going to give me any answers, then I don't want you following me again or I'll call the cops on you." I turn around, back to where I came from. I manage to take two steps before he finds his voice.

"Magnus Grant."

CHAPTER 8

The sound of that name freezes me on the spot.

Magnus is having me followed? What the fuck?

I turn to face him once again. "Did Magnus hire you to have me followed?"

"I can explain everything, but not here. I'm bloody freezing. There's a café just around the corner—"

"I'm not going anywhere with you! I don't even know who you are!" I interrupt harshly.

"So you think you're safer, talking with me in a half-lit alley than in a café where there are witnesses who can identify me?"

Damn it, he's right. "Fine, whatever. I need answers."

I start walking towards the café he's referring to, since I've been in there a few times before. I don't bother waiting for him, which doesn't matter anyway, since he manages to catch up with me in a couple of long strides. We walk side-by-side in silence. That's a good thing. I need to manage my anger down to a simmer.

We make it to the café, which is half-filled with students from the nearby NYU. My stalker-cum-Magnus's henchman stretches his arm out to open the door for me. I ignore the chivalrous gesture, walking in without as much as a 'thank you.' In the corner of my eye, I notice him raise his brows and shake his head at me.

Screw him, I don't need his approval.

He finds a booth next to the window, much to my relief. The more witnesses there are, the better. But then again, he suggested that, didn't he?

"You obviously know who I am," I comment as soon as he's seated across from me, "so you need to tell me who you are, and why you're working for Magnus."

"Well, *I'm* hungry. What about you?" he asks, ignoring my question. He calls the attention of the waitress nearby.

As soon as the waitress sees him, a flirty little smile appears on her face. "Hello, Jacob! What can I get you?"

Jacob. Okay, that's a start. He obviously comes around here regularly. Could it be because it's so close to where I work?

I need answers, pronto!

"Good evening Mindy," he greets her, before handing me the menu. "Go on. Order something. I'm sure that thwarted attempt of yours would have made you famished."

Excuse me?

He's laughing at me. How dare him.

He thinks he's so funny.

"I'm not hungry," I tell him pointedly.

He sighs aloud, and then turns to Mindy. "Well, I'll have the chicken parmigiana pasta, and the lady right here will have steak—medium rare—with fries and gravy on the side. And we'll have two lemonades, please."

What. The. Hell ... Seriously?

"Why did you order for me?" I ask, as soon as flirty Mindy leaves.

He shrugs and counters, "Isn't that what you usually order in here?"

"Yes, but how did you know?"

He raises his brows at me again, a crooked smile slowly appearing on his face. "It's what I do." Then he stretches his hand out to me. "Jacob Haynes," he says, but all I can do is stare at his hand.

"Go on, it's just a handshake."

Just a handshake. I guess he doesn't know me very well then.

I frown while staring at his hand in two minds on what I should do next. But he refuses to back down, his hand still on offer. So I take it, and my hand disappears in his. It should freak me out, but the first thing I realize is that his touch is pleasant. Not spine-tingling like Magnus's touch. It's just that—pleasant and not sickening or anxiety-inducing.

Interesting.

But I have questions that need answers, so I take my hand back. "So why did Magnus hire you to follow me around?"

"Magnus didn't hire me per se. He asked me for a favor. You see, he's an old friend of mine from back at Cambridge. After graduation, I decided to get into the Royal Marines. I served for over five years, until Magnus offered me an opportunity to start a private security company here. It was something I've wanted to do after my service. Of course, Magnus helped kick-start the initiative. Now I handle his security detail, as well as other bigwigs in the private and public sectors."

"You didn't really answer my question."

"I kind of did, actually. Like I said, Magnus is a good friend. And he wants the best to protect you, so here I am."

"I don't need protection, or security, or whatever the hell he's offering," I chide indignantly.

The mirth in his surprisingly light-hued eyes is replaced with sheer seriousness, and he leans over with his hands clasped in front of him. "Your safety was threatened three months ago. Magnus just wants to make sure that you and Ethan are both safe."

My eyes widen in panic. "Even Ethan? What?"

"Your son has his own very discreet, practically invisible, security detail. I personally chose the personnel," Jacob reassures me with a proud glint in his eyes.

I break away from his stare, looking out through the window, observing people passing by, going about their business. There's a light smattering of snow all over, and the streetlights reflecting on the tiny specks of ice glimmer like diamonds. I know I'm distracting myself because I should be upset that Magnus thinks it's his call on what is and what's not safe for me and my family. But just like yesterday, I know he's trying to show me that he's still there, that he never left me. That, in itself, tugs at my heart.

But the last thing I want is my heart tugged. It's bruised enough already. I want my heart to harden at the mere mention of Magnus's name.

The only problem is that when it comes to him, my heart and my mind just can't seem to reach a compromise.

Thankfully, our order is served. Mindy serves my steak first with a tight smile on her heavily made-up face, while Jacob gets the flirty smile and a wink with his parmigiana. I turn my attention to Jacob, who seems oblivious to all of Mindy's efforts because he seems more focused towards me. He knows I caught him staring, but he covers it up by turning his attention on his food instead. It makes me smile on the inside, and when he looks up at me again, I get a chance to study him further.

No man of his height and stature should have eyes in that gray hue, with lashes too long for any man, in my opinion. It's almost girly, but on him, paired with the hard line of his jaw, and the more prominent lines on his forehead, the combination just seems to fit. I have to admit it, he's ruggedly good-looking from afar, but up close ... he's a sight to behold.

I can just imagine women wanting a piece of his intensity. I'm sure Mindy will be first in line.

"Eat. Your food is getting cold," he mutters as he nods to me, his head now bowed as he cuts a piece of his chicken.

We eat in silence, but once in a while, I catch him studying me. That's when realization hits me.

"If you and your people have been following us for a while, this means Magnus knows where I live, doesn't he?"

Jacob hesitates, then nods, still chewing his food.

"If he knows where I live, how come I never saw him around the neighborhood?"

"That's something you need to discuss with him."

"Right. But how ... how's he been, if you don't mind me asking? I mean yes, I'm sure you know that we saw each other the other day because you obviously talk to him on a regular basis, so..." I sigh out loud so I can recompose myself.

What I actually want to know is if he's coping well without me. Or is he miserable every day like I've been in the last three months. But I'm unable to utter any of those words. Pouring my heart out to a virtual stranger, another *man* for crying out loud, regardless of the fact that he probably knows everything about me is not something I'm comfortable with.

Only one person managed to do that, and he betrayed me. So, excuse me for continuing to have trust issues.

Jacob leans back, surveying me with his sturdy arms stretched out and his large hands on the table. "Magnus has a different way of coping with difficult situations. But he's doing his best to deal, you know what I mean?"

I nod back at him, taken aback at the placidity in his voice but also wondering what Jacob means about Magnus's coping mechanisms.

"I should talk to him, shouldn't I?" I ask, knowing my question is more for me than for the man sitting across from me.

He regards me thoughtfully, then, I see that crooked smile I'm now getting familiar with. "Sounds like you just answered your own question."

We finally step out of the café after debating on who should pick up the tab. I insisted on paying because I was intent on assaulting him earlier with my walking stick. Jacob argued that it would take more than a walking stick to hurt him.

He also added that he should at least make up for the fact that I probably developed some sort of paranoia because of him following me around. I couldn't argue with that, and I, in fact, confirmed his suspicions. So I conceded, and I had a free dinner tonight, with my former stalker and now confirmed bodyguard, courtesy of Magnus Grant.

As soon as we leave the cafe, he calls out for a cab, insisting that it's best for my ankle's sake. I don't bother arguing, since my ankle still hurts. He relays my address to the driver before leaning back on his side of the backseat. It's weird hearing someone who I just met give out my address like it's a second nature to him.

The ride home feels a tad awkward, with only a few inches separating us. I can't help but feel dwarfed beside him. He's built like a brick wall, which I'm sure is useful in his line of work.

It leads me to wonder if he's got a girlfriend, or a wife, maybe. I wonder how she'd feel, knowing she's with somebody who can keep her safe.

Must be nice.

I used to feel that kind of safe with Magnus.

Used to.

Halfway through our trip, I find my voice again, "When I went over at Grant Corp, were you following me then? Is that why Magnus knew I was in the building? Did you let him know?"

He turns to me, his brows furrowed. "No … Magnus seeing you on that day was just sheer coincidence and luck on his part, and that should also answer your last question," he sighs audibly before continuing, "Magnus didn't want you, or Ethan, or anyone else close to you, to be alarmed with our presence. So he requested that under no circumstances, should we interfere, unless any one of you is under a genuine threat. I wasn't around that morning, but I had a couple of my trusted people shadowing you discreetly. My people only report to me, and they informed me about your visit to Magnus's building. But I instructed them to leave you and Magnus alone. I wanted to just let nature take its course," Jacob chuckles quietly, like he's laughing at his own private joke.

"I got hurt," I pointed out while pointing at my leg. "You could've saved me from him."

Jacob laughs again, and I frustratingly wonder if he thinks this whole thing is just hilarious. "I'm sorry that happened. Truly, I am," he shrugs sheepishly. "Look, I know he's a very good friend of mine, so I am partial, but Magnus is a top bloke. And the way he talks about you … I've never seen him so happy, and yet so broken up about you at the same time. After his divorce, he swore he'd never commit to anyone again But, you managed to change his mind. I reckon he's in it for the long run if you give him another chance."

The seriousness in his stare is making me self-conscious, and I can feel myself blushing. I don't know what to say to that, so I keep quiet and look out the window. Thankfully, Jacob leaves me alone until I can recollect myself and my thoughts.

"I'd like to meet Ethan's security detail. Can you make that happen, please?"

Jacob nods in understanding. "Of course, I can arrange that. You can meet them tomorrow morning. Eventually, with your approval of course, they can probably start taking Ethan and Tasha to and from their school. At least that leaves you, Ms. Adams, and Mr. Vasquez with more free time."

"I'm not that concerned about having free time. I'm more concerned about the kids' safety, especially my son's."

"You can rest assure that they are in safe hands, Ms. Morrison. I handpicked my own people. They are well-trained, honorable, loyal, and generously compensated. Pardon my French, but they're not the type to fuck around. They do their job, and they do it very well."

I believe him, so I nod in agreement. "Thank you," I reply, offering him a thankful smile, to which he reciprocates with his own. The way his smile softens his features is a sharp contrast to his otherwise daunting frame.

We make it to the front of my building, and Jacob instructs the driver to wait. He gets off and helps me out by taking my hand in his. Even with our gloves on, his hold is comforting. Not explosive like Magnus's, but nice. I can't help but smile inwardly at how pleasant this feels.

"So, are you still going to follow me around like a stalker or will you start walking with me from now on?" I ask with a raised brow and a sly grin, feeling more comfortable with him now than when we first came into the café for dinner.

"Well, it's up to you. I am a master at giving people their space at a safe enough distance. I've also been told that I'm quite an arm candy." He wiggles his brows at me, and I can't help but laugh out aloud.

"You should do that more often," he suggests with a smile.

"Do what?"

"Laugh."

"I'm just laughing at you. Do you want me to laugh at you more often?" I ask lightheartedly.

"Sure, if it means seeing your face lighting up like that. No wonder Magnus is so smitten by you," he answers with a shrug.

Even in the freezing temperatures, I manage to blush … again.

I choose not to respond back at his comment, thinking I'll ignore it instead. I don't know why his compliment affects me in that way. But I'll just put it down to a natural reaction when a man compliments a woman, especially when the man mentions the name that makes the woman's heart skip a beat.

"So if you're walking with me, do I call you my bodyguard, security, friend?" I ask lightheartedly.

He tucks his hands inside his jacket pockets. "No need for labels. I'm basically just here to keep you company. But the latter would be nice."

"I'd like that," I smile back sincerely. I really have a good feeling about this guy, and it's weird that I have come to that conclusion so quickly.

He smiles back and nods. "Well, the meter's running," he says, as he points at the cab with his thumb. "Off you go. Have a good night. I'll be here in the morning with Ethan's detail."

"Okay, great. Thank you, Jacob. Oh, and do you need my phone num … you have my number, don't you?" I purse my lips at my realization.

He shrugs, and almost looks apologetic. "It's part of my job."

"I know. You're only doing this job because Magnus requested you to do it, right? It's … it's cool. Good night." I turn and head towards the front door without waiting for his reply.

"Hold on," he calls out and catches up to me. Curious, I turn swiftly in his direction. "Here."

I take the business card he hands over and read its content.

"In case you want to talk," he adds.

"Okay, thank you … take care." I use the card to give him a small salute, and I turn back towards Nathan's brownstone.

I close the door behind me, and when I peek through the small glass panel, I can see Jacob standing there for a minute or two before going back to the cab. Then I notice him nod discreetly at a black nondescript van parked a couple of cars away.

Right, that must be the night shift. Shaking my head at Magnus's security overkill, I head upstairs to my apartment where Ethan and the gang are waiting.

It's definitely time for Magnus and me to have that talk.

CHAPTER 9

"C'mon, Billie, you can do this," I whisper to myself.

After tucking Ethan to bed, I'm left sitting alone on the couch, in our living room, holding my phone with both hands.

I'm terrified because I'm about to do something I thought I'd never have to do. But what Jacob said tonight, that Magnus is in it for the long run, stuck with me.

What if he's right? My past made me so untrusting, but when I finally opened myself up and allowed myself to fall in love, I was left brokenhearted.

And I still am in love with Magnus, no matter how much I try to deny it.

So before I change my mind, I search for Magnus's name on my Contacts list and press Call.

I hear the ringing, and I wonder if Magnus knows it's me who's calling. A part of me wants to hang up after the third ring, thinking this is stupid, even desperate. But something urges me to wait.

"Isabelle … hi," the familiar voice on the other end of the line manages to make my spine tingle by just speaking my name.

Damn ...

"Hi," I greet back, my pitch higher than usual. "Um, I'm sorry … are you busy? I hope I didn't disturb—"

"No. I'm not. Never for you. I'm just glad to hear your voice."

Pause. "Oh, it's good to hear your voice too. Um, sorry, but I was hoping that maybe …" I sigh. This is getting frustrating.

Focus, Billie.

"I think it's time we have that talk," I finally manage to say.

"We do. Thank you for finally giving me that chance."

"I'm sorry it took me so long to want to hear you out. It still hurts, you know, what you did. But I'm ready to listen now."

Magnus doesn't respond straight away, and all I can hear is my blood pumping as my ear is pressed a little too tightly against my phone.

"I know." I finally hear him speak. "I'm glad you haven't completely given up on us."

"That's only because you never did … so maybe I should give you the benefit of the doubt," I blurt out, my cheeks hot and red.

I hear his intake of breath. "So, can I pick you up tomorrow night at eight?"

"Sure. You know where I live, so I don't need to give you my address."

"Yes, I do," he responds quietly.

"I met Jacob. Actually, he almost met the end of my walking stick. He's a nice guy though."

"Look, about that—"

"It's okay. I was pissed off at first, but I understand now. I should be thanking you for thinking about me and our safety, not that it's your obligation to do so."

"Nothing about you is ever an obligation for me."

I know I have to end this call now, before I start crying my eyes out. "I … I have to go. Tomorrow, at eight then. Actually, I'll be working tomorrow. Maybe we can just meet up somewhere?"

"I'm working from home tomorrow, and where you work isn't that far. Maybe I can pick you up, and we can have dinner at my place?" he asks in a hopeful tone.

I hesitate, "Uh … I don't think that's a good idea…"

"You don't have to worry. I'm not going to try anything, except maybe impress you with my cooking skills," he reassures me lightheartedly.

"I'm already impressed, remember?" I pause, before continuing, "I want to trust you, Magnus. I really do."

"And I want that too," he answers back, and I hear the sincerity in his voice.

"Okay. Tomorrow then. Bye." And before he can say anything further, I end the phone call.

I'm still sitting on the couch, holding the phone, and realizing that my hands are sweaty and a bit shaky.

I did it. I made the call which could ultimately end up being the worst, or the best decision in my life.

But it was a decision I needed to make.

—

66

CHAPTER 10

I feel the rays of the sun licking with warm goodness all over the length of my bare arm and hip. The feeling is so delicious that it elicits a soft moan from me.

"My beautiful temptress …"

I hear my favorite moniker whispered against my ear, the voice so tender and endearing, that my whole body tingles from head to toe. That's when I realize, it's not the sun's heat that's making me giddy, but Magnus, and the feel of his gifted mouth on my bare skin.

He's here. He found his way back to me again. How he managed to sneak inside my bedroom and lie down next to me, unnoticed, should be worrying me, but instead I can't describe how delighted I feel that he's here. Right now, I just need him. No one else … just him.

I am lying on my side, so he gently urges me to lie on my back. No words are needed, just him and my compliant body.

I feel his every kiss traveling from my wanton lips, to that sensitive area behind my ear, down to my neck, my breasts, and my budding nipples, making me whisper his name, then down to my stomach, and finally to my apex—all wet and ready for him to do as he pleases.

The first sensation of the tip of his tongue on my slick crevice sends shockwaves through my system, and I gasp at how good it feels. I reach down to grip his silky, smooth hair, raising my hips up so I can gain more friction. Magnus continues to devour me, unspeaking, but focused. I missed that tongue, and my entire body screams with joy. His tongue is unrelenting, his mouth persuasive against my clit. It feels too damn good that I just can't hold back anymore. My body needs release. Before long, my heart thuds straight out of my chest and my breathing becomes shallow, like I'm running a marathon untrained, and I explode into a million pieces, coming so strong that I have to cover my mouth to stop myself from screaming to the heavens.

Holy shit, that was intense!

I try to reach for him, to pull him up so I can kiss him, and taste my climax from his lips. But Magnus is no longer in-between my legs … or on my bed.

What? Where did he go?

I had my eyes shut the whole time. I'm still breathing heavily when I open them, and I prop myself up, crashing back when I realize that I'm the only one here in my own bedroom.

That was all me. Magnus didn't sneak in my bedroom, he didn't surprise me like he used to. I dreamed it all.

I hide my face in my hands, feeling shameful, even though I know it's not an uncommon thing. But this isn't my first time to experience this either.

Not another sex dream.

Why are my dreams tormenting me in so many different ways?

The only time I ever slept untormented was when I'm lying on Magnus's arms. He managed to drive my bad dreams away, just by holding me close.

I'm fully dressed in my pajamas, lying down underneath my thick duvet, and yet, a cold chill runs through me.

I hate times like these because I don't want to dream about Magnus anymore.

I want the real thing.

I want Magnus back.

***

I'm sipping my coffee, waiting for Ethan to finish dressing up so I can take him and Tasha to school.

My ankle is healing remarkably well that I can actually do without a bandage. But I decide to rewrap it one more time as a preventative measure. I also have the walking stick, folded inside my purse, just in case.

My foot involuntarily taps like crazy, not even noticing it, until my leg starts to ache. I check the clock for the nth time. Jacob must be waiting downstairs already. I texted him last night and asked if he could hold off my meeting with Ethan's security detail until after I spoke with Magnus.

Last night, I informed everyone at home about the whole bodyguard situation. Michelle wasn't happy about Magnus doing all of this behind our backs, but she somehow understood his intention. After all, she may be pissed off at what Magnus did to me, but she still has a soft spot for him. I think she was also relieved, as much as I was that the guy I thought was stalking me is actually protecting me.

Ethan, on the other hand, was a lot more receptive, even telling me it's pretty cool to have a bodyguard. But then again, he's eight.

Nathan was not impressed that this sort of thing was imposed on us. He refused to be a part of it, and he was adamant that Magnus has gone mental and overprotective, not caring about our privacy, especially since we've already broken up. So I knew then, that Nathan had to see it through Magnus's eyes. So, I set him aside and told him everything. By everything, I meant just what he needed to know, nothing more. I knew Nathan can be trusted; however, I can't bring myself to tell him every filthy detail. What I did tell him though was enough that his hesitation was dispelled, and he understood.

He did make it clear though, that he'd still punch Magnus in the face for what he did to me, and in a way, I'm grateful for his protective nature. If Michelle is like a sister, Nathan is the closest thing I'd have to a brother.

I finally hear footsteps running down the hall, so I take a final sip of my coffee and place the mug in the sink.

"Let's go, Mom!" Ethan yells out as he passes by the kitchen.

I join him by the door and lower myself so we are face-to-face. "Are you ready to meet mom's new friend, Ethan? Tell me if you're not sure, and I can cancel it just like that." I snap my fingers in front of him in a comical way, earning me a cute smile from my son.

"You said he's also Magnus's friend?" he asks, leaning his head to one side.

I nod back to respond, "Yes."

"Does that mean you'll see Magnus again?"

"You ask too many questions, young man." I give him a playful squeeze, hopefully distracting him, so I don't have to answer his barrage of questions.

"Okay, okay I'll stop!" Ethan giggles.

"I love you, my sweet boy." I kiss his forehead and reach for his hand before locking the door behind us. Tasha and Nathan are waiting downstairs, with Michelle about to get up the stairs to see us.

"There you are. He's already outside," Michelle says, pointing at the front door, her brow raised. As soon as I pass her, she grabs me by the arm, "And damn, that's some stud, girl."

I roll my eyes at her as we make our way down, where Nathan opens the door for all of us. Beyond him, I see Jacob standing by his SUV. It's a black Range Rover, surprise, surprise. He strides forward to meet us halfway.

"You Jacob Haynes? I'm Nathan, Dr. Nathan Vasquez," Nathan introduces himself before I can say anything, his arm now outstretched. I'm sure Nathan feels the need to assert his position as the man of the house, which I completely understand, but I don't see the need for it.

Both men give each other a firm handshake.

"It's good to meet you, mate," Jacob says, then turns his attention to Michelle. "You must be Michelle Adams, good morning. It's good to meet you too." He shakes Michelle's hand as well before bending his knees so he's at the same level as the kids. "You must be Tasha, and this little man must be Ethan." He shakes Tasha's hand, making her giggle, then he fist-bumps Ethan.

"You sound funny, like Harry Potter," Ethan blurts out. Tasha giggles again.

Jacob chuckles and nods back at him. "I come from England. We all speak like Harry Potter back home."

Ethan nods back in awe. "Cool."

Jacob turns to me with his crooked smile. "Ready?"

"Yeah," I answer back, smiling. I feel Michelle's eyes on me, and as soon as I look up to her, she mouths *Wow!* with her eyes wide open.

I mouth back *What?* as I shrug subtly while Jacob's back is turned as he assists the kids inside the SUV. Afterwards, he opens the passenger door and waits beside it.

"And good morning to you, Miss Morrison. See that black car over there?" he nods at a shiny but generic-looking car close by.

"That's Ethan's?" I whisper, and he nods back.

"Okay." I give Jacob a quick yet tight smile. I'm on board about my son's protection, but it doesn't mean that I don't think this is over the top.

With all of our seat belts buckled, Jacob drives the kids to school. As soon as we're there, he insists on walking us inside, but I insist back that I walk them on my own. He agrees, thankfully, but takes us up to the entrance, telling me that he'll be at the same spot when I get back.

Once the kids are safely inside the school, I see Jacob waiting for me at exactly the same spot he said he would be. He reassures me that his people will be waiting outside and will check the grounds once in a while to make sure all is well.

This kind of security is reserved for high profile people, not a couple of kids from Brooklyn. I don't even know if there is a real threat from Cooper at all.

But I do know what he's capable of, and he knows where I am. New York may be highly populated, and it's easier to keep your anonymity, but when that person has resources readily available, staying anonymous can be short-lived. I managed to remain hidden for seven years, and all it took to bring me back to square one is one person.

All it took was Magnus.

Even lost in my thoughts, I'm still aware of Jacob's eyes on me. I can feel him turn to me once in a while as he's driving me to the shop. But he makes no attempt at starting a conversation, and I'm thankful to him for that. We make it to the bookstore with minimal traffic, and I sit patiently while he parks the car close by.

Once he switches the car engine off, I finally turn my head in his direction, and sure enough, Jacob's attention is on me. But what surprises me is the warmth in his eyes, and it puts me instantly at ease. Out of impulse, I give him a smile.

"Thank you," I tell him softly. He only nods back in reply, with one side of his mouth rising up to a hint of a crooked smile. Then he leans over, making me jerk back in surprise.

"I'm just trying to get something from the glove box," he explains with an amused smile. His scents of soap and mild aftershave hit my nostrils as he opens the compartment to get a small, narrow box.

He gives me the box. "Here, you need to wear this from now on."

"What is it?" I ask, eyeing the box suspiciously.

"Please open it."

I open the box, and inside it is a watch that looks exactly like mine.

Okay?

———

71

"It's the same watch as mine. Why would I need two watches of the same style?" I ask curiously.

"Because this other one has a microchip that will help us track your whereabouts, if the need arises.

"Excuse me?"

"The microchip in this watch has a GPS tracking device. So if you get lost, for example, we'll be able to find you. It's for your own safety and Magnus's peace of mind."

"Fine, I'll wear it."

"Every day. You need to wear the watch every single day."

I take the watch from the box and swap it with my existing one. He takes his phone out and taps on some buttons, before showing me the screen.

"Here, see? Right now, you're located in front of your store."

"Okay," I answer, nodding. "Is that all?"

"Yes, but make sure that you wear this watch every day, until we sort this thing out with Cooper Thornton. Do you have any questions?"

"No. It feels a little invasive, but I guess it doesn't hurt to wear it. I must admit though, wearing this makes me feel like a spy, so thanks, I guess."

Jacob chuckles, "Well, I wouldn't go that far."

I offer him a smile, but the way he's regarding me right now makes me feel a little shy, all of a sudden.

"Um, you probably know that tonight, Magnus—"

"Magnus will be picking you up. Yes, he told me so last night," he interrupts, his eyes now focused ahead of him, and not on me.

"Cool, so anyway, if you want coffee inside or whatever, just come in, and I'll hook you up," I prattle on.

Jacob nods back, "No worries, Isabelle." He opens his door and walks around to open mine.

"You can call me Billie, you know. I mean, you've been following me around for practically three months, so you should know that's what everyone calls me, right?" I chuckle softly as I get out of his car.

He nods again before flashing me a smile. "Okay, Billie then. I'll pop over later for that coffee."

"Good, see you, Jacob." I give him a small wave before I make my way towards the store.

I still have my smile on as I open the store. I don't know what it is about Jacob, but it's so easy to feel comfortable in his presence. Yeah, maybe that's why I'm reacting like this when he's around. He's comfortable to be with. Maybe, we can even end up as friends.

Imagine me … with a guy friend … the mere idea would've freaked the hell out of me before. Maybe I *am* making a headway. Maybe, I *am* on the road to recovery.

The thought leaves me with a smile on my face throughout the whole morning, putting me in a good mood and making me feel less nervous about meeting Magnus tonight. I welcome the distraction with open arms.

The early morning is busy, but very productive. Chris and I dismantle the Christmas decorations all over the store and replace them with decorations for Valentine's Day.

After everything is done, I give Michelle a quick call, reminding her that I may get home late tonight. She knows that I'm finally going to hear Magnus out, and we are going to have our talk. Since it's a Friday, Michelle said Ethan can sleep over at their place in case I don't make it home before his bedtime. I plan on making it up with Ethan on our Saturdate. I got us a couple of tickets to watch the Brooklyn Nets play tomorrow. The seats are at the nosebleed section though, but hopefully, Ethan and I will get a chance to bond over our favorite team.

Helen drops in after lunch to do some work at the back office. She is delighted to see the transformation of the store and gives both Chris and myself a kiss on the cheek. She's always been such a sweet boss to work for, and the small tokens of affection are becoming something I'm growing happily accustomed to.

It's almost closing time, and Helen and I are busy assisting customers with their purchases, when we hear the door's chime ring, signaling another customer coming in. Only this time, it's Jacob walking through the door, his large frame a little out of place in this quaint bookstore. As soon as he sees me, his face lights up. It leaves me with a warm feeling inside. When he sees Helen, who I assume he would know as the owner of the store, he hastily removes his beanie as a show of respect; a gesture I find endearing.

"Hey, stranger!" I call out as he walks further in.

73

"Hey back," he replies in return. He turns to Helen, whose brow is raised, with a curious smile on her face. "Ma'am," he greets her before she can speak.

"Who's that tall glass of water, Billie? Friend of yours?" Helen whispers discreetly, her mouth barely moving.

"Uh, yeah. I guess you can say that," I respond back, shrugging, tucking my hair behind my ear awkwardly. I think that telling Helen he's my personal bodyguard will hardly go down so well with her. She's healthy enough, but I don't know if her heart can handle it if I tell her the whole story.

Hell, even I can't handle it sometimes.

"I'm Jacob. You must be Helen, Billie's boss." Jacob firmly shakes Helen's hand.

Slightly flabbergasted, Helen replies, "Why yes, I am. It's lovely to meet you. Are you two dat—"

I abruptly cut her off, "Um, Helen, is it okay if I just sat down with him for coffee? I won't be long, maybe fifteen minutes or so?"

Thankfully, she nods back and smiles, "Sure. Take all the time you want. I know I would, for sure, if someone like *that* walks into the shop to see me."

I can't help the laugh that escapes my mouth. "You never cease to surprise me, Helen," I reply with my arm around her small shoulders.

"That's me, always full of surprises," she laughs back, elbowing my rib. "Now go have your coffee with that handsome fellow, dear."

Jacob just stands there, observing my tête-à-tête with my boss, with mirth in his eyes. His smile widens as soon as I approach. "So, I'm here for that free coffee?"

"Of course you are! Heck, I'll even keep you company."

"Ah, this must be one of the perks of this job: free coffee and great company."

I laugh softly, "Yeah well, don't get too used to it." I lead him towards the café where Chris is currently in the middle of making coffees for two customers. She looks up, and her eyes widen as her cheeks begin to blush. Then her mouth lifts into a sweet but flirty smile.

74

"I'll have a strong mocha and a strong cap for this guy," I request, pointing my thumb towards Jacob, who nods in approval, before giving Chris a smile.

God, now that's a smile that could charm the pants off of any woman. The way one corner of his mouth rises up, as he looks at Chris slyly with those long-lashed gray eyes is enough to make any woman's heart skip a beat.

My *own* heart skips a beat, and the smile isn't even directed at me.

Lucky Chris.

Not that I'm jealous or anything. Well, maybe I am jealous, but only at how confident Chris is with men. I wish I were confident like that.

If only my past hadn't made me so damned irreparable.

Chris is a woman who has the best of both worlds. She doesn't like to be pigeonholed into a category, and she prefers to be called 'impartial', which basically means she's bisexual.

Coming from a Bible belt town in Texas, I was a little unsure about the third sex in general. Back home, everything was black and white, with the gray area usually vilified or swept under the denial rug. So I was hardly progressive in my outlook towards gays, lesbians, and bisexuals. That is, until I met Remy and Clara, two of the most beautiful people I'm lucky enough to be friends with. They never judged me for my past, and they opened my cottonwool-covered eyes and made me realize that we couldn't help whom we fall in love with. True love is never judgmental or competitive, but unconditional and selfless.

I thought I had that kind of love with Magnus. But how can I even consider that what I have with Magnus is true love, when the foundation it's sitting on is unstable?

"So, are you having cake, Bills?" I hear Chris's melodic voice in the background, and I look up with dazed eyes. Jacob is staring at me with an amused look on his face.

How long was I lost in my thoughts?

"Um, no … but thanks," I reply back absentmindedly, tucking loose strands of my hair behind my ear.

Jacob leads us to an empty table by the window.

"You like sitting by the window, huh?" I ask, curiosity getting the best of me.

"Force of habit, I guess," Jacob answers.

"Here you go, strong mocha for you, and strong cappuccino for this guy." Chris puts our coffees on the table, her eyes lingering towards Jacob, who seems oblivious to her actions.

"So, does *this guy* have a name?" Chris finally asks him with a flirtatious wink, making me roll my eyes in response. Is she trying to pick up my bodyguard?

"Jacob," he answers briefly, before gazing back at me. "I'm sorry if I may sound too blunt, but I only have a few minutes with your friend here, so if you don't mind ..."

Whoa. I quickly look up at Chris, who seems taken aback by his dismissive attitude, and she gives him a sheepish smile before quickly walking away. I turn to Jacob and give him an evil eye.

"Seriously? She's a very nice girl. And she seems to like you, but you blow her off like that. I thought you were flirting with her earlier!"

He shrugs, shaking his head. "I was just being nice. I knew she was interested, but I'm not. I'm here to see you, remember?"

Okay, there might not be a diplomatic bone in his body. Possibly because there's no room, with all the muscles covering every available body space, but in some way, I find what Jacob just said, sweet ... and somewhat flattering.

I take a sip of my coffee, before blurting out, "So, is there a Mrs. Haynes?" out of the blue.

I really need to do something about my filter. That was way too personal a question to ask. "Look, sorry, I didn't mean to ask such a personal question. Sometimes my mouth runs off before I can stop it, then you refused Chris ... I mean no one refuses her, but—"

"It's alright, it's alright," he answers, seemingly amused. "I'm not married, nor do I have plans to be married."

"Maybe you haven't found the right woman for you yet," I mutter back before sipping my drink.

"Maybe I found the right woman, but someone else got to her first," Jacob answers, the deadpan tone in his voice, making me stop mid-sip.

Is he referring to me? Surely he's not. Then why am I blushing?

"Oh ... are you talking about —"

76

I'm just about to point to myself when Jacob cuts me off, "Oh, you thought it was you? Nah, I'm just being a smart ass," he says. I quickly look up to meet his stare, and the mirth in his voice matches the expression on his face.

Jerk. He's playing with me. Who does that?

But in my relief, I laugh, and he joins in, making it more comfortable between us. Even in his bluntness and brand of humor, I'm really beginning to warm up to Jacob. It makes me think that we can really be friends.

"Well, this was short and sweet, but I have to go back to work. Those books won't sell themselves, you know." I take a final sip of my coffee before standing up.

He stands up as well, but stays in his place. "You mind if I just stay here? It's nearly your closing time anyway, yeah?"

"Okay, sure. But please be nicer to Chris. You might score another cup of coffee and possibly her number."

That earns me a chuckle from him. "Hang on, are you pimping your bodyguard, Billie?"

"Bodyguard? Ugh, I hate that word! I'll see if I can get you out of this job so you can actually look after people worth protecting." I roll my eyes in frustration.

"You're not so bad. Other than that one-off walking stick incident, you're pretty easy to look after," he replies with a grin.

"Well, at least your reflexes are good," I laughingly answer back. "I'll be over there if you need me."

He answers with a nod and another grin, and I hobble over to the counter where a very curious Helen is waiting.

"Sooo, is that young man a suitor?" she asks with a glint on her eyes.

"Suitor? Who uses that word anymore?" I ask back lightheartedly.

"Well, in my day, a man who wants to see a woman and lingers around for her, means he's courting that woman. So is he courting you?"

I shake my head at my old-school boss. "No, Helen. He's just a … friend who's got my back, so to speak."

"Ah, he must be gay then."

"Helen!" I turn to her, shocked.

"Well, he refused Chris, who's blonde and gorgeous, and he's only here with you as a 'friend.'" Helen turns me, so I'm facing her directly; then she holds my hands. "Dear, you are a beautiful woman. Who in their right mind would not see that? You should be swept off your feet and experience a sort of romance that we can only read about in these books."

"That's what I'm trying to do. I just hope she lets me."

My breathing stops, and my heart starts thumping madly, just like it always does at the sound of his voice. Only one man has the power to render me powerless, and now he's standing only a few steps away.

CHAPTER 11

There he is. With only a counter separating me from him. "Magnus ... you're early," I manage to say.

"I couldn't wait anymore, Isabelle. And you know I waited long enough."

Oh my God.

He walks closer, and I do the same, the pull between us too strong to fight off.

"Well, that's my cue to leave," another voice behind him thankfully breaks the connection between us.

It's Jacob, who gives me a small smile before giving Magnus a strong pat on the back. But Magnus barely acknowledges him because his attention is focused on no one else but me, consuming me with the intensity of those striking blue eyes. Jacob just shakes his head, and with a casual salute, he's out of the store.

I wanted to keep my manners to at least say good-bye, but I can't even manage to breathe properly.

That's what Magnus does to me. I can't fight it, and I don't want to fight it ... at least not anymore.

"Now, who is this one? He's very handsome, Billie," Helen chimes in.

I blink my eyes a few times, trying to regain my composure.

Magnus, however, beats me to it. "Ms. Helen McMillan? I'm Magnus Grant. It's a pleasure to meet you. Your father was legendary on Wall Street."

Helen's eyes widen in recognition. "Why, thank you. Yes, he was. Did you say you're Magnus Grant? Of Grant Corp, Magnus Grant?" Helen turns to me, surprise written all over her face. "You know this man, Billie?"

"Yes," I answer back, nodding and biting my tongue before I can say, *'at least I thought I did.'*

"I've actually come to pick Isabelle up after her work, but since it's almost eight ..."

"Yes, by all means, Chris and I can close up. I was just telling Billie that she needs to find a man to sweep her off her feet, but it looks like she's found one already. And a highly reputable man at that."

"Helen, it's not what you think," I whisper back to her, trying to explain, but she waves me off.

"Please, child … I had my one great love, and it doesn't take a genius to see something great brewing between the two of you. Go, have a great night," she whispers back.

Even after all of my adversities, once in a while, I get to meet people like Michelle, and now, Helen. She makes me wish my own mother were like her.

"I owe you," I say and smile back at her.

She laughs in that singsong way she does, before shooing me off again. I grab my purse and coat, and I hobble my way around the counter, ignoring Magnus's outstretched arm. I don't think I'm physically prepared for another contact from him. I catch Chris and her gaping mouth as I wave good-bye to her for the night.

Everyone seems to see Magnus as this amazing man, and he is, by all accounts. But after that night, three months ago, I see him in a different light now. Underneath his handsome, sexy, power-playing exterior, lies someone who can be brutal and deceptive, just so he can get what he wants.

And yet, even after all the hurt he'd given me, I'm still here, walking beside him, towards his SUV … and still head over fucking heels in love with him.

That's why I need to know the truth. I need to see him the way I saw him before. Maybe it's just naiveté on my part, but right now, I want to be proven wrong. I want him to convince me that underneath that magnificent exterior of his, lies the person I've fallen so hard for.

And if he's not, at least I'll be ready this time around.

"You look beautiful as always, Isabelle. How is your ankle?" he asks in dulcet tones as we're sitting inside his car, with him taking the driver's seat.

I look down at my outfit, wondering if I subconsciously tried to dress to impress him. I'm wearing tight-fitting jeans, brown boots that stop just underneath my knees, a black knitted top that is surprisingly complimentary on my body, a black coat, and a printed scarf.

I look nice, but this is how I dress all the time anyway.

"Thank you, I guess. And my ankle's getting better, although I hobble around once in a while. These boots are helping," I answer feeling shy, all of a sudden.

"Good. That's good to know," he replies softly, and I see a glimpse of a smile on his face. Then he turns his attention back on the road, giving me a chance to just study him.

He's so close, and all I want to do is reach over and touch him. But I need to show some restraint. Just one touch from him is enough to keep me from thinking straight. And now more than ever, I need to keep a clear head.

Good luck to me.

Maybe it'll be an easier feat if he didn't look so breathtaking, with his rebellious black hair, hand-raked to the back, with strands falling across his forehead, a five o'clock shadow framing his well-formed jawline, the olive color of his skin, a contrast to the beige cable knit jumper he's wearing over slim, khaki pants, and tan desert boots. I'm mesmerized by his large hands, with long fingers now wrapped around the steering wheel. Just a few days ago, those very hands were touching me, and just a few months ago, those fingers were inside of me. I close my thighs tightly at the mere thought of it, not wanting him to see how he's affecting me from the inside. I divert my attention to his face instead, admiring every feature. His nose is aristocratic, and his eyes are as blue as the ocean. And those full lips … they have been responsible for my core tightening, every time he smirks. And every time he smiles … it's hard to describe the happiness I feel when I see his smile. And as soon as those lips are pressed again mine, so soft, yet firm and demanding at the same time, it makes me yearn for more. It makes me feel utterly greedy for him.

That's when I bite my lip, promptly turning away so I can take my mind off him, and what he does to me. I don't think I can take anymore without combusting from the inside.

God, he's magnificent, and for what feels like five minutes of my life, he was actually mine.

Listen to yourself, Billie. You had him for such a short amount of time. What makes you think his explanation will mean he can be yours for longer? What if the truth you're after is the final nail in the coffin?

We make it to his building in no time, and the heel of my foot starts tapping as he negotiates the vehicle in his very own parking space. The nerves are beginning to wreak havoc all over my body, increasing in higher increments with every minute.

He notices my bad habit as soon as he switches off the engine, leaning forward and placing his hand firmly on my knee, stopping me from tapping my foot. It makes me gasp, but I stop moving at once.

"You don't have to be nervous, Isabelle," Magnus says as he looks at me intently. "It's. Just. Me."

I nod back, albeit a little shakily. This is crazy. I've been here before, and I've given all of myself to Magnus in this very place.

Maybe that's why I'm so nervous. This is the place where I became most vulnerable … and the place where I felt free for the first time, in a long time.

With a deep exhale, I answer back, "Let's get this over with, okay?"

He regards me for a minute or two, before letting me go, and getting out of the car. "Wait here. I'll help you out," he instructs. He walks around and opens the door for me, offering his hand to hold onto as I carefully get out of his car, mindful to put more weight on the uninjured ankle.

As we start to make our way to the elevator, I feel his hand on the small of my back. He leaves it there, until we're inside the elevator. That's when I subtly move closer to the rails so I can lose his hold on my back. I can't allow him to cloud my judgment with his touch. The trip going up to the top floor is quiet, but the tension between us is so palpable that it's almost suffocating. He might not be touching me, but I can still feel the heat in the way he watches me. Thankfully, Magnus gets the message, and he lets me out first as soon as the doors to his floor open, keeping his hands off of me, even as he lets me in his penthouse.

"I never thought I'd step inside your place again," I tell him as he leads me down the hallway and onto the living room. "And your place still looks as beautiful as ever, Magnus."

I sit myself down on the nearest couch, while Magnus heads straight to his minibar. "Would you like something to drink?"

Definitely. "Please. Just a glass of white is fine."

He pours the white wine in each wine glass, before handing me one, and sitting next to me on the couch.

"I actually wanted to sell this place because it reminds me too much of you. But then again, that's also one of the reasons why I love this place. And selling this would just mean I've conceded … that I'd never have you back."

82

How the hell do I respond to that? "So, what are you saying? Are you just trying to prove something to yourself?"

Magnus shakes his head. "No, it just means I'm not going to stop fighting for us. You know this, Isabelle."

"I know that you keep saying you want to fight for us, and I keep telling you there isn't anything left between us that's worth fighting for."

"Then why are you here? What did you want to see me for?" he asks, leaning closer, and staring at me intently.

"I'm here because I have questions, and you need to tell me the truth," I answer back with conviction.

"I never lied to you, Isabelle." Magnus sighs, and looking away, he continues, "What do you want to know first?"

"Did you know how Cooper managed to find me?"

"I only found out when I beat the answer out of him."

"You ... you beat him up?"

"After you left that night, I came back for him."

"A—and?"

"Cooper apparently found out you were in New York because a friend of his told him, then he confirmed that we were dating. He scored an invite to the fundraiser through another friend. I didn't bother asking who. I was too pissed off."

"So were you pissed off because Cooper was there, or because I found out you were only using me?"

He turns to me, and I'm taken aback with the fierceness in his stare. "I said it before, and I'll say it again, and I will keep repeating myself, until you finally get it through your beautiful but stubborn brain. I *never* lied to you. What we had, what I felt, what I still feel about you is so fucking real, I can practically hold it."

My breath hitches, but I know I can't be distracted by what his words are doing to me. There is still one thing I need to know.

"How come you never told me you were buying my father's company? He's never going to sell his company. He built that from the ground up."

He slowly takes my hands in his, and for some reason, I just let him. "I have something to tell you, and I hope you're ready for this. Isabelle, your father is very ill. And that's why he wanted to sell his company."

My whole body suddenly turns cold.
Daddy's sick?

83

"What … what kind of illness?" I ask nervously, afraid to hear the answer.

"It's stage three cancer. They found out too late."

"Oh my God! Oh my God!" I take my hand back, covering my mouth in shock, as tears threaten to well up. Before I know it, Magnus's arms are around me, and he's whispering comforting words. I don't resist. My tears begin to fall, and I'm finding it harder and harder to breathe.

But my anger finds its way out. Magnus knew all along, and yet he never said a word. Not a single fucking word!

I push him off as hard as I can. "You never told me! How long have you known? How could you keep this from me?" I start hitting him repeatedly on the chest, but then he holds on to my arms to stop me.

"Let me go. Let me go!" I cry out, tears blinding my vision. How can it be possible to break my heart even more? What part of me is left to break?

"Stop it, Isabelle!" Magnus urges in a low, yet commanding tone. "I never told you because Michael made me swear not to. Will you please just let me explain everything before you jump into conclusions again?"

"Fine! Explain. Explain everything!" I stare back at him with daggers in my eyes, my teeth gritted in rage.

Magnus slowly lets me go, then he stands up and grabs some tissues from the minibar. He doesn't hand me back all the tissues, but sits back down next to me and gently wipes my tears himself, concern all over his face. My rage slowly dissipates, and my breathing finally evens out.

He pauses for a moment to exhale deeply before speaking, "I met your father about a month before I met you. The manager of Acquisitions was helping me scout for companies in Texas because I wanted a foothold in that state. He had a list of companies that were in trouble financially, and one of those was Bridges Builders. I thought that acquiring an established construction company, in a state where we can foresee a boom in property development in up and coming areas, would be a sound investment. I personally flew down to meet Michael Bridges. He's a proud man, with a very astute personality. But he also seems withered down, frail even. We had our meeting in his office, and something on his table caught my eye."

He smiles a melancholy smile and reaches for my face, brushing his thumb across my cheek. "It was your photograph … well, it was a teenage version of you … but it still took my breath away."

I can't deny the sincerity in his eyes, and it makes my chest tighten. But I don't utter a word.

Magnus continues, "Michael must have noticed me staring at your photograph, and that was when he told me that one of the reasons why he was selling his company was because he lost a lot of money exhausting his resources, trying to look for his daughter, the girl in the photograph … you. He said you ran away from home. He never told me why you did so, he just said that one day, you up and left, not even leaving a letter for them. He said, back then, that was about seven years ago, but looking at him, I could see it still affected him greatly. He's a father who lost his daughter. And as a mother yourself, you would know that it's not something you can move on from, at all."

He pauses, looking away. "And then he told me the second reason why he had to sell his company. A few months before our meeting, he found out he had cancer of the liver. He didn't elaborate, but it doesn't take a genius to see it's taking a huge toll on his health. We talked about the company at length, but eventually, he felt too tired to continue. That was enough for me, anyway. I knew straight away that I had to buy the company. I saw the pride he had for Bridges Builders, but when he talked about you … I saw how much he was hurting when he lost you, Isabelle. And the cancer just made things a whole lot worse. That's why I didn't want this company to go to someone else. I may be a shrewd businessman, but I'm not heartless like what you assume I am."

"But you didn't want to reacquire my father's company anymore, right?" I mutter out, my voice shaky.

"I'll get to that. First, I want to tell you everything." Magnus inches closer. "Your face stuck in my head, Isabelle, and no matter how hard I tried, I couldn't seem to stop thinking about that girl in the photograph. When I saw you for the first time at Le Bocca, I couldn't believe my luck. I didn't even think about your father. I just couldn't believe you were right there, working in the same restaurant I frequent. I asked about your schedule and booked a work dinner there on the same night you were working. I just wanted to see you again. And when I saw you enter Charles's office, it was like the universe was working in my favor. But your father was still at the back of my head. I knew he was still looking for you, and he was still ill, but I was selfish. If you want to get mad at me, get mad at me now because I was selfish."

"I don't understand. Why?" I whisper.

He inches closer once again, his fingers finding mine, my skin tingling at his slightest touch. "I was afraid—if I told your father that I found you or told you about him, then you'd fly back to Texas and never come back. Like I said, I got selfish … and stupid. I wanted you all to myself. I've never been insecure, nor have I ever had a jealous streak, not even with my ex-wife. But with you, even then," he rakes his hair back haphazardly with his free hand, "I wanted everything … and anything you were willing to give me. When you opened up to me, when you told me what happened to you those years back, and how your parents didn't believe you, it made me realize I can't be associated with your father, or with his company. I decided to pull out, but I wanted to talk to your father first, face-to-face. And that was the time I went for a business trip in Texas … do you remember? I actually was going to meet your father again. But by the time I got there, your father was confined in the hospital. I wanted to go see him, but your mother wanted to speak with me first. Your mother … I'm sorry, but that woman is a piece of work. She told me that her friend, who was also known to your family, was visiting New York, and she actually saw you with me while we were having lunch at the Bryant Grill.

I couldn't deny it because she said her friend sent her a photograph of us together, which she showed me from her phone. She told me she would tell her husband I'm keeping you from them, and then he won't sell the company to me if I didn't give you back to them. That basically confirmed I was doing the right thing. I wasn't going to allow her to use you as part of a blackmail scheme. So when I had the chance to talk to your father alone, I told him that I was done, that I was not buying his company anymore."

I'm listening to every single word he's saying with mixed emotions. I don't know if I should be angry, or sad, or happy that in some way, Magnus defended my honor, but at the expense of my family … of my sick father. But what he says to me next, makes everything clearer.

And makes me see Magnus more clearly.

"Isabelle ... I told your father that I found you."

"You *what?*" I ask incredulously, pulling my hand away.

"Please ... I need to tell you everything. I told him that I'm not pursuing Bridges Builders anymore because I've fallen in love with his daughter, and that I know he let her down when she needed him most. That I wouldn't like to be associated with someone like that ... someone who could hurt the most amazing person I've been so lucky to know."

Wait ... Did he? "Hold on, Magnus," I hold up my hand to stop him from going any further, "just ... just backtrack for me. You've ... fallen in love with me? You actually told my father that you ... you love me?"

"Yes," Magnus looks at me disbelievingly. "Isabelle, haven't I been obvious in the time we were together?"

I raise my arms up in frustration, still unable to believe what he's saying. "Why did you wait so long to tell me, Magnus?"

His voice rises in frustration. "Because I didn't want the L-word to get in the way of what we already had. When you told me you loved me that night, I wasn't sure you meant it. After all, you were half-asleep. When you denied saying those words the next morning, I realized that you weren't ready. And I can't deny that it hurt like a motherfucker. So I didn't push, I didn't pressure you, and I waited for that right time. I knew you needed to heal, and I wanted to be the one to help you do that, without you carrying the burden that a four letter word might bring."

My head shakes slowly, and I look away. This is becoming overwhelming. "I'm still trying to process what you just said. I spent three months trying to get over you because all that time, I thought everything that happened between us was a lie. I wanted to believe that it wasn't, that you couldn't care for someone like you've cared for me without an ounce of affection attached to it."

That's when I remember something that has been bothering me all along. "What about Martine? Why were you speaking with her privately in that room? Why does she know about your deal with my father?"

"She told me she wanted to speak to me about some sensitive information relating to their company, and she needed my help. But it was an ambush. She was drunk and tried to make a pass at me. I was able to keep her away, but I didn't want to let her loose because the last thing I wanted was for my mother's event to become tainted by her drunken behavior. But then she started talking shit about you, telling me she knew that I was just using you as a pawn. She was so drunk that she bragged she flirted the information out from one of my people in acquisitions. She didn't have all the information, but she decided to put whatever she had and came up with that outrageous conclusion."

"But you never denied it," I reply, shaking my head, my eyes welling up again, trying to put some distance between us once again. "I was there, and you never denied it. I was waiting for you to refute her, but you never did."

"Isabelle, I didn't even know you were there! I must have been on the phone because I was trying to call Alex to pick up Martine from the party. I needed her gone. Then I just heard this commotion outside, and as soon as I got out of the room, I saw some guy trying to chase you while you ran out of the door. I thought it was some fucking random prick hassling you. Something just came over me, and I didn't even ask questions. I fucking hit him in the face and knocked him out. Then I chased after you, and … well … you know what happened next."

I close my eyes for God knows how long, replaying the events in my head, the things I heard in that room, what Magnus said after, the confusion, the betrayal, the anger, the sadness, the jumping into conclusions … the stupidity.

Yes, the stupidity on my part.

Because I never asked him. I went on the defensive and concluded that Magnus betrayed me. He begged for a chance to explain everything, but I ran away.

I'm sick of running.

I have to stop.

For him.

For me.

For us.

I'm so damn stupid! So. Stupid!

"Stop … stop, Isabelle. You're trembling." In an instant, Magnus's arms are around me. I don't even realize I'm shaking from anger towards my own self, for allowing my pride to take over and not keep tabs on my parents, and when I finally found a man who actually loves me despite of my past, all I did was push him away.

"I'm sorry. I'm so sorry." And the dam bursts, and I cry in his arms, my body feeling limp from both relief and utter regret.

"Shhh," Magnus whispers, "I'm sorry too. I should have fought harder. I was just afraid that if I did, I might push you further away."

"Is ... is that why you never showed up anymore?"

"You moved."

"You knew where I moved to."

"I did, but I also wanted you to stay put," he tilts my head up with a finger under my chin, and I drown in his ocean blue eyes, and the beginning of *that* smirk. "And just because I never showed up at your doorstep, doesn't mean I was never there. I didn't need Jacob to tell me that you changed your hair color, or that even with you all rugged up, I could still see you've lost weight because you haven't been eating properly."

"Okay, that is some serious creeper stuff you just said there. Maybe I should be more worried," I reply, laughing shakily, and biting my lower lip to try to stem my mixed reactions.

Only Magnus can evoke this kind of emotional susceptibility in me.

It feels amazing. It makes me feel alive.

Again.

After three months of just barely breathing, he's finally resuscitating me.

But there's one thing that still bothers me, or should I say, some*one*.

"What about Martine? Where does that woman stand in your life?"

"Nowhere. I haven't seen her since the party, and I haven't been taking her calls. And the next day when she called, if you only let me stay, you would have heard that I told her to get over me and move on."

Another lost opportunity at happiness; all because I drew another conclusion without confirming the facts.

No more lost opportunities. The man I still love is right in front of me. I need to make this count.

I hold onto both of his hands, gripping them tightly. "I've made so many mistakes in my life, and the last thing I want to do is to make another one. So I'm just going to put it out there, okay? I love you. I never stopped, no matter how hard I tried. I'm still in love with you, Magnus Grant. I just hope you still feel the same way."

Magnus lifts our hands, still holding one another, and kisses both of my knuckles, filling me with warm tingles all over my body.

"I never stopped, and I never will. I am fucking in love with you, Isabelle Morrison. Just. You." The conviction in his voice is enough to make me want to jump up and dance with joy, but the need to have his lips on mine has never been more stronger than right now.

So, as I watch him lock his stare at my lips, I deliberately lick them slowly, delighting at the sight of his stare becoming hungrier.

"Would you like to kiss me, Mr. Grant?"

"Yes, I do. Very much," Magnus's last word becomes a mumble, as his mouth crushes mine. He's greedy, and I'm willing, as I open my mouth for him so he can taste me, making me moan with complete abandon.

That's when I feel my heart beating harder, stronger with every second, making me feel more and more alive.

Clear! ... Boom!

And just like that, Magnus brings me back to life.

CHAPTER 12

He tips my head back with his hand on the nape of my neck, needing a deeper kiss, our tongues teasing, and arousing each other's senses.

God, how I missed this. How I missed *him*.

So. Damn. Much.

My fingers find their way to the locks of hair I've been longing to touch. Three months felt like forever, and as he dips me down to lay me on the couch, I know that we have to make up for each and every day we spent apart.

But there's no rush.

We have all the time in the world.

I dove in, head first with Magnus before, and I crashed.

I don't want to crash anymore.

Shit.

"Magnus? Wait … hold up."

"I missed how sweet you taste," he whispers as he nibbles my lips, flickering his tongue here and there, and leaving jolts of electricity with every contact.

I place my hands on his chest, an unspoken signal for him to stop, which he thankfully, and regrettably, respects.

His eyes, now darkened with lust, are staring back at me questioningly.

"We rushed into this the first time," I breathe out as he pushes some strands of my hair away from my face, while I try not to get too affected by his sweet gesture.

"I just think that maybe, we should slow it down a notch."

He blinks a few times, then he slowly lifts himself off of me. I instantly regret the cool air that attacks my skin from the break in contact. "You don't want to rush. I understand," he says while nodding, raking his hair back.

He gets it. Even with the frustration written on his face, and the way he subtly adjusts himself, he gets it.

Damn it. It just makes me want him more.

Not giving myself time to doubt my next move, I quickly sit myself on Magnus's lap, surprising not only him, but also myself, at my sudden boldness.

"You know what? I'm done overthinking." I hold his head with both hands, enjoying his startled reaction and the smirk that slowly follows. I flash him a smirk of my own, before dipping my head and taking his mouth.

"I missed kissing you too," I whisper in-between nibbling his lower lip and grazing his upper lip with the tip of my tongue.

My hands are lost within his hair again, just as his hand finds the back of my neck, holding me firmly, while his other hand glides up and down my thigh, making my insides tighten in anticipation.

"I miss kissing every inch of you." Magnus begins its journey to my chin, nibbling the very tip, leaving tiny kisses along my jawline, until he finds that sensitive part of my neck. He gently bends it to one side, leaving more skin exposed for him to savor. I moan out as I feel tiny goose bumps all over my body, my skin now highly sensitized from Magnus's feather-like kisses and tongue lashes.

"I want you," I groan out to him, my hands now bunching the front of his sweater. "Please, Magnus … I want you," I plead.

"You don't have to ask me twice, baby." I gasp aloud as he stands up, with my legs still wrapped around his waist, his hands gripping me securely over my ass.

It doesn't take him long to climb the flight of stairs going up to the second floor, a feat in itself, considering my mouth has been busy working a trail on his neck. It still surprises me at how effortless it is for him to carry me anywhere. Not long after, I find myself still wrapped around him, still being carried, except now, we're inside his bedroom. I lift up my head, looking around, seeing if three months made any difference, thankful that everything is the same.

"I missed your bedroom," I whisper against his ear, nipping his lobe lightly, evoking a low, sexy chuckle from him.

"I missed *you*, in my bedroom," Magnus replies, his voice low and rough.

God, that voice. And judging by the heat between my legs, my body seems to respond to it so easily.

I don't get a chance to reply though, as Magnus lays me down his bed, my legs still tightly wrapped around his waist, refusing to let him go. He dips his head and pushes his tongue inside my willing mouth, undulating his hips against me, and driving me insane with the friction.

—

92

If he keeps this up, I know I'll come hard and fast.

And I don't want to come just yet, not when we're both wearing way too many clothes.

"I need to see you. Take off your clothes," I murmur against his mouth.

What is it with this man that always makes me act like a woman in heat?

He smiles, something I love feeling against my mouth. I loosen my hold on his waist, and he gets up and stands in front of me. I follow his lead and stand up just inches from him, unable to bear the separation. He steps forward, one arm wrapping around my waist and the other cupping my cheek, and we kiss once again.

With our lips locked whenever possible, both of us manage to take our clothes off, pulling apart slightly so we can take in each other's nakedness.

He's fucking beautiful. I can't even find the right words to describe him. Every line, every cut, every muscle is sheer perfection. He seems bulkier though, like he'd been spending more time at the gym.

"You got bigger," I croak out, biting my lower lip to stop myself from drooling, but not stopping my hands from exploring his torso, his pectorals, his abs, everything I can get my hands on. My eyes move further down, and my previous comment is even more apparent at the sight of his burgeoning appendage. I have dreamed of his cock so many times, that seeing it in front of me, in all its sizeable glory, seems almost surreal.

"And you, my darling, need to be fed," he replies, pulling me back to the present, as his hand follows the contours of my waist, and my now somewhat visible ribs. My arms instinctively wrap around my waist, and I bow my head, feeling self-conscious.

"Eating wasn't a priority for me. I focused all my energy on work and on Ethan," I counter, not explaining further.

I guess it's pretty obvious why.

"Look at me, Isabelle," Magnus urges, and I slowly look up at him, taken aback by the outright concern in his eyes. "I don't care what your shape is because you are still the most beautiful person I've ever seen. But I can't stand that I'm responsible for making you feel this way."

"It's done," I answer back, placing my hands on his shoulders, tiptoeing so I can plant a kiss on his neck, then his jaw, and finally his mouth. "And I did this to myself, not you. I'm responsible for my own decisions."

"Well then, I'm taking it upon myself to make sure that you're not leaving without getting fed. But not before I fuck you first because I can't wait another second. I'll fuck you deep, and I'll fuck you hard. I'll make sure you'll work up such an appetite, you'd have no choice but to eat every single dish I place in front of you, do you understand?"

I didn't think it was possible for him to turn me on even more, but he's just proven me wrong.

"Loud and clear." I take his hands and wrap his arms around me. "So what are you standing there for? Get me hungry."

He growls, the low rumbling reverberating through me. He hoists me up so my breasts are right in front of his face. He suckles one nipple, using his teeth to make me cry out from the shock of electricity it gives. He does the same with the other, licking and biting the hard nipple to submission. I can't help but close my eyes, and the sensation his mouth, teeth, and tongue on my skin seems to magnify a hundredfold.

"I want to taste all of you," Magnus roughly breathes out, as he throws me on his bed. He's gone primal, the hunger in his eyes turning me to putty in his hands.

He opens my legs wide apart, kneeling himself in-between. He bows and gives the distance between my pubis, to the valley in-between my breasts, one long, wet lick. The air hits the wet trail he leaves behind, giving me shivers and tiny goose bumps.

Magnus's head is now right in front of my wet apex. He kisses my inner thighs, torturing me with the wait.

But he doesn't give me a chance to get impatient. Before long, I feel his tongue on the length of my crevice, making me moan, and making me fist his hair.

"So damned sweet and juicy. You got me so fucking addicted," he says in- between licks.

He finds my clit, and he starts flickering his tongue against it, then sucking on the hardened nub. My lower stomach begins to pulsate, and if he keeps this any longer, I won't last too long.

"Magnus, I want to taste you too," I plead out, hardening my grip on his hair to get his attention.

He lifts his head up to look at me, his mouth glistening from my very own arousal, the sight turning me giddy with lust.

"You *will* taste me, my beautiful temptress, but I need to feel your tight little pussy, wrapped around my cock first."

Gah! How I missed that crude mouth of his.

He shifts his position so he's lying on top of me, his arms on each side of my head. With his legs, he opens me wider, his cock poised above my wetness.

"Take my cock with your hand and guide me in, Isabelle," he commands, as we stare at each other eye-to-eye. I do as he instructs, not breaking our eye contact.

I circle my hand around his hard, thick cock, and guide the head to my slick entrance. I let go of him as soon as I can feel an inch of him inside. Slowly, but steadily, he enters, and I can't help but bite my lip and close my eyes momentarily at the slight sting. Magnus doesn't move for a short moment, thankfully letting my channel stretch for his girth.

He starts to thrust slowly at first, and he calls my name softly, making me open my eyes for him.

"There you are, beautiful. Are you ready to be fucked?"

I nod, hooking my arms under his own and holding on tight. "Please fuck me hard, Mr. Grant."

That's all he needed to hear. He pulls away until he's barely inside, then he enters me once again with one strong thrust, moaning and murmuring how good it feels to be inside me. He does it again, and again, my cries of pleasure, intermingling with our slapping skin. My insides begin to tighten, and I can feel my orgasm building up like heated water going from a simmer to past boiling point. His pace quickens, and the increasing strength of his every thrust makes my body move like a rag doll. My breathing becomes labored, knowing I'm past the point of no return. Magnus's expert fingers begin to work their magic on my breasts and nipples, sending shock waves of electricity throughout my body, and making my eyes roll up from intense pleasure.

"I know you want to come, baby. Do it. Let me feel you come around my cock," Magnus commands with gritted teeth.

That's all it takes. I can't hold off any longer.

"Oh my God … *Magnus!*" And I explode, screaming out his name in-between ecstatic, garbled cries.

I can feel my insides contract and expand against his cock. He moans, lifting my hips so he can get deeper, with my slickness making every deep thrust increasingly pleasurable.

With a guttural moan, Magnus's body becomes rigid, and I feel him come so hard that even his eyes involuntarily shut. I feel every single twitch while he rolls his hips against me and empties himself inside. I tighten my core, trying to milk every last drop from him as well, making his pleasure known with every breath of my name.

Not long after, as his movements slow down, he slowly opens his eyes and fixes them on me.

"And to think, I only intended for us to talk," I groan out softly.

He smiles sheepishly, before answering, "Well, I can't say that I wasn't hopeful for more."

I chuckle softly, and he follows soon after. As our laughter dies down, I let my hands slide from his arms, stopping to cup his face.

"I can't promise you that everything will be perfect between us," I tell him somberly. "I will still have my moments, and I'm sure you will too. But if we remain honest with each other, then this thing we have right here, might just work."

Magnus takes one of my hands, and kisses my palm, letting his lips linger. "This thing we have here is very important to me."

"It is to me too."

"When you refused to hear me out before, I thought it was best if I moved on. But you ruined me for other women, Isabelle, and I'm so glad you did."

Oh. I think I just swooned a little.

Trying my best not to sound too elated, I brush off rebellious strands of hair from his forehead, a much-needed gesture to stop myself from melting against the passion in his eyes. "Good, because you ruined me for other men too. Thanks for that, you jackass."

That makes him laugh, and it makes me swoon all over again. That smile of his always gets me.

Yup, I'm done for.

"You're welcome, beautiful. I'm claiming you, and there is nothing you can do about it."

"Oooh, a challenge!" I answer mischievously.

He reacts with a scowl.

"You know I'm kidding, right? I *am* yours, Magnus. Just as you are mine. Martine can just kiss my ass."

"Nobody is kissing that luscious ass, except me." Magnus squeezes my butt cheek, making me giggle aloud.

But he's not laughing, and I quiet down.

"I love you Ms. Isabelle Morrison," he whispers, before touching his lips ever so gently with mine, making my toes curl.

"I love you too, Mr. Magnus Grant," I answer back, unable to hide my smile, pulling him to me so we can deepen our kiss.

And gosh, how different does this kiss feel? There's no hidden agenda, or a sense of desperation. It's a kiss between two people who are finally together, stripped bare, inside and out, with no walls keeping them apart. This is honest, yet extremely intimate, and all sorts of exhilarating.

This kiss is a kiss of two people who are completely and utterly in love.

CHAPTER 13

"I'm ready for another round. You ready, baby?" Magnus grabs my ass cheek and squeezes it hard … again … making me squeal.

Magnus is definitely a butt man.

"God, I can't believe you still have the energy after the last one. I'm getting really sleepy," I groan out.

"I told you, I won't stop until I'm fully satisfied," he palms my belly from behind in a sensuous way, then he lowers his head and starts kissing the crook of my neck, making me giddy like only he can.

"But I'm full!" I cry out as he walks over to the other side of the benchtop to retrieve a bottle of wine. "I've eaten so much, baby. I can't breathe," I add, sounding like a whiny, little child.

After fucking me, then making love to me in his bedroom, we're now in his kitchen, and I just finished meal three of Magnus's homemade degustation. He'd been reheating and even cooking random food for us to eat. So far, I've had pumpkin soup as my first dish, followed by an egg white omelet, and I just finished a small piece of steak with steamed vegetables. I haven't eaten like this in a long while, and my stomach is starting to protest.

Because the penthouse has great heating system, neither of us bothered to wear any clothing. Well, except for Magnus, who is currently wearing an apron while he's cooking, you know, because hot oil and bare skin never mix. Not that I'm complaining … from where I'm seated, I have the best view of his tight, muscular ass.

And as if a man who cooks isn't sexy enough, this man just upped the ante by doing it naked, well, except for that apron.

I just want to take a bite of that gorgeous ass of his.

Hmmm, does that make *me* a butt girl then?

Damn it, Magnus Grant. You just made me love you even more, and you don't even have to try. All you had to do is cook in the buff, and I'm done for.

He turns me around so my back is against the kitchen benchtop, and he leans his body against mine, so I can feel his arousal through the flimsy material of his apron. "Okay, dessert then.

I have an apple crumble in the fridge that I can heat up and serve with some whipped cream."

"Oh, what? You know how much I love that! But I don't have room anymore," I pout, wrapping my arms around his waist.

And just to prove my point, I burp, all of a sudden. My hand hastily tries to cover my mouth as I croak out an 'excuse me,' with Magnus laughing out loud.

"Ugh! At least *you* think it's funny," I continue pouting, but on the inside, I'm laughing with him.

"I think you're adorable," he muses, rubbing the tip of his nose against mine.

"Thanks?" I answer with sarcasm, but feeling tingly all over.'

The next thing I know, he lifts me up by my waist and sits me on the kitchen benchtop. I try to wrap my legs around his waist again, but he holds me by the knees and opens my legs apart.

"Well, I'm not leaving without 'dessert,' so I'm having this sweet thing in front of me." Magnus places my legs on his shoulders, making me lean backwards, leaving me completely exposed in front of him.

"I'm your 'dessert?'" I ask shakily, getting more turned on by the second.

He answers with a smirk, his hands on my thighs, firmly keeping me in place. Magnus dips his head down, and as soon as his tongue makes contact with my apex, my head throws back in bliss.

Oh my! I guess that answers my question.

***

My eyes flicker open to the sound of Magnus's voice in the background. After our late-night meal and his 'dessert,' we went back upstairs so we can take a shower, where I made sure to thank him for feeding me in my own special way. But by the time we got back to bed, I was completely exhausted and fell asleep as soon as my head is on Magnus's chest.

I must admit that after numerous nights filled with nightmares, last night's sleep was dreamless and uneventful, and all because I was lovingly ensconced in Magnus's embrace.

So I'm understandably disappointed when I wake to see myself alone in his bed, with Magnus standing by the window in just his boxer briefs, in a serious conversation with someone on the phone.

He sees me stirring and abruptly ends the call, before coming back to bed.

"Good morning, my beautiful temptress," Magnus greets me with a warm smile, leaving a light kiss on my lips.

"Is everything alright?" I ask straight away, rubbing my eyes slightly.

"Yeah, just having some problems with a project. But it's nothing that can't be solved with a phone call," he answers as he takes me inside his arms.

"Are you sure? Because if you need to be somewhere, I'll understand."

"It's the weekend. I don't plan on leaving this bed again for a while." Magnus's hold tightens around me.

"What time is it?" I ask.

"Eight in the morning," he answers calmly.

"Shit!" I exclaim, pulling away from his embrace before checking my phone. "I have to go."

"What? Why?" Magnus asks with a scowl.

"Ethan and I have our Saturdates, remember?"

The realization hits him, and he nods back, "Oh, of course. I'm sorry, it slipped my mind." He gets off the bed and walks over to his closet. When he comes back, he's carrying a gift bag.

"Before you go, I have something to give you," Magnus tells me with a smile.

I stop what I'm doing as he closes the distance.

"Magnus, what's this about? It's not my birthday," I remind him, eyeing his present suspiciously.

He places the bag on his bed, motioning me to sit down before continuing on, "I wanted to give this to you that night at the charity event ... but well, you know how that went."

"And you held on to it? Why? How do you even know that we'll get back together?" I ask, tilting my head to the side in curiosity.

"I never gave up on us, Isabelle. I gave you the space you needed, but I knew, well at least I hoped, that we'll find our way back to each other eventually."

"You truly believed that?" I ask, feeling overwhelmed by what he just said.

"It took us three months, but we're both here, right?" Magnus gives me a lopsided smile before pushing the gift bag closer to me.

"What is it?" I ask, feeling a mix of nervousness and excitement.

"If you want to find out, then you have to open the bag."

I tuck my hair behind my ear, feeling hesitant. But Magnus is sitting next to me, waiting. So with one deep exhale, I untangle the ribbon that was keeping the bag closed. Inside, there's a brand new, top of the line smartphone, a small red Cartier box—which I surmise has a jewelry in it, and a blue-colored envelope.

The phone and the jewelry are a weird combination, but I know expensive when I see one. And frankly, I don't feel comfortable taking these from Magnus.

"I already have a phone," is all I can say.

"I know, but I noticed your phone has a cracked screen from the last time we saw each other. I just added that the other day."

He takes it upon himself to get the red box from the bag, since I'm just sitting here, stunned like a deer on headlights. He opens the box in front of me, where a white gold necklace, with a pendant consisting of two, linked, diamond-encrusted rings, is sitting. It's beautiful. And even with all the diamonds, the whole piece looks simple and dainty. But it's still way too expensive-looking.

"I want you to have this, Isabelle." Magnus takes the necklace off the box, opening the clasp, waiting for me to turn around so he can place the necklace around my neck.

But I shake my head instead, moving away from it.

"I can't accept that. Why are you giving me expensive things? I'm not comfortable getting expensive presents. I just want you, that's all."

I know I must sound like I'm being difficult because what girl in her right mind would refuse such a gift?

Well, call me crazy, but I'm not a gold digger.

Magnus takes my hand and places the necklace on my palm, folding my fingers inwards to form a fist. "You *have* me, Isabelle. You have all of me. I just want everyone to know that I have all of you."

Oh.

I think I might be melting on the spot. How can I refuse his present now?

"Magnus, everyone will know I'm yours because I'll be right beside you … always. I just don't feel right accepting such an extravagant present."

"I'm giving this to you because I love you. And if I'm not right there with you, you'll at least have something that'll remind you of me," he answers quietly, as he stares solemnly into my eyes.

I'm definitely melting. And I can see my hesitation is hurting him. Maybe I should stop being difficult and accept his gift.

"Oh, Magnus," I sigh resignedly, offering him back the necklace before turning around and lifting my hair so my neck is exposed. "I'm accepting it because I love you too."

He positions the necklace around my neck and locks the clasp before planting a kiss where the clasp sits. He turns me around, and I let my hair fall back in its place.

"It looks stunning on you. Take a look for yourself." He takes my hand and takes me out of bed, fully naked, and leads me to a mirror, standing behind me so I can see it firsthand.

Magnus is right, the necklace doesn't overpower at all, nor does it look too flashy. It's exquisite, simple, and elegant.

And he chose this to symbolize his love for me.

Yes, the gift is a little too much, just like his love for me. Maybe that's why it's so beautiful.

I turn around to face him with a big smile on my face. "Thank you, I'll wear it every day. And thank you for the new phone. My old one's cracked, but it's still working fine, so I didn't expect you to buy me a new one."

"I noticed, just as I notice every single thing about you." His fingers graze just under where the necklace sits, leaving tingles in its wake.

"You're giving me the creeper vibe again," I tease.

"Creeper vibe, huh?" Magnus repeats in a low tone, as his hand travels downwards, finding my breast and squeezing it slowly, his thumb grazing my nipple, eliciting a sigh out of me.

With a smirk, he lets go of my breast, before walking back to where the gift bag sits. He takes the blue envelope out and hands it to me.

"And in case I forget, this is part three."

I accept his offering with a curious expression on. I open the envelope, and inside is a small piece of paper. I pull the paper, and on it are sets of random numbers.

"What are these numbers for?" I ask, holding the paper up.

"Those are your access codes for the elevator, the building entrances, and of course, the front door of this penthouse. We can set up your biometric access, but we need these codes first."

I'm stunned. And I continue to stare at the numbers.

"Wow, oh wow," I mumble out.

"I want you and Ethan to come over whenever you please."

"Are you sure? This is a pretty big deal, Magnus."

He smirks, as he grazes my cheek. "I am the master of big deals, or haven't you realized that yet?"

"I don't know what else to say, but thank you ... so much."

He regards me with affection, as I grab hold of his hand that's on my cheek, and I plant a kiss on his palm, my lips traveling to his bare arm, up to his shoulder, his chin, until they find his lips.

We kiss ever so tenderly, but then my eyes flutter open and find the clock.

"Shit, I really have to go," I exclaim, pulling away hastily, feeling the ache from being instantly apart from him.

"Let me throw something on, and I'll take you home."

"Okay," I agree, watching his amazing half-naked body disappear into his closet.

I use the time to finish dressing up, grabbing the phone and access codes, and placing them securely in my purse.

In no time, Magnus comes out dressed in jeans, a gray shirt, a scarf, and a dark tan peacoat.

So this is what he means by throwing something on?

I'll be damned.

He must have seen me ogling him, and he responds with a cocky smile. "C'mon, my temptress. Let's go."

After some time spent catching up on random things we missed at the time we were separated, Magnus is driving me back home, in comfortable silence.

"I think you should still buy my father's company," I suddenly blurt out.

"Excuse me?" Magnus turns at me, startled by what I just said.

"I think you should still buy my father's company," I repeat.

"I already declined, first of all. And how can you even ask me that, knowing what he … what *they* did to you?"

"Because you know as much as I do, that his company is sound and a good investment."

"And you know this because—"

"Because your company wouldn't have gone for it if it wasn't profitable, or at least viable to sustain growth."

He raises a brow, as he looks at me sideways, smiling, and possibly impressed by my answer.

"Are you sure, Isabelle?"

"He's still my father, no matter what he did to me in the past. I still love him, and if the sale will help him, then I don't want to be the one to stop that. And I know you'll take care of it, right?"

"Of course, I will. But he wants to see you, you know that." He takes my hand while still watching the road.

"I know, and eventually he will. But that will take more time," I contemplate.

He nods, checking both sides of the road before turning towards my block.

Magnus finds a space to park his Tesla; then he comes around and opens the passenger door for me. We walk up to the brownstone together, hand in hand tightly, until we find ourselves in front of Nathan and Michelle's door.

I sent them a message earlier that we're on our way, and she said to come straight to their place, so here we are.

Michelle opens the door, a ready smile on her face.

"Here they are!" Michelle shoos us in, and the next face I see is Ethan's—all lit up and excited, and running straight to us.

"Mommy! Magnus! Yay!" Ethan gives us both a hug, giving me a kiss on the cheek, and fist-bumping Magnus as well.

"I'm happy to see you again, buddy, you have no idea how much." Magnus gives me a sly wink, before lifting Ethan over his shoulder, fireman-style.

Nathan pops out from the kitchen just as Magnus sets Ethan down. He nods back at Magnus, though it's noticeable that he's still understandably apprehensive. But Magnus approaches him and offers a handshake.

"No hard feelings, man," Magnus says contritely. "And thank you," he adds, not needing to explain further.

Nathan offers him a small, yet friendly smile, before patting him on the back, and leading him to the living area. "Of course, man. I'm just glad you guys worked things out."

"Have you two had breakfast yet?" Michelle asks me, raising a brow in a 'read between the lines' sort of way. But before I can answer, her eyes zero in on the sparkler sitting just below my neck. "Holy shit. That's Cartier," she exclaims quietly.

I start playing with it absentmindedly. "Yeah, Magnus gave it to me. I want to wear it every day, but I'm not sure. Is it too much? It's too much, isn't it?"

"Hell, no, it's perfect. So what does this mean? Are you two …"

"I think so," I answer back, turning my head to see if he's listening. "Is it okay if we talk about what happened, maybe tonight, hopefully?"

"Of course, baby girl. But you must be tired from, you know, making up for lost time and all, so go park your ass next to your man over there, and I'll fix you guys some breakfast." Michelle winks at me, before turning to go back to the kitchen.

Ethan is sitting on the rug next to Tasha, and both are playing with their iPads. I finally gave in to my son's request and bought him a second-hand iPad for his birthday, and he absolutely loves it.

"Hello, babe!" I greet my son, before sitting next to Magnus. He's watching the news with Nathan, but as soon as I sit, he squeezes my knee and gives me a smile.

I try to compose myself from the effect of his touch and that smile, turning my attention towards my son.

"So, are you ready for what's in store for us today, buddy?" I ask my son excitedly.

"Can't wait, Mom. I'm going to wear my Nets shirt!" Ethan answers, obviously enthused.

"Man, I wish I can watch the game," Nathan cuts in, "but those animals won't heal themselves."

"Is that what you're doing today with Ethan?" Magnus asks me, an interested look on his face.

I nod back, shrugging, "Yeah, he loves the Brooklyn Nets, so I got us a couple of tickets to watch the game."

Magnus smiles back. "He'll have a great time, I'm sure. I'll get someone to keep an eye on you, just in case."

I study his face for a long second, and although he respects this special day I have with Ethan, the somber look on his face betrays his true feelings.

"What are you doing today?" I ask, placing a hand on his back.

"Work," Magnus answers in a low tone.

"No, you're not. I'm sure I can score another ticket. Would you like to come with us? It's the nosebleed section, but the atmosphere is unbelievable."

He leans close, and whispers, "You're amazing, you know that, right? But I really do have to catch up on some work today. Can I make it up to you tomorrow?"

"Breakfast is ready!" I hear Michelle yell out.

"It's a shame you have to work on a Saturday." I stand up, and Magnus does the same. I reach for his hand as we make our way to the dining table.

"Make it up with me tonight?" I whisper to him, feeling brave, all of a sudden.

"Hmmm, I'll be here by eight," he smirks back.

***

"Are you excited, buddy?" I ask Ethan as we make our way inside Barclays Center. People are already flooding the arena, and we can already feel the excitement in the air.

"Yup! Can I get snacks before the game, Mom?"

"You know what, let's get it now before it gets too crowded." I lead him to the concession stand closest to our section.

While waiting in line, I turn to the person standing right next to me.

"Thanks for coming with us at the last minute. I know you like keeping Saturdays off, so I'm surprised when you said yes," I tell our companion.

"Magnus only had to say Brooklyn Nets, and I'm here," Jacob says, with a grin on his face.

I laugh back. "Nice to know our incentive was good enough for you to say yes. But seriously, thank you. It's not easy for me to trust people, but you're the first person I thought of when Magnus said he's getting someone to keep an eye on us."

"Yeah, that's me, alright. A hot babysitter to Magnus's girlfriend and son," Jacob says dryly.

My brows wrinkle at his comment, but that's when Jacob bursts out laughing, a deep, hearty laugh that is utterly contagious. "I keep forgetting how Brit humor doesn't translate with you Americans. My bad."

My own laughter settles down, just in time for us to order our snacks.

With popcorn, hot dogs, and juice on hand, we head towards the door to where our section is.

"Actually, come with me," Jacob says, nodding for us to follow him.

"Where are you going? Our seats are this way," I tell Jacob impatiently.

"No, it's not," he insists.

"Mom, let's go. I don't want to miss it when it starts," Ethan urges.

Jacob bends down so he's face-to-face with my son. "Ethan, how do you feel about watching the game at a much closer distance?"

"What are you talking about, those tickets are expensive. We have tickets already, Jacob." I frown, when a thought hits me. "Wait, Magnus said he'll organize for the extra ticket …"

"He did, so what are you waiting for?"

I didn't answer him anymore, following him instead. Jacob leads us downstairs, handing three tickets to the burly guy at the door.

"Hold on, those are not our tickets." I tap on Jacob's arm repeatedly, but he ignores me.

Eventually, the usher leads us closer to the court. She points at three empty seats just one row behind the floor seats.

"Jacob, I can't afford these seats. What's going on?" I ask, while Ethan happily takes the first seat closest to him.

"What's going on is that Magnus has season tickets to the Nets and the Knicks," Jacob says, taking the third seat, so I'm sitting in-between him and Ethan.

"Why didn't he say anything? I mean, I have tickets, he didn't have to do this." I feel a mix of anger and flattery at another one of Magnus's extravagant surprises. Anger mostly, because he should know by now that he doesn't need to do this to impress me.

I *ran* from the shit that an extravagant life brings. He knows that.

"Take it up with the boss, Billie. And c'mon, just enjoy the game. Your son is ecstatic, see?" Jacob points at my son, fists pumping in the air, and his precious face, glowing with excitement.

This is for him, after all, right?

After sitting in a huff, I grab my phone, but notice the phone Magnus has given me first. Curious, I switch it on. It's already set up, and the only number on the Contacts list is Magnus's phone number.

Of course it is, I grin to myself.

Opening the message app, I type in my first message on my brand new phone:

> *You're sneaky ... thank you. Wish you were here with us though.*
> *See you tonight. I love you. X*

The game is exciting, the scores close, and watching it this close is just an entirely different experience. Ethan is beyond happy, which makes me happier. This is all for him, and it blows me away that Magnus understands it.

Before we know it, it's already halftime. While waiting for the game to restart, the Kiss Cam is back on, scoping the arena, looking for couples they can harass to kiss on the Jumbotron.

The camera finds an elderly couple, who doesn't need a lot of cheering from the crowd to pressure them for a kiss. It makes us all laugh, and I ooh and aah with the rest of the people.

And then the camera zeroes in on me ... and Jacob. I shake my head, refusing to succumb to the pressure. I hear the boos, but I don't care. Jacob seems to think it's hilarious, elbowing me, and laughing his deep laugh—the kind that rumbles even up to my stomach. Ethan keeps going in front of me, hamming it up for the camera.

The camera leaves us, thankfully, but not for long. It comes back to us after getting another couple to kiss. This time the crowd is more insistent, pushier, and beginning to stress me out.

Just then, Ethan nudges my arm. "Mom, you need to kiss Jacob!"

"No, I don't!" I bark back at him.

"C'mon, they're not gonna stop, until we do," Jacob pushes.

Raising my hands up in resignation, I shout out, "Okay, one kiss! One kiss and that's it! God, you two!"

I turn to Jacob, whose gray eyes are sparkling with humor and something else I can't pinpoint.

And it's mesmerizing, surprising even myself.

"Ready?" Jacob asks softly.

I nod, unable to speak.

This would be easier if his eyes aren't so captivating, or if his lips aren't curved so mischievously ... better yet, if he wasn't so damn attractive.

And then I feel his lips on mine. Soft, yet firm. Commanding, yet pliant.

A kiss different from Magnus's, but it still managed to make my stomach flip.

What the fuck?

I pull away immediately, having appeased the crowd. I didn't even notice Ethan hamming it up for the camera again. But Jacob seems as stunned as I was, staring at me like I just gave him the biggest shock of his life.

Surely, I didn't give him the same effect?

I'm usually able to resist men, especially the good-looking ones. The trauma I experienced from years ago, made me aloof and restrained towards them, even to the point of having panic attacks when they get too close.

Magnus changed all of that.

Now Jacob is getting me confused.

I don't need confusions in my life.

I hope Magnus didn't see that.

Shit.

"There. Done. Let's move on," I tell Jacob nonchalantly.

"Yeah. The game's back on anyway," he adds, sounding exactly like me.

CHAPTER 14

Magnus never texted or called me back.

We're home, just Ethan and I, after Jacob dropped us off straight after the game. The Nets won, and yet, only Ethan seemed enthused about it. Jacob tried to act like that small kiss didn't affect him, but he can't fool me ... because I'm just as freaked out as he is.

Or maybe I'm just blowing it out of proportion ... I'm not sure. But overthinking isn't helping either.

Jacob isn't Magnus. The kiss, though thankfully brief, was pleasant. Not mind-blowing like Magnus's, but pleasant.

Nothing more, nothing less.

It's also irrelevant that I kind of liked it.

Ugh.

If I want us to continue to be friends, then we *cannot* have this awkwardness.

After dinner, Ethan insists on going to bed. He must be very tired after today's game. So, after a story and a good-night kiss, he's asleep in no time.

I'm now sitting on the couch, watching TV, getting progressively concerned that Magnus hasn't called me back, or replied to my text message. I check the time, and it's already half past eight.

Maybe he's still caught up with work, but the least he could've done was call or text me. I decide to call him, but it keeps going to his voice mail. I send him a text message instead, thanking him once again on his surprise, which Ethan enjoyed fully.

I just don't understand him sometimes. He blows hot and cold, and it's confusing the hell out of me.

Is he regretting getting back with me?

Stop it, Billie.

My fingers touch the necklace he gave me this morning. Surely he wouldn't have waited three long months to give me this necklace, if he didn't mean the sentiment behind it?

By nine in the evening, I resign to the fact that Magnus isn't coming anymore. He said he'll be here at eight, and he's a no-show. And now I'm angling for a shower.

If I thought the shower can help me relax, I'm dead wrong. All I can think about is Magnus, wondering if he's okay, or if he's just being callous.

I hear the faint buzzing sound of my phone coming from my bedroom as I'm towel drying my hair. I hurry across the hall, just with my robe on, not wanting Ethan to wake up from the sound.

It's Magnus … and this isn't the first time he tried to call me either, judging from two more missed calls. I take a deep breath, before taking the call.

"Yes?" I answer, not bothering with niceties.

"I'm outside. Let me in."

I guess Magnus isn't going to bother with niceties either.

A part of me wants to just leave him there, outside, in the freezing cold. But a better part of me wants to put a stop to the pettiness … my pettiness.

"Okay," I answer back, walking over to the intercom so I can press the button to unlock the main door.

I open my apartment door to wait for him, and it doesn't take him long to come through the front door, walk up the stairs two steps at a time, and have both of his hands cupping my face and kissing me like I'm the prey to his predator.

I manage to pull away, still breathing heavily, removing his hold on me so I can lock the door behind him.

"What the hell, Magnus? What was that about?" I whisper harshly at him.

"Where's your bedroom?" Magnus asks, his breathing as heavy as mine, eyeing me hungrily.

And God, it's doing things to me that I need to keep at bay.

"Excuse me? Well, hello to you too. You're late. We already had dinner."

"I'm only hungry for one thing," he answers, his hand reaching out for the nape of my neck, pulling me roughly against him, adding, "and I'm sure you know exactly what I mean." He dips his head and gives the curve of my neck, one long lick.

"Oh God," I sigh out shakily, closing my eyes at the dizzying feel of his primal act of ownership.

That's when I feel the belt of my robe comes loose, exposing my naked front as the terry material settles on my sides.

Magnus wraps an arm around my waist, his stare hot and intense as he says, "Take me. To your room. Now."

The rawness in Magnus's command leaves my legs unstable, forcing me to hold on to his sinewy arms.

"Okay," I reply, stepping backwards, turning around as soon as my feet gain stability. Then, I grab his hand, leading him towards my bedroom.

He locks the bedroom door behind him, not even bothering to check out the surrounds, his eyes just fixated on me.

"Take your robe off," he commands quietly, and I do as he says, holding his gaze steadily.

He responds with a rise of his eyebrow, his eyes travel blatantly all over my nakedness, and he starts undressing himself.

Gosh, he's so beautiful naked. So damn beautiful.

And that cock ... his thick, hard cock.

So help me, God ...

I bite the bottom of my lip, trying to restrain myself from grabbing him and tasting every inch of his body outright.

After all, I should be angry at him, right?

"Why were you late, Magnus?" I ask.

He doesn't answer back, but he closes our distance, stopping so very close in front of me that I feel the warmth emanating from his own body.

Before I can say anything, his hand fists my hair, and he plants his lips on mine, his tongue pushing itself inside. I comply, letting out a moan because he tastes and feels so damn good. My hands reach up to touch him, but he pushes both of my hands off. It confuses me, but I soon forget about it because his kiss has the power to make me forget anything and everything.

He pulls away from my lips, just as roughly, leaving me stunned and breathless. Then his lips are back on my neck, licking and nibbling at the most sensitive part. He's sucking on one part of my skin, and I moan at the mix of that slight sting.

Wait, is he giving me a hickey?

"Magnus, hold on." He pauses for a moment, his lips now off my neck, but he continues his journey, bending as he moves further down my body.

He stops in front of my belly, and he proceeds to suck and lick me just above my belly button.

What the hell?

But before I can say anything, he continues on, until he's kneeling right in front of me, kissing my hips and giving my ass a hard squeeze, spreading my legs a little further apart.

Then I feel his warm tongue on my crevice, tasting me, making my legs turn to jelly. And as soon as his tongue reaches my clit, I lose all control, even throwing my head back and moaning out his name.

I try to hold onto him again, my legs already wobbly, but he won't let me hold him, taking my hands off his hair.

Okay, that is it.

I step back, needing the distance from his lips and the pleasure they give me. "What the fuck, Magnus? Why won't you let me touch you?"

He doesn't answer, but he stands up, his eyes pausing at certain areas of my body. I look down, and as suspected, he did mark me with a hickey on my belly, on my right, inner thigh, and I'm sure, on my neck as well.

"You marked me! What's going on? Why are you acting like this?"

He takes a step forward, and with gritted teeth he says, "Why? I just want to remind you that you're mine. Fucking. Mine!"

"What do you mean? So that justifies all of these?" I wave my hands at the parts he'd marked. "You gave me a necklace already, isn't that more than enough?"

"And yet, you're not wearing it."

"Well, excuse me, but if you haven't noticed, I just came from the shower!"

"Did you enjoy kissing him?" Magnus asks with his face fixed in a scowl.

"What? I don't know what you're …"

Shit … the game! The stupid Kiss Cam!

"You were watching the Nets game?" I ask.

"I watched up to that part where they showed you and Jacob, who, by the way, is *my* friend and *your* fucking bodyguard, *kissing* in front of everyone."

"That was nothing, Magnus. You have to know that by now. Is that why you're like this? Are you jealous?"

"Yes, I'm fucking jealous!" Magnus growls as he fists his hand in my hair. He takes my mouth once again, nipping my lower lip, and making my insides tighten. "I should be the one kissing you, in front of all those people. You're mine, Isabelle. Not his!" His kiss deepens, and it's too good that I succumb to him.

"I'm yours. You know that kiss meant nothing." I pull away, my hand reaching up to graze my thumb across his lips, locking his eyes with mine. "This kiss, our kiss? It means everything. Every … fucking … thing!"

That's when I pull his head towards me and kiss him. I kiss him in a way that will tell him, without a doubt, that I am only his. He lets me tangle my fingers in his hair, as I pull him closer, pressing up my breasts against his hard chest so I can kiss him deeper, my tongue dancing with his own.

"Show me how much I'm yours, Magnus," I whisper against his mouth, making him moan out my name.

He doesn't take me to bed. Instead, he turns me around, swinging my hair to one side, and licking the curve of my neck again. I close my eyes, sighing, as I feel his hands massaging my breasts, tweaking my already hard nipples, and leaving shockwaves all over my body.

"Bend forward, and put your hands on the bed," he tells me in a soft, yet commanding tone, gently placing pressure on my back to reinforce his instructions.

I bend forward with my legs apart, my hands on the edge of my bed for balance. Magnus's large hands are gripping my hips to hold me steady.

I can't see what he's doing from behind me, but as soon as I feel his warm tongue on my wet pussy, I let out a gasp. He licks the length of my pussy, his hands moving to grip my ass.

"This is mine … mine!" Magnus growls possessively, his tongue sweetly torturous on my pussy. He continues his primeval greed towards my body, grazing his teeth on my ass cheeks, his tongue tasting me from my lower back to my neck, until his whole body is fully covering my own. One of his hands is on my breast, kneading it, while the other is on my apex, building me up to boiling point, while whispering words of possession on my ear.

I've seen glimpses of this jealous streak before, authoritative, and primal … and I can't believe how much it turns me on.

I'm so damn close.

"Come for me, Isabelle. Now." Magnus's fingers are now rubbing against my clit … fast, hard, and demanding.

And … I'm gone.

I come so hard my whole body trembles, and my insides pulsating against his deft fingers.

This is him, taking control, torturing me for something that's been completely taken out of context; then making me come so easily— just like a switch.

I turn my head around so I can see him. His breathing is labored, staring back at me with a mix of anger … hurt … and definite satisfaction, mirroring exactly what I'm feeling on the inside.

I stand back on my feet, turning around so I'm facing him. My hands reach up to his chest, and to my relief, he lets me touch him. I leave small kisses around his neck, tiptoeing to reach him in the most sensitive of places. Then I kiss his pectorals, licking his perfect nipples, and drawing a moan from him. I continue my journey to his abdominals, licking every well-formed, square-shaped muscle of his six-pack.

"Isabelle," he whispers, as I go down on my knees, in front of his hard cock. My hand encloses his girth, still marveling at how the tips of my middle finger and thumb are barely touching. I look up to him as my hand slides to and fro, and I pick up the change in his expression. He seems vulnerable now, and the vulnerability tugs at my heart. But it's only momentary. He blinks once, and the control is back.

"Show me how much you want me," he whispers in that rough tone.

I take him in my mouth, inch by inch, until I can't take in anymore. His head tips back, hissing at the pleasure that I'm giving him, holding my hair back as I pull away ever so slightly, before doing the same thing, over and over again. I'm watching his reaction, reveling at the look of awe in his face.

His hips begin to rock gently at first, increasing in pace, until a growl escapes from him, "I'm coming … shit, I'm coming."

Magnus's body becomes rigid, and then I feel the first spurt of his come in my mouth. He holds on to both sides of my face, holding me steady, as he empties himself in my mouth, and I swallow each and every drop.

Once he's done, he carefully pulls out, watching me as I lick my lips, with a coquettish smile on my face.

As Magnus helps me stand up, his expression finally softens. "Well, I wasn't expecting that."

He walks to the edge of the bed and lifts the duvet, so we can slide inside the covers. Lying down next to each other, he pulls me in his arms so I can rest my head on the crook of his shoulder, with me looking up to him while drawing imaginary circles on his chest.

"I'm sorry if I hurt you," he says softly, his thumb grazing my cheek tenderly.

"I'm sorry if I hurt you too. It was never my intention. I think we both need to work on our trust issues, don't we? "

"I have my work cut out for me then."

"So do I."

"But I don't think I can allow Jacob to be your bodyguard anymore."

"Why?" I ask, lifting my head slightly. "Don't tell me it's because of that stupid kiss. I thought you understood?"

"Are you trying to defend him, Isabelle? He's a grown man. He can defend himself, " Magnus says with a curious tone in his voice.

"He's your friend though, right? And you know that I don't trust men in general, well, except for you. But I'm comfortable with him, and so is Ethan. He's become a friend more than a bodyguard. Plus, I get to ask him stuff about you."

Magnus chuckles, "You know you can ask me whatever you want. But you're right. Jacob *is* my most trusted friend, and it sets my mind at ease knowing he's keeping an eye on you when I'm not around."

"So, you're not going to fire him?" I ask hopefully.

"I guess you can say that but only on one condition."

"What's that?"

"Move in with me."

"Wh—what?" I ask, completely stunned.

"I understood when you said no when I asked you the first time, but your work is closer to my place, and I can keep you and Ethan safe."

"Are you asking me for practical reasons, or because you just want to keep an eye on me as well?" I ask, raising my brow.

"Both ... and because it's ridiculous that two people who love each other aren't living under one roof."

116

"But a lot of couples seem to do just fine living separately," I reason out.

Magnus turns his whole body so we're facing each other, then he kisses my shoulder lightly, leaving his hand on my hip.

"Look me straight in the eyes, and tell me you don't want to live with me."

I do what he asks, looking him straight in the eyes. "Magnus, it's not about me not wanting to move in with you, because I do want that—"

"But …" he cuts in.

"*But*, we just got back together. What if you decide that your girlfriend, who has a shitload of issues and has a son, is starting to cramp your style? I don't know if I can handle it, if you decide that it's too much for you."

"That'll never happen. You know—"

"Look, can we talk about this next time, please? I still have questions to ask you, like how come you were late? You never answered that question, you know."

He sighs, "It's because I contacted your father earlier in the afternoon, which led me to do more work afterwards. I didn't realize it was already late when I was done."

"Oh, you did?" I ask nervously. "And what did you talk about?"

"I took your advice. I told your father that my offer to buy his company is back on the table."

"Did he accept your offer? And … and how is he?" I ask, feeling a nervous tightening in my stomach.

Magnus's jaw clenches. "He's resting at home, but he also told me that he's got another serious offer, and he's considering accepting that."

"Another offer? Do you know who it is from?" I ask with my brows bunched together with worry.

His jaw clenches again. "You don't need to know who."

I feel an unwelcome twist in my gut. "You know, that just makes me even more curious. Is the other offer from someone I know?"

He nods, his expression hardening. "Apparently, one of his old friends decided to make an offer for his company, the kind of offer he can't refuse."

Old friend?

Oh God, no.

"Is it … is it the Thorntons? Please tell me it's not from them."

Magnus takes a while to answer, but he nods back at me, "They're offering more money, and according to your father, Cooper swore he'll bring you back to Texas … something I apparently failed to do."

"What? No!" my voice rises in full panic.

"That's why I was late. I've done my research on that family, and they have shelf companies everywhere which they use to launder political contributions. And granted that they also have legitimate companies under the RCT Group, they're not making money. But Cooper's father is up for a reelection, and judging from the polls, he's not going to win. I'm telling you right now, that if Bridges Builders falls into their hands, it won't be long before your father's business and its legacy will be gone because they will run that company to the ground."

"I can't have the Thorntons take my father's company. They took everything from me and my family already." My eyes feel moist, as my tears threaten to spill. "And what if Cooper comes for me?"

Magnus's hold on me tightens. "Your father's company will be in safe hands, Isabelle. I'll make sure of it. And Cooper won't be able to come near you. If he knows what's good for him, he'll stay away from New York City," he tells me in a voice menacing enough to give me the chills.

But *I* know Cooper Thornton. That animal can hold a grudge until it festers inside of him. He's doing this because he wants revenge … because I ran away, and because Magnus beat the shit out of him for me.

And Cooper learned his fucked up, manipulation skills from his father. My whole time growing up alongside the Thorntons, our so-called family friends, I've eventually come to realize how dirty they play. From politics to their personal lives, they don't know how to play fair.

I don't want Magnus's reputation to be tainted on my behalf, but now that Magnus is their competitor, they will use whatever resources, whatever connections they have against him.

Maybe it's my turn now to protect Magnus. He may have researched about these people, but I doubt if his researches showed the darkness and evilness of their souls.

And then there's my sweet little angel. What if the Thorntons already know that I have a son and know it's Cooper's.

He will never be Cooper's son. He lost his rights the day Ethan was conceived. I just need to make sure it stays that way.

I have to fix this, for Magnus and for Ethan. But how will I do it?

My thoughts are so focused on finding a solution to this problem, that I don't even notice Magnus regarding me with concern.

"Don't worry, Isabelle. Like I said before, your father's company will be in safe hands."

I wish it were that simple.

But I nod automatically, just to ease Magnus's concern. In my head, however, I'm already trying to think of ways to save Magnus's reputation, and destroy the Thorntons to nothing but rubble.

Maybe it's time for me to finally come out of the shadows.

CHAPTER 15

Eight Years Ago

I heard their conversation in Daddy's office at home. My dad wanted to speak with Mr. Thornton about something that couldn't wait. I was hoping they'd talk about what happened to me, but then again Mr. Thornton always came over because he was a good friend of my dad. They've been in there for a couple of hours, and for some reason, it was making me nervous. And what made it worse was that my dad sounded upset … angry.

I didn't like it at all.

I looked around me to make sure no one was around, and I leaned against the heavy wooden doors, cupping my hand over my ear to amplify the voices coming from the other side.

I could hear Daddy speaking, "Regie, I need to talk to your son, Cooper. My daughter came back last week from her trip with him, and something must have happened between them because she came back a completely different person. She's withdrawn, she cries without reason, and she screams at night. I tried talking to her, but she won't say anything to me, neither to her mother. Look, I'm not pointing any fingers, but Cooper …"

I felt cold all of a sudden, and I began to tremble. They were talking about me and Cooper behind those closed doors.

Since Cooper took me back home, I couldn't bring myself to talk to anyone about how he held me captive, doing vile things to me that made me feel like an animal. It wasn't because I didn't want to, but because I was afraid—afraid that Cooper would carry out his threat and bring shame to our family, destroying my father's hard work that got us to where we were.

"Aren't you? Be careful about what you're trying to imply, Michael." I could hear Mr. Thornton's authoritarian voice answering back.

"I'm not implying anything! All I want to do is talk to Cooper. Maybe it's something that's as simple as a fight between them, but I need to know the truth. Look, I hope you could appreciate my concern for my daughter. Maybe Cooper said anything to you?"

"You obviously love your family, am I right Michael?"

"Of course I do."

"And you take pride in being able to provide for not only their needs, but their whims as well, right?"

"Yes, but what does that—"

Mr. Thornton interrupted, sounding threatening, "Then, if you want to continue providing for your wife and daughter, I suggest you just leave your daughter and my son to deal with their own problems. If you continue to ask questions, or if you talk to Cooper or my wife about this, I will make sure to pull out every single contract I've given your company, and that's across all states, because I know people who owe me favors. Do you understand?"

"Now, old friend, aren't you overreacting just a little? Is there something you know? We've been friends for decades, and I've been nothing but loyal to you. All I want to know is if something happened between them, that is all."

"We have been friends for years, that part is true, and I know that my son is no saint. But I do not appreciate your tone of voice, or your insinuations. Autumn and Cooper are no longer children. They can deal with their own problems, do you understand?"

"To be honest, I find your reaction quite surprising, but ... I understand perfectly," my father answered quietly.

My stomach dipped, and I suddenly felt the urge to throw up.

"Good! Now that's settled. Let's talk about that golf handicap of yours. I think I'm starting to feel threatened by it!"

I couldn't bear to hear anymore. I backed away from the double doors and made my way up to my bedroom where I was staying in self-exile, after coming back home.

Why did I pick that day to leave my room?

I couldn't let Cooper get away with what he did. I needed to tell Mom and Dad everything. They have to believe me. Daddy already had his suspicions. Mom would be heartbroken, if she was sober enough to understand me. I just couldn't live with that festering inside of me. They both needed to know. Cooper had to go to jail. The only thing that was stopping me was that tape.

I still couldn't believe that Cooper would do something so wretched.

I stepped inside my bedroom, my haven in those past few days, and locked the door as soon as it was closed behind me. I felt tired, so tired, and so defeated.

How did my life get so damn complicated?

CHAPTER 16

"Wake up, beautiful," a low, sexy, familiar voice brings me back to the present. I open my eyes in slits and see Magnus, and his sea of blue, staring lovingly at me. I stretch out against his body, slinking my limbs over his, sighing happily when my leg brushes against his burgeoning appendage.

"Already?" I ask him coyly, my hand sliding under the sheets to confirm my suspicions.

"I woke up with you in my arms, naked, and you wonder why I'm hard?" Magnus whispers back.

"I think it's called morning wood. Isn't it common for men to wake up with a hard-on even when they're alone?" I tease, kissing parts of his chest that I can reach with my mouth.

"Yes, but it isn't normal for me to be *this* hard. *You're* doing this to me."

"Am I now? So it's *my* fault, isn't it?" Feeling a surge of mischief, I swing my leg over, so I'm now sitting over his crotch, but blatantly avoiding his cock.

"You bet your sexy ass," Magnus makes his point across by softly smacking both of my ass cheeks.

"Ow," I act out, pouting.

"Come here and kiss me before I go mad," Magnus growls out, fisting his hand on my hair, before pulling me down.

He doesn't care if I haven't brushed my teeth yet, and I don't give a damn if he hasn't.

But it's not enough.

I'm feeling greedy.

Still kissing him, I move my hips back, so I can hold on to his hard length. I begin to stroke it, inciting a deep groan from him.

Then I guide him inside my pussy, now wet and ready since the moment I opened my eyes and looked into his.

"You're so wet, baby. You feel so damn good," Magnus rumbles out against my lips.

"I woke up in your arms," I tell him, as I slide up and down his length, "with you all naked, and you wonder why I'm wet?" I bite my lip, trying my best not to giggle from my mirrored response.

"You. Are. One. Very. Wicked. Temptress," Magnus states, highlighting every word, with every upward thrust.

I close my eyes, tilting my head back, loving how perfectly Magnus fills me inside, immersing myself in the pleasure that he alone gives me.

"I'm right here, Isabelle. Let me see you," Magnus's voice is gentle but thick with desire, and as I open my eyes to meet his gaze, I realize exactly how much.

I can see it in his darkened eyes.

And I can feel it with his every thrust.

Now it's my turn to let him feel how much I desire him.

I take both of his hands from my hips, and lace my fingers with his. Then I raise his hands above his head, lowering my head down so I can kiss him, my mouth hungry for his.

With a moan, I undulate my hips so I can take him deeper, feeling him reach the very peak inside of me, welcoming the pain that comes with the intense pleasure.

My movements increase in speed, as does my breathing, as the fire inside of me is set to combust.

"Oh … oh … oh …" I gasp out, as my whole body convulses with the sheer force of this orgasm. My breathing is shaky, and my hands, which have been holding onto Magnus's for dear life are now loosened and limp.

"I felt you, baby. I felt every single one of them," Magnus whispers in my ear, as my whole body now lies exhausted on top of him.

Magnus shifts our positions, so I am now underneath him, our bodies still connected with him still inside of me. I'm breathing heavily, but completely ready for what he has in store.

At least I thought I was.

He places one of my legs over his shoulder, leaving my other leg on the bed. Then he twists me slightly to my side, before rolling his hips gently, and …

Oh my!

"Oh, holy shit, that is deep!" I exclaim, in shock.

This position makes his cock hit me in a different spot … a slightly more painful, yet *extremely* pleasurable spot.

"Tell me if this hurts?" Magnus asks while continuing one deep thrust after the other, making me fist the sheets.

"No. No, it doesn't hurt, but oh my God, that is so deep!" I whimper, as my eyes squeeze shut.

And then his thumb begins to play with my clit.

Game over.

I'm coming again, seeing stars all around me. I moan out in breaths, too shocked to find my voice, which is just as well, considering I'll probably scream out loud and wake everyone in the building.

Magnus's hold on my raised leg tightens, and I open my eyes only to see him squeeze his own shut for a mere second. I realize he's close, so very close.

"I'm coming! Holy. Fuck!" Magnus stills, and I feel his cock twitch, as he empties himself inside of me.

I gently take my leg off his shoulder, positioning myself so he's in-between my legs. We're both still catching our breaths, and waiting for our own heartbeats to settle down.

Afterwards, Magnus bends down and gives me a tender kiss, before carefully pulling himself away so he can get off the bed. He grabs a few tissues from the tissue box on the nightstand; then he proceeds with the intimate ritual I never thought I've missed … until now.

It leaves me with a big smile on my face.

"Thank you," I tell Magnus once he's done wiping me down.

"It's my pleasure," he answers back with a wink. He balls the used tissues tightly and throws them in the garbage, before hauling me in his arms once again.

"Hmm, morning sex with you is definitely up there as one of my favorite things in the world," I purr out as I once again stretch my limbs against his body.

"What's your favorite thing in the world?" he asks slyly.

"Well, if you think you're it, then you're mistaken, buddy," I answer back, patting his chest playfully.

He pulls away slightly to study my face, "I'm not?"

"Giving birth to my son will always top the chart, sorry. You come in a very close second though," I tease with a wink of my own.

"How close?" Magnus asks with that low voice that makes my insides contract.

I pull down his head towards me, and I lean up to him, so our lips are almost touching. "*This* close to being even."

Knock! Knock!

"Mommy? Are you awake? Your door is locked." A muffled voice from outside the bedroom, speaks with frustration.

"Speaking of," I say, abruptly pushing him off me, and making Magnus groan in protest.

"Give me a second, honey!" I yell out as I jump out of bed, putting on my underwear, a sweater, and track pants hanging by the door.

I sigh at the sight of Magnus scowling, still naked in my bed, his arm over his forehead, showing off his arm muscles without even trying.

He's a sight to see, even with a frown on his face.

But he can't be upset like this. If he wants to be in a relationship with me, he needs to realize that Ethan is part of this as well.

I walk back to him, "Hey," I whisper, "you knew that Ethan and I are a package deal, right? You had your chance to get away. Maybe you should have taken it, maybe you could've found someone far less complicated." I shrug.

Magnus stands up, his naked form never failing to make me salivate. But as he walks over to his clothes, still left on a pile on the floor, he pauses in front of me, taking me by surprise when he plants a deep, yet short kiss on my lips, leaving me breathless and wanting more.

"What do *you* want, Isabelle? Do *you* still want me and my complications? "

I'm taken aback by his question. "Of course, I do. It felt like death for me when we broke up, you know that."

"Then there's no need for 'could haves' or 'should haves' between us because right now, we actually have what we both want. *I* have exactly what *I* want, and she is standing right in front of me. I'm not going anywhere because your so-called complications will never scare me off. Do you understand me, baby?"

All I can do is nod, my mouth gaping, and my heart feeling like it just exploded with confetti and streamers.

I love this man so much, that my heart is throwing a party, just for him.

He smirks, "Good." Then in one stride, he grabs his pants and puts them on, nodding to me as a signal that he's halfway decent.

I open the door to an exasperated-looking Ethan. "What took you so long, Mom? I've been waiting ... Magnus!"

Ethan runs past me, without my usual morning kiss or anything. He fist-bumps Magnus, and Magnus hugs him playfully in return.

"Hey, little man!" Magnus greets, a big grin on his face. "Who wants to eat breakfast out with a nice cup of hot chocolate? My treat!"

"Me! Me!" Ethan jumps up excitedly.

I roll my eyes at Magnus, but can't help giving them a big smile. "Okay, well, we better get ready, don't we, Ethan? But you can't go back to your room without a kiss for me." I open my arms wide, and Ethan jumps up in my arms, looking adorable since his two front teeth have now fallen off. He kisses me all over my face, before running out of the room.

"Well, I have to go grab some spare clothes in the car. Can I get a kiss too?" Magnus asks as he walks towards me.

I place my arms around his neck, going on my tiptoes. "You don't even need to ask." After I plant a kiss on his lips, he leaves my room with a grin on his face.

***

The local café is buzzing with the usual crowd this morning. The son of the owner, Tyler, is a friend of Nathan's from way back, and since we're regulars now, we're always guaranteed a table even when the place is packed.

Tyler sees me first, and he comes around the counter to give me a hug and an affectionate kiss on the cheek. It doesn't bode well with Magnus, who is now sporting a frown on his face. Luckily, Tyler doesn't notice it, since he's giving Ethan a high five. So I lace my fingers with Magnus's, looking up to him with a reassuring smile just as Tyler turns his attention back to us.

"Tyler, I want you to meet Magnus." I notice his smile from the corner of my eye, but his mood is the same as he shakes Tyler's hand.

After the pleasantries, Tyler ushers us to our usual booth, telling us he'll be back to take our orders.

"Is everything okay now, Magnus?" I whisper to him discreetly, thankful that Ethan's too busy playing *Minecraft* on his iPad to take notice.

"No," he answers.

"Talk to me," I insist, rubbing his forearm gently.

"Tyler seems to have a thing for you," Magnus says flatly.

"Are you kidding me right now?"

He turns to me, and I can see that he's definitely not joking around. "Do I look like I'm laughing?"

"He's Nathan's friend, Magnus. And we're regulars here. Of course we're going to be friendly. And anyway, he isn't my type at all."

Magnus leans closer and places his arm over my backrest. "Really? What's your type?"

"You know what my type is. Tall, dark hair, great physique, voice that can melt butter, leads this band called The Doors …"

I chuckle at the obvious joke I played. But Magnus isn't laughing, his mouth is pursed, yet he's expressionless. His expression, or lack thereof, is enough to make me quiet down.

He leans forward, so his lips are grazing my ear. "Looks like I need to fuck some sense into you later. Let's see if your *type* will change then."

Oh, holy mother.

"I was just joking," I whisper back.

"I know," he answers, giving me a hint of his smirk, "I'm going to convince you anyhow."

Before I can comment any further, Tyler returns with our menus, as Magnus leans back like he didn't throw me completely off balance just a mere second ago.

"Please give us a minute, Tyler. I think my girlfriend here, needs a little bit more time before she can order," Magnus says, still with a light smirk on his face.

Tyler's pleasantly surprised expression mirrors my own. "Wow, girlfriend, huh? Nice."

Yeah, girlfriend … wow. I forgot how amazing that sounds.

As soon as Tyler leaves, I turn to Magnus, whispering, "Say it again."

"Say what again?" he asks.

"You know … that word."

He's regarding me with mirth in his eyes. "What word?"

He's playing with me.

I raise my brow.

He chuckles.

Magnus leans closer and speaks with that low, rough-whispery voice that I love to hear, "My girlfriend."

I smile.

"My beautiful girlfriend."

My smile widens.

"My beautiful girlfriend, whom I love so much."

My smile cannot get any wider, and the stretch hurts a little, but I don't care.

I'm happy.

I'm very happy.

"Mom, I'm hungry!"

I hear Magnus answer my son, "So am I. Okay, let's order. What would you like to have, little buddy?"

As I watch their exchange, I can finally confirm it.

I'm definitely very happy.

After a big breakfast teeming with hotcakes, eggs, and bacon, the three of us decide to stay local, with Magnus driving to one of the local Sunday flea markets so we can walk around and burn off what we've eaten.

Magnus is holding my hand, our fingers linked. It's amazing how our mere hands joined together can warm my whole body from the cold, but it does. I'm holding Ethan's hand, and I'm sure that from the outside, we look like a happy family ... a real family. I can't help but smile inwardly.

After all the shit I've been through, I never stopped looking for that silver lining. It keeps me hopeful that even in the darkest moments, something good will always come out of it.

This feels like one of those moments ... my 'something good.'

My silver lining.

I'm brought back from my reverie by Ethan, pulling my arm, and leading me towards the stall that sells toys.

"Ethan, we're not getting you a new toy," I tell him firmly, shaking my head.

"But Mom, they have—"

"It doesn't matter what they have," I cut in, lowering myself so that we're face-to-face, adding, "You just had your birthday, Ethan."

"But that was months ago."

"How about this," Magnus intervenes, bending down to Ethan's height. "I didn't get a chance to buy you a birthday present back then. If your mom agrees, we can go somewhere with better choices?"

I turn to him, speaking softly, "Magnus, you don't have to do this."

"I know," Magnus replies, "but I *want* to do this."

"C'mon," he says, "let's go for a drive. It's too chilly to be outdoors this long in the first place."

Magnus circles his arm around me, and I instantly forget the chill, as my whole body begins to warm up against him. He's also holding Ethan's hand this time, and as we walk back to his car, that's when I notice people looking at us. They aren't passing glances. They're openly staring at us.

The worst ones are the women, blatantly ogling at Magnus, even though he's obviously with me and my son. I try to ignore them, even telling myself that it's quite flattering because the man they're possibly fantasizing about actually loves *me*.

But it's the way they seem to look at me in disbelief, disdain even. Like Magnus can do a lot better than me.

Sometimes I don't know why there are women out there who have the need to put another woman down. We're already our biggest critics … I'm my biggest critic. I just don't need the additional hostility.

And then, just as my insecurities begin to get the better of me, I feel Magnus pull me closer in a tighter embrace, and he kisses my temple gently, in front of everyone to see. I can't help but look up at him, hoping to convey my gratitude with a smile. He smiles back, sweetly, affectionately, and all the negativity in my head just disappears in an instant.

That smile of his is a powerful stuff.

Yeah, my trust issues are still there, and so are my insecurities … as well as a whole catalogue full of other crap within me that I need to work on.

But I'll get there. I'll heal.

And with Magnus beside me, I actually believe it's possible.

CHAPTER 17

"No way!" I'm shaking my head, my arms crossed.

Seriously, I don't know how this man does it. One minute, he's making me swoon, and then the next, he infuriates me to no end.

He's lucky I'm madly in love with him.

Or is it the other way around?

Ugh.

"Isabelle, it's my present, and I have to make up for the lateness," Magnus insists in such a calm, yet firm manner that infuriates me more.

Earlier, Magnus drove us all back to his place, so that we could switch to his SUV and Alex could drive us. And now, we're standing in front of the biggest Toys R Us in Manhattan, with Ethan buzzed and ready to ransack the whole store.

I think he's even frothing on the mouth.

"You're spoiling him, Magnus. All those years of me keeping his feet firmly to the ground will be thrown out of the window."

"I want to do this ... for your son. I'll deal with the consequences, okay?"

"No you won't," I answer back. "I'm his mother, I get the envious job of keeping him in line."

My gaze moves from Ethan to Magnus—child to enabler—and judging from their expressions, this is not a battle I'm going to win.

"Fine," I cry out, raising both arms in resignation, "but I have to approve what you're getting, Ethan."

"Yes, Mom, I promise."

And so Magnus and I trail after Ethan as he does his rounds all over the toy mega store. After over a couple of hours of choosing, debating, and bartering, we leave the store with a big bag full of brand-new toys, thanks to his very own devil's advocate.

"I can't believe I allowed you to do this for Ethan. I just hope he doesn't expect this sort of thing every time it's his birthday."

"Ethan can be spoiled by me, for that one day, every year. He's totally yours to unspoil for the other 364 days."

I narrow my eyes at him. "I was talking about Ethan expecting *me* to do something like this for him every year. I'm not exactly a mogul like you."

He chuckles lightly. "I know. I am. So I'll be doing all the future spoiling for both of you."

What he says strikes me.

"So, you plan to stick around for a while?" I ask, my heart beating faster by the second.

He doesn't answer me, but he gives me a lopsided smile and a kiss on the corner of my mouth instead, increasing my heart rate. I want to take that gesture as a sign that he will be around because that's all that matters to me.

We all make it to his car, where Alex is patiently waiting for us. Magnus tells Alex to drive us back home, and we ride in relative silence, with Magnus choosing to sit in the front passenger seat. We're silent, that is, except for Ethan who keeps asking if we are almost home, obviously keen to open up his loot.

Magnus is texting someone, his face serious and focused. I take the chance to study him. A day-old fuzz has grown along his jaw, and just like the first time I saw him after three months, I find that it makes him look sexy, in a dangerous sort of way.

He must have felt my eyes on him because he lifts his gaze from his phone, and turns to me. I feel my cheeks heat up from being caught staring. His mouth twitches up slightly, but then he goes back to his texting.

Then my purse vibrates.

I take my phone from my bag—the new one he gave me.

It's a message from Magnus.

I turn to him, my brows raised in question while holding my phone up. He just shrugs back.

But my curiosity gets the better of me. I slide my finger on the screen to unlock my phone, and click on his message: *You looking at me like that is really getting me hard.*

Holy shit. Of course, he can't say *that* out loud!

I bite my lower lip as I text him back, trying to hold the grin that's about to break on my face: *And you sending this txt is making me wet.*

He snorts, then starts typing: *You have a dirty mouth.*

I reply: *You love my dirty mouth.*

Magnus replies: *You'll find out how much tonight.*

———

131

I practically gasp at his response. Not that he'd noticed since he was looking straight ahead as if our exchanges were not happening.

Does that mean he's staying over tonight as well? He did put a duffle bag in the boot of his car, after all.

My skin prickles at the thought.

"I'm feeling hungry. Who's keen for some burgers?" Magnus announces, turning to us at the back.

Luckily, Ethan answers in agreement, sparing me from talking since I'm still a little giddy from his last text.

After lunch at our local burger joint, Alex takes us straight to my place. Ethan, as expected, heads to his room so he can ransack his new toys. In the meantime, Magnus and I are relaxing on the couch. He reaches for my legs and places them over his own so I'm leaning back comfortably.

"Hmm, this is nice," I sigh. "Thank you ... for what you did for Ethan. I know I was kicking and screaming the whole time, but you just did make him very happy."

"And how about you? Are you happy?" Magnus asks, rubbing my leg gently, making my skin tingle.

"I'm happy when he's happy," I answer honestly.

He pauses for a moment. "I have to go away for a few days."

"You do? Oh. When?"

"Wednesday. Hopefully, I'll be back before the weekend. But there's a dinner function on Tuesday, and I would love it if you could go with me."

"Of course, I'll go with you." I pull myself up. "Is it a formal thing?"

"Yes, and if you need something to wear, I can—"

I cut him off, "I don't, so no need to buy me anything."

"I want to ... it makes *me* happy. Now, we can argue about this over and over again, but you can't change my mind about it anyhow, so just agree with me."

I try to pull my legs off him, but he refuses to budge.

"Do you always have to win at everything, *Mr. Grant*?" I ask, with sarcasm.

Magnus doesn't answer immediately. Instead, he slides his hand over my leg, and onto my inner thighs, his eyes following his hands. Even with the denim fabric, my skin still prickles from his touch, and my breath hitches.

"Oh, I've already won," he tells me in a low voice, turning to meet my stare with his eyes filled with mischief. "Everything else is just a bonus."

He parts my legs so he can slide in-between, our faces now inches apart, with the heat of his hardening member making *me* all hot and bothered.

"So, tell me, what exactly did you win?" I ask slyly, licking my lower lip slowly, knowing how much that affects him.

He dips his head to kiss the corner of my mouth, continuing on until he finds his way to my ear, his hands squeezing my breasts slowly.

"Guess," he murmurs, before burying his face against my neck.

"Umm, you won the lottery?" I ask, giggling softly, until the giggling turns into laughter when he starts tickling my ribs.

Magnus nips my ear. "Shhh," he teases, with another roll of his hips creating more friction against my sensitive clit, and shooting currents throughout my body.

I wrap my arms around him and bury my face in his neck as well, inhaling his masculine scent, and loving the roughness of his unshaved jaw against mine.

God, this man is a trip to the senses.

"You smell so good," I breathe out against his warm neck, lifting my hips slightly for more friction, knowing he can do the unimaginable and make me come with clothes on.

"Is my temptress about to come?" Magnus rolls his hips further, squeezing my breasts, rubbing his thumbs over my nipples, and doing it all over again.

It's too much, too soon, but he manages to make me come, my core pulsating like crazy. I leave my head buried against his neck to muffle my mewling.

"Wow," I whisper against his ear, feeling my cheeks and my neck turning red as I try to settle back down.

"You're welcome," Magnus smirks up at me, his startling blue eyes darkening with lust for more.

"I want to take care of you too." My hands slide downwards, fumbling on his belt so I can unbutton his jeans.

That is, until I hear Ethan's footsteps from down the hall.

"Shit!" I cry out, pushing a stunned Magnus away a little too roughly that he's now sitting on the opposite end of the couch.

What if Ethan caught us in the act? I shudder at the thought.

This is downright careless!

Magnus gives me a crooked smile as he buckles his belt and pulls his knit sweater down. But the way he's staring at me, tells me that what we have just started is far from being over.

He's going to make me pay.

I can't wait!

"Mom, Magnus, check this out!" I hear Ethan coming closer, completely oblivious to what just transpired here a mere seconds ago.

"What is it, Ethan?" I ask, inwardly cursing at my still-shaky voice and hoping that my skin isn't too flushed.

"Check out what this can do!" He proceeds to show us every single function his new toy can do. I try to act interested, but all I can think about is the man sitting next to me.

And the unconcealed hunger in his eyes just makes it worse … or better … I'm not so sure anymore.

But just after that, Ethan runs back to his room, possibly to check out his other brand-new toys.

Magnus takes his phone from his pocket, and I sigh, as he's reading a message. Then he turns to me. "I just need to make a couple of calls. I won't be long."

"No problem," I answer back with a small smile.

He stands and walks towards the window. He looks outside, his phone against his ear. I can't help but stare at him. Even in something relatively casual, like a pair of jeans and a knitted sweater worn over a button-down shirt, he still exudes authority and magnetism. Damn it, he just exudes sex.

I want him so badly it hurts in the worst places.

And those are the sort of things I shouldn't be thinking about while my son is just a few feet away from us.

I shake the dirty thoughts out of my head, deciding it's best if I let Magnus have some privacy. So I join my son in his room instead.

Ethan shows me the toys he's already opened, obviously uncaring of the packaging materials littered all over.

"Actually, Mom, can I show Tash my new toys?" he asks.

"Sure, but only after you clean up, okay?"

Once he's done his task, I watch him race down the steps, with selected toys on hand. As soon as Michelle ushers Ethan in, I close the door behind me.

Magnus is still on the phone, so I decide to start preparing dinner. After assessing the contents of the fridge, I decide on a simple pasta dish and a salad.

I'm in the middle of chopping some tomatoes, when I feel two arms circle my waist, making me jump.

"Shit!" I cry out. "Don't do that when I'm holding a knife, Magnus!"

He buries his head on the crook of my shoulder. "So jumpy."

"Can you blame me?" I ask back.

He doesn't answer, but he starts unbuttoning my jeans, and unzipping my fly.

I instantly drop the knife on the chopping board, and away from us. "What are you doing?" I ask out, near breathless in anticipation.

"Guess," he answers softly.

"I left the front door open for—"

"I locked it. Don't worry, they'll knock."

"What? You what?" I stutter shakily, as my jeans, together with my panties are pushed down to my ankles. He pulls my hips back towards him, and a moan escapes me when I feel his fingers on my moist opening.

"Always ready for me, Isabelle?"

"Always," I breathe out.

I hear the sounds of his jeans unzipping, and I turn my head, just in time as he's pushing his jeans down, and I'm gifted with a glimpse of his hard cock.

"And you're always hard for me, baby," I tease, rubbing my ass against his hardness, and making him groan out.

"Fucking always."

And without any warning, he's inside of me, filling me instantly and making me cry out. His hands are gripping my hips tightly, pulling me towards him to meet each hard plunge. I hold onto the edge of the kitchen bench, needing the leverage to stop my breasts from getting crushed.

"Hold on tight," he growls, as he practically lifts my feet off the floor from the force of his every thrust.

And every time, he hits that spot.

That. Freaking. Spot.

"Right there, right there, right there," I moan out repeatedly, my eyes squeezed shut, trying to restrain myself from shattering into a million pieces.

But Magnus feels too good.

He's too damn good.

"Oh ... oh fuck." And I come, climaxing so hard that my whole body shudders. He gathers me up, with one arm now circling just below my waist, and the other holding me in-between my clavicles, so that my back is curved against his chest.

Still holding me upright, he continues his thrusts inside of me. I gasp when I feel his warm lips against my neck, and I feel the vibrations coming from his voice when he groans. His movements begin to hasten, just as his groans turn into grunts. With one last thrust, he growls out my name. Then he stills, and all I can feel is the twitching of his cock as he comes inside of me.

Wow. That just happened.

Eventually, we manage to catch our breaths. Magnus gently pulls out, but when he does, the aftermath of our union starts trickling down my leg.

"Let me get that for you," he says, getting some paper towels and wiping me clean before tossing it in the trash can. Then with a peck on my ass cheek, he pulls up my panties and jeans.

"Always a gentleman 'til the end," I comment with a coy smile, turning to face him as we both straighten ourselves up.

"To what do I owe *that* pleasure, anyway?" I ask, fisting my hands playfully against his knit sweater.

Magnus shrugs, "The cock wants, what the cock wants."

My eyes widen exaggeratedly, in mock shock. "Magnus! And you say I have the dirty mouth!"

"Which is perfect for me, since I always have dirty thoughts on your dirty mouth," he answers, smirking, while holding me tightly against my waist.

Grinning, I cup my hands on both sides of his face. "Why do you think I like you so damn much?"

He smirks, and I plant a lingering kiss on his lips.

"Mmm, I know I'm supposed to do something, but this right here is distracting me," I mumble against his lips.

"Well, you better start on dinner, woman," he growls, "or I'm going to have to eat something, and it's not the kind I'm sharing with anyone."

Magnus cups my crotch, making me squeal in surprise. So, I push him away playfully.

"You are incorrigible, Magnus!" I bellow in my thick, Texan accent.

"Talk like that again, and I'll show you incorrigible," he answers, nodding suggestively at me, with that smirk.

I have to hold on to the benchtop to stop myself from melting in a puddle.

"Well, don't just stand there ogling me, you pervert. Make yourself useful and chop those peppers for me." I bite my inner cheek, to stop myself from giggling.

"Yes, ma'am," Magnus replies, tipping a nonexistent cowboy's hat, "and only because you called me a pervert."

I laugh out loud, but I stop as soon as he takes his sweater off, and rolls up the sleeves of his shirt. With muscled forearms now exposed, he proceeds to grab the utensils he needs to help me cook, and he starts getting to work.

For someone who's used to being in command, and a whiz at the kitchen, Magnus lets me run the show, doing what I ask him to do and making it fun for both of us at the same time.

We end up working together so cohesively, that dinner is cooked in record time. Maybe living with him won't be as daunting as I thought.

Dinner turned out to be a bigger affair. We invited Michelle and the rest of her crew to dinner at our place. It was noisy, happy, and a little bit messy. But now with Magnus adding to the mix, it just feels … complete.

"Hey, Billie … Billie!" Michelle calls my attention. "I was just saying to Magnus that we should all go out on a double date. Keiko invited us to her exhibition at that gallery in SoHo on Thursday night, and she said to bring our 'plus one.' What do you say? We can just get our usual babysitter to mind the kids as well."

Keiko is a very talented photographer/friend of Michelle's, and she has had her work exhibited in galleries all over the city. Her parties are always a hit, and they guarantee to draw in an eclectic mix of people.

It would have been great to go with Magnus, if he's not going away on a business trip.

"It would be amazing to go, but Magnus will be away on business," I confide, unable to mask my disappointment.

Magnus reaches for my hand and squeezes it tightly. "You shouldn't miss out if you want to go. I'll make sure there's added security for the kids as well."

Oh right, I almost forgot the whole 'security' thing. It makes me wonder if Jacob will still be a part of the detail, knowing what Magnus thinks of him right now.

"Don't worry, Magnus, we'll keep an eye on Billie as well," Michelle adds, covering her mouth from the kids before whispering, "and we'll make sure she won't be kissing any other boys either."

My head jerks up in her direction, raising my hands up as a general sign for 'what the fuck?' Sometimes I don't know if it's worth telling her my secrets. I can't help but notice Magnus's jaw twitching as well, his face now serious, his eyes hardened, as he stares back at me. But before I can say anything, he surprises me with his answer.

"I trust her," he says in a voice softer than his stare.

"I'm just joking, Magnus. Billie's not that kind of girl. You know that, right?" Michelle asks Magnus, her brow raised in a skeptical manner.

Damn it. Michelle isn't poking fun at me. He's testing Magnus.

Maybe she's on my side, after all.

"Like I said, I trust Isabelle." Magnus raises my hand, and plants a gentle kiss on my knuckles, the sincerity in his voice makes my heart skip a beat.

I squeeze his hand back, responding with a smile of gratitude.

After cleanup and coffee, the kids are starting to show signs of fatigue, so Michelle decides to head back to their place so the kids can sleep.

After tucking Ethan to bed and packing his lunch for school, I realize Magnus must have gone to bed. I open the door to my bedroom, only to stop at the doorway, my mouth agape.

He's standing by the bed, taking his shirt off, and is just about to unzip his jeans when he catches me staring.

"I'm just about to shower. Care to join me?" Magnus asks in that low, yet soft tone, possibly to avoid waking up Ethan, but most likely because he knows what that tone of voice does to me.

"Um … oh, there isn't a lot of space in the shower for both of us, so …" I stutter, feeling self-conscious but still unable to take my eyes off of his physique.

Yes, I'm openly ogling him.

It's okay if I do it, since I do it with love.

Okay, and with lust … I do it with *a lot* of lust.

"Are you sure? Would you like to shower first?"

"Still being a gentleman, I see. You're practically naked, and I don't want you to catch a cold, so you better go in there first. The towels are in the linen closet beside the bathroom door." I finally enter my bedroom, slipping off of my shoes.

Magnus shrugs, surprising me with a sharp slap on the ass on the way to the shower. "I won't be long, babe," he says before closing the door.

"Oh, Lordy, that man is too hot for his own good," I whisper loudly to myself.

A few minutes in and I'm preparing my clothes for tomorrow, feeling excited about my freshly showered, hot piece of ass who'll be sleeping with me tonight, when I hear a buzzing sound on the nightstand.

It's Magnus's phone, and judging from the continuous flashing of the screen, I can tell that someone is calling him. I pick it up, assuming it's work-related. The name on the screen, just says 'H.' I roll my eyes. Really? Magnus has this person down to a single letter?

I'm just getting peeved that someone would call him about work this late at night. Magnus may be a hands-on magnate, but right now, his hands should be on me and not on this damned phone.

I better set this person straight. Magnus will thank me later.

I tap the green button to answer the phone, "Hello?"

"You're not Magnus," a vaguely familiar, female voice answers back … and her clipped tone cannot mask her obvious disappointment.

"No, I'm not Magnus. That's a great observation, by the way," I answer back sarcastically, already beginning to dislike this person.

She sniffs, and retorts, "Well, I'll just call him when he's less … occupied." And before I can say anything, she hangs up.

Bitch.

But I can't help but think how familiar that voice is.

Then my stomach dips when it finally comes to me.

CHAPTER 18

I thought he had cut ties with her?

Magnus is still in the shower, and I'm tempted to just barge in there and give him hell for lying to me. But on the other hand, he wants me to trust him, just as much as I want him to trust me.

What if I'm reading too much into this phone call?

I don't think I want to see Magnus right now. He'll see right through me. He'll see me hurting … angry. So, I just walk out of my own bedroom and plant myself on the couch, switching on the television on low volume. I need the distraction so I can clear my head. I'm sure I'll find some idiotic comedy that can help.

But within a few minutes, I hear the soft padding of bare feet approaching. Even through my peripheral vision, I can see that it's Magnus, fresh off the shower, with only a towel hanging low on his hips.

Don't look, Billie. Once you look straight at him, you're done for.

Then I hear him call for me, now even closer, "Isabelle?"

"Yeah?" I answer back, but staring blankly at the television.

"Would you like to use the shower now? I'm done," he continues, stopping just inches from me.

Damn it, he smells good.

Don't look at him. You're angry, remember?

"I'm just going to finish this show, then, I'll shower."

I don't even know what the hell is on the screen right now. I just need some space from him.

"I can sit here with you." He raises his hand towards me, but I shift positions just in time to avoid his touch.

"I'm sure you have a big day ahead of you tomorrow, Magnus. You should try to get some sleep." I raise my legs up so my knees can cradle my chin, wrapping my arms around my shins as a form of protection.

From him … and his effect on me.

"I'm not sleeping without you in bed with me."

Before I can do anything, he takes my hand, holding it firmly and tugging me towards him.

But I have to resist it … I have to resist him. I try to pull my hand away, but my actions are useless.

"Magnus … let go. I want to watch TV," I insist, gritting my teeth as I continue to pull my hand away.

"Look at me, and tell me what's wrong."

Damn it, why am I so transparent?

I refuse to do what he says. "Nothing. Now, let me go."

Magnus does let go of my hand, but proceeds to tuck his arm under my bent knees, and the other on my back.

Shit, now he's lifting me off the couch!

"Let me down, Magnus! You can't manhandle me like this."

"You're being childish. Switch off the television, or I'll be forced to put you on my lap and spank the stubborn out of you."

The commanding tone in his voice stills me, but I'm pouting as I press the Off button of the remote control, before tossing it back on the couch.

"I have legs, Magnus. I can walk. Are you going to put me down, or not?"

"I will," he says, but he's walking off, and still carrying me … straight to the bathroom. He nudges the door gently so it closes, before letting me down.

"Now take off your clothes, or do you want me to do that for you as well? Trust me, I'd gladly do it." He plants his hands on his hips, cocking his head to one side, with no humor on his face.

"Trust you? That's fucking rich. And I'm not undressing until you get out of my bathroom." I cross my arms defiantly in front of him, meeting his stare, surprised that I managed to whisper it out.

"What the hell is this all about ?" Magnus asks in an equally low tone.

Before I can stop myself, I answer him back, "You told me she's gone from your life. But she just called you and she's completely surprised and possibly offended that I answered the call."

"Who are you talking about?" Magnus asks, looking confused.

"Oh my God, is there more than one?" I cry out.

"Who. The hell. Are you talking about?"

"Martine! Or should I call her H? Is that your nickname for her? Are there other women too, Magnus? Do you have nicknames for all of them? Oh yeah, that's right, you refuse to call me Billie, but everyone else gets to have a nickname!"

142

I know I'm blabbering, but I'm angry … so angry I want to hurt him.

But the change in his expression, from being furious to being relieved, surprises me.

"Are you done with your accusations? May I talk now, please?"

His voice sounds calmer as well, and he takes a step forward. But out of self-preservation, I take a step back.

I need to keep my distance from him.

Unfortunately, this tiny bathroom won't give me a lot of room to move.

"Don't come any closer, until you explain yourself." I put a hand up to stop him, and he does but he has the audacity to smirk back.

He's showing off that smile at the worst possible time!

"Fair enough. I don't know why Martine called. Yes, I have H on my phone's Contacts list, but that's not my nickname for Martine. I still keep in touch with her father for business reasons, and I have him under H for Harper. She knows that I don't answer her calls, so she must have used her father's phone instead, who the hell knows? It's probably a good thing you answered her call. Maybe now, she'll finally get the message. And I don't have other women with nicknames, nor do I entertain calls from any of them. None of them matters, Isabelle. You should know that by now. I think you're just finding an excuse to get angry with me."

He takes another step forward, though a little hesitant. But I stay in place, allowing him to come closer.

"Tell me, will you be happier if I called you Billie instead?" Magnus asks in a low tone.

"No. It doesn't matter. I'm just being an idiot," I answer back, feeling foolish, unable to meet his gaze.

And yet he steps even closer, close enough that we're mere inches apart. He tips my head up.

What hits me first is the affection in his stare. It causes my heart to flutter.

"You do have a nickname, you know. Or have you been so overcome by jealousy that you've forgotten?" he teases.

My cheeks redden, "I'm not jealous at all. I was … I was … I just thought you were lying to me. I can't be blamed for that."

"Temptress," he whispers, his thumb brushing at the reddened part of my cheek, making him smile slightly. "My beautiful temptress. You're like Eve who offered that apple to Adam. And when he took that delicious bite, he knew he'd broken all the rules. But that bite, that bite helped him see the world clearly."

"But Eve got Adam in trouble with God," I answer, shakily, trying not to sound like I'm swooning. "Does that mean I get you into trouble?"

Magnus leans down, so that our lips are practically touching.

"Oh, you *are* trouble. With a capital T. But it's the kind of trouble I need because it gives me clarity. It makes everything real. And you're responsible for that, or have you forgotten?"

Trouble, with a capital T ... sounds familiar.

Before I can protest, his lips find mine, and he softly nibbles them, the tip of his tongue slightly grazing my flesh. Then he pulls away, licking his own lips.

"See, baby, you taste absolutely delicious. Sweet and juicy ... like an apple."

I. Have. No. Words.

Well, except these words: "You can take my clothes off now." I place my hands flat on his bare chest, angling my head as an invitation to kiss me.

"Gladly," he mutters, rewarding me with a flash of that sexy smile of his.

Once again, I'm putty in his hands.

In no time, he takes every piece of clothing off my body, leaving a pile in one corner of the bathroom. Now I'm standing naked in front of him, anger gone, replaced with hunger for the man in front of me.

"So, you're not angry at me for answering your call?" I ask as my fingertips trace a line down from his chest to the happy trail above the towel.

"Tsk, tsk," he answers, shaking his head. "I should punish you for being naughty." He pauses, then shrugs, "Maybe I will, after all."

Slap!

"Ouch, shit! You slapped my ass!"

"I sure did, baby," he growls, as the same hand that slapped me is now circling my sore flesh in a soothing manner. "Wow, you're pink already."

"What did you expect?" I wince.

"Go have a shower now. I'm already hard, and that pink ass of yours is making my dick harder."

I look down at the obvious tenting under his towel.

"Suits you right for slapping my ass like that," I answer back playfully, sliding the shower curtain from the tub-slash-shower, and stepping inside.

With another sweep of my whole body, and a definite look of primal hunger on his face, he closes the curtain for me.

I hear the door open, but not before he says, "That ass is mine, Isabelle. And I'll slap it again if I want to, and I'll make you come while I do it."

Then I hear the door click shut.

Oh, holy shit.

Them fighting words.

I think I just came a little then.

I take a brisk shower, and it helps to cool me off from the effect Magnus's words has on me. By the time I head back to my bedroom, Magnus is already inside the sheets, his laptop on his lap.

And he's wearing nothing but those nerdy black-framed glasses, the ones that actually look hot on him. He seems comfortable, even though my bedroom is practically the same size as his bathroom.

I wish I were holding my phone right now so I can capture this moment.

"Are you just gonna stare at me, or are you coming to bed?" he asks, without even looking up from his laptop.

"Um, I just need to get my pj's on," I reply back, walking towards the dresser so I can get a pair.

"Why bother?" Magnus closes his laptop and takes his glasses off. "Come here," he says, getting out of bed and throwing me off when he reveals he's completely nude underneath the sheets.

He grabs me by the waist, pulling the towel off me, and making me shriek. I clamp my mouth with my hand. The last thing I want is for Ethan to wake up and walk in on us, both butt naked.

Those are the types of things you can't unsee ... no one deserves that.

I manage to free myself from Magnus's clutches, giggling, as I rush to the door to make sure it's locked. But Magnus grabs me by the waist again, growling like a wild animal as he does.

He turns me around and presses his body against mine, leaving me breathless for a second. With another growl, he fists my hair, before devouring my already open mouth. His tongue pushes past my lips and reunites with my own, his lips demanding, and I yield to him with no qualms.

My feet are off the floor, and within seconds, I find myself lying down on the bed, with Magnus in-between my legs. His lips are now nibbling my neck, and he tips my head to one side, so the tip of his tongue can glide along its curve.

It makes my skin feel tingly from the tips of my fingers to the tips of my toes.

But Magnus isn't done yet. He lifts himself off of me and turns me around, so my back is facing him. He moves my hair to the side, continuing his sweet torment on that sensitive part of my neck, making my nipples hard, and sending shockwaves of pleasure as they rub against the texture of the duvet.

The friction on my nipples is too much, driving me crazy, and getting me too wet down there. I curve my back in a cat-like position, lifting my chest off the bed, and Magnus uses this as an opportunity to hold on to my breasts, squeezing my nipples so tightly that my core clenches, letting me moan out.

"Magnus …" I cry out in whisper, losing my tether with every second.

"Not yet," he says, in ragged whisper, "I know what you want, but not. Yet."

He lets go of my breasts, and with one hand, he presses me down gently, my chest once again pressed on the bed.

"You taste too good to be true, baby," Magnus groans out, as his tongue makes its way down, stopping just over my ass.

He lifts my hips up, leaving my sex exposed to him.

"Oh … my God!" I cry out the moment I feel his tongue glide along my wet pussy. He does it again, before finally finding my burgeoning clit.

"So. Fucking. Tasty," Magnus rumbles in-between licks.

My entire body can't bear it anymore. I need the release.

"I want to come, Magnus," I plead.

"Do it, and make me feel it."

Oh, did I make him feel *it*. I bite on the thick duvet to soften my cries, as my core pulsates, and my body shudders in at my release.

Oh, damn!

This is becoming addictive too.

I'm slowly coming down from the high, when Magnus turns me around once again, so I am on my back. He crawls on top of me, a smug look on his face.

Let's see what happens if I do this. I reach for his hard cock, biting my lower lip as I enclose it with my hand.

"I want this inside of me," I purr at him with gritted teeth.

The smugness is gone, his vulnerable side now making an appearance, as he closes his eyes and breathes out my name. But as soon as he opens them back, the vulnerability is gone, replaced with carnal need.

"Take me," he dares.

"No," I answer, shaking my head, in another act of defiance. Then I place my ankle over his shoulder, licking my lips provocatively.

"I want *you* to take *me*. I want you to fuck me like you mean it."

His eyes widen in surprise, but the sexy, mischievous smile he's giving me becomes practically predatory.

"Then I suggest that you better hold on to something immediately, my temptress."

I am sore.

I wince as I change positions in bed.

Serves me right for challenging Magnus last night. I should know by now that he never does anything halfway.

Not that I'm complaining. I'd gladly do it all over again this morning.

But still ... *Ouch.*

It's Monday morning, and daylight is blanketing the whole room. Behind me, I hear the clicking sounds of a keyboard. I slowly turn around and sure enough, Magnus is already up, in deep concentration, typing away in his laptop.

But he's sitting beside me, and oh, he's wearing his glasses.

Yummy.

"Hey," I murmur to him, kissing the muscled arm next to me.

"Morning, gorgeous," he says, bending down, and kissing me on the temple.

"You look hot in those glasses."

"Do I?" he chuckles, closing his laptop, and placing it on the floor. He leaves his glasses on and hauls me in his arms.

"Very hot," I confirm, raising my head up to offer him a kiss, and sliding my leg in-between his, the dull ache in-between my legs, forgotten.

He sighs, smiling, taking my lips and sliding his hand down the length of my back, stopping on my ass. I rock my hips in response, inviting him for more.

I always want more when it comes to this man.

I'm greedy like that.

"After last night, I don't need to check to know you're probably sore, baby," Magnus breathes out, against the crook of my neck.

I groan in protest, "I'm a grown woman. I can take it … no matter how big it is." I reach for his hardening member, but Magnus laughingly shakes his head 'no' and takes my hand off, and making me pout back.

"Don't sulk." He presses my lower lip playfully.

I roll my eyes at him, pushing him off, and getting out of bed. "Okay, fine. Good luck trying to get all of this, next time you feel the *urge*." I wave a hand around my body to emphasize my point, before grabbing my thick robe and covering myself.

Magnus just chuckles softly, his fingers curled over his mouth. Then he gets out of bed, his eyes sweeping over my robed body in a way that makes me blush. He closes the distance and cups my face, sweeping the hair off my eyes.

Then he kisses me, devouring my lips passionately. My fingers curl in his hair, and I close my eyes, as I easily get lost in the moment … in Magnus's kiss.

And just like that, he stops kissing me and pulls away. I'm stunned, staring back at him questioningly, with a face flushed and breathing unsteadily.

He cocks his brow, looking smug. "You were saying?"

Damn it, he got me there!

"Ugh, you play dirty, Mr. Grant!" I cry out, pointing a finger at him in frustration. I turn to walk away, but he grabs me by the arm and draws me close.

"Oh, but you love it when I play dirty with you, Ms. Morrison," Magnus whispers against my ear, his voice and his words, sending tingles all over my body.

"Whatever," I answer back, doing my best to sound unaffected. "I have a son to feed breakfast to. And you … well, you can just feed yourself."

I huff away from him, exhaling slowly as soon as I'm out of the bedroom so I can compose myself.

I wake Ethan up, telling him his favorite cereal and a cup of hot chocolate are waiting for him.

It's never easy waking up in winter when it's so much nicer being in bed. But a good cup of hot chocolate always seems to do the job.

By the time we make it back to the kitchen, Magnus is already there, now dressed in lounge pants and a T-shirt, and making himself familiar with the percolator.

"Good morning, Magnus!" Ethan greets him with a high five.

"Morning, buddy. Looks like your mom prepared your breakfast already, lucky you!" Magnus says to him, before looking pointedly at me.

"Of course he is. He's my special little man." I bend down to give my son a kiss on the cheek, which he reciprocates sweetly before heading straight for his food.

I notice Magnus picks up two bowls from the benchtop, giving me one as he passes by. He's prepared us some cereal, even slicing up some bananas as topping.

"Aw, you prepared my breakfast, thank you," I express sincerely, touched by the gesture, knowing I wasn't quite as nice just a few minutes ago.

Magnus shrugs, before whispering, "I don't hold grudges, unlike this woman I know. She's incredible in the sack, but damn it, she's feisty when she doesn't get her way." Then he turns to me, winking, with a wicked gleam in his eyes.

Wait … what?

I narrow my eyes at him. It's a good thing Ethan's out of earshot, otherwise Magnus will realize exactly how feisty I can be.

After a rather enjoyable breakfast, we all get dressed and ready to go. As usual, I do a double take as soon as I see Magnus. He's wearing a navy blue suit that's tailored perfectly for him.

I don't think I'll ever get over how beautiful this man is.

After picking up Tasha, we exit the brownstone, and I start looking for Magnus's car, thinking he'll be dropping us off.

To my surprise, I see Jacob, with his arms crossed, grinning at us while leaning against his SUV.

I turn to Magnus, puzzled, as he walks ahead and gives Jacob one of those bro-shakes. But Magnus leans over and whispers something to Jacob, and his grin disappears as he nods curtly.

With a pat on each other's backs, they pull away. Magnus walks back to where we're left standing.

"Sorry to do this in haste, but I have a morning meeting today that I can't get out of, so Jacob will take you all to where you need to go. Then, Michelle and the kids will be brought back home by their detail, as usual. Is that okay?"

I shrug back, unable to hide the pang of disappointment with Magnus leaving so abruptly. On the other hand, he did listen and allowed Jacob to continue accompanying me.

He gives Ethan a fist bump and Tasha a wave as he helps them inside Jacob's vehicle. Then Magnus surprises me when he suddenly pulls me close, then kisses me in a way that leaves me feeling legless.

And just as quickly, he finishes the kiss, then he looks past me. I turn around to see Jacob witnessing the whole thing with an impassive expression on his face.

Except his eyes betray his annoyance.

That's when I realize that Magnus's kiss must've been for Jacob's benefit.

It's alpha male posturing at its best.

"I love *you*," I whisper to Magnus pointedly.

Magnus seems a little stunned, but his expression softens as he says, "I love you too, baby. I'll see you later."

"Sure," I answer back distractedly, giving him a half-smile.

Jacob opens the passenger door for me, and I smile sheepishly back at him, feeling apologetic about what just transpired, even though I know I don't have to be. Magnus is my boyfriend after all, and that's what boyfriends do, right?

Jacob nods back at Magnus, who is now getting in his own car.

"What did he tell you?" I ask as soon as Jacob is seated behind the wheel.

150

"Sorry?"

"Magnus said sorry?"

"Um, no," Jacob chuckles. "What I meant to say was, I beg your pardon? I didn't hear your question."

"Oh. What did Magnus tell you?"

His disposition changes, and his body stiffens. "Nothing," he says abruptly, looking straight ahead.

His reaction is telling me to back off. Maybe I should stop being too nosy.

I don't ask further; instead, I check on the kids to make sure they didn't notice the exchange. They didn't, with both of them checking out a book Tasha brought with her to school.

I drop off the kids while Jacob is waiting outside, noticing a couple of curious glances our way, some from the same mothers who were whispering with each other while staring at Magnus the other day. Now they're staring at Jacob and looking at me with judgmental eyes.

Seriously?

I try to ignore them as we walk past. I don't need to explain myself to them. I don't think they'll even understand. They need to walk in my shoes first.

"You okay?" Jacob's voice cuts through my thoughts as we're walking towards his car.

"Yeah, yeah. It's nothing. Some parents just seem so judgy, that's all."

He snorts, "Let them be. Gossiping is probably the highlight of their day."

That makes me laugh. "That's not very nice, Jacob," I counter.

"I never said I was nice, Billie," he says back.

"I beg to differ, actually," I say as he opens the passenger door for me. "See, you're even opening the car door for me. That makes you a gentleman."

He shakes his head, grinning. "No, this makes it my job."

Oh.

Okay then.

Jacob sits on the driver seat but doesn't switch the engine on. He exhales loudly, before turning to me.

"Magnus told me not to attempt to kiss you again, or he'll kill me. And I think he's serious about it."

Shut the door.

"What? Magnus wouldn't say that."

He sniffs, "You've never seen him angry."

"But … but he has nothing to worry about. And what do you mean by that? What happens when he's angry?" I ask, holding my breath.

"Don't worry, he'll never hit a woman. He's one of the most decent men I know. But when he saw us kiss on TV …"

"But that was innocent. No malice. I mean, I didn't even feel anything!"

That is a lie.

He turns to me, and curiously asks, "Really?"

"Um, yeah," I insist.

He looks away for a moment, shrugs, and remarks, "Good." Then he switches the engine on and drives off.

We make small talk on the way to the city, but it's hard not to notice that weird air between us, awkward even.

He parks his vehicle close to the shop, and I zip my puffy jacket up to protect me from the cold, just as Jacob is coming around to open the door for me. He then walks me up to the front.

"So I'll hang around here and come back in around lunchtime. Then maybe you and I can go to lunch, yeah?"

I look up to him, and he looks back at me expectantly, albeit a little nervously.

Is he asking me out on a date, or is this part of his job?

"Just so we're clear," I start, facing him, "you asking me out isn't like a date or anything, right?"

He mocks offense, "Of course not. I'm asking, strictly on a professional basis, or casually as a friend."

I chuckle at him. "Well, I prefer to be casually asked, so I'll casually say yes."

The relief on his face is apparent.

Gosh, he really is good-looking.

If I'm not so head over heels for Magnus, I probably wouldn't mind if Jacob asks me out on a real date.

But I am, so I shouldn't even be thinking about 'what ifs.'

I cut my stare, open my purse, and look for the store keys instead. He stands next to me while I open the store, even looking away as I press the alarm code. He steps in after me, grabs a chair from the café, and swings it around so he can sit bac-to-front.

I look back at him as I'm switching on the lights, and I instantly notice how his size just fills the entire store. He catches me staring at him, and he smiles back, so I look away, blushing like an idiot.

"Uh, Chris will be here soon. You can wait until she comes in, or you can hang out here until lunchtime and avoid the cold."

"I'll hang around until Chris comes in. I do go to my office during the day and switch with one of my people."

"Oh, right. Of course. I don't know why I thought you were watching me the whole time. I mean, how boring, right? Plus you obviously have your work—"

"It's not boring watching you. I can do it the whole day."

What?

"Pfft, as if. Yeah, right … whatever," I blabber on, like a complete idiot.

Why am I letting him affect me like this?

"Sorry, I hope I'm not making you uncomfortable with my remarks." He tilts his head to one side, studying me.

Feeling warmer in an instant and hoping it's because I switched on the heating for the store, I unzip my jacket, hurriedly hanging it on the coat rack at the back office. When I return to the store, Chris is just coming through the door. Her face lights up as soon as she sees Jacob.

"Oh! Hello, I'm Chris. Christina, actually." She reaches for Jacob's hand. He stands up from his chair and returns the handshake.

"Jacob. We've already had an introduction the other day."

Chris actually blushes, but steps closer to him. "Oh, I remember. I just wanted an excuse to shake your hand."

Jacob's eyes widen at her bravado. I'm personally used to it by now.

She's gorgeous, and she knows it.

I would give anything to have that kind of confidence.

"Right. Okay, then. I think I'll take my leave on that note." Jacob subtly nods at me to walk with him. I bite my cheek to stop myself from laughing.

"It was indeed a pleasure to meet you, Chris." He shakes Chris's hands again, holding it longer than usual. "There, now I have an excuse to shake yours."

Now that is some Brit charm at work.

Chris is practically melting like ice cream in summer.

153

Jacob leaves a still swooning Chris as I walk him to the door.

"Twelve good?" he asks softly, as if he's unwilling for Chris to hear him.

"Can't. Lunch rush. Let's make it two? And are you sure you don't want Chris to join you instead, Prince Charming? You can shake hands the whole time and everything," I tease.

He chuckles, leaning forward and whispering, "I'm already committed to our friendly lunch. I'm a monogamous like that, you see."

"I'm monogamous as well, so let's keep it just that, okay? Friendly," I whisper back, looking him straight in the eyes.

Those ridiculously stunning gray eyes.

He holds back my stare. "Of course, Billie." He pulls back, and I discreetly exhale with relief.

He waves back at Chris, before nodding back at me with a crooked smile.

And then, he's out the door. I notice him look to his left, where a generic-looking black car is parked. It's the same car as the one at our place.

Of course, the morning shift is here.

I turn away from the window. This over-the-top security is ridiculous.

"I'll just be at the office, Chris."

"Hey, Bills, wait up," Chris calls out, catching up to me. "So, um, I was wondering. Jacob's not your boyfriend, right?"

"No, he's not," I answer shaking my head.

"Is it the other guy? You know, the super hot and brooding one? And why does he look familiar by the way?"

I chuckle softly, "The *other guy* is Magnus, and it's still weird for me to say this, but yes, he's my boyfriend. You might've seen him on TV or something, because he owns Grant Corp."

Chris's eyes bug out in surprise, her mouth agape.

"Ho—ly shit. *Now*, I remember you! I've been trying to figure out where I've seen you since we've met!" she cries out.

"Wait, you remember me from where?" I ask with confusion.

"I remember a picture of you with him, in some charity gala. Magnus Grant was smoking hot in a tux, and you were wearing this gorgeous lacy black gown. You looked so beautiful, except your hair was darker, redder."

My hand reaches up to my hair.

"That felt like ages ago," I reply, smiling bashfully. "How can you remember so far back?"

"I don't forget a hot man and a gorgeous gown," she answers matter-of-factly. "It's a gift and a curse."

I nod slowly, "Of course, it is. Now I feel embarrassed." I start walking towards the office, not really wanting to talk about that night any further.

"Hold up, Bills. I still have a question for you."

I sigh audibly. "What is it, Chris? I have a shitload of paperwork to look into."

"Okay, so what I really wanted to know is, if Jacob's single? And oh, what does he do for a job?"

"Well, to be honest, I don't think it's my place to speak for him. Why don't you ask him yourself?" I answer back, getting a little impatient.

"Maybe I will," she answers, cocking her brow up with confidence.

"Good." I force a smile back before turning away. "Oh, and Chris, would you please …"

"Make you a cup of coffee? Bitch, please, you know I got you."

Feeling guilty at my snapping back at her, I smile back gratefully, thanking her before finally planting my butt on the office chair.

I start catching up on the mails, entering any invoices in the system, and posting promos on social media sites.

Now that Helen doesn't come to the store as often, she has been grooming me to take over the management of the store. It's a big task to eventually take, but I'm confident I can handle it. I love this store so much that I've been putting money away, hoping to own something like this, eventually.

I'm in the middle of finishing up a discount promo to post on all three social media sites, when my phone rings. I still have both my old and my new phones. It's such a hassle changing over phones, so I decided to just keep both.

It's my old phone ringing, and the caller ID is unknown.

I scrunch my brows, wondering who would be calling me that's not in my Contacts list. The phone continues to ring, so I press the Answer button.

"Hello?"

I hear background noise, then nothing.

"Hello?"

Still nothing. Whoever it was must have hung up.

What a dick.

I hate it when they don't even apologize for wasting your time.

After posting the promos, I return back to the store. There are a handful of customers already, with some of them regulars. I have a quick chat with a couple of the regulars, telling them about the new books we just got in, as well as some books that I've read which they might like. One of them decides to buy one of the new books I recommended, while the other buys a children's book for her niece.

I'm carrying my new phone in my pocket since this has only my loved ones on the Contacts list. I told Michelle to call me using my new number from now on. And, just in case Magnus decides to call, I'll be able to answer. Unfortunately, it's nearing lunch, and yet, no calls from Magnus. I'm putting it down with him being busy, but a simple text message wouldn't hurt either.

By lunchtime, Magnus still hasn't called me back. So, I decide to send him a text message myself: *Hello M. Busy? Miss you. XO*

I hit Send before placing the phone back in my pocket, and I'm bracing myself for the lunch crowd.

Nothing.

Out of curiosity, I try calling him … twice. My calls go straight to his voice mail. I leave him a message on both instances, telling him I miss him and if he could call me back.

Nothing.

Damn it.

I'm getting antsy, but I also know that I should slap the stalker tendencies out of my system.

A couple of hours later, on the dot at two in the afternoon, I hear the doorbell chime.

"Hey, Jacob!" I yell out, waving as he steps in.

"Hey!" He waves back, walking towards me while taking off his coat.

Holy, wow!

"Hold on, you were *not* wearing *that* this morning!" I shriek out, as I skim my eyes up and down his suit.

Jacob gives me a smirk. "Oh, this? I had meetings this morning with prospective clientele."

"Well, you look very dapper. Not that you don't look good in a bomber jacket, scruffy boots, and beanie too."

"My, my, Isabelle. Have you been checking me out?" he teases with a cocky demeanor.

"Please, don't flatter yourself," I answer back dryly, hiding the fact that yes … I have been checking him out on the down low.

"I hope we're not going anywhere fancy because …" I wave down at my choice of outfit for today: skinny jeans, brown leather boots, and a beige woolen jumper that's a little on the snuggly side across the chest.

"You look just fine," Jacob answers, his eyes lingering on the said chest.

"Thanks. Well, let me just get my jacket and my purse." I hurry over to the back office, making sure to zip up my puffy jacket right to the top.

By the time I'm out of the back office, I notice Chris staring at Jacob. She's too busy making coffees to get her flirt on, but she is definitely making eyes.

But Jacob doesn't seem to notice because his eyes are focused on me.

And now I'm blushing.

Why does Jacob keep making me feel self-conscious?

I choose to ignore it, giving him a big smile instead.

"Ready?" he asks.

"Yup," I agree, nodding. Then I turn to Chris and call out to her, "I'll be back in an hour."

She answers with a small wave for me and a flirty one for Jacob.

"So where are we going?" I ask Jacob as we head over to his car.

He smiles back, saying, "I hope you like ramen. Nothing beats the cold, like a hot bowl of fatty soup and noodles."

"Yummy! Can't wait!" I clap my hands excitedly.

He hails a cab, telling me he doesn't want to waste a good parking spot since we're coming back soon anyway. He tells the driver where to go, and before long, the cab stops in front of a nondescript shop full of signs written in Japanese. It's only a small shop and seems pretty popular because it's quite crowded, but we manage to find a seat at the back. The lovely server takes our orders and gives us a small bow, before heading back to the kitchen.

"Can't wait, I'm hungry!" I exclaim.

"Good, because the ramen here is amazing," he assures.

"So, how did you find out about this place?"

"One of my friends recommended it. I've been coming here for years. I can take you here again, if you want to. Trust me, you'll want to come back after you've tried their food."

"If I have a craving for ramen, you'll be the first one I'd call," I tell him with a wink, earning me a smile back.

Just then, my phone rings. It's my old phone, and the caller is from 'Unknown' again.

"Hello?"

I only hear background noise again, but it's nothing distinct for me to figure out where the call is from.

Then there's silence.

That prankster hung up on me again.

"Fucker," I mutter out.

"Everything okay?" Jacob asks.

"Yeah, yeah. Just some idiot playing pranks on me, I think. It's an unknown number, so there's no way for me to call him or her back.

"Didn't Magnus give you a new phone?"

"Yes, but I couldn't be bothered changing the contact details over. But if I keep getting calls like this I might just switch over."

"Have you been getting a lot of prank calls lately?"

"No, it's quite rare, but this is my second one today. It's just annoying. But I'm sure it's nothing to worry about."

Jacob nods but still looks concerned. "If you get more of those prank calls, you have to let me know, okay?"

I don't know what the big deal is, but I suppose it's part of what he does.

"Okay, I'll let you know," I tell him back.

By this time, the server returns with our bowls of ramen. The soup looks thick and rich, and it smells terrific.

"So, has Magnus contacted you at all today?" Jacob asks after slurping some of the soup.

I shake my head 'no' as I feed some noodles in my mouth.

"I'm sure he's just busy," I continue once I finish chewing.

"I know it's none of my business, but Magnus and I have been friends for years. And what I found out is that his work always seems to come first. I've seen it happen with Martine, and we know how that ended up."

I think I just lost my appetite the moment Jacob mentions her name.

I lay down my chopsticks and look him straight in the eyes. "I don't appreciate the comparison you're making on our relationship. First of all, I am not her. And I also understand that Magnus is a busy man, but I'm not the type to get in his way."

"I've heard those words spoken before as well. Look, I'm not comparing you with Martine at all. You two are chalk and cheese. But that's the problem … I just don't want you getting hurt."

"And I appreciate that, but this conversation is making me uncomfortable. Can't we just talk about something else … please?"

Jacob pauses and lays down his chopsticks. Then he surprises me when he places his hand on mine. "I'm sorry. You're right."

He pulls his hand away just as quickly and resumes eating his ramen.

It takes me a minute to get over how pleasant that felt.

"Jacob?" I start hesitantly.

"Hmm?"

"We're friends, right? I mean, I'd like to think that we've become friends."

"Of course." Jacob nods back.

"So you know that we can't—"

"Jacob?" A petite, cute, brunette approaches us, placing a hand on Jacob's shoulder.

"Anya. Fancy bumping into you in here." He stands up, and they give each other a hug and a kiss on the cheek. I couldn't help but notice how Anya's kiss seems to linger longer than Jacob's and how she's still holding on to him.

"We should catch up again, okay? I miss you," the chick called Anya says with a pout.

"We should, yes … soon." He gives her a smile that makes her swoon.

Heck, that smile is kind of working for me too.

"Okay. Sounds great. And just in case you lost my number …" Anya takes a business card from her purse and hands it to him.

"Thanks," he says, placing the card in his pocket.

Anya initiates another hug, and Jacob concedes, even whispering something in her ear that makes her giggle. She only acknowledges my presence when she starts walking away, only giving me a fleeting glance before passing me on her way out.

"Sorry about that, Billie. You were saying?" Jacob sits back down like *that* didn't happen.

"It's not important," I answer hastily. "I'd like to know who that woman was. You guys used to hook up or something?" I tease.

He shrugs, saying, "She's just someone I know."

"Obviously. She's cute, and she's clearly into you in a big way."

"She was fun ... that's all I can say," he answers quietly, his jaw clenching, before he reaches for his hot green tea.

Okay, I guess we're not talking about Anya anymore.

I decide to leave it at that because I know exactly how it feels when you want people to back off. So I change the subject, and we start talking about his work. That puts him in a good mood, and I like that I put a smile on his face once again.

We finish our meals, and I insist on paying, but he just laughs it off, saying Magnus pays him enough that he can treat me for lunch. I let it pass but insist on giving him free coffee back at the shop to compensate.

On the cab ride back to the store, my new phone rings.

It's Magnus.

"Hey," I answer, a ready smile on my face.

"I came by your store and you weren't there. The girl you work with said you left with Jacob."

"First of all, I'm *great*, thanks for asking. Jacob took me out for some ramen, and we're already on our way back."

"Well, I'm picking you up after you close. I'll tell Jacob he doesn't have to take you home," Magnus answers in a quiet tone. I can already picture him brooding.

"You can tell him if you want, he's right here." Before he can protest, I hand Jacob the phone.

First he doesn't call, and when he does, he gets all Mr. Bossy.

A bemused Jacob takes the phone, anyway. He nods, mumbles an answer, and then hangs up.

———

160

"What did he tell you?" I ask, as he hands me back my phone.

He sniffs, "Just Magnus being Magnus."

"What does that even mean?" I ask, puzzled.

Jacob turns to me. "All I can say is … that man is borderline obsessive when it comes to you."

"Yeah, well …"

I stare back at him for a moment, unable to continue what to say.

But nothing that Jacob said really surprised me though.

Why would it, when I'm also borderline obsessive about Magnus?

The cab drops us off in front of the store, and Jacob walks me inside.

I turn to him, breaking into a smile. "Thanks for the lunch. It was quite, um, interesting."

"Interesting. Yes, it was," he nods, rubbing his chin and giving me an awkward smile. "Well … see you." He taps my arm rather awkwardly, then gives me a mini-salute before walking away.

I watch him give a subtle nod at the same black car parked nearby, then he gets in his own SUV and drives off.

I try to keep myself distracted for the rest of the day, thankful that an event at the store tomorrow is keeping me busy with preps. A well-known indie romance writer is doing a release party of her latest novel, which includes a reading by her of some excerpts from the novel, followed by a book signing. We've placed promotional posters and displays on our storefront two weeks ago, and we have a substantial amount of interest generated by her fans. So now, we're in the middle of setting up the space for her reading and book signing. We've decided to set up the reading at the café area. At the other end of the store, we've set up her table, stacked copies of her books, and plastered more posters for good measure.

Chris has left for the night, and I'm alone in the store, doing some finishing touches on the signing table, when I hear the door chiming. Without warning, I feel two strong hands on my hips.

I jump, but the familiar tingling of my skin and his delicious scent are all the indications I need to know who's standing right behind me.

"Hmm, we don't usually allow groping in the store," I say, turning around to face him, "but you can be the exception, Mr. Grant."

Magnus's hands are still on my hips as he steps forward, so the lower half of our bodies are now touching.

"Good to know, Ms. Morrison." With a lazy smile on his face, he dips his head and kisses me slowly, tenderly.

"I'm almost done here. Give me a few minutes to close up?"

"Of course."

I give him a quick smile before heading to the back office.

As soon as I locked up the back office, I find Magnus checking out the new books that are on display. He looks up as I approach, staring at me with a smile rising from the corners of his mouth. There's definitely something about the way he's looking at me that makes me feel cherished.

I love it.

I love *him*.

"You love working here, don't you?" he asks, regarding me thoughtfully.

Closing our distance, I nod, "Yeah."

I credit a lot of the books in this store for helping me get through the rough moments in my life … and they were quite many. It's my dream to have my own bookstore someday and hopefully act as a conduit in helping inspire people. Helen told me that she will eventually sell this store since her kids aren't interested in running the whole thing. I'm hoping to buy it from her when that time comes. I've been saving money towards that dream.

"I can just buy this store for you, or whatever bookstore you want so you can have one of your own."

I stare at him like he's out of his mind, before shaking my head. "You know I won't let you do that."

We step out of the store, and he waits beside me while I lock up.

"And you know that I'll do anything for you, Isabelle."

"And I appreciate that, but this is my dream. Don't worry, if I need any business or financial advice, you'd be the person I'd ask, okay?" I tell him assuringly.

"I should be the first one you'd go to for anything," he advises quietly, taking my hand and walking me to his Bentley. "I needed financial backing when I started, and my father helped me."

162

I wait until Alex closes the door behind us, before I continue, "You know that's what I want, for you to be the first person I could go to. But sometimes, it's just not possible. You're busy running an empire, Magnus, and I love that you're hardworking, but," sighing, I add, "you can't even text me back, and when you finally called, you were angry at me."

Magnus reaches for my hand, leaving a lingering kiss on my knuckles. "I'm sorry, baby. But even if I can't text you back, I never stop thinking about you."

"I just worry. I know I shouldn't, and I'm being ridiculous —."

He pulls me on his lap mid-sentence, wrapping his arms around my waist.

"No, baby. Please, no more putting yourself down," he says, burying his face in the crook of my shoulder. Then he cups my face and finds my lips.

"I'm sorry ..." Magnus whispers against my mouth, caressing my lips gently, then more urgently, his tongue delving inside to deepen our kiss.

"I missed you," he continues, teasing my lips with the tip of his tongue. "That's why I got upset so quickly, when I found out you left with Jacob."

I pull away slightly, and I stare him straight in the eyes. "He's become a friend, Magnus. And he's meant to be the person you trust. Why do you have to be so jealous of him, even threatening him, when he's your friend in the first place? You had no problems with him before, so why is it so different now?"

"Because I'm a man, and I know the look that a man gives to a woman they are attracted to."

"Magnus, you have nothing to worry about. I'm. With. You." I take his hand and place it on the side of my head. "This brain of mine, only thinks of you."

Then, I take his hand over the left side of my chest. "This heart of mine, beats only for you."

Finally, I guide his hand down, in-between my legs, over my apex. "And this ... this only yearns for you."

"Baby ..." Magnus whispers, his eyes following our hands, before slowly making its way back to stare into mine.

"How many times do I have to tell you that I'm all yours, before your stubborn brain gets the message?"

"Stubborn brain, huh?" he says, his face lighting up in a smile, "Kind of reminds me of someone I know."

I smile back, hanging my arms over his shoulders. "Well, maybe that's why we're meant for each other, huh?"

My lips find his, with my heart tugging at this proud man's insecurity.

He's my beautiful, strong, vulnerable man.

"I love you, Magnus Grant," I sigh against his lips.

"I fucking love you back, Isabelle Morrison."

"Your hand is still on my crotch, by the way." I chuckle softly, nipping his lower lip playfully.

"It's found its way home, baby," Magnus murmurs back.

I giggle once again, before cupping his hand under mine, rocking my hips to create friction, and making me moan out with pleasure.

But before we can go any further, the car stops in front of my place.

"Damn it!" I mutter out, easing his hand off of me.

"You have no idea, how much I want to finish what I started," Magnus groans.

"But?" I ask shakily.

Magnus sighs, "But I have a morning meeting tomorrow."

"You're not even staying for dinner?"

"I have to go through the paperwork to prepare for tomorrow's meeting, and they're sitting on my desk at home. *But*, I would really love it, if you stay with me tomorrow night, after the charity event. I'll pick you up from work, then we can get ready at my place."

I hesitate for a moment. "I take Ethan to school every morning, that's my thing with him."

"One night, baby. Ethan will be fine. He's in good hands."

"Oh … okay. I'll talk to him. God, you make it so hard to say no to you." I roll my eyes at him, before giving him a smile.

The moment Magnus's face lights up, I know then that I have made the right choice.

"Thank you." He gently pulls my head down for a kiss.

After a few moments of kissing and fondling, we mutually pull away.

"I should go before I have you for dinner instead," I breathe out.

"Yes, please," he growls.

"So insatiable … I love it," I tease, planting one more kiss on Magnus's delicious lips, before uncurling myself off his lap.

I grab my purse, just as Magnus advises Alex that I'm ready. Alex comes around to open the door for me.

But just before I can step off, Magnus grabs my wrist and hauls me back to him for another kiss.

And oh, wow. What a kiss.

He pulls away first, leaving me stunned and swooning.

"Now, *that* is just an appetizer. Get ready for the next course tomorrow," he says, giving me a satisfied smirk.

"Hmmm, I'm hungry now."

"Tomorrow, baby. Call me before you go to bed?"

"Maybe," I answer coyly. "Good night."

I hop off the car, beaming at Alex, who gives me a slight nod and a warm smile back.

Magnus lowers his window, watching me climb the steps to the front door. Before I step inside, I blow him a kiss, and the smile he gives back to me as his car drives off makes my heart skip a number of beats.

And, as expected, the usual nondescript black car is already there. Curiosity and concern get the better of me, and I find myself heading towards the car, and knocking on the window, where two surprised men are staring back at me.

I motion for the man in the passenger's seat to roll down the window, and he does as I ask.

"Good evening, gentlemen. I was just wondering if you had your dinner? Would you like anything warm to drink?"

The man closest to me, speaks first, "It's okay, ma'am. We've already eaten. But thank you for asking."

"Well, I'll speak with your boss about this. It just doesn't feel right that you're waiting out here in the cold."

The second man, the one in the driver's seat, answers, "It's not a problem at all. We're just doing our job, ma'am."

I hesitate, before straightening up.

"Okay … well … have a good night."

"We will. Thank you."

I wave back at them as the man draws the car window back up again.

Gosh, the cold can't be good for these people at all.

Looks like I'm going to have words with Magnus and Jacob about this situation very soon.

CHAPTER 19

"What's the matter with you, Autumn? Why do you feel the need to destroy another man's future?" My father's voice, booming and full of disdain, drives me to cry tears of anger.

He doesn't know that I heard their conversation ... that I heard Mr. Thornton's threats. But I cannot keep quiet any longer. Cooper has to pay for what he did to me.

"Dad, I'll go to the police and tell them Cooper raped me. I didn't go on a fucking vacation with him! Check my passport. I have nothing—"

"You don't need a passport to go to Mexico, Autumn! You know that. And don't you dare swear at me, young woman. I am your father, for crying out loud!"

"If you are, then start acting like one!"

Without warning, he slaps me.

For the first time in my life, my dad slaps me.

I touch my cheek. It stings, but the hurt doesn't come close to the pain brought by a father's betrayal to his only daughter.

My own father is too caught up with Mr. Thornton's lies. He is too afraid to lose his business that he doesn't care if his only child ... his own daughter ... is crumbling in the process.

This isn't what a loving father does to his child who needs him.

Maybe I am a lost cause in his book.

I turn to the woman sitting on her usual armchair, a tumbler of whiskey in her hand, stoic and devoid of expression. I kneel in front of her, my hands on her thighs, as I try to get a reaction.

"Mom, you know I won't be lying about something like this. I was raped. Cooper did things to me that were sickening and horrible. Please, Mom, you have to believe me, I would never lie about this."

People used to tell me that I'm the spitting image of my mother, with our auburn hair, green eyes, and pale skin. But these are where our similarities end. She is a closet drunkard and a serial social climber. Status and reputation are more important to her than her own family's feelings.

I used to let her be, because it meant she'd leave me alone to do what I wanted. But she should realize when her very own daughter, her own blood, had been wronged. She is supposed to go past her own personal beliefs and be there for me, especially now that I need her support, her love more than ever.

But when her characteristic dead eyes turn to me, the fury in them is unmistakable.

"You ... you expect me to believe you now, when all you ever did was lie to cover your ass and give us grief?" Her voice is menacing when she speaks, and she is slurring from the hard liquor she's consuming.

She's beginning to scare me.

"But, but Mom, I changed my ways when I went to college. I was making something out of myself, away from all of these ..."

She raises her hand, stopping me from talking.

"You want to make something out of yourself? Stop accusing Cooper of rape. You are ruining our friend's reputation ... our family's reputation ... with your accusations. Cooper has been nothing but wonderful to you, even forgiving you for breaking up with him in the first place. His father will be a senator. And that's a clear fact. Do you seriously think we'll allow you to march over to the police with your ludicrous accusations and expect your family to come out of it unscathed? If you do, then you must be more foolish than I thought!"

"Why won't you believe me? Why would I lie, knowing I'd risk losing everything if I did?" I ask, my voice quivering as my tears flow freely.

"I'm standing behind your father, Autumn. Just forget about your fight with Cooper and move on. If you love your family, you will move on."

"No. Please ... don't do this."

"It's decided, Autumn," my father's voice commands from behind me, "and there will be no more talks about this, or so help me—"

"Or so help you what?" I interrupt him. "You'll disown me? You might as well, Dad. There's nothing left for me here."

I run towards the door while my dad tells me to stop the melodrama ... that I should just start growing up.

I'll get my act together, alright. I need to.

Away from this place.

168

Apart from everyone.
From this moment on, I am my own family.

***

I hate waking up like this.

My head is pounding, and my chest feels tight.

Why is it that only Magnus has the capability to keep my nightmares at bay?

I've been getting the same kind of dream about my parents in recent days.

What does it mean? What is it telling me?

Shit, it's only a little past six in the morning. I rub my eyes and stare unblinkingly at the ceiling.

That's it, I'm awake. Time to block away any remnants of that awful nightmare.

I get out of bed, feeling the immediate chill, so I run towards the panel to switch the heating on.

As I'm making my coffee, I think back at last night's phone conversation with Magnus, smiling to myself at the memory. Magnus always sounds so sexy on the phone, that it both excites me and frustrates me at the same time.

I told him how I disliked that Jacob's security detail had to stay out in the cold every night. He said the only way he'd feel comfortable about my and Ethan's safety at home was if he could get Jacob's company to install security cameras all over the house, or if Ethan and I would move in his place ... for good.

Again, with his offer to move in with him.

So I went for option number one reminding him that I'm still not ready for option two yet.

And, of course, Magnus was none too pleased with my choice.

If I only had a mind-set that'd allow me to be comfortable enough to say yes.

But unfortunately, I'm still mentally fucked.

I'm not sure though how Nathan will react with having surveillance cameras installed all over our place. But maybe if I explain to him that it'll only be for the time being, maybe he'll understand.

For the time being.

———

169

Until when, exactly?

Even I can't answer that question, so how will I expect Nathan to understand?

I sigh out loud.

Maybe I can ask Jacob for advice. After all, it's his company that's handling my family's security.

I take my coffee, walk to the living room, and check out the morning show on TV. But it's impossible to concentrate on what the hosts are saying. My mind still lingers on my conversation with Magnus and the dream I just had about my parents.

Before long, it's past seven, and Ethan needs to wake up soon. So I start preparing our breakfast of scrambled eggs and bacon on toast.

Once I'm done cooking, I wake Ethan up, a hard task on it's own due to the colder-than-usual winter season.

I already told Michelle last night that I'll be staying over at Magnus's tonight. She agreed, but only if I dish about it when I get back.

So, with one of his favorite breakfasts as bribe, Ethan readily agrees to a sleepover over at Michelle's. I don't even know why I was so nervous in the first place.

After a shower and some last-minute additions to my overnight bag, including the gown I personally chose to wear, Ethan and I are all set to go.

On our way out, I'm already wearing a smile to greet Jacob, but to my surprise, Jacob is nowhere in sight.

The only person waiting for me is a tall, sturdy-looking woman in a suit with her blonde hair tucked in a neat bun.

And she is unsmiling, it's almost scary.

"Ms. Morrison? I'm Lou. I will be looking after you from now on," she says in a professional, yet serious tone.

Like I said, scary.

Ethan and Tasha are inching closer behind me.

"Oh, good morning. What happened to Jacob Haynes? Is he alright?"

"Yes, ma'am. Mr. Haynes has decided that it might be more suitable for you and your son to be looked after by another woman. I can assure you that I'm highly qualified, with an army background as well."

"I see," I answer with a small nod.

170

Somehow, it's difficult for me to accept that this is Jacob's decision.

This has Magnus written all over it.

"Lou? It's Lou, right?" I ask, as she opens the passenger door for us, so I can usher the kids inside.

Lou nods her head, still looking impassive.

"After we drop the kids off, I'll need for you to take me somewhere else, before taking me to the store."

"No problem, ma'am."

After Ethan and Tasha are safely in school, Lou is now driving me to the address I've given her.

She parks the car and walks with me inside the building. It feels weird that I'm back in this place with a bodyguard in tow, knowing there's a chance I'll be recognized by some people I used to work with.

I reach the front desk, where the same woman I spoke with before is staring back at me with an obviously forced smile.

"Welcome to Grant Corp. How may I be of assistance?"

"Hi there, I'm here to see Mr. Magnus Grant?"

She stares back at me like I just said something completely nonsensical. But before she can utter a word, I hear familiar voices calling my name from behind.

"Oh my God, Billie! Is that you?" Jess's melodic voice yells out.

I turn to see Jess and Boyd running towards me, with big grins on their faces, and, surprise, surprise, with their hands held together!

Well, well, well!

I can't help the smile on my face as soon as they reach me, but Lou decides to block them from me instead.

"It's okay, Lou. They're friends of mine. Do you mind if I just talk with them in private, please?"

Lou pauses for a moment, before nodding and stepping a few paces away.

Both Jess and Boyd look on warily, before turning their attention back to me, their grins wider than ever.

"Ah, so I see you two finally found your way to each other," I comment happily, pointing at their intertwined hands.

Boyd turns to Jess, who beams back at him. "Yeah, we got together after you and Mr. Grant ... well ..." Boyd's expression changes from happy to solemn, and so does Jess's. "We're so sorry, Billie."

"It's okay. And Jess did warn me about the whole boss-employee thing."

"But you're here right now," Jess adds, her expression looking hopeful.

I smile back at them, assuring, "That's because we're back together."

"Oh, yay!" Jess claps. "You changed your hair color. I wasn't actually sure it was you. We had to make sure first."

My hand instantly holds on to the ends of my hair. "Yeah, but I'm going back to my original color. Blonde just isn't me. But hey, I have to go now. I work over at The Written Word, in case you guys are after a good book. I help manage the store. I'm there from Monday to Friday, unless I swap a weekend over."

"Oh, I've heard of that place before. Yeah, we'll definitely drop in," Boyd replies.

They each give me a hug and a peck on the cheek. Surprisingly, my reaction to Boyd's touch isn't as bad as the previous times.

Progress.

"Send my regards to Marla as well, okay?" I yell out as they head towards the turnstile.

"We will. She'll surely want a night out to catch up. We'll call!" Jess answers.

I give them a big smile and a wave, feeling even more relieved that it didn't turn out into a Spanish inquisition.

I walk back to the lady behind the front desk, who may have overheard our conversation because by now, she's looking at me with a surprised look on her face.

"So, as I was saying, please tell Mr. Grant that her *girlfriend*, Isabelle Morrison, would like to see him."

The woman's eyes widen, and for a short moment, she just sits there with her mouth agape. But then she nods back and says, "Of course, it won't be long, ma'am."

With her handset on, she dials a number and speaks with Denise. The woman looks up to me, before resuming her conversation. And then she hangs up.

"Just go through, Ms. Morisson. And please use the elevator on your right." She presses a button, and a small gate nearest to her, opens automatically.

"Thank you." I smile at her, and she reciprocates but not before sizing me up from head to toe.

I follow her instructions, with Lou right behind me. The elevator I was told to use is actually Magnus's private one. I've never used it before because when I was working here, Magnus used to take the main elevators with me. Now, I'm inside his private elevator, with my own bodyguard, on my way to Magnus's office while being addressed as Ms. Morrison.

Yes, this whole shift is definitely too surreal for words.

Denise is the first person I see as soon as the elevator doors open. Her usual prim and proper demeanor is thrown out of the window as soon as she sees me, with her wide smile and arms open, ready to give me a hug,

"Oh, Billie, it's so nice to see you again. Finally!" Denise is still hugging me tightly, surprising me with her strength since she's so petite.

"It's great to see you too, Denise. This is Lou, by the way," they nod at each other politely. After the pleasantries, Lou excuses herself and tells me she'll be at the waiting area.

I turn back at Denise. "So how have you been? Did I miss anything juicy when I left?" I ask her playfully.

"Oh, nothing much. But I have to say, Magnus was completely distraught when you two broke up. He buried himself with work, and mind you, he wasn't pleasant to work with either, always brooding, barking orders and giving unrealistic demands. But then, he started working on this new project for his foundation, and that negative energy he had, became positive. He was still brooding, mind you, but at least he wasn't so angry. It's like he was working with a purpose again."

New project? Magnus never told me about this project of his.

Denise reaches for my hands, saying, "And then of course, you two got back together, and my, oh my! He had a complete turnaround."

"He did?" I ask skeptically.

"I've never seen him like this. The way he's changed since he met you ..." she pauses. "He's like a son to me, so seeing him happy and focused again, well, it's just a relief."

Denise's words make my heart want to burst.

I need to see my man, right now.

Why did I come here in the first place again?

"I think I should go see him now."

Denise pats me on the arm, before waving me off. "Go on, he just finished with his videoconference, so he's in there, waiting for you."

I feel like skipping towards his office.

Except I'm actually here to address Magnus's jealous streak.

With my shoulders straightened and holding my head high, I open one of the double doors of his office.

And he's there, sitting by his desk. And just like Denise said, he's waiting for me, complete with his sexy smile, still wearing his equally sexy pair of glasses.

Shoot, I forget why I am here again.

"Hello, Isabelle. To what do I owe this visit?" He takes his glasses off and drinks me in, from head to toe.

I'm wearing a slightly tight turtleneck, tucked in a midi skirt—showing off my curves—with heeled, black boots. This outfit is flattering for my figure, and it makes me look professional … perfect for today's author signing.

I guess Magnus likes what he sees as well.

"I think you know exactly why I'm here." I walk towards his desk, aiming to sit on the chair opposite his. Except he makes room on his desk, right in front of him and taps it, suggesting for me to sit there instead.

I roll my eyes to let him know I don't intend to sit on the space he cleared in front of him, crossing my arms and leaning against the desk instead. Magnus surprises me when he leaves his chair and deliberately stands an inch from me.

"You miss me?" Magnus asks in a husky tone, his eyes following his hands as they slide up from my thighs, stopping on my hips.

"Guess again," I answer, my voice getting too breathy for comfort.

Magnus starts lifting my skirt up, and I let him inch it upwards, until it's barely skimming the apex in-between my legs. He bends down, until his nose is touching the hem of my skirt, making me suck in my breath.

He inhales deeply, closing his eyes.

And then he smirks.

"You do miss me. Don't even try to deny it, babe. I know you're all wet for me already."

Oh God, I can't really deny that.

"Um … I can't control what happens to me down there," I answer shakily.

"I want to see it for myself. Take your panties off," he commands, his voice thickened with desire.

This is not exactly how I've pictured this confrontation in my head.

And yet, I'm sliding my panties off and kicking it to one side.

Magnus stands up and holds me by the hips again. Then he lifts me up, and sits me on the edge of his heavy, wooden desk.

But then he lets me wait, as he takes his suit jacket off, folding his sleeves meticulously.

Damn it, this kind of waiting is making me even hornier.

He takes my legs—with my boots on—over his shoulders, fully exposing me to him. "Keep your boots on. I want the heels digging on my back as I make you come."

Damn his filthy mouth!

I don't get a chance to respond, moaning instead, as he gives my pussy one long lick.

"Oh … wow!" I cry out in ecstasy.

"I want my day to start and end like this, my temptress. With me tasting your sweetness," Magnus says in-between delicious lashes of his skilled tongue.

My head moves to one side, and I notice his glasses sitting on a pile of paperwork. I reach for his glasses and hand them to him.

"I want you to wear this while you're down there," I tell him, biting my lower lip in a sudden onset of shyness.

He lifts his head, and my insides tremble at the sight of his lips glistening with my wetness.

"Really?" Magnus smirks. "Getting kinky on me, Isabelle?"

"Please?" I ask again.

He takes his glasses and wears them, cocking his brow up, "Happy?"

I nod excitedly, "Very."

With a deep chuckle, he is back in-between my thighs.

I lift myself with my elbows, watching him as his glasses fog up while sucking my clit, sending jolts of electricity throughout my body. Then his tongue sinks inside my channel, mimicking the way his cock does. My hips follow the rhythm of Magnus's tongue as it lunges in and out of me, and it doesn't take long before my climax builds up. I hold onto my skirt, bunched up to my waist, needing something to hold onto before the inevitable happens.

And, oh my God, it does. As soon at Magnus's thumb starts rubbing my clit, putting pressure on it, I'm gone. I scream his name out, as wave, after wave descend upon me, overwhelming in its intensity.

I'm still breathing heavily, only realizing how my heels must have hurt him in some way.

"I hope I didn't hurt you," I pant out, as he gently takes my legs off of his shoulders, lifting me once again from my hips and pushing me towards the middle of his desk, crumpling some papers in the process.

"You'll never hurt me this way, baby," he says as he takes off his glasses and wipes his chin with the back of his hand. "Though I am hurting right now in a different part of my body, and only you can make it feel better." He adjusts the massive tenting on his crotch, before unbuckling his belt, and unzipping his trousers, pushing them down, and exposing him in all its glory.

"Come here, and let me make you feel better, Mr. Grant." I reach for his cock, so large in my hand, and I tug him gently towards my wet entrance, pushing its head inside, and making him moan for me.

He slides in slowly, allowing me to adjust for him. Then my legs wrap around his waist, urging him to give me more. And he does, moving back and plunging in hard and deep, sucking the breath out of me.

With one of his hands, he unties my ponytail, and grips my hair, pulling me upwards and meeting me halfway for a kiss, all the while continuing to undulate his hips and creating friction in all the right places.

"You feel so damn good, baby. *God*, you feel good," Magnus hisses with teeth clenched, his staggeringly blue eyes locking me in.

"It's yours, Magnus," I murmur back, moaning every time he hits that spot.

He nods, in a daze, thrusting inside of me, chanting, "Mine, fucking mine!"

His proprietary words get to me, and hitting that spot takes me over the edge. I come once again, my chest heaving and my insides, involuntarily clenching and unclenching over his cock.

"Isabelle ... fuck!" Magnus's body goes rigid, and he goes over the edge with me. I feel his cock twitching, his body shuddering as he empties himself inside.

He leans forward so our foreheads are touching. He closes his eyes momentarily, catching his breath like I do.

Once he's settled, he pulls back so he can look at my face. "Hi," he whispers gently, brushing strands of hair from my face.

"Hi," I reply back, chuckling slightly.

He kisses me tenderly before he strides off to his bathroom, and coming out with a small, damp washcloth, he proceeds to freshen me up.

I'll never get over how much I love it when he does this for me.

He helps me on my feet once he's done; then he grabs my panties, acting as if he's in two minds to give them back. Before I can grab them off his hands, he kneels in front of me and helps me put them on. Then he pulls my skirt down, leaving me to straighten up the rest of the way.

Once we're both done, he wraps his arm around my waist, leaving small kisses along my jaw. "Why don't you try to get today off at work? I'll get Denise to clear my schedule, and we can spend some time at my place, or we can head straight to The Plaza. I have a suite there under my name, so we can have a little fun before ..."

"But I can't take a day off, especially today," I answer.

Then my whole reason for coming here comes back to me. I remove myself from his arms, taking him by surprise.

"Why did you tell Jacob to swap with someone else?" I ask quietly.

"Oh, so you came here because of Jacob?" He steps back, clenching his jaw as he turns and walks to one of the windows, looking out into the city.

I follow right behind him. "I came here because you keep deciding what you think is good for me, without even asking *me*."

Magnus crosses his arms, his head tilting to one side. "And how is Jacob good for you, Isabelle?"

"I'd like to think he's my friend now too, just as he is yours, Magnus. And the kids like him. You're just doing this because you're reading more into something that's completely friendly and innocent ..."

"Lou came highly recommended by Jacob himself. Besides, aren't you supposed to be more relaxed around women than men?"

"Look, if you want me to walk around with a bodyguard, then you better make sure that person is someone I can trust. I trust Jacob and Ethan likes Jacob. I think you're just being petty."

His mouth is pressed in a hard line, looking unrelenting.

So I try to approach this in a different way. I place my hands over his still-crossed arms, unfolding them and wrapping them around my waist.

"Do you trust me enough to have male friends, Magnus?" I ask him, my hands cupping his face.

He exhales deeply, replying, "You know I trust you. But I don't trust any other red-blooded males around you."

"You're friends with Sofia, *and* you've slept with her," I point out.

"She's gay, and I've already explained that incident to you already," he answers back.

"And Martine?"

He looks past me, his eyes focusing elsewhere. "We have a history, but now, if we do talk, it's purely business-related, and only if her father's involved."

"She's still in love with you, Magnus. Even a blind person can see that. But I know you're not going to do anything to break my trust, not after what happened three months ago. Jacob knows I'm deeply in love with you, Magnus. We have nothing to offer each other *but* friendship."

The frown on his face dissipates, his scowl softening. "Deeply in love with me, huh?"

"Of course, that's the only thing you picked up from my entire speech," I answer, rolling my eyes at him.

"I heard everything you said. I just wanted to hear you say it again." He tightens his arms around me, pressing our bodies together.

"I'm deeply in love with you, my stubborn, possessive, presumptuous man." I prod my finger on his chest to emphasize my point, before planting a kiss where his heart lies, leaving a red lipstick mark on his crisp blue shirt.

"Oops," I mutter teasingly.

Magnus sees the mark, shrugs, and then closes his suit jacket. "I'm keeping that," he says, winking at me.

"You better!" I pat the area that's now covered. "So ... Jacob's back?"

He sighs, nodding, "Jacob's back."

"Thank you." I go on my tiptoes, and kiss him lightly on the lips.

"I'll pick you up at six?"

"Yeah, I'm sure it should be fine. I have to go. I'm supposed to open the store in like, half an hour. Thanks again, Magnus." I circle my arms around him, kissing his lips gently. But he has other ideas. He pulls me closer and deepens the kiss.

When he pulls away, I'm already flustered, and hungry for more.

"And in case you forget, I'm deeply in love with you too," Magnus whispers in my ear, and it's like a shot of adrenalin in the heart.

"Well, you just have to remind me all the time," I answer back, still breathless from his words.

He nods, winking back at me, and squeezing my ass cheek for good measure.

"See you later, Magnus." I kiss him on the cheek before grabbing my purse.

"Can't wait," he replies. "Sure you can't take today off?"

Do I really have to go to work? His offer sounds so tempting.

I check the time again.

Shit! I have to haul ass!

"I wish. Sorry, babe!" And I rush out of his office.

I give Denise a quick hug, telling her I'll see her again soon, before joining Lou once again. We're out of the building and on the way in no time.

I have to hand it to Lou. She may not be my ideal bodyguard, but she's an amazing driver.

We're almost at the store when my old phone rings.

It's from that same damned 'Unknown' person.

I press the button to answer the call.

"Hello?" I ask firmly.

Nothing.

Of course.

"Hello?" I ask again.

Still nothing.

"Either speak up, or stop calling me, you jerk!"

I end the call.

"Everything alright, ma'am?" Lou asks, checking up on me through the rear-view mirror.

"Yeah. Just a wrong number," I answer, still feeling annoyed.

On the screen, I notice I have two more missed calls from 'Unknown.'

Ugh, maybe I really should switch phones altogether.

Then a thought hits me, and a chill runs down my spine.

What if it's Cooper, or someone working for Cooper, trying to contact me?

It can't be. I've been very careful. And how could he get my number?

"We're here, ma'am," Lou's voice thankfully draws me out of my thoughts. "I'll just park the car, then I'll stay inside, if you don't mind. There's an event in your store, so the place will be crowded."

"Oh, of course, by all means. I was going to ask you, anyway. It's too cold to be anywhere but inside." I offer her a warm smile.

She only nods back, and her lack of expression makes me feel awkward.

How am I going to feel comfortable with someone I can't gauge? Maybe it's not so callous of me to ask for Jacob back, after all.

Mental note: Call Jacob about the unknown caller.

There's already a line of fans outside the store, which is always a good sign. It looks like this book signing will have a good turnout.

This promises to be one hell of a busy day today.

Good. I'm going to need the distraction.

I love hosting an event like this, and I especially love

---

meeting the author and the fans who share the same passion with reading as I do.

The only thing I don't love is cleaning up after everyone has gone.

Helen, Chris, and I are almost done putting everything back where they belong, with Lou even giving us a hand.

I asked Helen yesterday if I can leave a little early tonight. She asked why, so I told her that Magnus is taking me to a charity function at The Plaza. She willingly volunteered to be in the shop, but I think she has an ulterior motive. I picked up on that motive when she agreed for me to leave early, as soon as I told her Magnus is picking me up.

"What happened to that other fellow who was here with you last week? That very hot, very tall guy with the muscles?" Helen whispers while keeping a steady eye on Lou.

"Oh, you mean Jacob?"

"Yeah, him."

"Don't worry, I have a feeling you'll see him again," I answer with a wink.

"Oh, I hope so. He's so nice to look at. And he's available!" Helen teases.

"Hey, I have dibs on him! He's yummy!" Chris joins in.

"Ladies, he's not a piece of meat." I roll my eyes at them.

"Says the woman with a fillet mignon for a boyfriend," Helen responds.

I laugh at the comparison. "Fillet mignon? Seriously? C'mon, steaks are my specialty. If you were to ask me, I would say, my boyfriend is like Kobe beef: expensive and melts in my mouth. Mmmm …" I close my eyes, pretending to savor the taste. But as soon as I open my eyes, both women are looking past me, with wide eyes and pursed lips.

"So I'm a Kobe beef, is that right?"

I turn, red-cheeked, to find Magnus standing with his arms crossed and a self-satisfied smirk on his face.

"How do you keep sneaking up on me like that!" I exclaim, covering my hot cheeks with my hands.

"You were preoccupied when I arrived," he chuckles, placing an arm around my waist. "Besides, I got in just in time to hear you talk about your boyfriend. Believe me, your boyfriend is flattered." Magnus kisses my temple softly.

"Aww!" Both Helen and Chris swoon.

"And, on that note, I think it's time for us to go." I quickly grab my things, including my overnight bag and the suit bag holding my gown. Magnus takes the bag from me and speaks to Lou … possibly to advise her that her services are no longer required.

I feel guilty, knowing I'm responsible for Lou's dismissal. But I'm sure she's highly capable and won't have a hard time finding another assignment. But just in case, I'll ask Jacob to make sure she does get a good assignment.

Oh shoot, I haven't contacted Jacob yet!

I grab my phone from my bag as soon as I'm inside Magnus's Bentley, so I can send him a text message: *Hi, Jacob. We need to talk about the phone calls I'm getting. May I call you later? — Billie*

It doesn't take long and my phone beeps: *I'll be at Magnus's thing tonight. We can talk then. — J*

Oh. He'll be at the charity event. A smile rises on my face.

I feel Magnus's arm circle around my shoulder, his nose skimming the curve of my neck, and turning my smile into a grin.

"Hmm, I love how you smell, babe," he whispers, his breath tickling my skin and leaving tiny prickles all over.

"Thank you," I answer back, closing my eyes and letting Magnus envelope me with his arms. "Busy day?" I ask.

"As always. But my morning was pretty amazing," he answers, still in the crook of my neck.

"Oh, yeah? Why is that?" I ask, smiling.

"This hot piece of ass paid me a visit and had her way with me."

I giggle out aloud. "Had her way with you? Oh, please. She let you have your way with her … twice!"

He lifts his head, looking at me with a puzzled look on his face.

"Wait, are we talking about the same girl here, because I'm pretty sure …"

"Magnus, your joke sucks!" I pinch him on the side, my fingers barely holding on to the skin.

Seriously, this man has zero percent fat.

"Baby, don't pout," he runs his forefinger on my lower lip. "You know what that fiery temper of yours does to me."

I shift my position so I'm looking out the window. For some reason, his innocent joke really hit a nerve.

I never realized how jealous a person I am, until Magnus happened.

"I spoke with your father today. He's playing hardball," Magnus says out of the blue, as the car is pulling over the curb.

I turn towards him, brows furrowed. "What do you mean by hardball? He's still not selling?"

"Oh, he's still interested to sell. But he's ill and desperate to make amends with you. He believed Cooper when he said that he could bring you back. So, the only way for him to agree to sell to me is if I agree to help him reconcile with you."

The car door opens, just as I feel panic sets in.

"Call him back. Tell my father you're taking me back to see him."

I step out of the car and so does Magnus.

"I'm not confident that that is the right approach," he says as we walk inside his building, then stepping inside a thankfully empty elevator.

"But I don't want Cooper's family to get their hands on my family's business. They will destroy my father's hard work. I may be estranged from my family, and the possibility of seeing them again is scaring me half to death, but it doesn't mean I don't love them, Magnus," I answer back emotionally, my voice shaken and frustrated.

The elevator doors open, and we step out, heading towards the front door.

"There is something we discovered, upon digging inside Bridges Builders," he tells me softly, his expression serious, but wary. "It's something that Senator Thornton wants to make sure will stay buried, because it has a potential to destroy Thornton's chances for a reelection. It might even give him jail time." He reaches for my hand.

"But before we get into that, come here. I want you to do something for me."

"What is it? Magnus, what are you doing?"

"I'm giving you access to my apartment. Now, place your hand on top of this screen." Magnus gently flattens my hand on the flat screen, before pressing some buttons to start up the system.

"This is my way of letting you know that you will always have a place to run to, whenever you and Ethan feel unsafe," he says to me gently. "I've been meaning to do this for some time now, and this isn't something I'd do to anyone else. Only Rosa and Alex have this access, and now, I want you to have your own too."

My hand is screened, my fingerprints are recognized. He types a few more things on the keypad, until it finally confirms my identity.

I look up to him with uncertainty. "Magnus, are ... are you sure? I mean this is a pretty big deal."

"I was intending to do this after we came home from my mother's fundraiser, but," he sighs, "well ..."

He pauses, before speaking once again, nodding towards the panel. "Go on, try it, and see if it works."

I place my hand flat on the screen, and a digitized light scans my whole hand, before little circles form around each of my fingertips. Then a green light appears, and the screen says '*Access Granted.*'

"After you." Magnus opens the door and moves to one side, letting me in first.

Once we're both in his penthouse, he walks past me, down the hall, stopping at the living area.

"Make yourself at home. I have some white in the fridge as well, if you'd like a drink. I just need to send a couple of e-mails."

"Okay, no problem," I reply, smiling. "Thank you."

He responds with a slight nod and a genuine smile, his eyes lingering, before he finally makes his way back to his home office.

I walk over to the minibar, and even with the potentially bad information he's uncovered about my father's company, I can't help but smile.

Magnus just proved to me how much he trusts me by giving me access to his home. This is a pretty big deal.

My hand reaches over my pendant, and I gaze at it longingly, loving how the light makes the diamonds sparkle in a playful way.

Yeah, he really does love me.

I feel my heart soar at the thought.

But I still have questions that require answers.

Magnus is back by the time I've poured two glasses of pinot gris. I'm sitting on one of the couches, and he takes a glass and sits next to me.

I take a long sip, sliding closer. "You were saying something about Senator Thornton and my dad's business? Something you found out?"

Magnus regards me for a few seconds, before speaking slowly, like he's trying to choose his words carefully. "I think, and this is based on the information we gathered recently, that Senator Thornton is using your father's Bridges Builders to launder money."

It feels like a bucket of ice has been thrown over me.

It can't be true.

My father may be a lot of things, but he is *not* a corrupt politician's lackey.

Or is he?

Is that why he clings to the Thorntons? Why he betrayed me when I came to him for help? I thought it was only because he didn't want to lose his precious government contracts.

Oh dear God, not Daddy.

"I'm sorry …" Magnus says, concern all over his face.

"How long has he been aiding the senator on this? And how can I even be sure this isn't a lie? Do you have any proof?" I ask, my expression hardening, my body feeling numb.

"I do. It's been going on for over a couple of decades now, Isabelle. Your father has been in the thick of things basically from the word *go*."

I shake my head in disbelief. "No, that can't be true. My dad has a successful business. He worked so hard to get to where he is."

"And I'm not disputing his commitment to his business. But he's committed to the Thorntons as well. Isabelle, we're talking about money stolen through illegal tenders and unsubstantiated expenses. Two decades long of syphoning money through dubious transactions. I can't give you the exact dollar amounts, but from what I've gathered, they would have accumulated millions worth of taxpayers' dollars between the two of them. "

"No." My hands begin to shake, so Magnus takes the wine glass off my hand and places it on the coffee table.

I feel ashamed, angry, disgusted, a roller coaster of emotions going on inside of me that I can't easily ignore. I cover my face with my hands, and I start to cry, my whole body shaking from the shock.

That's when I feel Magnus's strong arms circle around me, holding me close against his chest.

"Maybe he was just set up, Magnus. What if someone planted this? It's possible, right?"

"I'm sorry, baby. I wish it were," he tells me softly, and I can't deny the sincerity in his voice.

I sob, my tears and smeared makeup messing up his shirt. So I pull away, trying to wipe my tears, but Magnus reaches underneath the coffee table to get the tissue box.

"Who else knows about this again?" I ask, grabbing the tissues he hands to me, blowing my nose, and not caring about how I might look or sound.

"Charles and myself. Just us. He won't talk to others because he's loyal to me. Not to mention the fact that he signed an NDA, just like all the people in my inner circle at Grant Corp."

"Will my father go to jail? They can't put a man in jail when he's got a terminal cancer, right? Oh, Dad, what have you done?" I sputter out in tears.

"He's not the mastermind of this whole scam. I think that he agreed to this, then had a change of heart, but was in too deep with Thornton, to get out without implicating himself. The senator knew that, of course, so he used it to his advantage."

I snort, "Like father, like fucking son."

"I can help him, Isabelle. I have the means and the connections to reduce the blow. He's too sick to be sent to jail, or stand trial, but the senator will try. Your father can get immunity, but he needs to cut his ties with Thornton and hand him to the authorities. I can help make that happen, and I'll start by acquiring his company and cleaning it up."

"I can't believe this, Magnus. I just can't get my head around it. I want to see the proof for myself. Will you show it to me?"

He nods. "Of course."

Then a sudden, chilling thought comes to mind.

"This can't be good on your image, for your *name*. A rape victim with a money-laundering father? I said this before, Magnus, I will not allow your reputation to be dragged in the mud because of me, and oh my God, my whole family. I'm not good for you. I will never be good for you!"

I slide away from him, shame riddling me. But Magnus moves closer, pulling me to him and holding me securely.

"There will be no more talks of this, you hear me? I don't give a *damn* about what the press thinks, or whether or not this will affect my reputation. I have people who can spin everything to my advantage. What matters to me now is you—your happiness. You're good for me, Isabelle, and I. Love. *You*. Christ, what do I need to do for you to understand that, you stubborn woman?" Magnus tightens his hold to emphasize that he means what he says.

A sudden sob escapes me, and I cry out once again. Not from fear, or shame, but from complete and utter love and gratitude for this man who is holding me now.

"I'm sorry … I'm sorry …" I whisper, my forehead on his chest once again, my hands over my eyes, trying to ebb away the tears that continue to flow.

"I'm gonna look like shit for your charity thing tonight. My eyes will be puffy as hell," I croak out.

His chest shakes in a low chuckle, "You'll still be the most beautiful woman in there. But if you stop crying now, maybe you won't get a headache. Would you like me to heat up some tea bags for your eyes?"

I sniff, staring up at him dubiously.

"You know how to fix puffy eyes? Did you learn that from your ex?"

"I have a younger sister … Regan … remember her? By the way, she threatened to kill me, when she found out we broke up."

"Oh. Tell her she doesn't have to now."

He cups my face with his hand, sweeping some stray tears away with his thumb. The tenderness of his gesture is overwhelming, that another tear escapes when I close my eyes.

"I'm sorry. I'm such a cry baby," I mutter.

He leans forward and plants a gentle, lingering kiss on my forehead.

"Sometimes, you need to cry. And I'll always be here to hold you, but also to give you space when you feel the need, okay?"

I nod back, so touched by his words.

He stands up and walks to the minibar, grabbing a small bottled water from the fridge, opens the lid, and hands it to me with a small smile on his face. "Here, drink this instead of the wine. Water will help as well."

I take the bottle from Magnus and drink the water as he instructed, watching him as he heads towards the kitchen to prepare my tea bags.

After several minutes, he comes back with a plate of warmed tea bags.

"These are still quite hot. Let's go to the bedroom so you can rest up for a little while." He offers his hands and helps me up, keeping them linked as he carefully takes me upstairs.

In his bedroom, he takes my coat and boots off, before laying me down the bed. Looking around me, I realize that I see no sign of my bags.

"Magnus! Oh no, we forgot to get my bags! My gown's in the trunk too."

Magnus is in the middle of taking his coat off, including his shirt and trousers. "Alex will take them straight to The Plaza. A limo will pick us up from here."

My brows furrow. "But like I said just now, my gown, heels, and everything else, are in that bag."

Magnus smiles a crooked smile, and it doesn't take me long to realize what he's doing … again.

"You bought me a gown, didn't you? What else did you get me?" I ask as I sit up, rolling my eyes, and getting off the bed.

"Uh, uh, uh. You're not leaving the bed. These tea bags are ready so you can lie down now." I comply to his instructions, then he gently places the tea bags over my closed eyes.

"You need to stop doing this," I tell him in frustration. "I'm perfectly capable of looking presentable for your peers without your help. Unless you think I can't?" I retort, crossing my arms.

God, how this man can make me giddy with happiness one minute, then angry the next is beyond me.

"I'm going to take your clothes off now so you're more comfortable," the gentle authority in his voice, telling me what he's about to do makes my skin tingle in anticipation.

From happy, to angry, and now, to horny.

Well played, Magnus.

The bed mattress dips next to my hips, and I can feel him unzipping my skirt. "You can wear anything and still be a fucking standout. But you have to see it from my viewpoint as well."

"So what, pray tell, is your view about this, and why does it hold precedence over mine?" I ask sarcastically, but my voice is too breathless from the feel of his fingertips over my bare skin.

"I don't buy you these things because I don't trust your taste. You have impeccable taste, and it shows because you chose me ..."

"Magnus!" I cry out in exasperation.

"But I just want to prove to *you*," his voice turns somber, "that I can take care of you and Ethan. The money is never an issue. Never will be. You know I have way more than I need. But I get a kick out of taking care of you, and seeing your face lights up over a present I personally chose. Now that is up there, with watching your face as you come for me. It's addictive."

"Oh, Magnus ..." my tone changes, now sweeter, my hands reaching out for him. "Take off your clothes and come here. I want to feel you on me."

I still have the tea bags over my eyes, and I'm wary that there may be a good chance I'll freak out as soon as I feel him on top of me.

It just brings back memories I've been trying so hard to forget.

It takes him a few moments, but as soon as I feel Magnus's near-naked body slide over me, with his hard body weighing me down, the anxiety I'm expecting to get is nowhere to be found.

In fact, I feel comforted, secure.

Safe.

"Are you alright, baby? Tell me if I'm getting too heavy for you."

I shake my head, taking the tea bags off of my eyes and placing them back on the plate. Then I wrap my arms around his shoulders, my legs around his legs.

"No, stay there. You feel good on top of me."

I slide my arms over his back but pull away just as immediately.

"I'm wearing way too many clothes for my liking," I tell him softly.

"We should remedy that problem, don't you think?" he smirks.

I raise my back slightly to make room for him, as he slips my sweater off, leaving me with just my underwear on.

Just like him.

"Hmmm … much better," Magnus says, as he lowers his head, pressing his mouth against mine.

I open my own, letting my tongue slide through his lush lips, loving how good he tastes. My hands flatten over his back, as my fingers caress every sinew, every line, until they reach that valley in-between, letting my fingertips trace its length up to his lower back. I pause just above the band of his boxer briefs, but the temptation is too much. So I slip my hand inside, cupping each smooth, muscled, butt cheek.

Definitely, zero percent fat.

He rolls his hips over mine, with my hands pushing him down further, making us both moan in unison.

"You feel too fucking good against me, my temptress," he whispers against my lips, gritting his teeth, "but we have to get ready for dinner."

"Do we have to go? Let's skip it, baby. I bet you and your cock agree with me." With my hands still underneath his boxers, I slide one hand around, confirming the hardness digging against my belly.

"See? Just as I thought," I say, biting my lower lip.

I wrap my fingers around it, tugging it gently, making him close his eyes.

"God, I wish we can," he groans, as he lifts himself up and off the bed, forcing me to let him go. Then he stands up and winces, as he adjusts himself.

That always gives me a little thrill, knowing how much I affect him as well.

"You know, you never told me what this whole dinner thing is about. Is it work-related?" I slide off his bed, unfastening my bra as I go.

Magnus just stands there, watching my every move intently.

Right now, his eyes are right on my breasts.

So I let him stare a little bit longer, silently enjoying the effect I have on him.

"Baby?" I call his attention, my hands on my hips.

His eyes finally rise up to meet my own. "I didn't tell you on purpose. I wanted to surprise you."

"Should I be scared?" I ask worriedly.

"No," he responds, closing our distance, gently placing his hands over my bare shoulders, sliding up to the curves on the sides of my neck, "because this is for you."

"Excuse me? But do I look like a charity to you?" I exclaim, not sure if I should be offended or flattered.

He shakes his head. "Baby, I'm raising funds to build a school in Texas."

"And that has something to do with me because …"

"Will you just trust me and wait until we're there? I want it to be a surprise."

"I trust you, but I—"

"There is never a *but* when you fully trust someone," he cuts me off, raising his brows as if to challenge me.

Damn him.

"You know that I trust you with my life, Magnus."

A slow smile rises on his face, like he's genuinely touched by what I just said.

"You've inspired me to do this. This *is* something good, I promise," he reassures me gently, his thumbs circling the sensitive part of my neck, instantly easing my doubts.

"Let's get ready then," I shoot back with a full grin.

***

"Did you know that I've been living in New York for quite some time now, but I've never actually been inside The Plaza?" I'm looking out of the window, as the limo is only a block away from the hotel. Even from this distance, I can see the press and photographers milling around the front, taking photographs of guests in their lavish gowns and dark suits.

This does not look like a run-of-the-mill dinner function.

Not by a long shot.

"Well, you're spoilt for choice in Manhattan. Where does your family usually stay?" Magnus asks, his arm reassuring around my shoulders, his fingers stroking my skin, helping ease the nerves that are starting to build.

"My dad always preferred the Waldorf Astoria every time we …" My chest tightens in agony, and I start shaking my head from side to side. "I'm sorry, just thinking about my family on happier times …"

Magnus kisses my temple, and I feel the warmth of his breath as he speaks, "You've been making great memories with Ethan too, right? Focus on that, baby, and not on the negativities. You have people who love you, who are helping to give you newer, happier memories. I'd like to be one of them, Isabelle."

I turn to look him in the eyes, and the sincerity in his eyes bowls me over. "All these years, I thought Ethan was my only silver lining, but I'm beginning to see that he's not the only one."

Magnus doesn't answer with words. He doesn't have to.

He reaches for my cheek to brush off a stray tear that has fallen from the corner of my eye. He regards me with such affection, smiling in a way that is only meant for me. Then he gives me the most tender of kisses. It's not primal, nor is it lustful, but it makes my heart want to jump out of my chest, and stand beside Magnus's own heart.

It's a special kiss. And like his smile, I know it's only meant for me.

As our mouths part, the flashing of cameras and the muffled barrage of chatter from the press make us realize that the limo has now pulled over at The Plaza's red-carpet entrance.

It's like I've been pinched hard, bringing me back to this part of my reality.

"Ready?" Magnus asks, with eyes showing gentle concern.

"I hope I don't have panda eyes," I half-joke.

"You look beautiful, Isabelle. And everyone out there will see that."

"You sure know how to make a girl feel special," I answer back, laughing nervously as the car door opens, making the camera flashes brighter.

"Reserve that comment until we're inside." And after a cheeky wink, he steps out of the limo first, before reaching for my hand and helping me out.

"Are you ready?" Magnus whispers close to my ear.

"I'm not afraid anymore. Not while you're here," I whisper back, and a smile appears on his face.

He holds my hand firmly, interlocking our fingers, and keeping me glued to his side. I'm holding a wrap around me to protect me from the cold, and as we stand against the media wall, Magnus helps me out of my wrap, and with a protective hand around my waist, he decides to proudly show me off.

Having a family friend who creates the most exquisite gowns must be so amazing. And I must say, Magnus chose well, and it's helping boost my confidence.

I'm wearing a long, deep red, full-sleeved gown. The material is sheer, but the delicate beadwork sewed in strategic areas gives the gown an illusion of being conservative, yet also sexy in parts.

And it makes the gown that I brought, looks like I sewed it myself.

I don't even sew.

I have my hair down and swept on one side—my personal favorite—putting in just enough curls to make it look romantic. It's just luck on my part that I almost forgot about my curling iron and dumped it in my purse. My makeup is simple, but I'm wearing a red lipstick that matches my gown. I didn't have any help from my friends this time, but judging from Magnus's compliments while I was getting ready for tonight, I must've done well.

I must thank Remy for those times when she taught me how to style myself. It was Michelle's idea to have makeover parties to get me out of my breakup funk, and it looks like I've learned quite a few tricks.

Mental note: I must thank my BFF as well.

"It's good to see you two back together!" one reporter from the press says.

"Thank you," Magnus answers politely.

"Mister Grant, this is a great initiative. Who or what was your inspiration?" one of the reporters asks.

I turn to Magnus, curious about his answer as well. He gives the reporter a smile, before answering, "I hold this project close to my heart, because the person who inspired me is very close to my heart as well. Hopefully tonight, we'll garner enough funds and help run, and even expand, this initiative."

"When did you and Miss Morrison get back together, Mister Grant?" a devious-looking reporter asks. "You two haven't been seen together since your mother's fundraiser. We heard that you broke up. Does this mean your playboy days are over once again?"

Magnus tightens his hold on me, saying, "Thank you for your questions, but we have to get inside now. Grant Foundation will be doing a press release tomorrow. Have a good night." I notice his jaw tightening, but he manages to smiles at the press on the way inside the hotel.

Magnus's hand is now on my back, and as soon as we're inside, he excuses us from the ushers and leads me to a quiet corner.

"I'm sorry about that fucker. He's from the tabloids, and his goal in life is to piss people off to get a reaction," he explains, concern all over his face.

"I'm not worried, Magnus. Yes, he's a dick, but he's not worth breaking a sweat on." I cup his cheek with my hand. "I know what we have."

He holds my wrist, kissing my palm tenderly.

"Good to know." And the worry on his face is gone, replacing it with relief.

Magnus takes my hand once again, allowing one of the foundation organizers to lead us inside the ballroom.

And wow, the Grants sure know how to put an event together!

The styling is high-end, though not as lavish as Miranda's but still quite striking. There are portraits of women all over the venue, propped on easels, some older, some of my age, and some who must be in their teens. There are women smiling, beaming even, while some girls have more haunted expressions on their faces, and some looking on with fear. I read the event signage on my way in: "Grant Foundation Dinner Fundraiser—Victim No More." These signs are everywhere inside the ballroom, as well.

"You haven't mentioned if your family is going to be here. Are they here tonight?" I ask Magnus, expectantly.

"My parents are currently holidaying in Europe. But they send their regards, together with a substantial donation. My sister is holed up in the school library, studying for her exams. And as for my brother, well," he exhales deeply, "he never comes to any of my events."

"I'm sorry they can't make it tonight. But if it's any consolation, you have my full support. I'm here for you."

"Your being here with me is not *just* a consolation. It's everything," he says, leaning forward to kiss me on the temple.

I didn't think it was possible to melt in the middle of winter, but right at this very moment, I might just be. All I can do is nod back, "Okay."

Magnus offers his arm, which I graciously accept. "So, are you finally ready to tell me what this is all about, or are you going to keep it to yourself? Am I the only person in the dark?" I ask Magnus curiously.

"Patience, Isabelle." Magnus takes my hand that is perched over his arm, and he kisses it before letting the usher seat us at our table.

"Well, guess who finally decided to make an appearance!"

I should be annoyed by the interruption, but I know that voice anywhere.

And I love her … and she's here!

I stand up straight away, and we both squeal like two teenage girls who haven't seen each other for ages.

Except that I just spoke to her this morning.

"Oh my God, Michelle, you're here! And with Nathan!" I hug my best friend tightly, leaning over to give Nathan a happy hug and a light peck on his cheek.

I step back from Michelle, holding her hands up to check her out.

"You look fabulous, girl," I cry out, admiring her purple, figure-hugging gown, with subtle gold trimmings.

"I know, right? Magnus invited us a couple of days ago, and he wanted it to be a surprise, so here we are!"

"Yeah, man. Thanks for inviting us. This is, well, pretty amazing," Nathan adds, scoping the room.

"This *is* amazing!" But my happiness turns to worry. "Wait, what about the kids? Is Ethan—"

"The kids are with their usual babysitter, not to mention Jacob's crew is keeping an eye on them as well." Michelle points at Magnus. That's when I notice his amused reaction.

I turn to the culprit. "You! How many secrets are you keeping from me?"

Magnus feigns innocence. "It's not a secret … it's a surprise."

A guy in tux, who seems familiar to Magnus, appears out of nowhere, and he whispers something to him. Magnus nods, before standing up and straightening his tuxedo jacket.

Did I mention how breathtaking he looks tonight in his tux? Not that he doesn't look good in whatever he wears, or doesn't wear for that matter, but …

Okay, I'm getting distracted.

"Looks like you're about to find out, Isabelle," Magnus tells me, before kissing me on the cheek.

"Wait, where are you going?" I ask, feeling wary that he's going somewhere without me.

"I have to get on the stage, baby."

"Oh, okay," I reply, nodding slowly.

I hear the host onstage, requesting the guests to please find their seats, which, he jokes, they should do very soon, and that inasmuch as they already paid over ten grand for each, they might want to make the most of their money.

"Holy shit, ten grand?" Michelle whispers a little too loudly, earning us some curious stares.

"That seems to be the running rate in this sort of charity events," I whisper back. "I still can't believe you guys are here," I add, squeezing her arm.

"I'm not about to miss this one, baby girl." She gives me a sideways glance, smiling and squeezing my hand in return.

We settle on our seats, and I watch as Magnus stands in the sidelines, waiting to be introduced.

The host first talks about what Grant Foundation is about, the charities it is affiliated with, and finally, a breakdown of projects where last year's donations went—from digging wells to provide clean, drinking water to third world countries, to building schools for the underprivileged children.

This is the first time I've heard about this, mostly because Magnus doesn't talk about his foundation as much, but I never realized how much it gives back to people who need help the most.

And as I stare at Magnus, still waiting by the side of the stage, there is no self-satisfied smirk on his face, nor is there any sign of cockiness, that I've come to accept as part of his confident personality.

After all, it's not like he can't back it up, right?

The Magnus I see is humbled, even a touch nervous as he listens intently at the host who, by now, is about to wrap up his introduction.

"So why don't I bring out the founder and director of Grant Foundation? He has a new, very important project that he would like to talk to you about tonight. This one is very dear to his heart, so he's hoping that it will be for you too. Let's give a round of applause to Magnus Grant, everyone."

The ballroom is engulfed in loud applause as Magnus climbs up the short flight of stairs, and makes it onto the podium where the host stood. His eyes immediately search for me, and as soon as our eyes lock, I can see his expression lightens up, and the confidence that I'm so used to seeing in Magnus is back. Why he's nervous in the first place, is anyone's guess. He's used to being the center of attention. Public speaking is one of his fortes, and one can't help but watch him and admire him in his element. And yet, for some reason, I'm feeling nervous as well, with butterflies in my stomach fluttering like crazy.

"Good evening, everyone. Thank you for spending your time here tonight, but most of all, thank you for sharing your hard-earned money for the cause. What can I say, I am extremely grateful."

Magnus pauses, right at the same time as my clutch vibrates. Surmising it must be the babysitter calling me, I take my old phone out to answer the call discreetly.

"Hello?" I whisper, with my head bowed down, pressing my ear to hear the voice on the other end of the line.

Nothing.

I check the phone's screen.

Unknown.

Without any hesitation, I end the call.

I definitely need to speak with Jacob.

The phone rings again.

Unknown.

Fucker.

I look up to Magnus. He's still onstage, talking about the other projects the foundation is currently working on.

Michelle and Nathan are both listening intently to Magnus.

Good. This can't wait.

I turn slightly away from my friends, before answering the call.

"Listen," I attempt to speak in a low, yet menacing tone, "I'm about to get someone to figure out who you are, so if you don't tell me what you want, so help me, I will get the police involved as soon as—"

"Please … don't." Even with the background noise on both sides, the voice on the other end of the call is clear.

It's a woman's voice.

A very scared, young woman's voice.

"Who are you, and what do you want?"

"I'm … I'm Kelly. I know you're pissed at me for calling, then hanging up, but I'm just … I have no one else to turn to."

I roll my eyes, before glancing back at Magnus, who notices that I'm on the phone. He slightly frowns with disapproval.

I have to end this call.

"I don't know who you are. I don't know of any Kelly. You have the wrong number, so stop calling me. Good—"

"Autumn. Your name is Autumn Bridges, isn't it?"

My breathing stops, and my body goes rigid.

"H—how did you know who I am? Why are you harassing me? How the hell did you get my number?"

I hear her break down at the other end, letting out a painful cry, "C—Cooper did something to me … he … he … oh God!"

My head begins to spin, and I feel a chill run through my body. Without thinking, I end the call, mindlessly placing the phone in my clutch with shaky hands. Michelle turns to me, looking concerned.

"Who was that? Was it the babysitter?"

You can't worry anyone else, Billie. This could just be a prank.

I shake my head, faking a smile. "It was a wrong number, sorry. All's good."

Seemingly satisfied, she doesn't ask further and switches her attention to Magnus once again. I sigh in relief.

I know Magnus is now giving a backgrounder on his latest project, which is the focal point of tonight's event. I can't concentrate, not after that phone call. What if it's a trap? What if Cooper told her to do this, in order to draw me in?

But what if it's legitimate?

And how the hell did she know my number?

I try to shake the thoughts out of my head, at least for now. I need to focus my attention on Magnus. And now that I finally understand what he is talking about, it suddenly occurs to me that this new project is not about giving clean water, or feeding the hungry. Magnus is talking about young women who were victims of assault, sexual or otherwise, and have nowhere else to go to. And his plan is to build, not only a school, but also a home for these women, to help educate them, and empower them, so they can rebuild and better their lives. And if these victims of rape ever bear children, then they will also be cared for.

My heart is beating stronger than usual, I'm feeling shortness of breath, and the ballroom suddenly feels too enclosed.

Surely, I'm not the person who inspired him to do this.

But does he know anyone else that has gone through what I had?

People will know it's me.

Magnus, what have you done?

"The foundation will build the flagship center here in New York City. Then, if this initiative is successful, we're hoping to branch out into other states, eventually going international in the near future."

Magnus pauses after a few moments for the applause. Then he turns his head in my direction, his enthusiasm apparent.

"Ladies and gentlemen, sometimes, we're lucky enough to meet someone whose inner strength is evident even after surviving appalling forms of abuse. These people inspire us to look back at our more fortunate circumstances, and so in turn, we can help better their lives. This project is very close to my heart because I have met such a person. I'm choosing to keep the person's identity a secret to protect that person's privacy, but nevertheless, this project was inspired by this one very special human being. Our aim is for these victims of abuse to rise up, with support, legal or otherwise, education, and even a place they could call home. Ladies and gentlemen, I bring you Autumn's Haven."

There are a lot of clapping and cheers of approval. The room dims, and a video about Autumn's Haven begins.

What ... the ...?

"Oh, wow. He named the shelter after you," Michelle says in awe.

I'm too stunned to speak.

Michelle turns to me, looking concerned. "Are you okay, baby girl? You're shaking, do you need some water?"

"Did you know about this?" I ask her in monotone.

"No," Michelle answers, shaking her head, "but why are you getting upset? This is an amazing thing Magnus has done. And Billie, you're obviously the inspiration for this. "

"I didn't know. I just wish he gave me a heads up." I pause, shaking my head. "I need some air."

I stand up a bit shaky, still giddy with shock from that phone call … and now *this*. I don't know why I feel used, but that's what I'm feeling right this moment.

I falter backwards, before correcting myself. And then I grab my wrap and my small clutch hastily.

"Billie," Michelle calls out in whisper, managing to hold my wrist, "don't freak out … please," she insists.

But I'm having hard time breathing. I really need some air.

"Let me go." It must have been the tone of my voice, but she does as I ask, and I do what I do best.

I take advantage of the darkness, and I run out of the ballroom.

CHAPTER 20

Shit, where am I gonna go?

I can't even go outside. The press are right there waiting.

Oh God, what if they link this project to me?

Why did Magnus do this?

I have to talk to him. I need to hear his explanation.

But not right now.

Right now, I can't even be in the same room with him. I have a feeling I will have the urge to walk up that stage and slam my fists on Magnus's chest, right in front of his distinguished peers.

God, this is so embarrassing.

I don't know how my legs manage to get me to the nearest bar inside the hotel, but they do.

I find a seat at the corner part of the bar. It doesn't take long before a tall, good-looking barman approaches me.

"Hello, what can I get you, Miss …?" He hangs the last word, obviously asking for my name.

"I'd like a whiskey, neat, please," I answer back, discouraging any small talk. It's been a while since I drank the strong stuff, but I really need this right this minute.

He nods back and gives me a coy smile. "You've got it, beautiful."

I ignore his remark, and I focus my attention on him pouring my drink.

He hands me the tumbler but takes something from his trousers pocket.

It's the bar's business card and a pen with it.

"You can write your name and your phone number if, you know, you need company." He leans forward, trying to make himself look charming, but only succeeding in getting me nervous. "But if you're staying in the hotel, you can always give me your room number? I'm sure I can wipe that sadness off your face."

"How about if you give me your name, and I'll have you fired on the spot?"

The familiar static is back, and my heart lurches in attention.

As soon as I feel his hand on my nape, an instinctive act of proprietorship, it doesn't take a rocket scientist to realize who is right behind me.

The barman's expression goes from playful to terrified, in no time at all.

"Apologies, Mr. Grant. I didn't know the lady is with you. That's on the house." Then he backs away to the far end of the bar.

Magnus swings my bar stool around to face me. I stare at him with defiance. He stares back broodingly, his sculpted jawline twitching.

I break it off first, taking the glass of whisky onto my lips. But Magnus grabs it off of me and slams it on the bar.

"You, my dear, are not drinking that." His low, commanding tone makes my insides clench.

He firmly takes my hand, tangling his fingers with mine.

"Get off the bar stool, unless you want me to carry you over my shoulder," he adds in the same tone of voice.

I do as he says, not keen on becoming a spectacle. I carefully slide off the bar stool, while unsuccessfully trying to take my hand back. Still holding my hand, he leads me out of the bar.

"Where are you taking me? I need to be alone, right now."

He walks on, not even giving me a glance.

"I can't go back in there, Magnus. What if they find out it's me? Why didn't you ask me first? Magnus, I'm talking to you."

Magnus's jaw clenches, but he still doesn't answer me. Instead, he leads me towards the elevators, and presses the button going up. As soon as the elevator doors open, he takes me inside, still silent, but looking thunderous.

Other guests, unfortunately, join us inside including two young, beautiful women who instantly zoom in on Magnus, completely ignoring the woman he's firmly holding hands with. But Magnus doesn't see them, because even through the reflection from the elevator doors, I can see that he's only looking at me.

And yet, he still refuses to speak.

He is angry. He is furious at me for walking out on him.

I told him I'd never run, and I did.

But he told me he'd never hurt me, and yet he just did, by pulling a stunt like this in such a large scale.

I may as well be a poster girl for rape victims everywhere.

First that horrid prank call, now this?

Why can't the universe allow me to be happy for a little bit longer?

All the other people with us in the elevator had left, and we are all by our twosome.

"Why did you do it, Magnus? Why did you do something like this without even telling me first?"

He still refuses to speak.

It's beginning to make my blood boil.

The elevator finally stops on the twentieth floor, and with Magnus's hand still holding mine, he takes me out with him. He leads me to the end of the hallway, and he uses his entry card to open the double doors.

"Holy shit!" I exclaim, looking around me as he takes me inside a massive suite, stopping next to a flight of stairs leading upwards.

But he continues on, going up the stairs, down another hall, and into one of the most beautiful hotel bedrooms I have ever seen, with doors leading out onto a massive terrace, with views of the Central Park.

"Oh my God, Magnus, it's beautiful here."

"I want you to sit on the edge of the bed." Magnus finally lets me go, but the tone of his voice gives me no option but to follow what he says.

With a sideways glance at him, I make the few short steps towards the bed, and I sit at the bottom of the bed, facing him.

If he starts reprimanding me like a little girl, I might lose it.

"Look at me, Isabelle," Magnus commands in that deep, yet rough voice of his that makes my insides clench.

I look up at him.

He's still brooding, but his blue eyes tell it all, the intensity in them as they stare back at me, makes me thankful that I'm already sitting down.

"Magnus ..."

"Take your panties off."

"What? I don't think—"

"I said. Take. Your. Panties. Off. Slowly."

My breath hitches, but my body takes over my brain, and my hands are now pulling up the delicate material of my dress, up to my crotch.

Then with my eyes still fixed on his, I slowly take my panties off, letting them drop off my forefinger when I'm done.

He closes our distance, and he takes my flimsy underwear, stuffing it straight into his trousers pocket.

"Open your legs." He's looking down at me as he commands, an intimidating figure, the moonlight highlighting his handsome face.

"I want us to talk first," I answer back, a little too meekly for my liking.

"I want *you* to listen to *me*. Open your legs. Now, Isabelle."

With another deep breath, I do as he says, letting my dress fall on its sides, with my hands supporting me from behind.

He's making me wet, and he knows it, and as he slides not one, but two fingers along my crevice, he can also feel it.

I watch him as he unzips his trousers, not even bothering to take his tux jacket off. He pulls his trousers and underwear down, exposing his hard cock in all its glory.

All my anger dissipates, replaced by my yearning for him, for what is right in front of me … for what is mine.

I reach for his cock, but he steps back.

"You don't get to touch this," he whispers roughly. "I want you to stand up, turn around, and put your hands on the edge of the bed, feet on the floor.

I search his face for a clue on what he's thinking, but find none.

I stand up, and spread my legs apart, my feet flat on the floor, like he wanted. My dress fell back down when I stood up, but now, I feel the dress hitching up once again, the sensation of the material against my skin has me tingling all over.

He holds on to my hips, fingers gripping on my skin. Then all of a sudden, he's inside me in one hard plunge. No warning, no waiting for me to adjust to him, just pure rawness with that single thrust.

Yet even after the initial sting, it still feels good.

Too. Damn. Good.

That single thrust becomes two, then three, then four, the tempo increasing. I find myself moaning with every thrust.

Magnus grunts in unison with me, his grip on my hips digging deeper.

I push back against him, our skin furiously slapping against each other.

Then he fists his hand in my hair, pulling me upwards, and grazing his teeth on the skin of my neck.

There is no affection in this, nor are there any words of love.

This is an angry fuck.

And the bad part about this is that I don't want him to stop, because with every angry thrust, Magnus fills me completely, hitting the right nerves, and driving me close to a climax.

"Magnus, I'm so close," I moan out.

And then he does something I'd never thought he'd do, even in anger.

I hear him let out a deep groan, and then he comes inside of me.

He came before me.

Magnus always lets me come first.

He pulls out, then walks away, leaving me feeling cold both inside and out.

My chest tightens.

Damn, it hurts like a motherfucker.

Still stunned by what just happened, I do my best to straighten up, reaching for a box of tissues so I can at least clean myself. But just then, I feel Magnus's hand over my arm, as he gently holds me, then turns me around so I'm facing him.

In a move that stuns me even more, he says, "I've got you. Let me clean you up." Then he gently lifts the front hem of my skirt, and he starts wiping me clean with a warm, washcloth.

"You don't have to do that." I try to grab the towel from him, but he refuses to stop and hand the towel to me.

Once he's finished, he lets go of my gown, so it cascades in front of me. Then I follow him with my gaze as he walks back to the bathroom, and he tosses the towel in the sink.

All the while, I'm standing on the same spot, confused as hell. He manages to upset me with his initial act of selfishness; then, he shows me his caring side immediately after. With my legs still wobbly, I manage to sit on the edge of the bed, just as Magnus is walking back to me.

"You never did that before, so I know you're furious. But I hope you know that I'm just as angry with you too," I tell him softly, but looking down at my shoes.

Magnus sits next to me. "I expected you to be surprised by what this event is about, but I never expected you to walk out on it, just as I was in the middle of the presentation," he says, with an edge in his voice. "And when I finally found you, I caught you flirting with another man."

"Let me clarify something. First of all, Magnus, that guy was hitting on me, yes. But I never flirted back. I thought you would've trusted me by now."

"Like how you trusted me right before you walked out?"

"Oh, this doesn't even compare—"

"You're right, it doesn't. You never even bothered to sit through the last five minutes of the presentation," he interrupts.

"What for? Seriously, Autumn's Haven? Didn't you realize that people will eventually put two and two together, and figure out that I'm that person … that I'm the rape victim. This will make me the fucking poster child of abuse!"

"But you're looking at this the wrong way. I wanted to build this shelter because these victims have no place to run to. This school will be a safe place for them. Wasn't that what you would've wanted when you ran away? A place you'd feel safe in? Where you can find a support system?"

With my lips trembling and my eyes pooling with tears, I manage to answer, "But what you don't understand is that what happened to me will always live with me, no matter what kind of help I get. And eventually, when everyone realizes that I *am* Autumn, that your girlfriend is *actually* a rape victim, then my name, my face, will always be associated with rape, and I'll always be seen as the fucking victim!" My whole body shivers at the thought.

"Isabelle, haven't you realized it yet? The moment y*ou* stopped becoming a victim was the moment *you* stood up to your parents and walked away to start a new life. I know it wouldn't have been easy, but you fought hard for yourself and your son. You had your nightmares and your traumatic memories, but yet, you never let them hold you back. Some victims of abuse would've gone the other way. You moved forward, the best way you could. So Isabelle, you're *not* the poster child of abuse. You're the poster child of survival, or resilience. You're the epitome of strength. And *that*, my darling, is the reason why I named this Autumn's Haven."

I turn to him with wide eyes, allowing tears to fall down my cheeks. All this time, I never looked at myself the way Magnus sees me. I thought it was too hard to survive what happened to me those years ago. But now I realize it's because I always saw myself as the victim, and I clung to that word and made it a part of my being.

Magnus sees me differently. He sees the strength I never realized I possess. He sees the fighter side in me.

Why did I even doubt this man's intentions, when all this time, all he's ever been to me is nothing short of amazing?

God, I really am such an idiot sometimes.

Without a word, Magnus's arms circle around me, and he lays my head on his chest. In silence, my tears continue to fall on my dress and over his crisp white shirt.

"I understand now, and I'm truly happy that you're doing this. You're right, I never had a place to run to when I left home, and you're giving these women hope for a better life. Maybe ... maybe one day, when everything isn't so complicated, I'd like to be able to come over and help out?" I look up at him, attempting a smile.

The smile he reciprocates back makes my heart leap out of my chest.

"Of course, I was hoping you would. But only when you're ready."

Smiling wider, I answer, "You should head back down, Magnus. I'm sure people are looking for you. And you still have some moneyed asses to kiss. I want Autumn's Haven to succeed, I really do."

He reaches up to gently wipe the last tears from my cheeks. "The only ass I ever need to kiss is yours, babe."

"Damn straight," I answer with a shaky laugh.

"I'll get Michelle up here to stay with you, until you're ready to come back down, alright?"

I nod back beaming, "Sounds great."

He straightens up, a crooked smile plastered on his face. Then he takes his phone, and types a text message, waiting momentarily, until he reads the response.

After reading, he looks at me and says, "She'll be right up," he assures, before placing his phone in his pocket.

"Um, you're not going back there, with my underwear in your pocket." I point at his pocket, raising my brow at him.

"Oh … you mean these?" Magnus pulls my undies out of his pocket, takes them to his nose, closes his eyes, and takes a deep breath.

My mouth drops. "Oh my God, you did not just do that! Give them back!"

He gives me a self-satisfied grin and teases, "You'll get them back downstairs."

Then he dips his head and lays a kiss on my lips. "I'll see you soon? Your bags are in the closet, by the way."

"Okay. I'll see you downstairs. I'll be the one in commando."

He leans forward, whispering in my ear, "Don't worry, I'll make it worth your while, I promise."

"It better be a good one. You *owe* me."

"I'll pay you back in full very soon." He winks at me, smirking, as he makes his way out of the door.

With a smile still on my face, I linger on the bed while listening to Magnus's footsteps going down the stairs. Once the room is quiet, I hear my stomach rumbling, realizing I've yet to eat dinner. I might as well head back out soon. Maybe they're still serving some food at the event.

It doesn't take long before I hear Michelle calling out my name, telling me that Magnus let her in. I yell out that I'm upstairs, in the bathroom, and it doesn't take long before I hear shrieking.

"Damn, girl, this place is ridiculous!"

"Yeah, I was thinking the same thing, as soon as I stepped inside."

Michelle dramatically saunters in the bathroom but stops short, once she sees my face as I'm reapplying my makeup.

"What happened? Oh my God, did you guys have a fight?" She rushes to where I am and starts fawning at me. "Wait, he ran after you. I mean, he was discreet but during that video, he left the same way you did."

I can't help but feel a little guilty about my panic attack. "He found me at the bar. I wanted to get out of the hotel altogether, but there were press outside. Not to mention that I …"

"That you what?" Michelle asks.

I stop myself from going any further. Michelle is like a sister to me, but the part about the phone call I received has to wait until I'm sure it's not a prank.

"The important thing is we've talked it out, and I understand that his project comes from a good place. I found it confronting at first, but now I'm loving that Magnus did this."

Michelle smiles in understanding and squeezes my upper arm.

"He's a good man, Billie."

"I know."

"Then we better get you down there, shall we?"

Michelle and I are arm-in-arm as we make our way inside the ballroom. Luckily, the servers are just into the third course of the five-course dinner.

"Good, I'm famished!" I plant myself on the same chair I ran off from just a little over an hour ago, my eyes scanning for Magnus.

Michelle, on the other hand, starts talking to Nathan about the suite upstairs that Magnus had booked.

With my stomach calling my attention on the delicious-looking salmon in front of me, I decide to take heed and eat up.

And the wine matching the food isn't too bad either.

After the plate is picked up and the wine glass is drained, it's dessert time. And yet, there's still no Magnus anywhere. I try to make conversation with Nathan and Michelle, but my mind is too distracted. I know Magnus needs to network, but knowing he's around, but not seeing him is not putting me at ease.

I'm just about to send him a text message, when something tells me to look up. I smile instantly, as soon as I see him sitting at a table closer to the stage, staring back at me with a slight smirk on his face. That's when I see him slipping his hand inside his trousers pocket, the same pocket he shoved my panties in. Then he gives me a smile that would put my panties in a twist.

If I were wearing one, that is.

He's speaking with two people, whose backs are facing me. I'm trying to see who they are, but a large man is now blocking my line of vision.

Annoyed, I look up, only to see that it's Jacob, with his self-assured smile, looking like he was born to wear a tux.

"Well, aren't you a sight for sore eyes," he says, eyes focused solely at me. He exchanges pleasantries with Michelle and Nathan, before coming around the table, standing near an empty seat next to me.

209

"This seat taken?" he asks, which is obviously a jibe since he's already pulling the chair out.

Sighing, I nod towards Magnus's direction. "Oh, you know it is, but he's too busy schmoozing it up over there with those two."

"They are Mr. Harper and Martine," Jacob says dryly.

Stunned, I ask, "She's here? Magnus knows how I feel about Martine, no offense to you since she's your friend and all, but then he invited her here?"

Jacob shrugs, "None taken. And it's not Magnus's fault either. Mr. Harper is a major contributor to the Grant Foundation, so he's a fixture in these events. His wife passed away two years ago, so sometimes, Martine comes along with her father at certain events, as his plus one. And since this is Magnus's event, well …"

Jacob doesn't finish his sentence, and he doesn't have to. Of course, Magnus doesn't have a choice but to play nice with Martine when her father is around.

It doesn't mean though that seeing them together doesn't get me nervous.

The host is back onstage, introducing the entertainment for the night. It's a band that is quite well-known, so I'm looking forward to hearing them play.

They start off with something slow, an original from their last album. It gets the couples dancing on the dance floor, Nathan and Michelle included.

And that's when I realize the truth in what Jacob said, something I knew all along. Martine reaches out for Magnus's arm, as he tries to stand up and excuse himself, like she's asking him for a dance. But what surprises me is that Magnus isn't resisting Martine's groping, nor is he pulling away. He stays in his seat, and he engages her in a conversation instead.

And not once, after that one time, did he look back in my direction.

I swallow hard, trying to push down the hurt I'm feeling at seeing Magnus charming Martine. But what makes it worse is that they look so damn well together.

And why wouldn't they? They were childhood sweethearts and at one point married, for goodness sake!

Anyone with half a brain will notice the chemistry between the two.

So fucking perfect together.

210

My first instinct is to leave. Magnus knows I'm right here, and yet he chooses to stay with *her*.

Well, he can stay with her then.

I'm not running away though.

I'm staying right here, next to this stunning man beside me, and I'm going to shoot daggers at Magnus until he realizes I still exist.

"This song is great," I hear Jacob says casually.

I lightly lay my hand on his arm, instantly feeling the hard muscles underneath.

This is definitely better than shooting daggers at Magnus.

"C'mon then, I love this song too!" I pull myself on my feet, forgetting how much I'll probably regret what I'm about to do in these heels. But as soon as Jacob stands up, I know the extra inches will help.

He offers his arm for me, which I graciously accept, leading me to the dance floor halfway through the song.

If Magnus wants me, he knows where I am.

That is, if he cares enough to look for me.

That man just drives me insane.

And yet, I can't stop loving him so damn much.

I allow myself one final glance before I let myself enjoy another man's company.

I can't deny though that it's kind of surreal not having any feeling of anxiety, as I place an arm over Jacob's shoulder, while holding his hand up with the other. Even Jacob holding me firmly by the small of my back doesn't faze me.

This can't be anything but good, right?

"I like that I don't freak out around you," I say out aloud, but kicking myself at the same time. My lack of filter never fails to dismay.

Luckily, he smiles warmly, his eyes honed in on my face. "I like that I don't freak you out."

"I never picked you for a good dancer though," I continue candidly.

"Uh, thanks? If you'd like to know, I have taken a dance class or two when I was in primary school," Jacob answers matter-of-factly.

"Really?" I reply, pleasantly surprised. "No way! I studied dance too. What type of dance was it?"

"The waltz," he murmurs closer to my ear. "I lasted two classes."

I can't help but giggle at the sight of cute, little five- or six-year-old Jacob waltzing away. "Aww, Jacob, you must be so adorable!" I muse, placing my hand on his arm.

Wow, this arm is all hard muscles ...

But before I can take my hand off, Jacob surprises me by giving me a graceful twirl. Then, he dips me, just as the final notes of the song are playing.

It takes my breath away, how someone so solid can be so graceful at the same time. Jacob smiles his cocky smile at me, and I find myself blushing.

"Jacob," I start shyly, "you can lift me up now."

The band is now playing the introduction of a new song. It's a version of Adele's cover of "Make You Feel My Love."

"Are you sure, Billie? I'm kind of enjoying dipping you like this," he says with a flicker of mischief in his eyes.

"She's sure, Jacob. So if you don't mind, I'd like to take this dance with my girlfriend," Magnus's firm voice surprises both of us, and Jacob stands me up.

Jacob concedes, albeit unsmiling, and backs away, his hand waving me off towards Magnus with grace. "She's all yours, mate."

"I know," Magnus whispers back, but his attention is solely on me. I look away, but I let him bring my arms to wrap around his neck. He then caresses me with his fingertips as they make their way downwards from my arms to my waist, and onto my lower back. He inches even closer, using his hands on my back so our bodies are pressed closer together.

"Look at me, my temptress."

I'm still hurting from the way he ignored me, which was made worse because he ignored me for Martine. But it's Magnus, and he has this power to draw me in—to make me feel like I'm the only person important to him.

Like what he's doing to me right now.

Why does he make me feel so much, all at once, all at the same time?

I tilt my head up, allowing myself to drown in his eyes.

"I finally get to dance with my girl," Magnus says, a small smile on his face.

"We've danced in your club before. Well, I suppose that felt more like foreplay than dancing." I pause, because now, he's smirking at me. "*But*, this is nice. I love this song." I close my eyes and press my cheek close to his shoulder.

"I'm glad you like this song," Magnus whispers against my ear.

"Mmmmm."

"I want you to hear this song, and listen to the words."

So even though I've heard this song numerous times before, I listen to the words intently, with my eyes closed, while Magnus sways me effortlessly around the dance floor.

Wow … is this how he really feels about me?

"You're such an asshole," I blurt out halfway through.

"*I'm* an asshole? I never expected that reaction, to be perfectly honest." Magnus is chuckling softly, lifting my head up by my chin.

"For this … this hyperbole of love you're showing to me, I can't match this. I wouldn't know how to begin," I whisper.

He shakes his head at me. "I'm not asking you to match this, Isabelle. You gave me a second chance. That's all I ever needed."

I stare up at him, and there is no ounce of humor in those eyes of his.

It makes me smile. "Next time, will you please try to keep things simpler?"

"Sure."

"Promise?"

"Sure."

"You won't ever keep it simple, will you?"

"Sure."

I smack him lightly on the chest, making him chuckle, and I chuckle with him.

But my laughter disappears as soon as I notice Martine staring from her seat, her arms folded.

And if looks could kill, those daggers she's shooting at me will most likely give me a slow and painful death.

I meet her stare for a moment longer, not allowing her to affect me. Then I turn back to Magnus. "Why didn't you come to me when you knew I was back? I saw you with Martine and her father."

He sighs deeply. "You've no idea how much I wanted to. But I also want this school to happen. Martine's father is one of the most generous contributors to my foundation, so I have to make sure his support is still intact."

I know Magnus can see the hurt return to my face. "Does that include pimping yourself to Martine?"

He frowns, taken aback. "I *tolerate* Martine. There's a difference," he says, then he pauses, his eyes searching my face. "That's why you danced with Jacob just now? To make me feel jealous?"

"Excuse me?"

"You know what that will do to me. If Jacob wasn't a good, trusted friend of mine, I would've decked him for dancing with you like he did."

"Well, Martine isn't a good friend, so maybe I should deck *her*."

He raises a brow, looking smug. "So, you *are* jealous. Just admit it."

"Eat me," I mumble out.

Magnus raises his brows, eyes darkening. "Gladly," he answers.

Grabbing my hand firmly in his, we weave out of the dance floor, and out of the ballroom.

"Where are you taking me?" I ask, as he leads me down the hallway, and into the ladies room.

He checks to make sure it's empty, and he locks the door. Before I can speak any further, he grabs me by my waist and kisses me, pushing me back against the wall, undulating his hips, so his crotch is rubbing against my thinly clothed one.

With his lips still on mine, his hands find my breasts, and he squeezes them gently, then roughly. I feel my insides coil with excitement, that I find one of my legs rubbing against his side, the hem of my dress sliding up to the top of my thighs. Then one of Magnus's hands finds its way in-between our bodies. He lifts my dress up further, his fingers finding my bare, yet wet apex.

"Oh God," I groan out, as soon as I feel his fingers slide against my slickness.

"Wet already?" he whispers, with a voice thickened with desire.

"I'm always wet for you," I whisper out.

"Mmmm, I'm going to enjoy this, my temptress."

He leaves me confused when he places my foot back down on the floor, stepping back and leaving a distance far enough that it makes me feel vulnerable.

"Magnus ..." I start, standing awkwardly against the cold wall.

"Stand with your legs parted for me."

I stare back at him, curious, but I do as he asks.

"Now, I want you to lift your skirt up to your waist, but slowly ... I want to enjoy seeing every supple inch of your legs."

With my chest heaving, I slowly lift up the hem of my skirt, bunching the delicate material until it reaches just below my belly.

I'm fully exposed down there, right in front of Magnus's stare.

And yet, I feel no embarrassment, not from the way he's looking at me right now with those lust-filled blue eyes.

He steps forward once again, cupping me by the chin and smashing his lips on mine, his tongue pushing its way inside. And just as quickly, he stops the kiss.

Then he bends down, until he's kneeling in-between my legs, his hands holding me securely on my inner thighs.

My breath hitches, and Magnus looks up to me with a smirk that drives me wild, with his forefinger over his lips, alluding me not to make a sound.

I nod slightly, still unsure what to expect but can't wait to find out.

And as soon as his tongue greets my pussy in the most intimate way, I cover my own mouth with my hand, muffling the cry that escapes me.

It's a miracle I'm still standing, much credit to Magnus's hands holding my legs firmly. But it's nearly impossible to stand straight for longer. My belly twitches with every flicker of his tongue against my clit, and my legs begin to quiver unsteadily.

The sight of Magnus, jaw-droppingly handsome and well-groomed to perfection in his custom-made tuxedo, a powerful force in the business world, a generous philanthropist, now kneeling in front of me and using his expert mouth and tongue to pleasure *me* ...

"Oh, my God!" And I fall ... I fall off that edge with such speed that the cries of my climax has become completely voiceless, just air coming out in silent screeches.

"Oh yes … that's it …" Magnus's muffled words of encouragement only adds to my climax, my body jerking as I ride out every single wave.

And as I'm slowly coming down from the high he's brought me, Magnus leaves light kisses on my inner thighs, before producing my panties from the pocket of his trousers.

"I believe I have something of yours?" He waves the tiny piece of material in front of me, and I coyly nod back.

He helps put on my panties, planting a kiss on my now concealed sex, before standing right back up.

I smooth my skirt down, just as he circles an arm around my waist and presses his lips on mine.

It gives me a thrill to taste myself on him.

But I can't let him out of here like this, no matter how much it would satisfy me that other women, particularly a certain ex, will know he's got *me* on him.

Like I've marked him in my own way.

Because he *is* mine, after all.

"I didn't think you'd take what I said so literally," I tell him softly, still on a high from what has transpired barely a minute ago.

"And I told you I'd make it worth your while when I took your panties."

"Oh."

He nods, smirking and answers in a low tone, "Yeah. Oh."

"Well, we better head back to your event. But … not before you clean this up," I use my thumb to wipe off the moisture just under his lower lip, still getting a kick out of knowing it's me who put it there. But he grabs my hand and kisses the same thumb, his mouth lingering on it for a moment.

"I'm only staying on so I can properly show you off to my guests. After that, I'm going to take you upstairs and ravage you all night."

My insides clench at the thought.

Easy, girl. You have all night.

"Then show me off quickly," I answer back.

But then again, I get very impatient.

After a couple of minutes straightening ourselves up so we look presentable, we hear a knock on the door by one of the security staff of the hotel. Magnus unlocks the door of the ladies restroom and speaks with him, apologizing for the inconvenience. Then, hand-in-hand, Magnus and I step out of the ladies room, but not without seeing the aghast expressions of the more conservative patrons of the hotel. A couple of these patrons recognize Magnus, but are too flabbergasted they quickly turn their heads away.

Back in the ballroom, Magnus hooks my hand on the crook of his arm, and with me on his side, he begins to introduce me to his peers.

As his girlfriend.

I just love hearing him say that word alongside my name. And the look of endearment he gives when he does, just makes me feel like I've grown wings.

The general reception to this introduction is mixed, albeit expected. There are a few surprised expressions—some delighted and some awkward—as they scan the room, silently acknowledging, but not addressing the elephant in the room.

Not that I'm referring to Martine as an elephant.

Because she's more like a … cow.

Sorry, cows.

One person who is apparently keen to meet me, however, is Sofia Meier. At first, I am intimidated. She's taller, blonder, and every inch a supermodel. But it's hard not to like her. She has an infectious personality, a straight talker, down to earth, and very, very gay.

Thank goodness for that!

Sofia introduces me to her girlfriend, a complete opposite of her, physically. She's petite, even shorter than I am, but she's just as bubbly as Sofia.

I'm so glad I met her and saw first-hand the dynamics between her and Magnus. They treat each other like brother and sister, and it's so refreshing to see, not to mention a huge relief as well.

We're getting along so famously that they invite Magnus and myself over to their place for dinner. Just then, I spot Michelle waving at me with her purse in hand, so I excuse myself from the gorgeous couple and make my way over to my BFF.

"Babe, I'm so sorry for not staying with you as much as I wanted to," I tell her apologetically, while giving her a hug. "Where's Nathan?"

"Oh, he went to the little boys' room first. But hey, it's alright, girl. It's not like we don't technically live under the same roof, right?" She pauses, before tilting her head, her eyes inquisitive. "Everything's okay now?" she asks.

"I overreacted as usual. I'm still working on my trust issues, I know that. But Magnus and I are—"

"Obviously okay now. Hello, you're oozing happy juice. So are you sure there's nothing troubling you anymore?"

I hate it sometimes that Michelle can read me so well. Maybe I should switch it around.

"How are you and Nathan going?" I ask, noticing from my peripheral vision that Nathan is about to join us.

"I'm so happy, Michelle. It hasn't been easy sometimes. His ex-wife is just an asshole," she exclaims, raising her hands up.

"Amen, girl. Ex-wives suck," I answer, knowing first-hand how she feels.

"What sucks?" Nathan asks as he stands beside Michelle, holding her affectionately close to him.

"Hey … never interrupt a girl-talk, boy!" Michelle juts her hips to him, and all three of us laugh it out.

"Tell you what, I think Michelle and I are overdue for a catch up. Let's do one over dinner. Just us two."

"Well, if you want to do it on Thursday, so I can get out of Keiko's exhibition," Nathan suggests.

"Fine, you can stay home with both kids." Michelle squeezes Nathan's chin playfully, while he just shrugs like it's no big deal. These two will go the distance … I can just feel it.

"It's a date then," I confirm.

"We better get going," Nathan says. Then he adds, "Please thank Magnus for having us. I'd tell him myself, but he looks engrossed in a serious conversation over there."

Nathan discreetly points over to where Magnus is standing, arms crossed, brows bunched with his serious face on, now talking with two older gentlemen.

"I will. And I'll pay you back tomorrow for the babysitter."

Nathan shakes his head, "Nah. Don't worry about it, Billie. We'll see you tomorrow."

I give both of them a kiss on the cheek, before whispering to Michelle, "Please give my boy a tight hug and a kiss for me?"

"For sure, babe. G'night. Love you."

"Love you too."

And with a wave, they make their way out of the ballroom.

With my friends now gone, I can't help but feel a little out of place, as I'm looking around me, standing next to my table. I just don't feel like interrupting Magnus when he's talking business. But other than Magnus and Jacob, I know no one in this party.

Thankfully, I find Jacob standing by one of the doors, having a conversation with one of his security staff.

With Magnus still preoccupied, I figure this might be a good opportunity to speak to Jacob about the phone calls.

I make my way over to him.

"There you are." I place my hand on his shoulder, giving it a squeeze to get his attention.

Okay, those are most definitely traps, bulging on those broad shoulders of his.

I resist the temptation to squeeze his shoulder again to confirm my suspicion. Jacob turns and gives me a warm smile as soon as he sees it's me. He nods at the guy he's talking to, a signal of the end of their conversation, before facing me once again.

"I hope I didn't disturb you, but I was hoping we could talk?"

"About?"

"You remember how you told me to speak to you if I get any weird phone calls again? I just had a really, really weird one tonight."

His expression turns serious. He looks around, before taking my elbow and guiding me to somewhere quieter and less crowded.

"Right. Talk to me," he asks in a low tone.

"I was just wondering, are you able to trace unknown callers?"

He nods, "I can, but why do you need to?"

I hesitate for a second, before continuing, "I need to know if what I'm getting are prank calls or not. And whatever the outcome is, I need to find out the identity of the caller."

"Have you spoken to Magnus yet about this?"

"No. Not yet. I need to confirm this first. He has too much on his plate, and I don't want him worrying if it's just an idiotic prank. Please … I just need your help. I'll pay extra if I have to." I hold my palms together, pleading for his help.

He reaches for my clenched hands and covers them with his own, making them disappear underneath the size of his hands.

"You don't have to pay me, Billie. I *will* help you. But I'll need your phone. I have the equipment at my office and my place."

"Well, maybe I can come over after work tomorrow? Which one's closer from the store?"

He eyes me curiously. "My home. Are you sure though? I don't think Magnus will be pleased. Regardless of our friendship, he still doesn't trust me around you."

I study him closely. "I don't understand that whole trust issue. He obviously trusts you enough to keep me safe, but he doesn't trust you as my friend?"

"Because he has good reason not to trust me," Jacob pauses and lets out a deep sigh. "He's going to kill me for telling you this, but fuck it. After he got divorced, I took him out so we could make up for lost time. We weren't looking for anything serious, we were just two lads having a good time. And sometimes, that involved wagering on who would end up sleeping with the hottest woman in, let's say a club, or sometimes, with how many women," he pauses and shakes his head in shame. "It wasn't our proudest moment."

"*I* don't even know what to say to that. I'm speechless," I blurt out, shocked and hurt by this revelation.

Wait, does that make me …

"Okay, I can see the cogs in your brain, turning. Before you jump into conclusions, you need to realize that he's changed when he met you. And if I may be perfectly honest," he regards me sheepishly, "I can't blame him. You're just different from any woman I've met. And believe me, it would have been game over for me too, if I met you first."

Oh.

Uh-oh.

"Jacob, I'm really flattered by what you just said, truly I am. But you also need to know that all I can offer you is friendship. You're a great guy, but Magnus is just … well … there really is no one I want but him. If it's any consolation, you and Nathan are probably the only guy friends I have. Magnus isn't the only one with trust issues."

"I know. Understood," he says, shrugging and placing his hands inside the pockets of his trousers.

I reach for his forearm. "I really want us to be good friends, but this means no more innuendos, or double entendres. You have to tell me right now if my friendship isn't enough. I sure hope it is because I'd be sad to lose you as a friend." I let my hand slide off his arm, suddenly feeling sad at the thought of losing him.

Call me selfish, but there's something about Jacob that makes me want to have him around, and I don't want to lose that.

He stares back at me for a long moment, before offering me his hand.

"What's this for?" I ask, as I hesitantly accept, watching in awe as my hand virtually disappears out of sight.

"Friends." Jacob motions to shake our hands, and I can't help but smile.

"Good friends?" I add, hopefully.

"Me, in a platonic relationship with a beautiful, remarkable woman? There's a first time for everything, I guess," he gives me a crooked smile, squeezing my hand slightly.

"Jacob …" I remind him gently.

"Good friends," Jacob finally concedes.

"I've been looking everywhere for you, gorgeous." A familiar hand slides over my belly in a possessive way, that familiar pull leaving me with no choice but to break my handshake with Jacob.

Magnus's lips find that spot on my neck that makes my body tingle, and he lingers there. I sneak a glance at Jacob, who understandably looks on awkwardly.

It doesn't take a genius to realize that this is Magnus's display of proprietorship, more so than a show of candid affection.

It irritates me, and it turns me on at the same time.

Like I want to slap him and climb him like a tree, all at the same time.

Magnus finally lets go and gives a still uncomfortable Jacob, a friendly smack on the shoulder. "Great job once again with the security, J. And thank you for keeping my woman company."

Woman? Is he serious? I turn my head towards Magnus, whose friendly banter hides the tension on his jaw.

"Well, you hired the best. And it's easy to keep her company because we're buddies. Right, bud?" Jacob puts his arm on my shoulder and gives me a playful squeeze, earning him a bemused stare from Magnus.

"Well, your *buddy* and I are about to leave," Magnus says, before tangling our fingers together. I know he's doing it again for Jacob's sake, but it doesn't mean I don't feel the flutters.

He continues, "We're staying here tonight, so tomorrow, I'll take her to work. If you can make sure Ethan and Tasha are safely brought to school tomorrow morning, that would be appreciated, man."

"It's definitely not a problem," Jacob answers, with a resigned smile, before turning to me, "I'll see you tomorrow at your work, yeah?"

"Tomorrow, then. Good night." Without thinking, I lean forward to lightly kiss Jacob on the cheek, whispering, "Thank you," before pulling away.

Jacob answers with a single, slow nod, then he gives me a warm smile, the kind that's warm enough that it makes me happy on the inside.

"Let's go," Magnus whispers as he tugs at my hand so we can leave. Then he picks up my clutch and wrap, before we make our leave.

"Congratulations on a job well done, Magnus," I tell Magnus, as we're walking towards the elevators.

"That's partly because of you, babe." Magnus leans forward and kisses my temple affectionately.

We step inside the elevator, with another older couple stepping in with us.

Magnus and I are standing behind them, and we can see their hands intertwined, much like ours, with the lady's head pressed against her partner's arm.

And even with the emotional roller coaster that comes with my relationship with Magnus, all I can wish for is for us to be like them when we're their age.

I look up at Magnus and catch him looking at the couple as well, a pensive look on his face. Then he meets my gaze and smiles at me affectionately. He bends his head closer to my ear.

"Me too," he says, before straightening up, still with that sweet smile on his beautiful face.

And I can't help but smile back at him.

My beautiful man.

Yes, he's possessive and frustrating as hell sometimes. But I wasn't lying when I told Jacob that Magnus is different from other men.

He loves me, even at my damaged best. He understands me and my unspoken words. And now, it seems that he wishes for the same future that I want.

Growing old together.

Or am I just overthinking again?

The couple reach their floor, and they warmly greet us 'Good night' to which we reciprocate in kind.

As soon as the doors close, Magnus pulls me closer to him, his arm around me, and both of my arms around his waist. He leaves a lingering kiss on my temple, only easing off when the elevator stops on our floor.

Inside our suite, with our hands linked, and words no longer needed, we make our way upstairs, straight into our bedroom. As soon as we're inside, he turns me to face him, his hand cupping my face, our eyes locking, and our lips inching closer.

As soon as our lips meet, I melt like snow on a sunny day. His scent, his eyes, his warm breath against my skin, and his taste make all of my senses hyperaware.

He's addictive, and I can't get enough.

Still, with no urge to exchange any words, we start taking each other's clothes off, and every article of clothing I remove from his body, building up the excitement. He turns me around and unzips my dress, slowly and deliberately. It's torturous because I want his naked body against mine, and yet he makes the wait so desirable, leaving the skin of my whole body prickling with impatient anticipation.

Now naked in front of each other, he leans down to kiss me, leading me towards the bed, and only pulling away to catch our breaths.

And inside the room bathed only in moonlight, Magnus makes love to me. And the only sounds uttered are of pleasure … only broken once in a while by a single word he whispers over and over again.

"Mine."

CHAPTER 21

Ugh.

I hate waking up in the middle of the night, especially while I'm comfortably ensconced in Magnus's arms.

I pry his arm off my body, trying to get off the bed as carefully as possible to avoid waking him.

After emptying my bladder and washing up, I crawl back on my side of the bed, with my space next to Magnus, still waiting for me to assume my position.

But I get distracted at the sight of him lying naked, with only the lower half of his body covered by the sheets, the moonlight illuminating his every feature, his every muscle. My eyes linger momentarily on his face, so peaceful in sleep, the dark lashes of his closed lids sweeping his cheeks, and his full mouth slightly open and oh so inviting. I resist the temptation to suck his lower lip, still enjoying this opportunity to study him further. My eyes travel down his neck, then down his chest, and the way it moves up and down in steady motion from his steady breathing. I start chewing on my bottom lip as my eyes count each square-shaped muscle on his abdominals.

Yes, there are definitely six highly-defined muscles on these sexy abs of his.

And his abs are only highlighted by the V-cut that seems to point towards one of my favorite parts of his body.

I know I shouldn't do it, but when it comes to Magnus, my self-control is close to nonexistent.

I have to taste him.

With the tip of my tongue, I proceed to trace the muscled line on his hip.

Oh my God. I can't believe I'm actually doing this!

This is not like me, taking advantage of Magnus in his sleep. But goodness, I'm only human.

I'll stop if he wants me to.

Magnus stirs, and I lift my head up slightly. He shifts positions, his back now flat on the bed, exposing more of him to me, and making me hungry for more.

Like I said, I'm only human.

I lower my head, leaving the lightest of kisses over his chest, using my tongue to trace the groove in-between his pectorals. My heart beats faster, knowing this is taboo, taking advantage of someone in his sleep. Yet, I'm unable to stop myself. He stirs again, this time his legs seem to kick the sheets down, exposing all of him to me.

And I mean, all … of … him.

Magnus may be sleeping, but his body is responding to me.

With renewed confidence, I move further down, my heart thumping harder, my body humming with nervous energy at what I'm about to do next.

I've been fantasizing about this, and now, there's no turning back.

Do it.

My hand reaches for Magnus's cock, my fingers carefully enclosing over his length, thrill building inside of me as he hardens further with my touch.

I lick my lips, biting my inner cheek to gain some form of control. But it's pointless. My hunger to taste him again overwhelms every single cell on my body.

I'm giving in. My desire for more of him is overruling the last remnants of my hesitation.

Keeping my eyes locked on his face, I lower myself and close my mouth over his thickened head. I pause to check him again, before sliding his hard length inside my mouth. I lick its tip, making my movements downward and back up again. I repeat my movements, slowly, carefully, with each stroke of my mouth and my hand making me braver and hungrier at the same time.

My eyes close as I get into the moment, my strokes gaining momentum. But then he moves his leg, and I pause, releasing him in panic. That's when I feel his fingers brush my cheek, making me gasp, and forcing me to turn to him with widened eyes and a ready apology.

But there he is, eyes still half-open, with the beginnings of a smirk on his face.

"Come here, baby," he whispers, his hand reaching for me.

My cheeks redden, embarrassed at being caught. I cautiously crawl back to him, leaving a sidelong glance down at my unfinished business. But when I look back up to him, even through the cloudiness of sleep, I can already see desire in his eyes.

225

Without a word, he turns me around as I lie down, with my back pressing against him, my breath caught in my throat.

Maybe he wants me to stop. Maybe he doesn't like it. Maybe it's not desire I saw, but displeasure. Maybe ...

Oh. Oh, holy shit.

So preoccupied was I with the maybe's that I failed to realize that Magnus has shifted himself behind me, and now his cock, my unfinished business ...

Oh ... he feels so good inside.

"I need to come inside you, baby. But you need to come on my cock first," these are the last words he mutters, before he starts thrusting from behind me, his mouth leisurely nibbling that sensitive part of my neck. His fingers tweak my nipples, before making their way down, finding my clit, and rubbing it in a way that makes my whole body feel like tiny fireworks are shooting out of my pores.

This position hits me in a different spot inside, and the friction is amazing. But it's the intimacy in this position, and the security he's giving me when he's holding me like this that hit me straight to my heart. My whole body tenses, and I let out a breathy groan, as the tiny fireworks form into one colossal explosion.

But there's no time to settle down from the high. The hand that was just on my clit is now clutching me by the waist, holding me so I am pressed deeper against him. His rocking becomes more feverish, his breathing now in short spurts. Then he just stops moving altogether, and finally, with a deep groan, he climaxes, and the only movement I can feel is his chest breathing as heavily as mine, and his cock twitching inside of me.

Wow. That just happened.

After a few seconds of stillness, he gently pulls out, and once again, he holds me securely against him, kissing me affectionately on the lips.

"Baby ... you should do that more often," he murmurs, his eyes closed, a satisfied smile on his lips.

"Hmmm, okay," I purr back, my eyes doing the same.

Magnus quiets down, and as his breathing grows steadier, I soon realize that he's gone back to sleep ... with me heading the same route soon after.

My eyes flicker lazily, squinting, as they adjust to the blinding brightness of the morning sun. Magnus is already up and out of the bed, and he's standing by the window wearing nothing but his boxer briefs. He's holding a cup of coffee while looking out towards Central Park, his expression thoughtful.

My mouth salivates at the sight of his silhouette, and I take a moment to drink him in before he figures out that I'm awake.

Just as I sit up, he turns towards me, and I react by pulling the blanket up to my chest, earning me an amused gleam in his eyes.

"Good morning, beautiful," he says, a smirk forming on those sexy lips of his.

"You're on the wrong side of the bed," I answer back, my brow rising up.

"But I'm not in bed."

"Exactly. Wrong. Side."

Magnus bites his lower lip, trying to curb the sly smile on his face. He sits on the bed, placing his cup on the nightstand next to me.

"So, that thing you did last night …" Magnus trails off, as he tries to tug my blanket down, his smile turning to mischief.

But I clutch on the blanket, now feeling embarrassed, my cheeks hot. "I know! I can't believe I did that. I'm so sorry. I know it's wrong. You're asleep, and—"

I don't get a chance to explain, as Magnus's lips are on mine, and he's kissing me in a way that makes me forget about the blanket I'm clutching, and now it's pooling around my waist.

"I want more of *that*. Feel free to do more of *that* to me," he murmurs against my lips, the tip of his nose brushing lightly against my own in an intimate way.

"Ah … oh, so you're not angry?" I whisper.

"No, I'm not. And as you may have ascertained before we both fell asleep, I enjoyed what you did immensely."

"Oh," I breathe out.

Magnus still has a smirk on his face, while his eyes travel down to my neck.

"I love that you never take your necklace off." Magnus brushes his fingertips over the chain, lifting the pendant before planting a tender kiss on my lips.

"And risk people not knowing that I'm taken? This stays on, buddy," I tease, smiling coquettishly. "I'm never taking this off."

A satisfied grin brightens up his face, making me smile with him.

He leans closer. "I ... fucking ... love ... you ... Isabelle ... Morrison ..." he murmurs as he plants a kiss with every word.

Still giddy from his kisses, I hold on to his face, looking him straight in those blue eyes of his, so he knows I mean every word.

"With all my heart, I love you too, Magnus Grant," I affirm softly, saying each word clearly.

He reciprocates by locking his lips with mine, and leaning his body forward so that I'm lying on the bed again, with our bare chests pressed against each other.

The phone rings, and he growls in frustration. It stops, but just as we're about to resume what we were doing, his phone rings again.

"Fuck," he exclaims.

"Maybe later?" I say, half-jokingly, but fully frustrated on the inside.

"*Definitely* sooner," he raises a brow at me, his expression showing me that he means business.

With a resigned sigh, he stands back up and reaches the desk in a few short strides. Without him, I suddenly feel cold, so I pull the blanket back up, reaching for my phone so I can call Ethan.

I've been feeling guilty lately for not always being there for Ethan, now that Magnus is back in my life. But he's been very understanding, and having Michelle, Nathan, and Tasha helps.

But it doesn't erase the fact that my son should be the priority.

All I need is to find a happy balance.

Michelle answers the phone, "Hey, Billie."

"Hey, back! Is Ethan there? I'd love to speak to him before he leaves for school. Hope he was okay last night?"

"You know Ethan loves sleepovers. We're about to go actually. Your stud of a bodyguard is taking the kiddos to school, and he's waiting outside for us right now. Let me get Ethan for a sec. Just hold on."

While waiting, I tuck my phone between my head and my shoulder. I get out of bed, and head to the bathroom to retrieve the hotel's robe. I hear Michelle tell Ethan that I'm on the other line, and after a couple of seconds of silence, I finally hear my special guy's voice once again.

"Mom? Hi, Mom!" Ethan answers excitedly.

"Hey, buddy! Are you ready to go to school now?"

"Yeah. Jacob's outside waiting for us. Mom, are you coming home tonight?" Ethan asks in a voice that makes my heart dip.

"Of course, and I'll try to be early, okay. I missed you last night, honey."

"I missed you too, Mom. See you. Love you!" he distractedly tells me, and before I can answer back, I hear Nathan's voice call out to the kids, followed by some shuffling noises.

"Sorry, hun. Nathan just called the kids. He didn't know you were talking to Ethan on the phone."

"It's alright. Please just tell him I love him very much and that I'll see him for dinner tonight."

"Sure thing. Oh, and *dish* … tonight!"

"Fine, will do. Thanks again, Michelle."

"For what? You know I love Ethan like my own."

"That's why I love you, babe. See you later."

"You're cooking tonight."

"Or buying. I'm buying dinner."

Michelle laughs, before I hear silence.

When I end the call, I notice that I have a text message sent from last night.

Shrugging, I press on the Message tab, finding the one unread message.

From Unknown.

With one deep breath, I press open the message: *"This is not a joke, or a prank. My name is Grace Peterson. I know I'm taking a huge risk here, but I have a feeling you can help me with Cooper Thornton. He needs to pay for what he did. Please, please call me. My number is -----."*

A painful gasp escapes me, and I cover my mouth to muffle the sound. Magnus doesn't notice since he's still on the phone and about to leave the bedroom.

Looking back at the screen, I read the message again.

It's from a Grace.

My *Unknown* now has a name, and it's Grace … Grace Peterson.

It's a good thing Magnus has just left the room because I don't think I can tell him about this yet.

I know he said he didn't care about the bad press this could give him and his company, that he wanted to help me, no matter what.

229

But I care.

And I know the Thorntons well enough to recognize what they're capable of doing, just to get what they want. If this Grace person's accusation is fictitious and it becomes public, the Thorntons will make sure this will blow up in our faces.

So I need to be sure. And when I am definite, then I can go to Magnus.

Jacob can help me. This is his forte. He'll be discreet ... and thorough.

I search for Jacob's number on my phone, and I send him a text message that I need his help, and soon. I don't think this can wait. If Grace is truly one of Cooper's victims, then she will need all the help that she can get, and fast.

Question is if she is, will I be ready to help her take Cooper down?

After eight years of hiding, am I ready to finally come out and risk everything so Cooper can finally get the justice he deserves?

And what about Ethan? What happens if he finds out?

One thing at a time, Billie ... one thing at a time.

My phone vibrates, with Jacob confirming that he'll be picking me up by lunchtime. I just need to convince Helen to give me the rest of today off. She's going to be in the whole day, so hopefully it won't be a problem.

After brushing my teeth and washing my face, I decide to venture out of the bedroom, making my way down to the main floor. Magnus is still on the phone, but he gives me a sheepish smile before signaling me towards the dining table where a breakfast of cereal, French pastries, and sliced fresh fruits are waiting to be eaten, alongside a pot of freshly brewed coffee.

But instead of listening to my already grumbling stomach, I walk over to Magnus, leading him to seat on one of the chairs. When he does, I make myself comfortable on his lap, straddling him so he can't get away. He raises a brow, as he listens on to whoever is on the other line, while holding me securely on the waist.

I reach for a croissant and rip off a crusty piece, holding a piece in front of him. He gives me a smirk as he accepts my offering, and he chews. But a crumb is left on the corner of his mouth, so I pick it up with my tongue, nibbling on that corner a little longer than

I should. When it's his turn to speak, I rip off another piece from the croissant and prop it in-between my teeth, inching closer to him. He stops mid-sentence and takes the piece off my mouth, licking my lips before pulling away and chewing, his eyes not leaving my lips.

"Listen, Charles, do you mind if we continue this discussion when I get to the office?" Magnus tells the guy on the other line, his eyes still focused on my lips, which I deliberately lick for his benefit. Then he continues, "Yes. Well, my sexy girlfriend is feeding me breakfast, and right now, what you're saying sounds like white noise." And then he hangs up, leaving me wide-eyed and blushing.

"You did *not* just say that! Was that my former boss?" I exclaim, giggling.

"Yes. You're right here on my lap when I said it. Now where were we?"

Smiling, I offer him another piece of croissant.

"From your mouth, Isabelle," he whispers huskily.

Excitement building, I place the piece on my mouth and inch closer. He accepts my offering and shows me the same courtesy.

It doesn't take long before I feel him hardening underneath me, and he starts nuzzling on my neck. I adjust the way I'm sitting, now straddling him so we're face- to-face. With the croissant eaten, I take his face with my hands and begin kissing him, grinding myself against him, both of us moaning softly against each other's mouth.

I don't know how this man can turn me into a horny nympho so quickly, but he just makes it so damn easy.

"Baby, you feel so good," he murmurs against my mouth, "but if I don't stop this right now, I won't be able to get to work at a respectable time, and you won't be able to fucking walk."

"I'm sorry, but was that supposed to be a threat?" I ask, before grazing my teeth over his stubbled jaw. Then I wrap my arms around his shoulders, my head on the nook between his neck and shoulder.

"I wish we could just stay here and forget everything that exists beyond these walls. We could forget about our pasts for one day, maybe talk about our future together, but most of all, just *live* in the present … together. At least for one day, I want it to be just you and me … just us," I sigh out, my eyes closed, and my mind drifting off to that make-believe place, the type of place I read about in books.

His arms hold me tighter across my back, exhaling deeply. He remains quiet and continues to hold me close, not letting me go.

I'm the first to untangle my arms, knowing reality is kicking in, and we can't stay like this for the rest of the day, blissful as it may sound.

"We better start getting ready, huh?" I say as I straighten up.

Magnus just nods, untangling his arms off me so I can stand up. But his expression is unreadable.

Did I say something wrong?

"Is everything okay, Magnus?" I ask, unsure of what I did or say, or if I'm just being paranoid.

"Yes, of course. Your bag is in the closet upstairs." Magnus seems distracted, preoccupied somewhat.

I hesitate for a second, tempted to ask why his mood changed. But as soon as he grabs his phone and turns away, I sense it's a signal for me to leave.

As I'm climbing up the stairs, that's when I realize that, of course, it *was* what I said that made him react that way. I slap myself on the head for the colossal fuck up.

"Talk about our future together, Billie? Are you insane? You freaked him out!" I whisper to myself with gritted teeth as I enter the bedroom.

Shaking my head at my tragically nonexistent filter, I head straight to the closet to grab the clothes I packed in my overnight bag—my favorite skinny jeans, a light pink button-down shirt, and a navy blazer which I hastily toss on the bed. I take out my dark brown, high leather boots and a pair of socks as well. Looking around, I realize that my gown and Magnus's tuxedo suit are nowhere to be seen. I make a mental note to ask him later, when his mood is better. Then I quickly toss clean underwear on the bed and head for the shower.

After mixing in the temperature of the water, I step inside, closing my eyes, and planting my hands on the wall. I let the warm flow of the water envelop me, the steam opening my pores and coaxing the negativity to pour out of my body.

So focused am I at engulfing my senses, hoping to forget what just happened, that I don't hear him coming in the bathroom, nor do I feel his presence when he steps inside the oversized shower.

So as soon as I feel his warm lips on my shoulder, I gasp, jumping out of my skin. But his arms circle around my waist, holding me firmly, until the beating of my heart slows back down, and I feel calmer again.

Well, as calm as any woman who embarrasses herself can be, anyway.

"Magnus ..." I whisper, as my arms move up behind me, holding him by the nape of his neck as his lips rest on my shoulder. "I'm ... I'm sorry for freaking you out, talking about the future like I did. I hope we can just pretend that I didn't say those things."

Magnus turns me around, brows furrowing. "I wasn't upset because you wanted to talk about our future."

"But your mood changed, so it was clearly because of what I said. I was thinking too far ahead."

Magnus cups my face, forcing me to look up at him.

"Stop it. Stop thinking the worst, Isabelle. Can't you see that I want what you want, or have I not made myself clear?"

Still cupping my face, Magnus inches closer, our bodies touching.

"If you thought my mood changed, it wasn't because I didn't see my future with you. I was just in shock because you finally said it. Baby, I will spend the rest of my life, making sure that you're loved. I've envisioned our future with that in mind from that time I met you."

My chest tightens, and I'm finding it hard to swallow. He just told me that he saw our future together from the first time we met, when I thought no one in their right mind would ever love damaged goods.

"How you stayed single this long after Martine, really blows me away, especially since you keep showing me what you're capable of. No wonder Martine wants you back," I reply with a shaky voice, staring at his chest, unable to look him in the eye for fear that I might break down.

"I stayed single by choice. *You* made me change my mind. And I don't care what Martine wants because she will *never* have me back." Magnus gets the small bottle of shampoo and squeezes a dollop on his palm. "Come on, my stubborn temptress, let's get you nice and clean."

"Not when you're around, I won't be," I mumble as he turns me around.

233

Without any warning, I feel a sharp slap on one of my ass cheeks.

"Ouch, what the f—?" I cry out in shock.

"That's for implying that I get you dirty," he says before laying another sharp one on the other cheek, "and *that's* me, showing you that you're right."

Oh, God. I know I'm not supposed to like getting my ass slapped, so why did that make my naughty bits tingle with pleasure?

Magnus thankfully doesn't do it again. Otherwise, I have a feeling we won't be able to leave this shower, or this bedroom for the rest of the day.

We dress up in relative silence, giving each other sidelong glances, smiling when we catch each other's eyes.

Did I mention how much I love his smile?

"By the way, I'm just curious, where are our clothes from last night?" I ask Magnus while brushing my hair into submission.

"I had the staff pick it up for dry cleaning this morning. The hotel will deliver the clothes to my place." Magnus is watching me while I fix my hair. He's sitting on the foot of the bed, already dressed in a perfectly fitted charcoal suit, a matching crisp white shirt, and a dark tie. His hair is well-groomed, but he didn't shave, making him look distinguished and roguish at the same time.

I like it. No, scrap that. I love it. Shaven or not, he sure knows how to turn up the heat. I'm sure that if my eyeballs can only talk, they'll thank me every single day.

"You're staring," he says, his arms are crossed, legs stretched out in front of him, and he's trying in vain to hide his amusement.

"You like it when I stare," I remark playfully at him through the reflection of the mirror, "and trust me, I'm not the only one who does, and I think you're fully aware of that."

He stands up and walks towards me, pulling off the hair tie I just secured on my hair, watching as the strands fall on my back.

"I don't care about the others. Do you?" he asks my reflection.

So he does know, but he doesn't care. Maybe I shouldn't either.

"At least I get to touch the merchandise," I answer back with a grin.

He laughs out aloud, "You get to do more than touch the merchandise, baby."

I'm still beaming when I happen to check out our reflections, and I must admit, we do look good together, no matter what other people might think. But my reflection isn't the real me. Changing my hair color might be trivial to some people, but to me, it's like I stripped away the last reminder of who I was. It was a necessary evil to keep me and my son under the radar. But with Magnus with me, and now, Jacob helping to keep us safe, maybe I don't have to hide anymore.

It's time to get the old me back.

The store is already open by the time Magnus drops me off. I hate not seeing him, even if it's just for one day. But he's going to convince my father again to sell his business to Grant Corp. I just hope my father will do the right thing.

Chris doesn't have the keys, so Helen must have come in earlier because there's still half an hour to spare before our actual opening time.

"Helen?" I call out as soon as I close the door, locking it for now. Feeling the warmth of the heater, I take my coat off on the way to the back office.

I find her sitting in front of the computer, checking out inventory. She looks up as soon as she sees me, smiling excitedly.

"What time did you come in?" I ask, as I hang my coat on one of the hooks at the door.

"Early, because I'm too excited. I have to tell you some wonderful news. And trust me, this is good news, okay, though it may sound bad at first, but you'll know what I mean as soon as I tell you. But gosh—"

"Helen … Helen, just tell me already!" I'm laughing softly when I put my hands up to stop her from tattling on. But my laughter is a fake. Instead of the excitement, I'm actually feeling nervous, my gut instinct telling me that this might be an opposite of the good news.

"Okay, I know that I've told you a million times, that I will only ever sell this store if I'm on my deathbed."

"Yes, but you're not sick. You're the healthiest, liveliest, seventy-six year old woman I know."

"Don't forget the sexiest too," she says, winking at me.

"That, too, of course. So what's the big news? Wait, you're checking our inventory levels. Are you ... selling the store?"

She divulges, "I didn't have any intentions to sell. So when this man, who sounded like he's from the south, calls my house last night, telling me that their company is interested in buying my store, I told him I wasn't interested. I'm not even sure if he's serious. You see these scam artists on television, and I thought he was one of them. Plus, I'm an elderly woman, so he probably thought I was easy pickings—"

"Helen ..." I raise my palms up, exasperated that she's just not getting straight to the point. I check on my watch as well, making sure we still have enough time before we open the store.

She has obviously picked up on my worry underneath the smile that I'm trying to keep on.

"Sorry, you know how words just seem to spill out of me. Anyway, he said that their company is interested in purchasing this store because they want books from independent authors to be marketed to the mainstream, but the business model I have is exactly what they're after. What they're proposing to me is that they want to start a chain of stores that would be similar to my store now, you know, with the café and a more reader-friendly atmosphere. Imagine, a chain of The Written Word stores all over the US?"

She clutches her chest in a melodramatic fashion, her excitement is apparent. "Oh my God, I almost fell off my chair with what he told me!"

"I would too. That's a great news, Helen!" I cry out happily, my worry turning into excitement for my book-loving boss.

Sure, this means I can't buy her store, and that makes me sad. But it just means it's not the right time for me yet.

"But I'm not an idiot, Billie. Once they send me their proposal, I'm going to get my lawyers to look into it with a fine-tooth comb. I haven't given them an answer yet. But if I'm happy with their proposal and everything is up to scratch, then I will definitely sell."

"I just can't believe it. This will help out a lot of indie authors, getting their books out to a bigger audience. I hope they won't change the integrity of your store."

"Oh, I'll make sure of that, don't you worry."

Just then, we hear the bell chimes, signaling someone coming inside the store. I take a quick peek, and Chris waves to me on her way to us.

"Is that Chris? Don't tell her yet, okay? Let's keep this between us for now until everything's set in stone," Helen tells me with a cautious tone.

I only manage to nod back and pretend to check the mail, just as Chris enters the back office.

"Good morning, girls!" Chris greets us, beaming.

"You're way too cheerful for a weekday, child," Helen comments while giving Chris an amused stare.

"It's hump day, and I got some last night."

"Ah," I wiggle my forefinger at her, grinning. "I see what you just did there."

"Yup! You're not the only one who hooked up with a hot man." Chris gives us a coy wink before leaving the room to go to her side of the store.

"I tell you, that woman's sex life will get her in trouble one of these days," Helen clucks as she shakes her head with dismay.

"Oh, she's a grown woman. I'm sure she's had her share of lessons learned."

Helen only snorts, making me chuckle at her response.

"So, who's the buyer, Helen? You said they weren't local?"

"No, and that's what I initially thought as shady. But then the man I was speaking to, I think his name is Harrison or something or the other, told me their company has varied business interests all over the states. You may have heard of them since your *hot man,* as Chris would put it, owns Grant Corp. This company's called RCT Group. Have you heard of them at all? Apparently, their head office is based in Texas. The former owner of the company is this oil magnate. He's a senator now, so his son has taken the reigns. Young blood with new ideas, I suppose ..."

RCT Group.

Oh my God.

No.

I can still hear Helen talking on the background, but my brain seems to stop functioning after hearing the company's name. All of a sudden, I'm feeling light-headed, with my legs buckling underneath me.

"Oh, dear me!" I hear Helen cry out for Chris as I try to correct myself but failing in my attempt and collapsing on the floor.

"Billie! Oh, shit!" I hear Chris's panicked voice, as soon as she sees me.

"I'm ... I'm okay," I croak out, as I correct myself with her help.

"Chris, why don't you get Billie a glass of water?" Helen's firm, yet calm voice helps relax my shattered nerves. "And you, I won't allow you to work in this state. This could be low sugar, or goodness knows if that man of yours kept you up all night, but you're best to just rest this one out."

I pause, considering what Helen is offering me. I know I can't stay here and work right now, especially after this bombshell has just been dropped in front of me.

Chris comes back with a glass of water, and she hangs around until Helen instructs her to mind the store. I take a long sip of water, and it helps me clear my head and think things a little more clearly.

Cooper Thornton Jr. has taken over his father's company, and it's no coincidence that out of the blue, RCT Group offers Helen this amazing opportunity.

This is fucked up ... *he* is fucked up in so many levels. He knows I'm here, but he can't get to me, so he's trying other means. I don't know what he's planning, but I'm not going to sit down and just wait for his next move.

I have to make my own move now.

Slowly but steadily, I stand up, politely refusing Helen's help. I grab my purse, taking my phone out.

"I should give you some privacy," Helen says as she starts walking out but not before I gently hold on to her by the arm.

"Helen, please promise me that you won't consider the proposal. I'll speak with Magnus. I'm sure he can offer the same if not more than what RC ... what RCT Group is offering."

She stares back at me looking confused. "I don't understand. Do you know something I don't about that company? You do, don't you?"

"I need to check my facts, but please trust me, and put this thing on ice for now?" I try to plead with her, and I hope that she takes heed.

"Well, it's not like I'm desperate for the money … okay, I will. Now I want you to go home and rest. Can somebody else take you home?" She covers my hand with her dainty one.

I nod back, "I'll get someone to take me home. Thank you."

With a kind smile, she walks out of the office.

I unlock my phone and press the Contacts list. I know exactly who to call.

"Hello, Billie?" The distinct accent confirms I've called the right person.

"Where are you?" I ask, not bothering with pleasantries.

"I'm a block away. Miss me already?" he answers, mirth lacing his voice. "Sorry, I know you said—"

"You told me before, that you have the equipment to trace people and their real identities, addresses, that sort of thing, right?"

"Yes, at my place and the office. Why? Is this about the phone calls?"

"Yes, but there's more. Your place is closer, right?"

"Yes."

"Can you pick me up at the store? I'll wait for you."

"Come out now. I'm already here."

CHAPTER 22

"Thank you for doing this for me, Jacob," I tell him, as we walk towards the direction of his home.

"Don't thank me yet. I don't even know what the rush is about. Does Magnus know you're going home with me?"

Even in my panicked state, Jacob manages to make me blush.

"I thought you were going to stop with the innuendos?"

"C'mon, I'm just trying to make you smile." He bows down to face me, making me aware of our height difference. But he's grinning, and surprisingly, I do the same, lifting some of the burden off my shoulders.

"Ah, much better. So seriously, why did you go to me and not to Magnus?"

"Because I don't want him to worry over something that I'm hoping would be nothing. Plus you are more qualified to help. But can we talk about it when we get to your place? I have things I need to tell you, and I really don't want other people overhearing me." I look around, trying to see if anyone's following.

I thought I was close to getting rid of my paranoia, and then this happens.

"We're almost here," Jacob says, after a few blocks of walking.

We turn to a street lined with beautiful brownstones, and unlike Nathan's, these particular ones are larger, very well-maintained, and obviously expensive.

Jacob opens the front gate of his place, letting me in first.

"Wow, so which floor is yours?" I ask as I look up the three-storey building, following him up the stairs and stopping in front of the black front door.

"The whole house is mine," he says nonchalantly, as he presses a few keys on a panel similar to Magnus's.

He chuckles at my gape-mouthed expression, and steps aside to let me in first. "What? The security business is quite lucrative. Money and power makes you a target, and my company has benefited from it."

"I must say though," I utter as I let my eyes wander around, "that your place is very impressive."

"Thank you," he says with a reluctant smile on his face. "So do you want a tour of the house, or do you want to get straight onto it?"

"As much as I'd love to check out all of these, I really need for you to help me trace this girl responsible for all the calls and messages."

"Of course. By the way it doesn't take long for the heater to kick in, so you can hang your coat here if you want." Jacob takes off his usual thick, puffy jacket and beanie, and he hangs them on the rustic-looking line of hooks on the wall. Then, as if that wasn't enough, he also takes off the denim, button-down shirt he's wearing, leaving only a T-shirt on. I've only really imagined what his arms would look like, having only felt it in a couple of instances. So my eyes practically bug out at the first glimpse of his muscular arms, with one whole arm showing a detailed, intricate-looking tattoo which gets cut off where his shirt sleeve ends.

I don't know if it's the sight of his muscular, tattooed arm that has gotten me feeling a little hot and bothered, but it's safer to blame my sudden onset of warmth and reddened cheeks, to the heater.

Yeah, I'm definitely blaming the heater.

I turn away from him as I take my coat off, hanging it next to his, hoping that by the time I turn to face him, the color of my cheeks must have subsided enough.

He's watching me with amused curiosity, as he waves me into his living area, which surprisingly looks like something out of an interior design magazine. It's masculine, but not overtly so, and with Jacob standing in the middle of the room, his size and physique seem to complement his surroundings.

"I take it, you had someone help you do all of this?" I wave a forefinger around, a knowing smile on my face. "I mean no offense, but that puffy jacket and beanie you love to wear is not exactly stylish like your house."

"None taken. It's just one of the benefits of dating someone who's an interior designer."

"Oh …" I say, not expecting that answer. "So, are you still seeing each other?"

He chuckles but shakes his head. "The interiors stayed, she didn't."

"I'm sorry about that."

"Don't be. We both accepted what we had for what it was." Jacob pauses, but doesn't elaborate. So I decide not to ask anymore, only giving him a smile that I hope will show that I understand, even if I don't.

"Before we start, can I offer you some coffee or maybe a cup of tea?"

"Does it come with little cakes and cucumber sandwiches, served by the Queen?" I ask jokingly.

"Of course, is there any other way?" he jokes back, making me chuckle.

"Sorry, I'm a closet Downton Abbey fan. Whatever you have is fine, Jacob. May I come with you? I'd like to see your kitchen. I love kitchens," I babble on, following him as he makes his way down the hall towards the back.

My mouth pops open once again, as soon as I see his kitchen. It's massive and well-designed ... neat and clean.

Very clean.

"I love your kitchen. Do you do a lot of cooking in here?"

"No. I don't cook, I reheat." He puts some water in a kettle, before placing it back onto its heating pad and pressing the button to Boil.

"That's a shame," I comment, as I sit myself on one of the barstools next to the massive marbled benchtop. "You know, a man who knows how to cook is a pretty big deal. Women fall for that sort of thing."

He gives me a sidelong glance and a smirk, before reaching for the tea in the overhead cupboard, giving me a front row ticket to the view of his ass.

And even with his jeans on, it's obvious that it's muscled and well-formed.

"I suppose it won't be hard for you to attract women, I mean look at you," I blurt out, my eyes still glued to his backside.

He pauses and slowly turns to face me, and my eyes quickly move to his face, only to see his smirk turn to a self-satisfied grin.

Shit. Think before you speak, Billie. *Before* ... not after!

"Sorry. I didn't mean to sound like—"

"Like you find me attractive?"

"What? No! That's insane."

"You're human, Billie. You can still find other men attractive, even if you're committed to another," he teases.

242

I shake my head a little too furiously. "No, that's the thing. This never happens to me. Men used to freak me out in the worst kind of way for years. And before that, I was monogamous." I stop myself from speaking any further and digging myself into an even bigger hole.

But I've always wondered how much he knows about me.

"Jacob, before you took on this job, what did Magnus tell you about me?"

He doesn't react immediately, placing some tea leaves in an infuser and pouring boiled water inside. He lets it sit on the benchtop, and he turns to me, leaning over on the opposite side, his expression unreadable.

"Enough. But the main thing he told me was that you're very important to him, and that he needs to make sure you and Ethan are safe."

"That's all he said?"

"He doesn't have to tell me the whole story. If he needs my help, I'll help him. He's a good mate of mine, as you know."

I nod back, "So you're looking out for me all this time without asking why?"

He gives me a crooked smile. "Have you seen you? It wasn't exactly a tough task, you know."

"Jacob ..."

He exhales out loudly, "Sorry. I know I said I wouldn't do that." He fetches two cups and two saucers, laying them in front of us, before grabbing the tea, and pouring it steadily without saying another word.

I guess this is my chance to just lay it out in the open. I trust him, and he's been keeping me safe. It's the least I can do. And maybe, once he finds out about my past, he'll see me differently, and whatever crazy energy there is between us will hopefully disappear.

Here it goes.

"Over seven years ago, I was ... I was raped ..." I begin to relate.

I told him everything, right to the part where my ex kept me until I was clear of any evidence of rape, then dropped me off at my home like nothing happened.

And throughout my recount, Jacob's expression changes from curious to angry, to concerned, in a span of seconds.

With a deep breath, I continue on, "And you know what the best part is? My ex-boyfriend, the guy who did this to me, is a son of an influential politician ... a mayor during that time and now a senator."

His jaw clenches, his face hardening. "Let me guess. Cooper Thornton Jr.?"

My eyes widen. "H—how did you ..."

"Three months ago, that night you and Magnus broke up at his mother's fundraiser, Magnus called me up because he needed help. He did a number on that motherfucker, and Magnus told me his name was Cooper Thornton. But all he said was that he's bad news, and if I don't help to get Cooper out of his sight, he might kill that son of a bitch." He pauses, and I notice his knuckles turning white as he grips on the edge of the benchtop too tightly. "Maybe I should've just finished the job. The world would've been a much better place without people like him. How the fuck did he get away with it?"

Because I was afraid.

"I didn't report the incident to the authorities because he threatened to hurt me and my family, and I believed him. He also said he filmed the whole thing and will release it online, but eventually I didn't believe that. I mean, wouldn't that incriminate him as well? I tried to get my parents to help me, but I guess their priorities didn't involve helping their only child. So I ran away, and I came here thinking no one from my hometown would find me. I also changed my name from Autumn Bridges to Isabelle Morrison. I was still getting used to my new life here when I found out I was pregnant. Cooper is Ethan's father. But Ethan cannot know that he is. I'd rather die than allow Cooper to get his hands on my son."

"Shit, Billie. I didn't know. I can't believe that fucker's still walking free after what he's done to you." He comes around to me hesitantly at first, almost unsure if he should. Then he stops just inches from where I'm sitting.

"May I?" he asks, as he takes my hand and gently helps me down the barstool, before enveloping me in his arms.

"I'm so sorry," he says softly, his arms firmly around me.

I hesitate for a long moment, before finally giving in and wrapping my arms around him. Without thinking, I close my eyes and accept all the warmth and the affection Jacob is openly giving to me. As I take in a deep breath, the first thing that hits me is his scent.

He's not wearing any aftershave, but I can smell the scent of soap with his very own musk. He smells clean and downright masculine. He also feels larger than Magnus, with bulkier muscles, giving him a wider girth on his upper back. His bulk and his much taller stature make me feel like I'm being engulfed by him. And yet, there's no awkwardness, no feeling of anxiety emanating from me.

It feels ... comforting. It feels nice even.

But beyond the comfort of this embrace, I can't help but be afraid of it as well.

This shouldn't feel this good. Only Magnus should be able to comfort me like this. No one else, especially not someone like Jacob, who's supposed to be one of Magnus's best friends, hired for one specific reason.

To protect me.

His friendship is something I want, but that's as far as I'm willing to go.

Nothing more ... definitely nothing more.

So why am I not stopping him, as he tips my head up, just as his head dips down so his lips are now inches from mine. The longing in his gray-hued eyes is there, even when partially covered by his long lashes.

"I'm sorry," Jacob whispers again, his lips a hairs breadth away. And I can't tell if he's saying sorry for my past, or for this particular moment.

"Jacob ... we can't ..." I finally find my voice, my hand over his chest as a gesture for him to stop.

It seems to stir something inside of him, and his body goes rigid, then he hastily pulls away, letting me go as if he's been burned.

The sting I feel from his sudden denial surprises me, which is further reason why this moment needs to end.

"Fuck!" he mumbles under his breath, shoving his blonde hair back in frustration. He turns the other way, about to walk off. But he stops when he feels my hand on his shoulder.

"Please, don't walk away. I'm not angry."

He turns to face me once again. "Well I am. I'm angry at myself because I almost took advantage of you."

"But you stopped. That's what counts."

"I'm sorry, Billie. I'm not usually like this, especially since I know how Magnus feels about you." He stops pacing, and he bows his head, placing his hands on his hips, looking defeated.

My chest tightens as I look on. But I do not dare comfort him with a touch.

When he finally looks up to me again, he seems calmer, yet remorseful.

"I don't know what came over me. But I swear to you that I won't do anything idiotic like that again."

I take a step closer to him, tucking my hands in the back pockets of my jeans. "I meant it when I said I want us to be friends, so I'm going to let this pass. Let's just move on from this. Is that okay with you?"

He nods back, and walks towards the door of a walk-in pantry. He takes a packet of biscuits and places it on the benchtop next to the tea.

"Tea and biscuits? Can you get any more cliché?" I chuckle lightly, trying to lighten up the mood. He thankfully smiles back with relief.

We take a quiet moment to sip our teas, allowing our nerves to settle from the craziness of what could have happened just a few minutes ago.

"Jacob," I finally say as I stare down on my tea, "I think Cooper may have assaulted another girl."

His head jerks up, and I meet his gaze, noticing his brows are now furrowed. But he stays quiet, so I decide to continue on, "That girl who's been calling me, she left a text message on my phone. Her name is Grace Peterson, and she gave me her phone number, at least I'm hoping it really is her phone number."

"So I presume, you're having doubts about her, and you'd want me to check if she's legitimate?"

"I wasn't in a hurry to find out at first, until this morning. Helen, you know, the owner of the bookstore? Out of the blue, she received an offer to franchise a chain of The Written Word, and the company that's offering the deal is RCT Group. RCT stands for Reginald Cooper Thornton Sr. His son Cooper has now taken over the company."

"He's a persistent little fuck, isn't he?" Jacob shakes his head in disbelief, muttering something between gritted teeth. "So he really has found you."

I nod back, "I told Helen to hold off on pushing forward with them because that company is not to be trusted. She agreed after I told her Magnus is interested as well. Although it's not actually a big lie because Magnus did offer to buy the store for me, and I of course declined that offer. Anyway, I had to say it because I panicked. I had to say something to divert Helen's attention."

"What do you plan on doing with this information? Why haven't you gone to Magnus about this?"

"I came to you first because I need to make sure Grace is really who she says she is. If she is, then it means she's desperate and wants to reach out. But what's bugging me is why she thought I could help her. I need to know how she found out I was raped, and if she really is another victim of Cooper's, then I think I know how to finally end this."

Jacob doesn't say anything, but from the worried look etched on his face, I can sense he won't hesitate to help me out.

But I'm the one with hesitations. "I'm just scared that my plan will destroy Magnus and everything he's worked for."

"Let's just take this one step at a time, Billie. The first step, is giving me Grace's details."

"This is like something out of the movies, Jacob," I exclaim in amazement as I look around his 'office.'

We're in the middle floor of his house, inside a room that from the outside, seems like any ordinary bedroom, except the room feels more like a command center, with several screens, computers, and gadgets that I've never seen before. We even had to use a similar biometric access as Magnus's to be able to get in.

"*This* is a big part of what makes me good at what I do," he relates with pride. With my phone in his hand, he takes his seat at a customized desk, and plugs my phone in. He wheels a spare office chair so I can sit next to him, and I tuck my hands under my legs to stop myself from touching anything. Before long, he's typing some code, then, details about Grace Peterson show up on the large screens.

Jacob manages to gather Grace's police records, phone bills, and other information that I'm sure breaches a lot of privacy laws.

But I'm not about to call him out on that.

And if I'm being honest with myself, I can say that what Jacob has come up with is pretty impressive.

"Damn," I whisper out, as I stare in awe at the information he was able to gather so easily. "You're not just muscles, are you?"

He turns to me, raising a brow and giving me a sly smile. "Oh, there are a *lot* of muscles. But the biggest muscle I have is my brain."

I laugh softly, before focusing on a screenshot of Grace's license. It's surreal to be able to put a face on an otherwise distraught voice. But I can see that she's pretty—brunette, perky nose, and big, brown eyes. She's Texan, just like me. No criminal record. And her address shows that she's not from any of the affluent suburbs. She actually lives in an area that's mostly lower middle-class.

How did she meet Cooper then?

Jacob unplugs the phone and hands it back to me, handing me another phone. "Why don't you call her, and discreetly verify the intel we've got? That line is secured so there's no chance of anyone listening in."

"Is it okay if I spoke to her in private?"

He considers it for a minute, before nodding, "No problem. I'll be outside until you're done."

Once he's out of the room, I tap Grace's number on the other phone's keypad, breathing out deeply, before pressing the Call button.

"Hello?" the woman on the other end answers, and it sounds like the same woman who called me before.

"Hi. Is this Grace Peterson?"

There's a long pause, then she answers back, "This is Grace. Is this Isabelle Morrison?"

"Yes, it is. I'm just going to get straight to the point, and you don't need to be scared because this is a secured line. You obviously wanted to connect with me for some reason, and it has something to do with Cooper. How do you know him, or me, and my phone number?"

"I knew you fled Texas and changed your name because of Cooper. So I took a chance and called you because I have a feeling we've gone through the same shit and want him to pay for his crime."

A cold chill sweeps through me. "I don't know what you're talking about," I sniff, not wanting to give myself away.

"I think you do. I think he did something to you, and you ran away."

———

What the hell? She's taking a stab in the dark, taking a big risk based on assumption. She doesn't even know me!

And yet, she's right. She may just be guessing, but she's completely right.

"What did he do to you?" I ask, trying to maintain my composure.

"He raped me."

There it is. The same words I've uttered just a few minutes ago to Jacob. But now, I hear it coming from another girl.

Another. Victim.

How many are there? Were there any before me?

That motherfucker.

"How did it happen?" I want to know, my voice cracking.

She sighs, "I only met Cooper that night, a couple of months ago, and one other time a week after that. My friends and I were at this bar in Dallas. It was one of those classy ones, you know. But we dressed up real good, real posh, so we could attract the loaded ones, and maybe score us a rich boyfriend, or at least, a date. I know it sounds awful, but I'm not even going to pretend that I wasn't looking at having a comfortable life for myself. He was there with his friends ... two other guys. But he stood out. He's very handsome, but you probably know that, anyway."

She pauses but continues when I maintain my silence, "Anyway, he must have caught me eyeing him, so he and his friends approached us. He introduced himself and his friends, and he oozed charm. I was clinging to his every word. He told us his father was Senator Thornton. But to be honest, I had no clue about politics, so I had no idea what his father even looked like. But I have heard that name before. I just thought it must be pretty kick ass to know someone who's so influential. Anyway, we ended up going to his place ..."

She sighs out aloud and continues, "Eventually, one of his friends came out with the booze, then later, coke. And I'm not talking about the soft drink either. We drank, and so did my friends. They all snorted a line or two ... I didn't. I tried it before and I can't stand that shit. It didn't take long for Cooper to get high. But he was still charming, and attentive, and well, he made me feel like I was the only one in the room. It felt great ...I felt special. I thought we were on to something. I know, it sounds so stupid, right?"

I remain quiet, she sniffs, once, before continuing, "The TV was on, and it just so happened that Magnus Grant popped up on the screen. Naturally, my attention became divided. No offense, but I was majorly crushing on him, and I was vocal about it. He's handsome, successful, super rich, the whole package. Well, that pissed Cooper off. And that was when he told me that that asshole Magnus was dating his ex-girlfriend. That piqued my interest, so I asked him to tell me more. By that time, he was already hyped up and talking shit because of the booze and the coke. He said he knew you as Autumn Bridges, that you were childhood sweethearts. Then you broke up with him, then moved to New York, and got too big for your boots. He said he found out later on that you changed your name to Isabelle Morrison. So he went to New York because apparently your father's been looking for you. He knew one of the organizers from the charity event that Mrs. Grant was hosting, and he scored an invitation. But when he saw you, he said you were a major bitch, pretending like you didn't know him, even got your boyfriend to beat him up. At first, I asked him why he didn't sue Magnus Grant. He just mumbled something I couldn't really understand. But he was obviously still pissed off. That night, I actually felt sorry for him."

This is killing me. None of what he told her is true. I want to scream at her, and tell her Cooper's lying, that *he* wanted to hurt *me*.

But an outburst like that might scare her off.

So I try to keep my cool, refusing to say anything so she can reach the end of her story.

"Eventually, they all left, my friends, his friends ... I stayed because he practically begged me to. And by then, I was pretty wasted and felt kinda sorry for him as well. That's when he started getting all charming again. Eventually, we made out, and I actually enjoyed it. But then, he wanted to take things another step further, and God, he was pretty forceful about it. It freaked me out, and I wanted to leave. His mood seemed to change after that. Then he said he'd make some coffee and insisted that I have some too before he drives me home. He said it was the least he could do for being a dick. I believed him. He sounded so genuine. I remember drinking the coffee, but I don't remember finishing it. I think I blacked out. The next morning ..."

She pauses, and I hear her exhale loudly, shakily. "I woke up at the front door of my apartment, but my underwear was missing. I didn't know how I got there, but my body felt sore. I managed to get inside my apartment, and when I undressed, that's when I saw the bruises beginning to show all over my body, even down to my inner thighs." Grace's voice cracks, and she starts to sob.

The sorrow I hear in her voice reflects the sorrow I feel in my chest.

"Listen, you don't have to continue—"

She seems not to have heard me because she goes on, "I was in so much pain down there that I could barely walk. I tried to recall what happened to me, but I kept drawing a blank. And I couldn't even prove that he brought me to my place in that condition because we had none of those fancy CCTV crap. The only thing I could think of was maybe I was raped. Cooper must've drugged me, raped me, and possibly beat me up while I was unconscious. I mean how deranged was that?"

I can hear her sniffling on the other end. "I wanted him to pay, so I went to the hospital, and underwent a medical examination that confirmed I indeed had an intercourse. That, with the bruising, was enough to convince them to report the matter to the cops. But then the cops reminded me that before I start accusing the son of a senator of something that serious, I had to have solid proof. I didn't even have any proof that I was with him in the first place! And Cooper made sure he left no traces on me, except for the bruises that he could easily refute and assert as somebody else's doing. He knew what he was doing. He. Knew. And those damned cops are too spineless to start an investigation. And the way the authorities were looking at me ... like I'm some slut after a payday." She starts sobbing hysterically, and all I want to do is hug her pain away.

"I'm so sorry ..." I whisper, my eyes brimming with tears at the thought of what Cooper did to her, as well as the memories of what he did to me.

I could have stopped him from doing this to Grace.

Why didn't I think he'll do this to someone else when I let him get away with it in the first place? Why did I allow myself to be intimidated by his threats?

This is just as much as my fault too.

"He did that to you too, didn't he? He raped you too."

I'm nodding even if she can't see it, as I admit, "Yes, he did …"

But I'm not like Grace. I can't bring myself to elaborate the shame from all the degrading things he did to me, still imprinted on me like an ugly tattoo.

"It's not too late. We can still get the justice we deserve."

"Much as I want to, Grace, I have so much at stake if I did."

"What if there are others? Who knows, maybe if we go after him, others will eventually surface, and we'll have a chance to take him down."

The idea has played in my mind before, that there might be others whom he had victimized too, women who are now damaged because of his sick actions.

But maybe they have a lot to lose too, just like me. I have Ethan and Magnus to think of. I'd rather be the one who suffers inside than put them in harm's way. I don't think I can ever live with myself if that happens. It will destroy them.

"Give me time to think about this."

"I don't know why you need to think about this. He ruined me, and he obviously did a number on you if you just up and ran from home. I can't just let Cooper get away with this."

"Then I'll do my best to help, I promise. But right now, I can't have my name linked to this. I'm so sorry."

"I have no one to turn to. I have no family left, and the girls who went with me to Cooper's house are not exactly reliable witnesses. I work as a stripper … just like them. Well, I was a stripper. Now, stepping inside the club makes me want to throw up. And who the fuck will believe a stripper anyway? Either way, I lose."

I feel her agony on the phone, and it's the same agony I experience every day. I know in my heart that we need to do this. Maybe if we could put Cooper to jail, it might help emancipate us from the torturous memories.

But I also know Cooper and his family, and the lengths they'd go to clear their name. We have to think this through, and I need Grace to understand it.

"I've known the Thorntons for a long time. I know what they're capable of. That's why we need to be smart about this, Grace. Please, just give me time to think of a plan."

There's a pause on the other line, and I hear her sniffle a couple of times. "Okay. I believe you. But please, don't allow him to get off scot-free again."

"I won't. I promise. But I need to know one more thing. Cooper told you who I was, I get that. But how did you get my contact number?"

"I called in a favor from a friend who is, well, really good at finding things just by using his computer. That's all I'm gonna say because I don't want to get him in trouble. He's just a kid."

That scares me. If a kid was able to locate me, it won't be hard at all for one of Cooper's people to do the same.

What if he already knows about Ethan?

I reluctantly say my good-bye to Grace, but not before thanking her for being so brave. I just hope that she'll be true to her word and not do anything foolish.

I take a few moments to get my wits together, before asking Jacob to join me back inside.

"Are you alright?" he asks with concern as he walks inside.

"Yeah … actually, no. Grace … she was raped too, and I believe her. That animal raped another girl." I feel numb, but my chest still feels tight, like only a good, long scream can give me relief.

Jacob's hands turn into fists, his expression pained.

"I want to help her take Cooper down. I just don't know where to start. All I know is that I'll need your help." I look up to him with pleading eyes as he stands a few feet away from me.

"You know you can count me in, Billie. But Magnus needs to know what you're up to."

"I *will* tell Magnus. I have no plans of keeping this a secret from him. I just don't know how I can involve him without hurting his name."

"When it comes to you, I don't think he'll give a shit about his reputation."

"That's exactly the problem, Jacob."

His expression begins to soften as he continues to regard me thoughtfully. "So, what do you want to do now?"

I let out a deep breath. "Right now, I don't want to talk about this anymore. I just want to go home, catch up on the latest gossips with Michelle, surprise Ethan by picking him up from school, then, cook our dinner." I offer, with a weak smile. "I just want everything to be normal right now, if that's okay."

"I wish I can just ..." He raises his arm and takes a step forward, with me standing on the same spot. But as soon as he gets closer, he drops his arm in obvious resignation.

Does he want to hold me? Is that what he's trying to do?

So I reach for his hand instead, the same hand he wanted to hold me with, and it still astounds me how large his hand is, compared with mine. He seems unsure of my intention, and frankly, so am I.

I know he wants to give me some comfort after what just unfolded a few minutes ago, and I'm not about to deny him that, because I need it, just as much as he wants to give it.

So I give his hand a squeeze, before quickly pulling away with a small smile that leaves him without doubt that the gesture is purely platonic.

No hugs—this is as far as I'm going with Jacob. I can't allow whatever this is between us to become something we'll both be unable to control.

The awkwardness is broken by the sound of the doorbell. Frowning, Jacob approaches his desk-cum-command station and taps on the keyboard, where one of the screens changes to a view from the outside, just by the front door.

Waiting there is a bombshell with straight, black hair, red lips, and big boobs ... at least I think they're big, judging from the way they jut out from her coat.

"Oh, wow! Who is that?" I ask with interest.

"Shit. Wait here, I'll deal with her," he says, unable to hide his annoyance.

"Oh no, I'm not staying here. I want to see this for myself!" I tell him playfully. He pauses and turns to me.

"Stay here. Please," he says gently, yet firmly at the same time.

I stop walking, shrugging back at him, unable to deny the slight irritation that I suddenly feel.

But I've never been the obedient type. I follow Jacob as soon as he's downstairs, keeping myself hidden near the stairs as he opens the door.

The buxom woman steps in. "Surprise!" she says, before throwing her arms around Jacob. He doesn't fight her off, but he doesn't hug her back either. Eventually, he takes her arms off, earning him a red-lipped pout.

"What are you doing here?" Jacob asks quietly.

"I just flew in. I'm here for a day before I have to fly out again. I *was* gonna call you first, but I saw your car outside, so here I am."

Jacob is still wearing his T-shirt, and the woman, whom I presume he had shared his bed with on more than one occasions, deftly slides her hands inside his shirt, gliding from his stomach to his chest, and on his back.

"Hmmm, so warm. I can't wait to get my whole body warm against yours," she purrs, stepping closer.

I roll my eyes at both of them. I can't believe I actually think we have some sort of chemistry.

Jacob is obviously spreading that chemistry around.

Player.

Really? This surprises me?

"You need to leave," Jacob's gruff command at the woman pulls me back in full attention. He holds her by the wrists and gently pulls her off him again.

"Why? I just got here. Come on, you've never said no to me. I missed you, baby," she purrs again, surprising me when she grabs him by the crotch.

"Please get your hand off my crotch. I'm just about to leave. I'm working." Jacob steps back, exasperated as he glances towards my direction.

I guess he must have realized I'm listening in.

But the woman is persistent, and she steps forward again, now pulling him by the waistband, trying to unbuckle his belt.

"Come on, show me your dick. I can't stop thinking about it since the last time we fucked." I gasp as she tries to get her way, unbuttoning his jeans before kicking the door closed with her high-heeled boots.

"No!" Jacob's booming voice makes the other woman jump backwards, almost losing her balance, but quickly correcting herself. "Leave. Now!" Jacob glances back at my direction, his face clouded with frustration and anger.

She follows his glance, and realization hits her. "You have another woman here, don't you? Where is she?" She turns towards the stairs, straight to where I'm watching them.

Before she can get upstairs, however, Jacob blocks her way, "I told you from the beginning, to never come in here unannounced. I have rules, and you broke one of them. So get the hell out of here now and don't come back!"

Did he just say he has *rules*?

The hurt in the woman's face makes me feel awful for her, and angry towards Jacob. She obviously wants more from Jacob, and he just rejected her so callously. I don't know what I'd do if I were in her position.

Since I have my things with me, I stand up from where I am hiding, and I take each step down, until I'm in full view of the woman, whose heart Jacob might have torn to pieces.

But as soon as the other woman sees me, the hurt on her face is gone, now replaced with anger.

Anger directed at me.

Uh—oh.

"I knew it! Who the fuck are you?" Her thunderous eyes are focused on me, that I instinctively step backwards.

"You will never talk to her like that, do you hear me?" Still blocking her, he moves towards the door, forcing the other woman to walk back in that direction.

"No. Jacob, that's enough. *I'll* go." I hurry down but pause in front of her. "You have no reason to be jealous. He's protective of me because it's his job."

I ignore the steely look in Jacob's eyes. "Thanks for your help, Jacob," I tell him as I grab my coat and head out the door, not looking back.

"Isabelle!" I hear him call out for me, but I choose to ignore it, walking off in the direction of the nearest subway station that will take me home.

I don't know why that whole thing pissed me off. I don't like being an unwilling participant of some nonexistent love triangle. Putting this distance will be good. And I highly doubt that something dangerous will happen to me between here and my apartment.

I'm about to turn a corner when a strong hand grabs me by the shoulder, making me cry out with fright. I try to run, but an arm is now wrapped around my waist. I try to take it off, about to scream for help, when I notice the familiar-looking tattoos on his arm.

"Calm down, Speedy Gonzales, it's just me," Jacob's voice from behind makes my heart jump, but not out of fright.

I can't believe he came after me.

"What are you doing? You should be with your girlfriend right now."

"She's not my bloody girlfriend," he sighs as he lets me go, but he places his hand on my back as he walks me back to where I came from. "Magnus did warn me you're a runner. I'm driving you to your place, so let's go."

I turn to face him, and I frown at the sight of him with just his T-shirt on, his belt still unbuckled, while he's outside in the freezing cold of winter.

We must look ridiculous to the people around us.

"Could you please wear your jacket? It's freezing right now. And buckle up, for goodness sake." He gives me a lopsided smile, doing what I asked, but deliberately doing it slowly.

My eyes narrow at him, "And what's this 'rules' thing about? You have dating rules? Seriously?" I raise my brows, crossing my arms indignantly. "What woman in their right mind would agree to that?"

"Those *rules*, Isabelle, help me avoid any future complications. If these women know where I stand and what I'm about, then they know not to expect anything further than what I'm willing to offer. But once they break one of my rules, it's over. Trust me, there are a lot of women out there who prefer things in black and white, especially with someone like me."

"But it's never black and white with relationships."

"First of all, relationships are not for me, and I doubt that they ever will. But with me, they know what to expect." We stop by his Range Rover, which he promptly disarms, and he opens the passenger door for me.

"What are your rules?" I ask as I get inside.

He smiles coyly, before closing the door. He walks around and gets in the driver's seat.

But I'm not going to let him ignore my question. "What are your rules, Jacob?" I ask again, staring at him intently.

He smirks at me, before turning on the ignition and driving off. "I don't just give those away to anyone, Isabelle."

"I thought we're friends."

"Exactly. We're friends. We're not lovers, nor is there any chance of us being one, so you, my *friend*, are not qualified to know my rules."

"Fine," I answer, crossing my arms and looking straight ahead. "I still find it degrading and think it's preposterous that women are willing to give in to your demands, oh, sorry, I meant *rules*," I add with sarcasm.

"You'll be surprised at what these woman will agree to, after spending one night with me," Jacob says and shrugs nonchalantly.

"Really? What do you do to them?"

He doesn't answer, but he gives me a sidelong glance and a sly smile.

Oh.

That was a dumb thing to ask, Billie.

"Who knows, maybe you would've been the exception," he says, instantly making my cheeks feel warm, and he adds, "but I guess we'll never know."

I turn my attention outside. "You're right. We'll never know."

On the way home, I ask Jacob to take me to the supermarket for some supplies I need at home. By the time we reach our destination, he parks his SUV, and things have become pretty awkward between us. I let myself out without waiting for Jacob to open the door like he usually does.

"You can just wait for me here, Jacob. You don't have to come with me," I tell him, as he's getting out of his vehicle.

"Not a chance," is all he says. Before long, he's walking beside me, his hands shoved in his pockets to keep them warm.

Inside the supermarket, I put everything I've listed in my head straight inside the basket. Jacob is also quite helpful, carrying the basket for me, and getting the items I can't reach, because they are placed on shelves that are way too high for someone like me to reach.

He's placing the latest item inside the basket, when an elderly woman approaches us, with an endearing smile on her face.

"Oh, it must be so nice having a tall husband. My Gerry used to do that for me too, before he passed away five years ago."

"I'm sorry to hear that, ma'am," Jacob apologizes, his expression unreadable.

"My goodness, and with an accent too? Sweetie, you're one lucky lady."

"Oh, we're not—"

"Thank you, ma'am. I'm sure, she feels the same way," Jacob cuts me off, and they both have a good laugh.

I wait until the woman walks away, before slapping Jacob's arm.

"Ow, what?" He feigns getting hurt, rubbing his arm.

"You let her assume we're a couple, let alone married!"

"So? Did you see how that pleased her? There's no harm in it."

"But I'm with Magnus, not you. What if she sees me in the news, and with Magnus? She'll probably think I'm cheating on you, with him!"

"So what? You bloody overthink things."

"Whatever, let's just drop it."

"Sounds good to me."

Just then, my new phone rings. It's the one Magnus gave me.

Thank goodness. Jacob is starting to get under my skin in a bad way.

"Hello?" I answer the phone, and I can't help but smile, knowing exactly who's on the other line.

"I miss you," the deep voice on the other end pipes up.

"I miss you too," I echo, the events of this morning telling me how much I really do. I notice Jacob rolls his eyes and turns away, focusing his attention on some random brand of cereal on the shelf. I turn the other way, ignoring Jacob. "So what do I owe this phone call?"

"I want to hear your voice. Is Jacob there? I've been trying to call him, but he's not answering my calls. It's beginning to piss me off."

"Um, I'm actually on my way home and Jacob was taking me. We just had to stop over at the supermarket around the corner from my place."

"Why? Are you okay? What happened?"

I half-chuckle, "I'm okay now. I kind of felt faint this morning. But now, I'm fine. Helen told me to go home."

"Why didn't you call me?"

"And what would you have done? Aren't you in Texas?"

It takes him a few seconds to answer. "Actually, I never left New York. It was a last minute change of plans. I just spoke with your father on the phone, and I think I'm back in his favor. I was about to surprise you with lunch so I can tell you all about it. Is Jacob there with you now?"

"He's here, but don't get upset with him. I told him to take me home and not to worry you anymore."

"I'm on my way with our lunch. I'm calling Jacob. Please tell him to answer his phone."

"Okay, I will."

"See you soon."

I take a few steps away, somehow not wanting anyone, let alone Jacob, to hear me say what I'm about to say.

"I love you, Magnus," I whisper.

"I love you too, my temptress. Wait for me."

"Always," I answer, smiling once again.

After hanging up, I walk back to Jacob, just as I hear the buzzing sound coming from his jeans pocket.

"That'd be Magnus," I tell him, pointing down at his pocket.

Jacob sniffs, before taking the call. I choose not to hang around to wait for him, opting instead to head to the cashier's to settle my purchases, while sending Michelle a text message to let her know I'll be coming home shortly. She responds quickly, telling me she's home.

Jacob rejoins me in time to help me carry the bags.

"So Magnus is coming over, huh?"

"Yup. You're welcome to stay. If Magnus isn't bringing enough food, I can always cook extra."

Jacob helps place the bags inside the trunk of his SUV, before opening the passenger door for me.

"Are you sure? I don't want to be the third wheel," he confides, hanging his solid frame over the door.

"Don't be silly. Michelle will be there too."

"Ok, if you insist," he gives in with a small smile, and drives the short distance to my place.

At home, even as Jacob is helping me with the groceries, I can't avoid noticing how distant he seems. I don't know if it's just me, but his mood changed from the supermarket to my place.

Does it have anything to do with his conversation with Magnus?

The awkwardness is thankfully broken, with Michelle's entrance.

"Hello, everyone!" she yells out as she closes the door.

"We're at the kitchen!" I yell back.

"Hey, babe." Michelle gives me a kiss on the cheek, before waving a greeting at Jacob, "Jacob … it's nice to see you again."

Jacob nods back, saying, "Likewise."

"Magnus will bring some lunch, but he didn't specify if it's good for four, so I'll just whip up something quick before he arrives.

"I'll help. Jacob, do you know how to cook?"

"I'm afraid my kitchen skills are quite limited," Jacob answers with an embarrassed smile. "I'll just park myself on the couch—"

"Oh no, you wont." Michelle veers him back inside the kitchen, his frame making it harder for all three of us to move.

"I'm going to cook fried chicken. Is that cool?"

Jacob smiles, "Yum. Tell me what I need to do, great teacher."

"You guys can handle that. I'll just cut some fruit for after," Michelle says.

Time passes and we're almost done with the dish. Jacob is actually a pretty receptive student, which surprises me, considering that the only appliance he uses, basically does the cooking for him.

We hear the doorbell ring, not long after the chicken is fried. Michelle offers to open the door, checking first to make sure it's Magnus. I hear him call for me as he makes his way to the kitchen. I turn around to greet him as soon as I feel him close. But as soon as I see him, the expression on his face surprises me. Magnus's eyes are hardened towards Jacob, who's standing beside me, with a dish cloth on one hand, and stainless steel thongs on the other.

God, he's reading this wrong.

I steel myself for an outburst. Instead, Magnus surprises me again, by purposely walking towards me, sweeping me in his arms, and kissing me … no, *devouring* me. His lips are definitely hungry.

By the time we come up for air, my limbs feel like jelly, my eyes are glazed over, much like Magnus's. But there's no mistaking the smugness in those eyes of his.

That's when I realize that Jacob is no longer in the kitchen with us.

Oh, Magnus.

"Was that for me, or for him?" I ask in whisper, my hands on his chest and my eyes watching him closely.

"I just wanted to kiss my girlfriend, that's all. And I want more," he dips his head once again, his lips on mine in no time.

My hands fist on his hair, just as he presses his body closer, pushing me back against the kitchen benchtop.

"Oh, come on! Not in front of the food. Get a room, will you?" Michelle's voice brings us back to reality, and we pull apart, laughing softly like it's an inside joke between us.

"Sorry, Michelle," I answer, still giggling as she walks out.

"I must admit, I'm really happy you're here, even if it means you not seeing my father in person."

"Why? Because you'll miss me?"

I nod back, shyly biting my lower lip.

"So will I baby," he whispers, leaning forward to give me another kiss that makes my toes curl.

"What did you bring us for lunch?" I ask Magnus, as soon as we pull away.

"Well, my Texan babe loves her meat, so I got us a varied selection of roasted meats and some cold cuts, cheese, bread ..." He opens both paper bags and takes out enough food to feed a small army.

"You bought all of these?"

"Denise ordered all of these from this really good deli, and Alex picked them up on our way here."

"Well, I should thank them then."

"I paid for all of these, so you're welcome."

I reply by rolling my eyes at him, and he responds by smirking back.

As I'm setting the table with Michelle, Jacob and Magnus seem to be catching up at the living area. Jacob looks up momentarily and catches my eye. I offer him a smile, hoping it's an acceptable form of apology for Magnus's earlier display of ownership. Jacob only gives me a slight nod back, before turning his attention back at Magnus. Magnus must have said something funny soon after, because both of them laugh. It's strange, but without me in the mix, I can actually see genuine camaraderie between the two of them.

So it is true. They really *are* great friends.

"Jacob's crushing on you," Michelle whispers from behind me.

"No, he isn't," I answer back, knowing I don't sound convincing enough.

"You know he is, and I'm sure I'm not just seeing things, but I saw it last night, and I saw it earlier. Jacob likes you, and I think you kinda like it that he does."

"I do not!" I exclaim, leaving one last glance at Jacob and Magnus, before dragging Michelle by the arm to the kitchen.

Inside the kitchen, I let her go, but she carries on, "It's okay, Billie. I mean, come on, you'd only be blind if you don't find Jacob hot. Even I get all hot and bothered around him."

"It's not like that, Michelle. Okay, he's not bad to look at, but it doesn't matter. I love Magnus, and Jacob and I are just friends. And in case you haven't noticed, *they're* good friends."

"I'm just saying—"

"Look, my life just got even more complicated these past few days. Can you please just drop this?"

"How did your life get more complicated?"

I sigh out aloud, "Now's not the best time to talk about this. Let's just eat our lunch, so I can pick up the kids after. I promise we'll talk when the time is right."

Michelle nods, her expression somber, "Okay ... okay. I totally understand you, baby. But I'm just here if you want to talk, okay?" She reaches for my hand and squeezes it.

I must be so transparent to her right now.

"I'll tell you everything soon, I promise."

She nods and gives me a smile. "Okay. Just don't carry this on your own, like you used to. I am here."

"I know you are. That's why I love you."

"So do I, babe."

Suddenly, her face lights up. "Hey, I'm really excited about tomorrow night. Our dinner date before Keiko's thing, remember?"

"What? Oh yeah," I answer back, distractedly. "Actually, is it alright if I skip tomorrow night? I'm just not feeling up to that kind of socializing right now."

"Oh, okay. How about Friday, will you be game to go on a girls' night out? I miss our night outs, and the girls miss you too."

"That's an excellent idea. Friday sounds good."

"I'll call them and organize everything. C'mon, let's get these boys fed."

Lunch was thankfully uneventful, but productive in a way. I spoke about my concern for the security watching out for us during winter, agreeing to Magnus's option to replace the security with surveillance cameras. Magnus seems pleased, and Jacob tells us it's possible. But we can't go ahead without Nathan's approval, so Michelle will help me on that part. She also announced that Nathan is in the process of adopting a German shepherd, a former K-9 who became terribly injured on a police raid turned ugly. The dog's handler is unable to adopt the dog, so Nathan put his hand up, since he became quite attached to him, having treated him previously for other injuries, and experienced the dog's sweet side. I think it's a great idea, having additional security as well as a companion for the kids.

After lunch, Michelle decides to go back to her place after helping me with the dirty dishes. She has to work on a project which is due by the end of the week. Not long after, while I'm still in the kitchen, Jacob decides to make his leave as well, saying he needs to go back to his office. Since I'm still cleaning up, Magnus offers to walk him downstairs. Jacob comes over and gives me a quick hug, and I reciprocate by quietly thanking him for his help. He gives me a smile back and a wink, before walking out with Magnus.

I'm already sitting on the couch when Magnus returns.

"Hey," he says, sitting next to me.

"Hey back," I answer, unable to resist the urge to sit on his lap.

His smile widens as soon as I'm straddling him, and he stretches out his arms on the back of the couch. I waste no time in lowering my head and leaving slow, lingering kisses on his neck, moving upwards onto his mouth.

His arms circle around me, holding me tightly as his own lips respond to my own. He doesn't take over the kiss, instead, he lets me take the lead, fully compliant to my demands.

A girl can get used to this.

But my eyes catch the time on the wall clock across from me.

"We have about half an hour before I have to go pick up the kids."

"No problem," he answers, nipping my lower lip, "we can do plenty in half an hour. Then, we can pick up the kids."

"So you're not going back to work?" I ask, unable to mask the smile growing on my face.

"Is that what you want?" Magnus asks back, his finger gliding over my nose.

"Yes, if it's okay."

"I'm sure I'm not going to get in trouble for it."

"Are you sure? I hear the boss is a real hard ass," I tease.

"His girlfriend loves his hard ass."

That makes me giggle, and his smile widens, making me feel delicious flutters in my stomach.

"So what do you want to do, baby?" His hands slide downward and over my ass, giving it a quick squeeze.

But my plan for that half hour is different from his. "I'm hoping we can talk? I have something to tell you, and the first thing I want to ask is for you not to get upset and jump into conclusions, okay?"

His mouth thins into a line, just as I'm lifting myself off his lap, sitting beside him instead.

"Just tell me what it is," Magnus says quietly.

"This morning, you know how I told you I felt faint, and Helen told me to go home? I collapsed because Helen just had an offer to buy her store from this company, and they want to build franchises across the states."

"That sounds like a great offer."

"The offer came from RCT Group."

"What? That's Cooper's company."

"I think he's doing this to get to me. He's trying to send a message. I told Helen not to trust them and that I'll talk to you first. Maybe you can make a counteroffer or something? I know it's a big ask, but I just need to buy some time."

"You don't even have to ask me twice. You know I'll do it."

"Thank you. Oh God, thank you so much." I jump up to hug him, and he wraps his arms around me, holding me close.

"Now, why would you think I'd get upset over that?" he asks against my hair.

"Because that's not all."

He sighs, "Tell me."

"When Jacob came over the store, I asked if he could take me to his place, only because it was closer from the store. I needed his help, and he had the equipment in his house to help me."

Magnus's body goes rigid. "You went over his house?"

"I've been getting calls from an unknown number. I tried to ignore them, but at times when I decided to answer, no one was on the other line. So the last time I took the call and the caller didn't speak, I warned that I was going to get the phone traced. Then during your charity event, I got a text message from that person. It was from a girl, a certain Grace Peterson, and she was asking for my help to get Cooper thrown in jail. She also gave her contact number.

"But how did she get your number?"

"That's why I had to go to Jacob's. You probably know that he has one of those top of the line computer softwares that can trace calls and confirm identities. I wanted to be sure that she's a real deal. I can't afford to be gullible again."

"What happened after that?"

"We confirmed she's legit. I called her using Jacob's phone, and she explained everything. She told me she was raped by Cooper and how it happened, how she found out about me, how she got my number. She didn't get my number through Cooper, so that was a relief. But she needs my help to take him to court ... and I think I want to help her."

"She can build a case on her own. Why does she need to involve you?"

"Because she comes from a not-so-respectable background. She's a stripper. The police basically told her she has no chance in the world to sue someone like Cooper unless she has proof. And like I told you before, Cooper was very careful."

Magnus looks in the distance, the wheels turning in his head.

"What are you thinking about?" I ask.

"First, I'll get in touch with my lawyers to see what we can do to help you and Grace. But before I make that step, I want you to be sure about this."

"That's the problem, Magnus. I'm not sure about this. Cooper knows how to play the system, and what about Ethan? He can sue me for custody."

As soon as the words spill out of my mouth, I start freaking out. But Magnus holds me close, not letting me go.

"I cannot allow that animal to come close to me, or my child." My voice is cracking, now that the realization of the consequences of seeking justice against Cooper hits me.

"My lawyers will make sure that doesn't happen, Isabelle. But right now, I can think of two ways of stopping Cooper from coming after you and Ethan, at least while this case is taken to court."

I look up at him with wide eyes and ask, "What is it?"

He regards me with a look that veers on uncertainty. "First, we can take a restraining order against him, for you and Ethan. We can also file one for Grace. He won't be able to come near you. If he does, he will go to jail."

"Okay, that sounds good," I nod back in agreement. "Let's do that. But you said there are two ways?"

Magnus looks away, licking his lips, like he's trying to stretch the time.

I'm beginning to have butterflies in my stomach.

Why is he stalling?

"What's the second option, Magnus?"

"The second option is for you to marry me."

CHAPTER 23

I don't think I've ever been lost for words this long.

I'm stunned, staring in space, my heart is beating a mile a second, and I can't seem to catch my breath.

Magnus resumes, "With us married, we'll have a stronger case against Cooper. The judge will see that Ethan will have a more stable life with us, not with an accused rapist. And it doesn't have to be a big wedding either. Just a small one will do. City hall, with Michelle and Jacob as our witnesses—"

"No," I blurt out aloud, cutting him off.

"No?" he asks, sounding surprised.

What did he expect?

"No. We're not getting married. Why did you even suggest that?" I tear myself out of his arms, and he mercifully lets me go.

I stand up and walk away from the couch, distancing myself from him.

"Is it really such an unappealing idea to marry me?" Magnus stands up as well, his expression a muddle of bewilderment and hurt.

I close my eyes to stop myself from getting affected by his reaction. "I know that you only suggested that because it will help keep Cooper away. But that's not fair to you, nor is it fair to me and my child."

"Isabelle …"

"Please, just hear me out. The moment you told me your second option, I wanted to jump out of my skin, and literally do a cartwheel. I thought I was dreaming it all up. But then I realize you probably wouldn't even suggest that if my current situation weren't in dire straits. I don't want you to marry me out of convenience, or because it will help me keep Ethan," I pause, blinking back the tears that are ready to spill. "I want you to marry me because I'm the only person you will ever love for the rest of your life, not because it seems to be a good idea to do so. When I get married, it's going to be for life, Magnus. So, if you're not prepared to spend every waking day of your life with me, then option two is off the table."

He just stares at me after my whole spiel, possibly contemplating what he's going to say next.

"You know what? Let's just drop the whole thing, forget I even mentioned it," he says ... a little too calmly for my liking. He turns away from me, which is just as well, so he won't see the moment when his words leave a crack on my already battle-weary heart. He grabs his coat from the rack next to the door, and puts it on. "I'll talk to my lawyers about how we'll approach this." He takes my own coat from the rack and closes our distance, handing it to me, "We have to go."

I stare at the coat, before taking it from him. I don't want to look at his face. I don't want him to see how his words affect me.

Funny how we both gave each other two choices, and we both end up hurting each other with our decisions.

Actually, it's not funny at all.

It's déjà vu.

But the difference is that we're still here, together. He hasn't left, and I haven't ran away.

"Are we okay?" I ask precariously, suddenly anxious of his answer.

The brooding expression is gone, softening as he closes our gap. He cups my face in his hands and kisses my forehead, before tilting my face up and laying a single, tender kiss on my parted lips.

"I'm not going anywhere," Magnus whispers, with so much affection in those blues, that the hurt I feel starts to ebb away.

"Good. Actually we both have to go somewhere, you know, so we can pick up the kids?"

He laughs softly, his face brightening up like sunshine pushing all the storm clouds away.

I can't help but smile back. It's just automatic when it comes to him.

On our way to his car, Magnus tells me that Jacob is giving the kids' security detail the rest of the afternoon off, as soon as we pick up Ethan and Tasha.

Thankfully, our car ride to school is not as tense as I thought it will be. In fact, it's surprisingly tender. Magnus keeps our hands clasped, only letting me go to change gears, or if he needs to turn the car. I have to chew on the inside of my cheek to stop myself from grinning like a lovesick idiot.

"My parents will be back from their trip on Friday," Magnus says, looking straight ahead. "Mother can't wait to catch up ... with you mostly. She never really had a chance the last time."

"No, I suppose not," I answer back wistfully, as I recall the events that occurred after Miranda and I met for the first time ... events that I wish never happened.

"She invited us to spend the weekend at our family home upstate. I'm hoping you and Ethan could come with me?" He gives me a sideward glance, possibly noticing my brows rise up in surprise.

"I have to be honest. I'm a little bit nervous meeting your family again after we broke up."

"I don't see why. Regan will never let me hear the last of it if I go up there without you. She gave me hell when we broke up."

"Ah, so us going with you is a ruse to keep you out of trouble?"

By this time, we're in the parking lot of the school ground and Magnus is negotiating an empty parking spot.

Once he's done, he turns to me and answers, "I don't think I can stand being away from you the whole weekend. I'm going to go mad without you there."

"Really?"

"Yes, really." Magnus leans closer, until he's only inches away. "Say you'll come with me."

"We'll come with you," I answer back, smiling. "I guess it'll be nice to just get away from all of the craziness of this city."

We make our way to the school, hand-in-hand once again, relishing our couplehood and not giving a damn who sees it.

In a matter of weeks, or maybe even days, I'll be coming out of my self-imposed exile, to go against a man who nearly destroyed everything about me. And the only reason I've even gained enough strength to do this is the reassurance that I won't be doing this alone.

And Magnus holding my hand is my proof.

Amidst the gawks and stares from other teachers and parents directed at the man right beside me, I immediately see the auburn hair of my son, bobbing up and down as he's running towards us.

"Mom! Magnus!" he hollers out with delight, with an equally delighted Tasha, running right behind him.

"Hey, little man. Surprise!" I open my arms wide enough to give them room to jump in.

"I didn't know you were going to pick us up," Ethan rattles on excitedly, with a wide grin on his face.

He fist-bumps Magnus, and in his excitement, he gives him a hug as well.

The expression on his face as he looks down at Ethan is enough to warm my heart. I only realized how much it affected me, when I notice that my hand is now clutching my chest.

"Hey, Tash." I give Nathan's daughter a brush on the cheek. "I hope you guys had a good day today. What'd you get up to?"

We're walking back to the car, with me between the kids, and Magnus behind us. I turn back to check on him, and he's looking back at me thoughtfully, with a contented smile on his face.

"Yeah, it was alright. Math is *hard*, Mom," Ethan mumbles.

"No, it's not," Tasha adds.

"Well, we'll just have to work on it together, buddy," I assure him, adding, "and maybe, Tash can help out as well?"

Tasha beams at me, obviously happy with my suggestion.

With the kids secured at the back of the car, Magnus drives back to my place. He's been quiet for the rest of the trip back. But the small, very subtle smile on his face tells me that there's nothing to worry about.

At home, Ethan and Tasha head straight to Nathan and Michelle's to do their homework so they can play straight after. It's a ritual they're used to, so I'm not about to break it.

Magnus and I are left at the hall, outside of Michelle's apartment.

"So, I did tell Ethan that I'll help him out with his Math," I tell Magnus, chewing on my lip, adding, "but you're welcome to stay if you want."

"Hmm, I do have to get some work done, so how about this. I'll be upstairs so I can catch up on some work, and I'll ask Rosa to fetch me some clothes so Alex can drop them off."

My heart wants to leap for joy at his suggestion, but I try to play it cool. "What makes you think I want you to stay over, huh?"

He leans forward, a smirk already on his face, and he whispers in my ear, "The way your cheeks are turning pink right now. And I think I can safely assume that the mere idea of me … in your bed … is already turning you on."

"Oh my God," I croak, handing him the keys to my place.

He knows me too well.

Damn him.

"Sounds like a resounding yes to me," he answers back in that rough, low tone that reverberates through me. "See you soon, babe." Magnus leans to kiss me on the cheek, and with a smug smile, he glides up the stairs and into my apartment.

"Yeah ... see you," I answer back distractedly, as I open the door to Michelle's apartment, wondering how I'm going to be able to help Ethan now.

Good luck to me.

The rest of the afternoon flies by, or at least I did my best to make it fly by, trying to maintain some sense of normalcy because, subconsciously, my head is buzzing from thoughts of Magnus upstairs, to what I'm about to do in the next weeks.

When the kids are done with their homework, Michelle fixes them a light snack and prepares coffee for us.

Michelle and I are seated on the couch, with the kids happily snacking in the dining room while playing with their iPads.

"So, how's your project going? Is it almost done?" I ask Michelle, before sipping on my coffee.

"Yeah, I should be done before Friday. But c'mon, let's not talk about that. I still can't get what you said out of my head. What's going on, baby girl?"

I sigh, knowing how inevitable this conversation is.

So, after checking the kids and making sure they're too preoccupied to hear us, I tell her everything that has been happening these past few days—from the prank calls, to the RCT Group's schemes, up to the present when I've finally decided to do get the justice I wasn't brave enough to pursue all those years ago.

Michelle keeps quiet throughout the whole thing, only nodding, or frowning at certain points. Afterwards, she opens her arms and gives me a hug.

My usually outspoken best friend is hugging me tightly, with no words or opinions being uttered. When we both pull away, I can see her eyes are teary.

"Babe, you're crying. Don't cry," I gently urge.

"I'm just so damn proud of you for finally doing this. But, on the other hand, I'm also very, very afraid for you and Ethan. You know how much I love you both."

"I know. And I want to keep Ethan protected from all of this mess. But he's old enough to realize when something's wrong. What would it do to him, if he realizes that his biological father is a rapist? It will break him, Michelle. So the best I can do is to soften the blow for him when I go after Cooper."

"If you want, Ethan can stay with my parents. They can keep him safe. And he's only a child, the media can't touch him."

"Cooper can. His family can. God, they have enough power to shut this whole lawsuit down."

The heel of my foot starts thumping on the floor, and it doesn't stop until Michelle places her hand on my leg.

"Billie, speaking up and exposing him and his family will sully their image. Even if they're able to throw your lawsuit out, it will already leave an imprint on the people's minds. The public's confidence on them will be tarnished, and it'll be all over for them I can assure you."

She holds on to my hands. "And you have someone like Magnus who's going to be there for you, just like me, Nathan, and the girls would."

"I know. I just hope this doesn't end in a bad way."

"It won't, because all of us won't allow it, okay? Oh, and speaking of the girls, I rang them earlier, and they are all in for Friday. It's gonna be epic!" Michelle ends in a singsong voice.

"God, I sure hope so. I do miss them. But let's not tell the girls about this for now, okay? I don't want to put a damper on the fun. I just want to catch up on gossips and drink enough to calm my nerves and forget, at least for that night." I let out a loud sigh, as Michelle squeezes my hand and looks on with empathy.

Then her eyes light up, a smile showing up on her face.

"I have something to tell you, but don't tell the girls yet. I only want to tell you this because it's not set in stone yet."

"What is it?" I ask, suddenly intrigued.

"Nathan's thinking of selling his practice. He wants us to move upstate, possibly Long Island where it's quieter. He wants to open a new practice there."

"What? Where did this come from?"

She smiles back sheepishly. "Believe it or not, I'm actually excited at the idea of moving. Mom and Dad will be closer, and the area is more stable for Tash. I mean, Nathan and I, we've been talking about starting a family of our own. I know it all sounds like we're rushing—"

She doesn't really need to explain anything. I can see the explanation I need in her eyes.

"You should do it," I tell her.

"You're … you're not upset?"

"I can't deny that I'm not going to miss you, because I will. But I love you, babe, and Nathan's not so bad," we both giggle, "I want nothing but for both of you to be happy. You both deserve it."

"You've found happiness in Magnus too, baby girl."

I answer with a big smile, hoping to mask the tightness in my chest from the argument I had with Magnus only a couple of hours ago.

Speaking of Magnus…

"Hey, do you mind if I just go upstairs? I just want to check on Magnus, and possibly get a head start on dinner. You guys are welcome to join us if you want?"

Michelle smiles, but shakes her head. "Thanks, but Nathan's taking us out to dinner tonight. He'll be home in a couple of hours. Don't worry, I'll tell him about the surveillance cameras."

"You think he's gonna go for it?"

"Babe, he's going to go for it, if I say he should," she sasses.

"That's great, thank you!"

On my way out, I approach Ethan, "Honey, I'm just going upstairs, okay? I'll call you when it's dinnertime, or just come up when you're ready."

"Yes, Mom!" Ethan yells back.

I give Michelle a quick peck on the cheek and my son a quick hug, before making my way out.

Since there are only two apartments in Nathan's brownstone, and with the kids always going back and forth between apartments, we don't bother locking our doors during the day, since the main door is always securely locked anyway. Thankfully, Magnus didn't lock the door this time.

The first thing I see is him, sitting on one of the dining chairs, his suit jacket draped on the backrest. His tie is loosened, and the top button of his shirt is open. He's also wearing his sexy black-rimmed glasses, reading something from the laptop in front of him. He must be speaking with someone on the phone about something serious, judging by the brooding expression on his face.

Wow, I can stare at him like this for hours.

He looks up and gives me a distracted smile, just as I'm closing the door, locking it without thinking.

Hmmm, I wonder what I can do to take his mind off work right now.

I push myself off the door, straight towards him, lifting my leg over his lap so I'm standing in-between his legs, blocking his view of the laptop screen. Magnus stops mid-sentence, but only for a second, resuming his conversation as his eyes slowly make their way up to meet mine. I lower myself, cupping his face gently, and grazing my lips against his, but standing right up, just as he starts to reach for me.

He narrows his eyes playfully, trying to anticipate my next move while trying not to sound distracted on the phone.

Yes, he's still on the phone.

But he won't be for long ...

He pushes his seat back, giving me more room, as if encouraging my next move. Biting my lower lip, I kneel in-between his legs, my hands slowly, but deliberately running down his inner thighs, from his knees towards his crotch. All the while, Magnus is watching me, still composed, as he listens and responds back to the poor sap on the other end.

He even opens his legs a little wider for me, subtly pushing his hips forward, not just to display his impressive bulge, but as invitation for me to continue.

Without a word, I unbuckle his belt, unbutton his trousers, and slide the zipper down carefully. Then I pull down the waistband of his boxer briefs, and there, in all its hard glory is his beautiful cock.

And it's all mine.

I lick my lips in excited anticipation, wrapping my hand around his hardness.

I hear him suck in his breath.

But surprisingly, he's still holding his phone.

As my mouth closes around its perfect head, I hear him breathe out a curse, before dismissively apologizing at the person he's talking to.

Now, he's too distracted, watching me slide my mouth over his length. I witness him squeezing his eyes shut momentarily, like he's trying to gain some form of control.

I got him where I want him.

And he knows it.

As my tongue slithers languidly on the underside, he finally speaks up, "We'll talk tomorrow. Nothing you're saying makes sense right now. There's someone more important in here that I need to take care of … yes, I said *someone*."

He finally hangs up on whoever he's talking to and throws his phone on the table. "Fuck! That was torture."

"And this?" I ask coyly.

"I love you so fucking much, Isabelle," he whispers, eyes glazed with desire.

His words seem to stoke the fire inside of me, and my tempo increases.

Not long after, his body goes rigid. And, with one deep groan, Magnus explodes, and I take every last drop until he has none left to give. He whispers my name, as I continue to stroke him, slowing down at the same time as his breathing.

And as he looks at me with awe and affection, I whisper up to him, "I love you too, baby."

Soon after, he helps me stand up before he fixes himself. But he doesn't let me go far though, hauling me back in his arms, and letting me sit on his lap.

"Now, what the hell did I do to deserve that?" he asks me as he brushes strands of hair away from my face.

"Well, you know what you, sitting there with your glasses and looking all serious, do to me. I just couldn't help myself," I answer with a shrug, trying to act casually.

He raises a brow, smirking, "Is that right? I better keep that in mind for next time then."

"Baby, you can just sit here, doing absolutely nothing, and you'll still manage to turn me on."

His hand begins to skim over my neck, down my breasts, and over my stomach, stopping just above the button of my jeans.

"I want to return the favor," he whispers over my neck, making my skin tingle all over. Then he unbuttons and unzips my jeans.

But I hold on to his wrist, stopping him from taking my jeans off. "Wait, we're going to have company soon."

"Okay … fair enough. But I always have a Plan B." With my jeans still open, he positions me so that I'm facing away from him while straddling one of his legs. Then, he circles one arm around my waist, while his free hand begins its downward journey underneath my jeans.

"Magnus, what are you … oh!" I exclaim, as soon as I feel his hand squeeze inside my panties with ease, and his digits begin sliding over my already moist folds.

A whimper escapes my throat, as one of his fingers begin to make slow circles over my sensitive clit. As the circling increases in speed, so do the shots of pleasure emanating from every nerve ending of my body, turning my body into jelly, with my head lying helplessly on his shoulder.

It blows my mind that even with us fully clothed, no dirty talk being uttered, and no means to kiss him, Magnus can still make all of my senses fully aware of him, of what he's doing, all with just the tips of his fingertips.

My breathing changes into short spurts, my heart thudding like it's about to leap out of my chest.

"I want to feel you come all over my fingers," Magnus whispers roughly against my neck.

Oh …

And almost automatically, I climax, repeating his name out loud with gritted teeth, riding every single wave of pleasure, as they wash away my worries … even my fears. Right at this moment, it feels like I'm being cleansed of every single anxious cell from my body.

Maybe Magnus was right all along. That when I climax, I actually feel free.

I close my eyes, with my head still on Magnus's shoulder, allowing my whole body to settle down.

"That. Was. Wow," I whisper, still feeling short of breath.

Magnus slides his hand from under my panties, and as I stand up, he lets me witness him clean off his fingers with his mouth, with a smug grin on his face.

Holy shit, that's so hot.

With still-shaky fingers, I zip up and button my jeans.

"I think I better get started with dinner." I make my way towards the kitchen, still on jelly legs, but before I even make it halfway, I stop, and I run back to him.

Cupping his face, I lean down and give him a lingering kiss before scurrying back to the kitchen, with a big smile on my face.

I'm in the middle of preparing the ingredients for the burger dinner, when I hear knocking at the door and Ethan's voice calling for me.

Magnus opens the door, and in come the kids and Michelle.

"Why is the door locked? You never lock the doors, Mom!" Ethan shouts out as he plops himself on the couch.

"Yeah, Mom. You *never* lock these doors during the day ... ever!" Michelle adds, her expression telling me she knows exactly why.

"Sorry, my bad. I'll remember that next time." I narrow my eyes at Michelle, before sneaking a glance at Magnus, who's watching on with interest.

"I better get some cooking done. Have fun with your dinner, Michelle." I give her an air kiss and a wave, just as she and Tasha are about to go.

"Hey, Ethan, guess what? We're having burgers for dinner."

"Cool! I'm just gonna be in my room to play, okay?" Ethan shouts out excitedly, before turning to Magnus. "Would *you* like to play with me?"

"Sure, buddy. Then I'm going to go help your mom out. Is that okay?"

Eventually, Magnus comes back to the kitchen while rolling his sleeves up, exposing more of his toned, olive-skinned arms, ready to help.

Even with all the shit I've been through, this is probably one of those moments when I've never felt so lucky in my life.

After dinner, Ethan asks Magnus if he can read for him before he goes to sleep. It throws me off, but in a good way. He's starting to be really good in reading, but he lacks confidence to read in public—only reading to me, or Michelle. So you can imagine my surprise when out of the blue, while in the middle of his burger, Ethan asks Magnus if he can read to him later. Magnus, also surprised, looks to me first, and when he sees me nodding back, he answers, "Of course, buddy. I'm quite honored that you asked me to hear you read."

"Yay!" Ethan cheers, before asking, "What does honored mean?"

"Ah, it means grateful, thankful."

"Mom always tells me she's thankful that I'm her son. That means she's honored to have me?"

"I am, Ethan. Very," I muse as I reach over to squeeze his hand.

"Just as I'm also very honored that your mom seems to like me for some reason," Magnus adds, winking at me.

I smile back at him, saying, "Likewise."

And even with us eating away, Magnus's intense blue eyes are focused only at me, as he regards me with enough love to make my heart swell up to ten times its size.

I feel it all. He makes me feel it all.

And it's beautiful.

God, he's beautiful.

After dinner, with the plates and cutlery in the dishwasher, I help out Ethan get ready for bed, while Magnus is watching the news on TV. Once Ethan is tucked in, we swap over so that he can read a story to Magnus before going to sleep.

I'm watching TV on the couch when Magnus returns, and he pulls me close as soon as he sits down next to me, my head resting comfortably on his chest, with my arms around his waist.

"You know, it's a pretty big deal for him when he asked you to listen in on him reading. He only reads to me and to Michelle."

"I felt very privileged. I don't know what I did to deserve his confidence."

"He was asking for you, even after we broke up."

He gives me a tight squeeze. "Baby," he whispers, as I feel his lips press on my forehead.

I soak in the comfort that kiss gives me, my eyes automatically closing, not realizing that I have just allowed sleep to take over.

***

Thursday came and went in a blur. I kept myself busy at the store to make up for the previous day's fiasco.

Magnus, unfortunately, had to fly to Cali in the late afternoon because of some very urgent issues that needed his presence. As much as I admire and love how hardworking Magnus is, it doesn't mean having him away from me doesn't kill me. He promised he'll be back as soon as possible, but soon just isn't quick enough.

Jacob, on the other hand, had become distant the whole day of Thursday. Sure, he was with me almost all the time, and we'd talk, but there were no more wisecracks, no joking around ... no flirting. The latter, I could accept. Maybe seeing Magnus and me together that way the previous day just brought it home to him. But still ... I missed his friendly, mischievous side. I tried to ask him if everything was okay when he dropped me off after work, even joking that I missed my friend. But he snapped at me, telling me I couldn't have the best of both worlds. When he saw my shocked expression, he backtracked, and he apologized immediately, but he did not explain any further.

By the time I went home after work, Michelle and a not-so-enthused Nathan had gotten ready for Keiko's gig. Because I begged off from attending the exhibition, Michelle insisted that Nathan had to come with her instead. I insisted on taking care of the kids so they could both spend quality time together. This meant having the kids do a sleepover at my place. I kept mum about what Michelle told me, not wanting to say anything to Nathan until he's comfortable enough to let me know about their plans to move.

And now it's Friday, thank goodness. I needed to be normal last night, and I got it by spending the night with the kids. Now I'm ready to have some fun. I'm really looking forward to tonight. This is going to be a girls' night out, in its strictest sense—venting, drinking, bitching ... the works!

I *cannot* wait!

"You look so pretty, Mom. We have the same hair color again," Ethan says while he's sitting on my bed, already wearing his pajamas, and ready for his sleepover tonight, this time at Nathan's.

As soon as Jacob dropped me off this afternoon, I didn't waste any time dying my hair back to my original hair color. It just felt right to finally do it.

"Thanks, honey. I never felt comfortable as a blonde anyway. Now I really look like your mother," I answer back, grinning at my son.

"What do you think of my dress?" I ask Ethan through the reflection at the mirror.

"It's pretty too," he shrugs, unable to hide his growing disinterest, especially now that he's playing with his iPad.

Sighing, I check on myself one more time. Michelle lent me the dress, and I'm not quite sure if it works. It's all black and split in the midsection. The top is long-sleeved and ends just on my stomach. It also shows some cleavage, but not too much, especially since I'm wearing a chunky, gold necklace on top of the necklace which Magnus gave me. The skirt is high-waisted so even with the midrib top, only a thin line of pale skin is exposed. The skirt also ends above the knees, but it's super tight, and it emphasizes my rounded hips and butt. I finish it off with a pair of heeled ankle boots and a gold clutch.

Overall, I think I look good, especially with my auburn hair back, the colors just align really well.

The front door opens, and I hear Michelle's heels clicking on the hardwood floor, towards my bedroom.

"Billie? Let's roll, baby."

Ethan runs out of the room as soon as he hears Michelle's voice, with me not far behind.

"Hey, little man! Nathan and Tash are waiting for you. Say bye to your mom."

Ethan comes back around, just as I lower myself so I can get a big hug.

"Be good, okay?" I whisper to my son, as I enclose him in a tight squeeze.

"I will," he answers. "I hope you have a good night, Mommy."

"I'll do my best. I'll miss you though." I jut my lower lip out, showing him how sad I'll be.

Ethan pats my arm as he gives me a comforting smile. "Don't worry, I'll see you tomorrow. And we're going with Magnus."

"Yes, we are. Good night, my love. Mommy loves you so much."

"Love you too." And with one last kiss, he's off. Not long after, I hear Nathan's voice welcome Ethan inside.

"Ready, gorgeous?" Michelle asks with an excited smile.

Hooking my arm with hers, I answer, "Ready, and by the way," I make it a point to let my eyes wander over her skin-tight number, "you look amazing."

"Well, duh!" And we giggle ourselves out of the room.

I lock the front door behind us, and we head down, where Nathan is waiting at the bottom of the stairs.

"Have fun, ladies. But not too much, alright?" he says, staring right at Michelle.

"Shoot, babe, like you have anything to worry about." She winks at him before giving him a kiss to remember her by.

It makes me miss Magnus even more, so I discreetly look away.

Outside, a limousine is parked in front of the building, with a stocky-looking driver already waiting for us. A guy of equal build, who is also wearing a dark suit, opens the passenger door for us.

When I told Magnus that we were going out tonight, he insisted on having us chauffeured to ensure our safety. I didn't bother protesting. I know how important it is to keep safe right now. The kids have their nightly security detail already parked outside, so it shouldn't come as a surprise that Magnus wanted me and my friends safe as well.

"A girl can seriously get used to this life, Billie," Michelle declares as we take our seats in the car.

I thank the guy before he closes the door, and I turn to Michelle, whispering, "It has its perks, but it also has its downsides."

"Well, I don't know about you, but I'm focusing on the perks," Michelle says amused, as she checks the bar fridge on the side. "Ooohh, girl, there is champagne in this bitch. Look!" She raises a couple of bottles of Krug Grand Cuvee's. "These are off the chain! We *have* to drink this with the girls!"

"Oh hell, yeah!" I answer back, grinning widely.

As soon as Remy, Clara, and Tahni are in the limo, we tear into the first bottle of Krug like nobody's business.

This is already starting to be a great night!

"Hey, Tahni, who's running your kitchen tonight?" I ask the petite chef sipping champagne beside me.

"Rufus, of course. Henry's sleeping over at Ma's tonight. God, I'm just so happy for a break. And I miss you, girl!"

Rufus is Tahni's husband, and also the sous chef of their restaurant. You'd think it would be weird having your wife as your boss, but Rufus has never been the type who is bound by social opinion. He's a cool cat, and he obviously loves his family to no end.

"I miss you too, babe." I give her a sloppy kiss on the cheek. "But enough talk of men, it's all about us girls tonight!"

"Oh, yes. Say it like you mean it, girl!" Remy chips in, as we clink our glasses for yet another toast.

We finally make it to the city, and the limo stops in front of W Club. According to Remy, this place is pretty exclusive, with high-end clientele. So chances of us getting groped at by assholes should be reduced significantly. She scored a membership after a great job, styling for one of the shoots of *Rolling Stones* magazine. And because of that membership, she's able to invite us all.

Stepping inside the club is like stepping inside another era. It's like *The Great Gatsby* in here, with its black and white tones and art deco interiors. Clara tells me it's called W Club, because they mainly serve whiskies of any kind, especially the rare and expensive ones. But they also have alcohol inspired by the book itself.

"Wow, talk about decadent," I whisper, as a leggy blonde wearing a flapper dress sits us over at one of the booths.

Remy remarks, "I know. I like how people here look at me with their noses up in the air like their shits don't stink. They're probably wondering how I managed to score an entry in here."

I have to laugh. Remy's outward appearance can be quite polarizing. You'll either love her, or walk the other way, covering your children's eyes so they don't get any ideas. Her tattoos have increased since I last saw her and so did her piercings. She also dyed her half-shaven hair a bright pink. We love her look though, and Clara finds it sexy as hell. But judging by the way the people here are dressed, it's not surprising that we keep getting stared at.

"Fuck 'em," Michelle blurts out, standing up. "I'm going to the bar. This round's my treat."

We all give our drink orders, and just as Michelle is walking off, the music changes to a song I've never heard before but want to dance to.

"I wanna dance. Who's with me?"

"I am!" Clara chimes in. We slide out of the booth and head straight to the dance floor. Clara's a great dancer, and we dance without a care in the world. We're twirling each other, dancing back-to-back, and just being carefree. Then some men join us, but we shoo them off. A group of jerks attempts to dance with us, and Clara tells them we're not really women. The look on their faces makes us crack up laughing. They eventually realize we are joking, but they are too pissed off that they decide it's not worth it, and they just walk away.

I notice Michelle is back with our drinks, so I grab Clara so we can head back. On our way to the booth, someone bumps against me from behind, and I feel a splash of cold liquid on my back.

"Oops, didn't see you there," a woman's voice laughingly speaks up.

What pisses me off is that she sounds sarcastic.

And it's only when I turn around to confront the bitch, do I realize that this woman did it on purpose.

"That wasn't an accident. You knew it was me."

CHAPTER 24

I'm not sure if it's the alcohol that's giving me the self-confidence, but I'm not about to get treated like a piece of shit by someone like this woman.

I don't owe her any kindness.

Clara steps forward, using her height to stand above the woman who spilt her drink on me, including two of her friends.

"Who the fuck is this bitch? You know her?"

"I happen to be Magnus's wife," her voice is clear, but spiteful.

Clara turns her head towards me, shock registering all over her face.

"Wife? You must be delusional, Martine. You and Magnus had been divorced for over five years. Why don't you just accept *that*? He's moved on, so I suggest you do the same."

"Oh, is that right? I'm delusional? Magnus is only using you. He'll be back in my arms after he's gotten what he wants."

"Bitch, you better back the fuck off before I put my knuckle across your jaw." I catch Martine's frightened reaction at Michelle's intimidation. I'm so focused on Martine that I didn't even notice my friends standing behind me.

We're already drawing attention, and the last thing I want is for our girls' night to be ruined by this wretched woman.

Better put this bitch in her place.

"It's alright, girls. I got this." I step forward, standing tall, even though my best effort is still a few inches shorter than Martine's.

In my calmest of voices, I start to speak up, "Listen well, because I'm not going to repeat myself. I know *everything* because Magnus told me everything. You had your chance with him, and he actually loved you. But you betrayed him in the worst possible way. Yes, I know *that* too. I know what you did to him … how you *blew* it. So maybe you did manage to break us up that one time, but guess what? Thanks to you, we're stronger than ever. And don't you fucking dare make it appear that Magnus is callous and heartless. He's not *you*. You're in a class of your own. So I suggest you walk away before I make you pay for this dress you ruined."

Am I hearing my friends clapping? Holy shit, they are.

Did I just say those words without breaking down? Holy shit, I did.

High-five, Billie.

"Oh, we're not staying," Martine huffs, looking like the pedestal she's standing on has been knocked off her. "It appears the caliber of this club has gone downhill, anyway."

"Must be the stench of your defeat that did it, bitch," Clara adds, and even with my blood boiling, I can't help but laugh.

I have awesome friends.

Just. Awesome.

Martine gives Clara a sideways glance, before turning her attention back to me. "Oh, and by the way, I notice you're wearing a Cartier necklace underneath that gaudy piece of jewelry around your neck. Magnus may have given you an upgraded version of that necklace, but you are not the first person he gave that too." She lifts what appears to be a necklace from under her closely buttoned shirt. As soon as I see it in full view, my breath catches, and the pang in my heart is instantaneous.

The necklace is practically a doppelganger of Magnus's present, except hers has a much simpler design, yellow gold, and with only one band covered in diamonds.

Martine sees my reaction, and with a smug smile she continues on, "That's right, he gave me this necklace when we were together. Now he gives you the same thing? Who knows who else he's given this to, right?" She places her necklace back inside her top. "Well, I hope you have a good night," she says before turning to go.

I'm at a loss for words as I watch Martine and her equally smug minions walk away. What if she's right? What if there are other women out there, walking around with a similar necklace that Magnus gave them?

But on the other hand, Martine's a manipulative bitch, who'll stop at nothing to get Magnus back.

"Girl, that was boss. You owned that bitch!" Michelle places a hand on my shoulder, squeezing it.

"Is she really Magnus's ex-wife? Damn it, I missed most of it. I was in the restroom!" Tahni raises her hands up in frustration.

"Don't worry, I'll tell you everything, blow by blow." Remy places her arm over Tahni's shoulder, as she walks her back to our booth.

"Look, girls, she already left. I just don't want to talk about her anymore. That just felt like high school all over again," I remark.

Clara says, "We're so proud of you, nonetheless, finding the courage to stand up to her like that."

"I've just had enough of her trying to break up Magnus and me." I raise my cocktail, and the girls follow suit. "You know what? The night is young, so let's make the most of it. Let's toast to tonight, to friendship, and to getting rid of toxic people in our lives. Oh, and the next round is on me!"

We clink our glasses, cheering as we take a drink. Then we dance, toast to the most ridiculous things, then we drink some more. I laugh with them, cry happy tears with them, trying to forget the bomb that Martine just threw at me.

All I know right now is that I love Magnus Grant, and he loves me. It will take a lot more than one woman's manipulation to break what we have.

I'm ready to fight for him, for my son, for my life.

No more hiding.

No more running.

But tonight, with my girls, all I'll be doing is drink.

Oh. My God. Why the hell did I drink that much?

I wake up with an extremely bad pounding in my head, my mouth feels like dried fruit, and my whole body feels like it's weighed down.

I don't even need to see my reflection to know that I look how I feel.

Like shit.

I can't even remember how I got home, but I'm going to have to thank Magnus for arranging the chauffeur and the security. Who knows where any of us could've ended up if we didn't have them?

But hold on, is that the blood pumping in my head I'm hearing, or is that really someone knocking at my door?

Knock, knock!

Oh, damn it! I scramble for my phone — it's almost nine in the morning.

The knocking stops, and I hear the sound of footsteps leading to my room. I clutch on my sheets, until I hear Magnus's voice calling for me.

"Isabelle? Nathan let me in." I hear a deep, low tone speak my name, and the butterflies in my stomach immediately respond, fluttering about like crazy.

"There you are, beautiful." Magnus is now standing by the open doorway, looking like he just stepped out of a Ralph Lauren fashion shoot, with his collared shirt, knit sweater, scarf, and pea coat.

Come on. Seriously? No one should look that good at this time of the day, on a weekend, especially when I feel and probably look like a worn-out chew toy.

I pull the sheets further up. "God, why do you look so good in the morning?" I ask, my voice muffled under the sheets, but I don't care. I know I look like the complete opposite of Mr. GQ, over there.

I feel a dip on my bed. "And I missed you too," he answers back with mirth.

Just having him this close is almost torturous. I want to touch him so badly, kiss that lush mouth of his, but I want to at least look presentable when I do.

"I see you've gone back to auburn."

"What? Oh … yeah. I'm so sorry, Magnus, but I've got a massive hangover. I can barely move. And I'm sure I look like roadkill, right now. Could you please wait for me outside while I get ready?" I feel the bed rise once again and hear him leave the room.

I sigh with relief, but relief is immediately replaced with a tinge of dismay. Do I look that bad that he can't stand looking at me?

Great … just great.

I lie in bed for a couple more minutes, trying to find the motivation to get up.

But before long, I hear footsteps coming back to my room. Magnus is back, and the heavenly smell of coffee hits me first.

"Drink some coffee. It'll help."

"Okay, I'll drink it but only when you leave the room. I'm serious, Magnus. I look like shit. And … oh God! I stink!"

But Magnus refuses to leave. Instead, I hear clothes rustling, and my bedroom door locking.

Still with the sheets hiding my face, I hear him padding around the bed and over to the other side. He lifts the sheets, and he lies down behind me. That's when I feel his hand on my shoulder, gently urging me to turn around.

"Don't be shy. It's just me."

"I know it's you. But I can't face you looking like this."

"You think I fell in love with just your face?"

"Ugh, it's not that. I just ..."

"Turn around, Isabelle." The authority in his voice leaves me with no choice but to do as he says. I turn to face him, but I'm still too embarrassed to show my face.

"Don't cover your face. Look at me," Magnus demands.

I reluctantly uncover my face. "See, I look like shit, don't I? My makeup's probably a mess. I can't face your family like this. Remind me to never drink that much again."

"Baby, first of all, you don't look like shit. You never look like shit. My family already loves you, so don't you worry about them. But, you do look like you need a shower. Come on, I'll help you shower." Magnus gets off the bed, his hand holding mine in a gentle, but firm grip.

"You don't have to ... wait, you're, um, undressed." Even with hazy eyes, I can see every single detail Magnus has on show.

It's like a shot of vitamin B on the ass.

"I told you, I'll help you take a shower."

"Are you taking advantage of my vulnerability?" I slowly push myself off the bed, keeping a keen eye on him, you know, just because.

"No."

"Boo! Wrong answer," I answer back, wrinkling my nose at him.

He smirks at me, a wicked gleam in his eyes. "Shower. Now."

I stick my tongue at him, but even with that childish response, I head straight to the shower with him right behind me. And, true to his word, and much to my annoyance, he doesn't take advantage of me at all. Instead, he shampoos my hair, even massaging my scalp. Then, he leans me against him and takes great care in soaping my whole body, even down to the most intimate parts.

When it's time to rinse me off, Magnus turns me around so that we're facing each other, and all I want to do is just stare right at him, taking in the way his brows furrow in concentration, how his lashes catch tiny droplets of water, and how he licks his well-formed lips absentmindedly. When he catches my eye, he gives me a subtle smirk, making my heart skip a beat.

Martine can talk shit all she wants, but surely, this is real.

What Magnus and I have is definitely real.

Feeling refreshed after the shower, I insist that he dresses up while I brush my teeth and dry my hair. It takes me a little longer to find an appropriate 'meet-the-family' outfit, with Magnus just sitting back and watching me with amusement. I finally decide on a pair of black leggings, long black boots, an emerald green top—to hopefully brighten up my eyes—and a black coat, belted at the waist.

"So how do I look? Is this okay to meet your family, or should I change?" I speak to his reflection in the mirror, completely unsure of my choice.

He stands up from my bed and walks up behind me, laying his hands on my hips. "Don't change a single thing."

I feel my cheeks blush, and I realize he might not just be talking about the clothes I'm wearing.

"All set?" he asks.

Thank goodness I packed my overnight bag and Ethan's yesterday.

Speaking of Ethan …

"I better check on my son."

"I'll take the bags to the car. I'm driving us there."

"Okay. Oh, and by the way," I run over to him, and I give him a small, but prolonged kiss. "Thank you," I whisper.

Just as I'm about to pull away, he cups my nape, pulling me back to him. And he kisses me with ten times the intensity, making my toes curl, and my heart flip.

"You're welcome," he answers back with a smile.

It takes a second before I can finally manage to step back, exhaling slowly to regain my composure.

Why do I even bother with drinking alcohol, when Magnus gets me all sorts of drunk with just one kiss?

And I haven't even mentioned how good that kind of hangover feels.

Downstairs, as expected, Michelle is still asleep while Nathan and the kids are up and having breakfast. Ethan is already quite excited with our weekend getaway, so as soon as he sees Magnus waiting by the front door, he hounds him with nonstop questions.

"Where are we going, Magnus? Are we going to have fun there? Is it far?"

Magnus chuckles, "We're going to my family's house upstate, and it is right in front of the beach. Have you been to the beach?"

"We've been to Coney Island," Ethan answers, as he wears his seat belt on, "but I've never tried swimming in the ocean."

"We usually just go to the local YMCA to swim. Even in summer, ocean water can be a little on the cold side," I divulge.

"Well, one of these days, I'll take you both to Hawaii. They have one of the best beaches in the world."

"Magnus ..." I turn to him, brows furrowed. I don't feel comfortable with putting my son's hopes up, unless I know for sure I can fulfil it.

"I'm serious, Isabelle. Do you trust me?" Magnus asks in a low tone, so only I can hear.

I stare back at him before nodding, "Yes."

"Good to know," Magnus states with a smile.

After two and a half hours of driving and almost nonstop conversations ranging from work, to Ethan's favorite Transformers characters, we stop over a quaint café for brunch. After another half an hour on the road, we finally make it to the Grant's family home, to where, I've learned, the East Hamptons is—Further Lane, to be exact. In my years of stay in New York, I've never really been at the Hamptons before, mostly because it's not exactly a place I can afford to spend our weekends at.

The Grant's family estate is breathtaking. Situated by the beach, it is gated, with a long and picturesque, landscaped driveway. The house itself is enormous and very classically designed, complete with shingled roofs ... just like the kind I see on TV or in the movies. There's a fountain right in front of the entrance, and luxury cars are parked around the path.

It's opulent and lavish, and it takes me back to my old stomping grounds back home in Texas.

"Wow," I whisper, surprised at the good energy emanating from the house.

"Oh. My. God." Ethan exclaims, his jaw drooping and his eyes bugging out.

"It's just a house," Magnus mutters as he takes off his seat belt and gets out of the car, then opening the passenger side doors for Ethan and myself.

Ethan wanders around, checking the fountain first, before moving on to another point of interest. So, I follow Magnus, just as he's taking the bags out of the trunk. "I'm sure it's more than just a house, I can tell you had great childhood memories here, the kind that shape you as the person you are now."

His expression softens as he asks, "You can tell that, just by seeing the house for the first time? And what kind of person did this house make me?"

"A good person, Magnus. Definitely, a good person." I tap on his chest to emphasize my point, and before I can pull away, he covers my hand with his, and he stares into my eyes so deeply, that it touches the deepest recesses of my being.

"After all that's happened between us, you still see me that way?" He gives me a crooked smile, making me smile back.

"I never stopped loving you. Even after all that's happened, my heart believes that you *are* good. Maybe if I listened to it more, we probably never broke up."

Magnus drops the bags on the ground, and gathers me in his arms, holding me tightly. And I cling to him, loving the warmth of his embrace, loving *him*.

Just then, one of the double front doors opens, followed by a woman calling out Magnus's name. Surprised, Ethan rushes to my side, and Magnus and I break from our embrace.

"Yay! You finally made it!" Regan approaches us with a big smile and open arms. She hugs her brother first, before turning to me and letting out a squeal of delight, then giving me a hug as well.

"Oooh, I'm so glad you gave my idiot brother another chance, Billie. He's back to being tolerable again."

"Hey, I'm right here, Regan. Can't you at least wait until we're inside before you start throwing insults at me?" He offers his hand to Ethan, which my son takes without hesitation.

"That's my sister, Regan," he tells Ethan, and he carries our bags with his other hand as we make our way up the front door, adding, "and she's usually very nice. Usually."

"Don't listen to him, Ethan." Regan offers Ethan her hand as well. And possibly because Regan is gorgeous, my son chooses her over Magnus. She also takes Ethan's bag, overtaking us as they make their way to the house.

"Come on, don't worry about them. I can show you to your room. It's pretty awesome, and it's got the view of the beach. Oh, and do you know we have an indoor pool? It's heated!" Regan's voice, as well as Ethan's laughter, trail off as they disappear in the huge interior.

"She's great with Ethan," I opine, lacing my fingers with Magnus as we enter the front door.

"She'll make a great pediatrician," he comments proudly.

"Oh, is that what she …" I pause, totally lost for words at the sight before me. I'm only standing at the foyer, and it's already like I've just stepped inside a *Vogue Living* magazine, complete with high ceilings, plush furnishings, and panoramic views of the ocean.

"This house is amazing. And that view," I wave at the windows where I can see the ocean swells from where I'm standing, "you can't get sick of looking at *that*."

With a shrug, Magnus leaves the bags next to one of the large leather couches, and he guides me towards the kitchen with his hand on my lower back.

"This house *is* a work of art, I'm not denying that. My grandfather had this built as a home away from the busy life of Manhattan. But my mom decided to make this as our home base. They only stay in their townhouse in the city when they have an event to go to. Anyway, I'll give you a tour a little later, I promise. Right now, I can hear my mother's voice coming from the kitchen, and she'll kill me if we don't show our faces first."

I swallow slowly as we make our way towards the other end of the house, trying to calm the nerves—as they're starting to get jittery. Magnus must have picked up on it because he starts to rub my back in a soothing way.

"You'll be fine, baby," he calmly assures me.

As soon as we're in the massive kitchen, I can see a tall, lithe woman with dark curls flowing from her back, stirring something in the pot in front of her. Next to her is another woman, who's much older and wearing a uniform. They're joking with each other, their laughter contagious enough to make me smile.

Magnus lets out a cough, and they both turn around, their faces lighting up as soon as they see us.

"Magnus! You're here. And oh, Isabelle, I'm so glad you two are together again! Magnus told me not to talk about it, but for what it's worth, I'm truly sorry for what happened that night." With arms open, just like Regan's earlier, Miranda gracefully walks over, and she gives us both a big hug.

"Mother ..." Magnus warns, before I place a hand on his shoulder, squeezing it to let him know it's okay.

"It was all a big misunderstanding. To be perfectly honest, I should be the one apologizing. I shouldn't have caused a scene."

"You didn't. And even if you did, I wouldn't hold it against you. I'm just glad you two found each other again." She holds both of our hands, sighing. Then, her eyes widen, as if she's reminded of something.

"Where's your son, Isabelle? Magnus told me about him ... Ethan, isn't it?"

"She's actually with Regan. She's giving him the grand tour," I reply, smiling sheepishly.

"Ah, I see," she nods, seemingly satisfied with my answer. "Well, I hope he likes cookies. I baked a couple of batches for him."

"Oh, wow! But you didn't have to go through such an effort—"

"Nonsense, it's my pleasure," Miranda says with a wave of her hand. She looks away, and sighs, "It's been awhile since we've had a child in this house. I remember Magnus running around the halls half-naked, with either his top off, or his pants at the other end of the house."

"She doesn't have to hear that, Mother," Magnus sternly says, with a voice that seems to dissuade Miranda, as she laughs out in a light, airy tone.

And I can't help but laugh with her, thinking how adorable that must have been to see little Magnus Grant running around and being silly.

"Guess who's excited about swimming in the pool?" Regan announces as she finally makes an appearance in the kitchen, with an excited Ethan holding her hand.

"Ah, so this is Ethan! I'm Miranda, Magnus and Regan's mother." Miranda bends down so they are face-to-face. "Did you see the pair of swimming trunks in your room?"

Ethan nods at Miranda, and shyly answers, "Yes, I did. Thank you."

"Swimming trunks?" I ask curiously.

Ethan turns to me with sparks in his eyes. "Mom, I saw their pool, it's awesome! It's inside the house, it's heated, and you can see the beach from there. Can I swim please? I have new trunks in my room. Please, mom? Pleeaase?"

Regan adds, "I told him to ask for your permission first before he can go to the pool. But you don't have to worry, I'll stay with him the whole time."

"If it's not too much to ask, then yes, he can go swimming. Are you sure it's okay for you to keep an eye on him? He knows how to swim, but just in case?"

"Don't you worry, Billie. He's in safe hands. I used to be a lifesaver," she says and smiles proudly, putting my worries at ease.

"And she'll continue to be a lifesaver in the future." Miranda looks on to her daughter with pride, and Regan, in turn, regards her mother with sincere fondness.

Their exchanges leave a sting in my heart. Maybe if my own mother were half as supportive as Miranda is to her children, maybe my life would have turned out differently.

And as my gaze returns to Magnus, I realize that maybe my mother's lack of parenting may have been the best thing that's ever happened to me.

"Where's Father?" Magnus asks his mother.

"Where else? In the study," and Miranda rolls her eyes. "You should let him know you've arrived." She waves her hand towards the direction of what I'm assuming is the study. "I won't keep you any longer. We can chat about our trip to Europe, but I really don't want to be a bore. Dolores and I still have a bit of cooking to do. Make yourself at home, Isabelle ... sorry, Billie," she says, patting my arm lightly. "We'll be here if you need anything, alright?"

"Thank you, Miranda. I really do appreciate the hospitality," I answer, extending my gratitude towards Dolores with a smile.

"Oh, I'm only like this to people I like." Miranda playfully winks at me, before turning back to her task.

Magnus places his hand on my lower back once again, as we make our way to his father's study.

"Your mother is really nice. I can see glimpses of you in her."

"I'll take that as a compliment." Magnus pulls me closer, just as we're standing outside the study. He knocks at the door, and a low, timbered voice tells us to come in.

Carlton is on the phone, standing by the window. Even from afar, I can see that nothing much has physically changed from the first time I met him, except that today, he's wearing a chunky knit, a blue sweater, and jeans. As soon as he sees us come in, he ends the call, putting on a smile, albeit strained.

"Son. Been a while." Carlton closes the distance, and shakes Magnus's hand.

I always find it weird when family members shake hands. My own father did it to his brother, and it always looked awkward.

But then again, my father and my uncle were not exactly chummy either.

"Father, you do remember my girlfriend, Isabelle?"

Carlton turns his attention to me, saying, "Of course. How can I forget such a beautiful face?" He takes my hand and kisses my knuckle, just like the last time. I take my hand back as graciously as I can without being offensive. He may be Magnus's father, and although my reaction is not as bad compared with how I'd react to other men, it's still not my favorite thing in the world.

"I heard you had a great trip to Europe," I tell him.

"Why yes, we did. It was mostly just a skiing trip, but if you ask Miranda, she'll probably say we only went so she could do some shopping. Have you ever been to Austria or Switzerland?"

"No, sir. I've been to Paris and Italy with my family, but that was practically over a decade ago."

Back when Daddy used to spoil me and treat me like a princess.

"Ah, I see. Well, maybe you'll get your chance again, now that you're back with my son. So I suggest you hold on to him tight this time."

"I'm … I'm sorry?" I stutter, unsure whether Magnus's father is being nice, or being sarcastic. But something in the tone of his voice is unsettling me.

Carlton chuckles, "Well, my son is consistently in Forbes's top ten richest bachelors list every year since his divorce, which comes to no surprise. He's extremely successful, and he has the looks that women seem to go for. Don't get me wrong, you are a beautiful woman, but a single mother with a questionable background?" he contemplates, as he shakes his head at me.

I feel my insides turn cold, and I bow my head, the shame of my past, forcing me not to look at him directly.

"Wherever you're going with this, you need to stop." Magnus steps forward, as if shielding me from his own flesh and blood.

"Magnus, *you* need to be more protective of your interests. I'm just trying to make sure you're not wasting your time on—"

"Enough!" Magnus cuts off his father, putting his hand up at him. "You do *not* talk to Isabelle like that, or question her intentions. Ever. Do you understand, or should we just leave this house now?"

"Magnus, it's okay," I insist, holding onto his arm. I notice the opened bottle of scotch on his desk, with an almost empty tumbler beside it. "I don't want to be the cause of any trouble between you two."

"You won't be, baby. He doesn't know who you are, or what you've been through, so he's not entitled to form an opinion about you."

"Have you forgotten whom you're talking to, son?" Carlton's voice rises a notch, a scowl forming on his face.

Magnus takes another step closer towards his father, towering over him. "I know exactly who I'm talking to. You want me to protect my interests, right? So that's what I'm doing right now. *Isabelle* is my main interest, and so is her son. Therefore, I'm guarding them … from you and your spite."

My breath hitches. So this is what it feels like to have the person you love so dearly, defend your honor with no thought of consequence.

Magnus protectively places his arm around my shoulders, and we start to walk out of the room, just as a worried-looking Miranda runs straight inside the study. "What happened? I heard shouting?"

"Father's been drinking again," Magnus whispers as he walks past her mother, who, in turn, sighs out audibly.

"Leave him with me. I'm sorry, dear. He's usually better when he's sober," Miranda's apologetic tone and expression, help calm me down. So I nod back and offer her a faint smile, before leaving the study with Magnus.

I understand what she's saying.

Been there, done that.

"Are you okay?" Magnus asks, still with me in his arms, as we turn the corner, and walk past the kitchen.

"Yes I am. Thank you ... thank you for defending me and my son," I say softly, looking at him with brand-new eyes.

"We can leave if you want to. Just say the word."

"And disappoint your mother and sister? No way."

Magnus pauses and faces me. "So, my father hasn't scared you off?"

"Me? Scared off by a wealthy, intimidating man? I have been surrounded by men like him, almost all my life. I can hold my own. In fact, I actually fell for one of those wealthy, intimidating men."

"Really?" He circles his arms around my shoulders, raising his brow as he looks down at me.

"Only because he's hot," I answer with a shrug.

He cocks his brows. "Hot?"

"Well, I'm not repeating that."

He chuckles, then lays a kiss on my temple. "Speaking of hot, want to go for a swim in the pool?"

"Um, I didn't bring a bathing suit."

He wiggles his brows at me suggestively. I laugh out aloud, before slapping his chest. "I'm not skinny-dipping with you, especially since my son and your sister are swimming there with us. That's just wrong in so many levels!"

Magnus laughs out, and his whole face brightens, making me giggle.

I don't even notice that Magnus is leading me upstairs, since my focus has been solely on him. And only when he opens the door, do I realize that we are now in his bedroom.

And holy cow, what a bedroom!

It's bigger than my two-bedroom apartment, with two French doors opening to a balcony overlooking the ocean.

"This … is …" is all I can manage to say. The room is furnished in the same neutral colors as the rest of the house, and yet, Magnus has clearly put a stamp on this one. The bed is enormous, with some artworks hanging on the walls, which remind me of the pieces of art in his penthouse.

Oh, and speaking of the bed, laid at the center are two sets of ladies' bathing suits—one of them is a conservative, black one-piece, while the other is just two scraps of red Lycra. I lift up a piece that is supposed to be the bikini bottom, waving it at him questioningly.

"What the heck is this?"

Magnus stands in front of me, his hands clasping my waist, and pulling me closer to him. "Wear the one-piece today. That one's for us … tonight."

"But there's not much of me to cover with these."

"Exactly. That's why I bought it, then had it sent to this address. Just thinking about you, wearing that bikini is already making my cock hard." He presses his crotch against my belly, boldly confirming his statement.

"Well, I better wear the family-friendly swimsuit then." Smiling coyly, I playfully push myself off him, taking the top half of my clothing off, except for my bra. Magnus watches me, as he saunters off to his walk-in closet, coming back out, holding a pair of swimming shorts. I shimmy off of my leggings, before grabbing the black suit, silently grateful that I waxed where I needed to.

I can't help but watch Magnus, as he starts taking off layers of his clothing. He catches me and smirks, but he doesn't stop until he's down to his underwear.

His body, with muscles cut in the right places, is so perfect that I find myself licking my lips instinctively, checking to make sure I'm not drooling.

"Turn around," he says in a thick, low tone. I follow without protest.

I feel him coming near me, stopping only a couple of inches away. He moves my hair and swings it over my shoulder, his fingertips leaving a hot trail on my skin. The same fingers are now on my bra, and they deftly unhook the strap. With two hands, he slides the flimsy material over my shoulders, down to my arms until they fall on the floor. I breathe in quick, shallow successions, the anticipation of his next move making my mind reel.

I feel his lips on my shoulder, his warm breath tickling my skin. His kisses travel down, tracing the valley on the lower part of my back.

He slides my panties down, joining my bra on the floor. With his hands now flat on my back, he urges me to bend down, with my hands on the bed, and my feet, flat on the floor.

"God, you're beautiful from every angle," he growls, making me giddy from his touch and adulation. His hands make their way down, stopping just at my hips, holding me steady. I suck in my breath the moment I feel his tongue glide over my sex. Then his tongue flickers over my clit, teasing it, and making me moan from the shots of pleasure.

Then he moves his hands over my ass, squeezing the cheeks to the point of pain. "Oh, God!" I whisper, welcoming the pain and the pleasure it brings.

I want him inside of me now. My insides are already clenching, and it's only a matter of time before he brings me to climax.

So, with him still holding me, I stand myself up, turning around to face him.

Oh, my.

The hunger in his darkened blue eyes takes my breath away.

"I want to come with you inside of me," I hear myself speak the words, but too mesmerized by his eyes, his face, and his glistening lips.

Unable to help myself, I go on my tiptoes, lifting my head so I can kiss him, the tip of my tongue licking around his lips, tasting what he just tasted.

I realize he's taken off his boxer briefs because his hot, hard length is now pressing against my stomach.

I'm still lost in our kisses when Magnus suddenly lifts me up, letting my legs wrap around his waist. He crawls over the bed, laying me right in the middle. He pushes up slightly, staring at me, while I stare back at him with equal desire.

His knuckles brush gently on my cheek, his touch is so tender that my eyes instantly close. My hands move up to his arms, loving the feel of his sinews under the palms of my hands. Then I fist my fingers in his hair, pulling him down so he can kiss me once more.

And then, without notice, Magnus enters me, making me moan against his lips, as he fills me up wholly, stretching me inside like only his cock can do.

"I can never get over how good you feel around me," he whispers against my lips, as he slowly begins to thrust inside.

"Take me there, Magnus," I answer back with pleading eyes.

"I will … and I want you to feel it."

I cry out at the strength of his first thrust, his cock hitting my very core with every consecutive undulation of his hips. The sting makes the walls of my pussy clench around him, making us both cry out in shock and in bliss.

It doesn't take long before I reach that peak, my cries of ecstasy, now muffled by the pressure of his lips on mine.

I'm still coming down from the high, just as Magnus's thrusts escalate in speed. He is so close. I can see it in the way his handsome face winces, in the way his eyes are glazed as he focuses on me, and the way his whole body goes rigid.

"Fuck!" Magnus roars out, and in one last, deep plunge, he climaxes. His thrusting becomes short and shallow, as he empties himself inside of me. Then he dips his head and kisses me with a tender passion that makes my toes curl.

"That was amazing," I sigh out, trying to get my heart rate to slow down.

"You're welcome," he smirks back. The smirk turns to laughter as soon as he sees my reaction.

"Arrogant 'till the end," I tease, shaking my head in mock disappointment.

"It's just confidence, which you know, I can back up," he insists, smiling teasingly as he plunges inside of me one last time, instantly making me moan.

But when he raises his brows at me, as if he's just proven his point, I roll my eyes back in response, "Whatever, I still love you anyway."

"And I. Love. You." Magnus kisses me with every word, before carefully pulling himself out. He gets off the bed, and jogs to the en suite, with me enjoying the sight of his ass in action. He returns with a damp towel, so I open my legs, knowing exactly what he'll do next.

I'm dressed in my family-friendly bathing suit in no time, making me giggle on the inside knowing we just did something not so wholesome a few minutes ago. Magnus is only wearing his swimming shorts, and as I follow him across the house to the pool, I'm doing a little happy dance in my head because someone this hot actually wants someone like me.

I can hear Ethan laughing already, with the constant sounds of water splashing. When we get there, I see Ethan splashing water at Regan, while Regan seems unsuccessful in defending herself.

"Thank goodness you guys are here! Rescue me from this water-bot!" Regan pretends to swim away from Ethan, who laughingly chases her the best way he can.

"Sorry, Regan. I'm with the water-bot on this one." Magnus gracefully dives in, then, he rises up to dunk Regan underwater.

Who'd have thought that Magnus could be this playful? It's an eye-opener for sure, and I love seeing this side of him.

I'm just sitting at the edge of the pool, watching the three, roughhouse each other while my legs are wading in the heated water.

"C'mon, Mom ... join us," Ethan asks as he waves at me excitedly. "You can be in Regan's team. She's human, so you can be human too. Magnus and I will be water-bots."

Magnus leisurely swims towards me, then he pulls himself up, like one of those hot male models you see in ads that do it in slow motion.

Those male models have nothing on Magnus.

Not. A. Thing.

"Yes. C'mon, Mom. Swim with us." Magnus places a wet arm around me, his chin on my shoulder.

How someone can look equally hot while brooding in a suit, can look completely adorable while wet, and half-naked is beyond me. But this man seems to handle these transitions with ease.

"Did you just call me Mom?" I ask, turning to him, and half-smiling. I hear a lot of fathers calling their wives 'Mom' or 'Mommy,' just like their children. Weird as it may sound coming from Magnus, I like it ... a whole lot.

It's actually scary how much it thrills me to hear him say it.

"You don't like it?"

"I didn't say that," I answer, smiling back at him.

He smiles back, but his eyes betray the mischief behind it. Before I can react, he jumps in the water, taking me with him.

I shriek as soon as my ass leaves the ledge, and I plunge underwater. Strong arms pull me back up, just as I hear Ethan and Regan guffawing.

"That's mean, Magnus," I nudge at his chest, but he holds me firmly, a smug smile on his face.

"I can't believe you didn't see that coming," he remarks.

"Oh, you'll pay for that Mr. Grant. Trust me." I lean closer, my lips against his ear, "Who knows, maybe I won't join you in my bikini tonight." That's when I push off, swimming away from him, smiling smugly and enjoying his gaped-mouthed expression immensely.

"Well, well, doesn't this look cozy?" the sarcastic, but familiar voice, sends me crashing back on the ground.

I turn towards the voice, where none other than Martine is standing with her arm hooked around Gerald.

"I was in the neighborhood. My friends and I are spending the weekend at the family estate. I heard Miranda and Carlton are back from their trip so I thought I'd drop by. I hope it's okay?" Martine asks a little too sweetly for it to be sincere. But her eyes are only set on Magnus.

And Magnus ... it's a shot in the dark what's running in his mind at this moment. His expression is unreadable as he looks on. Ethan swims closer to where I am, and I reach out to hold him in my arms.

"You came with Ger?" Regan asks, her tone suspicious.

"No, I actually saw her car pulling up, so, as gracious as a gentleman that I am, I offered to escort her to see our parents." Gerald and Martine both chuckle like it's some shared, private joke.

"Well, Mom's in the kitchen, and Dad's in his study, as always," Regan says, pointing beyond the doorway. "You can say hi to them there."

Am I noting a hint of hostility in Regan's voice? Or am I just hoping it?

"Thanks, Regan. Let's catch up soon, yes?" Martine gives her a saccharine smile, then she completely ignores me as she focuses back on Magnus. "And Magnus, aren't you even going to say anything to me?" she asks with a pout.

I glance over at Magnus, and I can see his scowl forming, and yet, he's been silent this whole time. He turns to me, and the scowl on his face is now replaced with a calming smile, instantly easing my nerves.

"Next time, call first. Good-bye, Martine." And without a final glance at Martine, he swims closer to me, stopping with his back almost facing her.

"Are you alright?" he whispers to me.

"I am now," I answer, unable to stop smiling.

On the other hand, Martine's reaction is the incensed, open-mouthed kind.

"Oh … burn!" Regan whispers, chuckling.

"I think Martine deserves an apology. She's nice enough to come over and say hi, and this is how you treat her?" Gerald scoffs.

"And I don't know what she told you," Martine adds, "but your girlfriend and her friends threatened me and my girlfriends last night. That's why we're here so we can de-stress. *She* should apologize to *me*."

My blood runs cold. My son is right here, and Martine is telling flat-out lies about me! I hold my son closer, who by now is beginning to feel anxious.

"Mommy, why are they shouting?" Ethan mumbles, holding on to my waist.

"You didn't tell me you saw Martine last night," Magnus whispers at me.

To avoid Ethan from feeling more anxious, I answer back in the calmest voice I can muster, "Yes, I did see her, and I'm not going to talk about that with my son here. There's a lot more to the story than what she's implying. Yes, I fought back, but I was *not* the aggressor. And I'm not going to allow my son to hear any more of these lies. It's not fair to him." I swim my way to the steps with Ethan in tow.

"Regan, can you deal with this, please?" I hear Magnus instructs Regan, as he follows us out of the pool.

"Gladly," she answers back.

Magnus makes his way up the pool steps, grabbing two folded towels off the table and handing Ethan and me, one each, and another one for himself. Regan follows as well, taking a towel and walking towards Gerald and Martine.

"Okay, okay, there's way too much drama in here. I'll come with you two and we can all go to Mom and Dad, okay?" Regan lays an arm on each of their shoulders and turns them around. As they start walking out, I hear them complaining about getting their clothes wet.

It's actually funny, if I wasn't so upset.

"Mom, who are they?"

Magnus answers for me, "That's Gerald, my younger brother, and Martine, my ex-wife."

"Magnus," I warn, but Magnus offers me a reassuring smile.

"You're married?" Ethan asks, bug-eyed.

"No, not in a long while, buddy."

"Okay. Is that why you're with Mom?" he persists.

Oh, dear. "Ethan …"

"Yup, that's why I'm with your mom. And I hope to be with your mom for a long, long time. Now who's hungry?"

"I am!" Ethan raises his hand.

"Let's go and change then, so we can have some lunch," I add, while drying him off with the towel. Getting another dry one, I wrap it around him like a cocoon. "Here, wrap this around you, so you won't feel too cold."

He does what I say and starts to walk past us.

"This isn't how I expected this weekend to be," Magnus tells me quietly, as he wraps a towel around his hips, leaving his now dry, upper torso, bare. "I'm sorry, about my father, and now this."

"You don't have to apologize, Magnus. *I'm* sorry I hadn't told you about Martine. But if I told you what happened last night, it'll end up with us fighting." With a towel around my waist, I start to walk off, but Magnus grabs my hand, preventing me from moving forward.

"Fighting? Why would we end up fighting?"

With a deep breath, I turn around, holding the necklace he gave me.

"Because of this." I lift the necklace up, trying to hold my anger to a simmer. "She showed me the necklace you gave her. It's the same, Magnus. Exactly, how many women did you give this kind of necklace to?" I sigh, trying to walk away again, but his hold on my hand is firm.

"What? She must have bought it from the store. The necklace I gave you is Cartier's signature design, and it's readily available in store. But I had yours especially made with yellow diamonds. You have a one-of-a-kind design. Only you have it. Just. You," he pauses, looking away. "I was never the sentimental type ... even when I was married. It wasn't my thing."

He brushes my cheek with the back of his hand, before taking the pendant with his fingers. "But with you, it's just different. I needed you to know how much I love you, to be reminded every day, even if I'm not around. I just hope Martine didn't ruin that for us."

Shaking my head, I answer back, "She didn't, no matter how hard she tried. But this needs to stop. I know she's still your friend, and I shouldn't impose, but it's so obvious that she wants you back. She told *you* flat out that she wants you back, and what if she ..."

I can't continue anymore. I'm too afraid to say the words. Magnus laces his fingers with mine, and I let it happen. With hands held, he tips my chin up so I can face him.

"Why are you even entertaining the idea? She will never have me again. You *have* me." His fingertips move down to graze over the necklace. "This necklace is your reminder. I still do business with her father, but if it means your happiness, then I'll cut ties with him as well."

"I didn't ask for that, I just—"

"I'll do it because I'd rather lose the money, than lose you," he stops midway and cups my face with his hands. "I can get the money back elsewhere. That part is easy. But I can't afford to lose you, Isabelle. I'd rather get rid of everything I own, rather than lose you. I just love you too fucking much."

I hold on to his arms, my heart beating fast and tightening all at once.

How could someone this amazing, love someone like me?

"You won't lose me, Magnus. I won't let you."

He closes his eyes, bowing his head so it touches mine. We stay like this, hearing each other breathe. The silence is only broken by Ethan's voice calling for us and telling us he's hungry.

"Welcome to my life," I groan out, rolling my eyes, then smacking the palm of my hand on my face.

Magnus grins as he playfully plants his arm around my shoulders. "Come on. Let's get dressed so we can feed your water-bot."

Ethan's room is just a door down from us, which also happens to be Magnus's childhood room. It's a definitive boy's bedroom, with green and blue hues, lots of sports paraphernalia, and toys still neatly kept on shelves. Miranda apparently kept all of the kids' rooms intact, and according to Magnus, it's mostly because she wants her future grandkids to have a room to stay in when they're visiting their nana and pop.

It's a good thing Magnus and Regan take after their mother. Yes, she may be borderline presumptuous, as is Magnus, but her intentions come from a good place.

Martine is thankfully gone by the time we've showered and dressed up. Miranda insisted that we all eat lunch together, so here we are, seated rather awkwardly around their huge dining table, with the sound of the waves breaking some of the silence. To Miranda's benefit, the food is fantastic and all inspired by their trips to Austria and Switzerland.

Thankfully, Regan's gift of the gab pretty much saves lunch, even helping Ethan come out of his shell more. Carlton seems less hostile, and he keeps to himself during the lunch, only speaking with Gerald most of the time. Miranda seems more interested in getting to know more about me, which, normally, would be quite flattering. But I can only elude so much of her questions without them getting suspicious. I know that in the coming weeks, they will come to know exactly who I am, and what I've been through, including who is Ethan's real father. How they'll react when they find out really scares the shit out of me, because it can be a deal breaker for most people.

The rest of the afternoon is spent doing absolutely nothing, and it's great. Magnus decides to take Ethan out for some sledding. It's something my son has never done before, so naturally, he jumps at the chance. Regan uses the downtime to study and FaceTime her boyfriend. Miranda is already preparing dinner with Dolores, while Carlton and Gerald decide to go to the local country club, Maidstone, which is just as well, since I don't think I can handle another confrontation with either one of them.

As for myself, I'm at the balcony of Magnus's bedroom, seated on one of those fancy egg chairs, all rugged up with hot chocolate and Miranda's cookies, an open romance novel in hand. And as I look out towards the sea, I can't help but smile.

This feels perfect.

So I take all of these and store them into memory. Who knows when, if ever, I'll get to experience this kind of serenity again?

I haven't really checked my phone in the whole time since I got here, and when I do so, I see two missed calls and a couple of voice mails, one from Michelle, asking how it is living the pimp life in the Hamptons. There's one from Jacob, who just wanted to check up on me, which I find quite sweet and surprising—especially after the way he snapped at me.

Suddenly, cold, icy wind forces me to go back inside the house. Maybe I'll help Miranda and Dolores with the cooking. Yes, that will be a perfect opportunity for me to get to know Magnus's mother a little more.

So I head straight to the kitchen, offering my services to the women who seem to already have things handled in the kitchen. But they welcome me wholeheartedly, with Miranda happily getting me to work in no time at all.

Miranda is an amazing woman. Cooking alongside with her and Dolores, without the awkward dynamics between the Grant men, is quite enlightening.

She wasn't born into money, I've learned. In fact, she was from the Bronx, born and bred, with parents who are Greek immigrants. But she dreamed of becoming a dancer since she was a little girl. It wasn't easy, especially since she had two other siblings with parents who worked two jobs each so they could support their ambitions and put food in their stomachs. At a young age, she subsidized her ballet lessons by working part-time at a local store. But her natural talent and persistence paid off. She got accepted with a full scholarship at Julliard, and she rose up the cutthroat ranks and became a prima ballerina.

She met Carlton when he watched her show, the *Swan Lake*. He was actually there with another date, surprisingly. But he decided to cut his date short, and he waited at the backstage to meet her. Miranda jokes it was lust at first sight on Carlton's side, but to be honest, I zone out that part. They got married after six months of courtship, then, she retired after giving birth to Magnus three years later, so she could take care of him full time, with little to no help from nannies.

"It was practically a whirlwind affair," Miranda says dreamily as she looks out into the ocean. "There was just something about him that I just couldn't shake out of my system. Until now, I'm still trying to figure it out." She shakes her head and chuckles softly, and so does Dolores.

"How was Carlton then?" I ask, wondering what happened to him through the years that turned him into a bitter man.

"You wouldn't have known it, just by looking at him now, but he was actually quite the rebel."

"We're talking about the same Carlton here?" I ask jokingly.

"Yes," Miranda says, nodding. "He didn't really want to work as his father's lackey, so he worked as a barman for some time when he was younger. Unfortunately, it also got him hooked to hard liquor. It got so bad for him at one point that his family had to step in to help him sober up. To show his gratitude, he started working for his father, and he actually realized that it was what he wanted to do. He took the helm before his father died. And now, he's grooming Gerald, since his firstborn—your boyfriend—decided to do his own thing. I think Carlton saw a lot of himself in Magnus, especially his need to find his own way, professionally. But where Carlton failed, Magnus succeeded. Maybe, I don't know, that's why he's extremely protective of him. But he's a good man, Billie. Once you truly get to know him."

"I hope he gives me a chance to get to know him."

"He will. That man is as bullheaded as his son. That's why they get into these disagreements all the time. They're alike in a lot of ways."

I'm cutting some carrots, listening to her talk about Carlton, and from the tone of her voice, it's obvious that she's still head over heels in love with him.

But as much as I want him to see that I'm actually good for his son, I have a feeling his hostility towards me will just get worse in the weeks ahead.

"I must be boring you already with my nonstop talk about my husband!" Miranda exclaims, sounding apologetic.

Oh no, she must have mistaken my lack of response with boredom.

"No, I love hearing about other people's love stories. I think yours is absolutely beautiful," I counter, offering a smile.

She comes over and gently places a hand on my shoulder, her voice soft and understanding, "You and Magnus are still writing your own love story. I know it's been rough these past few months because I saw how it affected Magnus. I don't know the whys and the hows because I feel it's not my business to ask. But I'm glad you gave him another chance. You're good for him."

"You—you think so? I mean, we haven't really been together that long."

"The length of time you've been together is never an indication of your strength as a couple. You've met Martine, obviously. And all I can say is … good riddance. We may be friends with her family, but I never felt at ease with her. It took Magnus quite a while to figure that out, but I'm glad when he finally did. Otherwise, he wouldn't have found you. And Regan told me what she just did this morning. I'm so sorry about that. And I'm also sorry about Gerald, and even Carlton's behavior towards you. Sometimes Carlton needs to be reminded about our own history." She offers me a kind smile, her eyes twinkling against the light.

Like I said earlier, this woman is amazing. I feel like giving her a big hug.

So throwing caution in the wind, I wrap my arms around her, as I say, "Thank you … for being so nice to me." I blink back the tears threatening to descend.

My own mother never showed me this kind of compassion.

But whether or not she feels the same way after she finds out my past is something I'm not ready to think about.

Just then, I hear Magnus's and Ethan's voices. It looks like they've come back from their sledding escapade.

"It's decided. I have officially found my sledding buddy." Magnus gives his mother a peck on the cheek, Dolores a squeeze on the shoulder, and me, a tender kiss on the lips.

And it's yummy as always.

"Did you have fun, honey?" I ask, placing the chopped carrots on the plate beside the chopping board.

Ethan answers excitedly, "Yes! And I went down the hill so fast, so many times and only fell off twice!"

"Looks like this little guy is hooked," Miranda cheers, clapping her hands. "Well, Billie, thank you for your help, but you're still a guest of the house, so go on and have fun with your boys and we'll do the rest of the cooking." She gives me a playful wink, before shooing me off.

The three of us relocate to the games room, where we decide to play an old-fashioned game of *Monopoly* by the warmth of the fireplace. I try to teach Ethan how to play it, but he prefers to watch us play first. Regan joins us not long after, having thrown in the towel with whatever it is she's studying for tonight.

She throws the dice, then, looks over at her brother curiously. "I've not seen you check your phone, or call someone about work today. What's up with that?"

"It's Saturday."

"Exactly. You used to be on call, twenty-four seven. It didn't matter what day it was, or who you were with, it was work, work, work with you. So, I'm going to repeat my question. What's up, big brother?"

"Nothing's up. I just want to enjoy my downtime." Magnus avoids looking at me, staring at the board instead.

"Downtime was never in your vocab. I think you're turning a new leaf, Magnus." Regan turns her attention to me, "And I think I have you to thank, Billie."

"What? Why? What'd I do?" I ask, thoroughly confused.

"He doesn't prioritize work as much as he used to. And I think it's because you cast a voodoo spell on him. It's a beautiful thing, so keep it up!"

I look over at Magnus, who must have felt my eyes on him because he stares back at me with a hint of a smile on his face.

"Is that true?" I ask Magnus.

It's his turn on the board. He throws the dice and answers without looking at me, "My priorities may have changed, yes." Once he moves his token, he continues, giving me a sidelong glance, "But it's not exactly a hard decision to make."

I think I may have melted just a little bit right now.

We didn't get a chance to finish the game since Dolores announces that it's time for dinner.

Carlton and Gerald are back, and they seem to be in better spirits. I'm not sure if the talk Miranda gave them after lunch was the key, but they're even civil with me. Regan and Miranda keep the conversation flowing, while Ethan is happily eating his dinner of veal schnitzel and cheesy spaetzle.

Magnus, however, is a different story. I don't know what it is, but he seems quieter, even distant. Sure, he joins in on the conversations, even squeezing my thigh once in a while. But when he smiles, he seems far away from here, distracted.

I wonder if something's happened that has gotten him worried. Or is he itching to check his work messages and e-mails, but he couldn't do so since I'm with him? People don't just change their ways so quickly, right? Maybe I'll ask him later, when I get to speak with him alone.

I help Miranda clear the plates, even though she tells me that I don't need to do so since I'm a guest. I insist, saying it's the least that I can do for her, for showing Ethan and myself so much kindness during our stay.

After the cleanup, as I'm about to head back to the games room to hang out with Ethan, I hear voices coming from another room, next to the kitchen. They're Magnus's and Regan's voices, and they seem to be having an argument. I want to leave them to it, thinking it's none of my business.

Until Magnus mentions my name.

Maybe I should have learned my lesson, but unfortunately, my curiosity wins out, so I tiptoe close enough so I can hear what they're saying, placing myself in a spot where I won't be seen.

"But you two just got back together," I hear Regan speaks out.

"And what's your point?" Magnus asks.

"What if she freaks out? You might scare her off again. "

"I know it's a huge risk, but it's not something that can wait."

"I like her, Magnus. Why are you in such a hurry anyway? What if you lose her again?"

"That's why I need you to keep this between us, at least for tonight. I just need to figure out how to do this without upsetting her or making her want to run."

"Okay, I will. I just hope you know what you're doing."

I make my way to the games room in haste, my heart beating fast, and my head throbbing.

What did I just hear back then? What is Magnus keeping from me?

And God, why does it sound like something awful is going to happen to me?

I think I'm going to be sick.

Stop overthinking this, Billie.

No. I heard what I heard, and it sounds awful.

Is it Cooper? Is he here, and he's not telling me? Or does it concern Martine?

It sounds bad enough that even Regan thinks I might freak out.

What. The hell. Is going on?

I can't ask Magnus because he'll know I listened in on a private conversation.

Why does this feel like déjà vu?

Ethan is showing me something from his iPad, and I go through the motions of nodding and speaking monosyllabic words. But my mind is racing, thinking the worst will happen very shortly.

Magnus enters the room, with no Regan in sight. His brows are slightly furrowed, but as soon as he sees me, the worry lines disappear, replaced by a smile that can easily melt any woman with a pulse.

I try to smile back, but on the inside I'm worried, with awful scenarios in my head, of us breaking up once again.

What are you hiding from me, Magnus?

"There you are. I've been looking for you."

Sure you were.

"I helped Miranda out, then came straight in here."

He sits beside me, draping an arm over my shoulder.

"You know what, it's getting late. I'm going to get Ethan ready for bed, okay?" I try to stand up, but he gently squeezes my shoulder, leaning closer to my ear.

"I can't wait to see you wearing your bikini in the hot tub."

I pause for a second, before replying, "Actually, I'm feeling kind of tired tonight. Maybe next time?"

He tips his head, studying me with curiosity. "Is everything okay? What's wrong, baby?"

"Nothing," I answer, shaking my head. "I really am tired."

I turn my attention to Ethan. "Honey, let's get you to bed, okay? We have a long trip back home tomorrow."

"But I'm not tired yet," Ethan whines back.

"You will be tomorrow, if you don't sleep now."

Ethan gives me a small pout, but he does what I ask, following behind me.

"Good night, Ethan," I hear Magnus say.

Ethan stops and jogs back to Magnus, giving him a hug.

"Thanks for taking me sledding, Magnus. It was freezing, but I had fun."

"Glad you enjoyed it, little man."

It tugs at my heart and right now, I hate that it does because I don't know if after this weekend, they will do anything together again. After Magnus pats him on the back, Ethan pulls away and comes back to me.

Magnus watches on, leaning forward, with elbows on his thighs, and his hands clasped together. Then his eyes focus on me, his lips are slightly open, like he wants to tell me something, but is holding back. And as for me, all I want to do is kiss those lips of his. Instead, I offer him a polite smile, leaving the room with Ethan as quickly as my legs can take me, without looking suspicious.

After Ethan is showered and tucked in bed, I take a seat on an armchair next to him so I can read him a story from one of Magnus's old books. I watch my son as he eventually gives in to sleep, and I can't help but smile as his breathing starts to even out, and his face, a picture of serenity.

He's happy, and he was radiating it the moment he came back from sledding with Magnus. Magnus took the time to get to know him, to bond with him, and I know that that kind of male bonding is what was lacking in my otherwise perfect relationship with my son.

I just hope this doesn't end up becoming another heartbreak for him. I don't know how I'd cope if that happens.

How long I've been sitting next to Ethan is beyond me, but I must have fallen asleep. Suddenly, I feel myself being lifted off the seat and carried by strong arms. My eyes flutter open, and I see Magnus looking straight ahead, taking me back to our bedroom.

"Magnus," I whisper, "you don't have to carry me."

"You're sleeping in our bed … with me. If I have to carry you to make sure that's happening, I'd gladly do it."

Magnus lays me down on the bed and takes my shoes off. Then he pulls the sheets over me. He bends down so his face is inches from mine. He doesn't speak a word, but just gazes into my eyes. There's a nervous energy about him, and it kills me that he can't tell me what it is.

Before I can ask him, he leans over and kisses my forehead tenderly.

"Good night, my beautiful temptress. I love you ... so much," he whispers, before standing up and disappearing into the en suite.

I hear him turn on the shower, as I lay there, staring at the ceiling, replaying the conversation I overheard just over an hour ago.

What is Magnus hiding from me? And why is he hiding something from me at all? I thought we were done keeping secrets?

What if his secret is truly horrible that it might drive me away?

On the other hand, when I told him about my own horrible secret, he stayed. He didn't run away from me. Not only that, he vowed to protect me.

And even when I broke up with him, and I didn't want to have anything to do with him, he continued to protect me.

All because he loves me.

He. Loves. Me.

And how do I repay his love?

By running away from him at the slightest hint of trouble.

I can be such an asshole.

An asshole, with serious trust issues.

But I'm also an asshole who loves Magnus with all my heart.

I jump out of the bed, and I quickly take my clothes off. Now completely naked, I head towards the en suite, which has now become steamy from the shower. There, I can see Magnus, naked in all his muscular glory, his hands covering his face, as water trickles down his body.

I open the shower door, and Magnus turns around to face me as soon as I'm inside. The shower is huge, so I take a few steps to close our distance. He stands still, as my hands slide up from his abs to his chest, locking my fingers at the nape of his neck.

"I thought you wanted to sleep," he says in a low, yet slightly surprised tone.

"I did. But I realized that I wanted you more." I tip my head up, opening my lips slightly as an invitation for him to kiss me.

Magnus doesn't make me wait, smashing his lips onto mine with so much passion that it takes my breath away. He moves me further from the water, leaning me against the glass screen.

"I love you too, Magnus," I mumble against his lips, my arms now hooked under his arms, my hands clinging desperately on his back. "I just want you to know I love you so much."

Magnus cups the side of my neck as his kisses become deeper, his tongue chasing my own, then suckling it, and making me moan. Then he moves to the side of my neck, licking the droplets of water, mumbling, "I know," every so often and making my insides clench.

He snatches my wrists and holds them above my head with one hand, while the other hand starts moving downwards. He plays with my breasts, tweaking my hard nipples, as he continues to kiss me. His fingers find my apex, and he proceeds to work his magic. I suck in my breath, my entire body feeling the little shocks of electricity. He smiles against my mouth before slightly pulling away. He's giving me that killer smirk, his eyes locked with mine, as his fingers continue their wicked ways against my sex.

He can tell I'm close, from the way I'm moaning, and the way my hips involuntarily jerk in response to him. His smirk is now gone, replaced with intense focus at giving me pleasure.

I try to reach for his cock, wanting him to feel the same satisfaction he's giving me, but he shakes his head, not letting me to do so. "No, I'll do the touching for now. I want you to come so damn hard, that when I'm finally inside of you, I'll still feel your pussy trembling around my cock. So come hard for me, baby."

"Oh, God!" And like a marionette to its puppeteer, I succumb to Magnus's demand. I whimper as my whole body rocks from my climax, then cry out, as soon as I feel Magnus's hard cock inside of me. He lets go of my wrists so he can lift both of my legs, plunging himself deeper.

"So good, baby. You feel so fucking good, it's driving me insane," he groans against my neck.

"I thought I'm the crazy one," I breathe out, as I hold onto him tightly.

This position may not be easy for him, but Magnus's every thrust is strong and relentless, with no signs of slowing down.

"As long as you're crazy for me, baby. Just. Me." After a number of strong thrusts, his body goes rigid. Then he groans out my name as he climaxes, making me feel every twitch of his cock, as he empties himself inside of me.

After a few moments of catching our breaths, he pulls out, and he helps me on my feet, before kissing me once again.

He pulls me back under the shower, so we can shampoo each other's hair, treating each other with back scrubs, then towel-drying each other off. After brushing our own teeth, he leads me back to bed, holding me snugly in the crook of his arm.

It's the sort of thing normal couples do.

I know I still have that issue about Magnus's secret to worry about, but right now, as he holds me close before we sleep, I know that I love him enough not to run away from him so easily.

I have to take that leap of faith, to trust in his love. He did so with me. It's time for me to do the same.

***

"Wake up Isabelle. Baby ... wake up." I hear Magnus's voice against my ear, followed by kisses on my bare shoulder.

I open my heavy lids, only managing to squint. The room is still dark, so it must still be in the middle of the night. I turn to face Magnus, and I'm surprised to see him fully dressed in warm clothing.

"Why are you dressed? Where are you going?" I ask with some apprehension.

"I want to show you something."

"What time is it? It's still dark outside."

"It's almost the crack of dawn. Come on, I'll help you get dressed."

"But why? Can't it wait until later, around the time when most civilized people wake up?"

He stands up, offering me his hand. "Please, Isabelle."

He seems a little on the edge, nervous even. That and the expression on his face are enough for me to take him seriously.

"Okay, okay, just give me a second." Holding on to his hand, he helps me get up from the bed.

"Your clothes are ready for you to wear. But you can change them if you prefer something else."

Magnus points to the clothes laid at the foot of the bed—cream-colored pants, thick, navy blue knitted sweater, and a puffy hooded jacket.

I look back at him curiously. "But these clothes aren't mine."

"Of course, they're yours. I bought them myself with the help of Bergdorf's personal stylist. Now, would you like me to help you dress up?"

"Hey, I'm an adult, and I'm perfectly capable of dressing myself," I protest, before sighing out, "but, thank you ... I appreciate it ... I really do."

Magnus seems in a hurry, so I get on the task of washing my face in cold water to help wake me up. Then I brush my teeth and tie my hair in a ponytail. I put on the new clothes that Magnus gave me, mumbling a thank you again, pleasantly surprised at how comfortable and well-fitted they are.

After putting on my gloves and boots, Magnus takes my hand and leads me out of the bedroom, down the bottom floor towards the back door, and out towards the long jetty leading out onto the ocean.

As we walk closer, I can see the jetty has been transformed, with lit candles right up until the end. And as I step on the wooden planks, I can also see what appear to be pink petals, scattered all over the deck.

My hand covers my mouth involuntarily, shocked at the sight before me.

"This is beautiful, Magnus! Did you do all of these while I was sleeping?"

"Yes, but I also had help."

"Who?"

"Uh, let's get to the end of the jetty first." Magnus is beginning to sound a little shaky, and I can't confirm if it's due to the cold weather, or nerves.

But then again, why would he be nervous?

Thankfully, it's not that windy, so the candles maintain their luminosity. But, it's still freezing outside—so cold, in fact, that there's snow over the sand. So I can just imagine how cold it must have been when it was pitch dark. By this time, the sun is beginning to illuminate the sky's expanse, giving the skyline beautiful and contrasting hues of orange and blue.

"Did you take me here to watch the sunrise?" I ask him, as we make our way towards the other end of the jetty, with me still shocked at how beautiful this whole setup is.

"Partly, yes," is all he answers back at me.

At the end of the railed jetty, there's a picnic blanket with a large wicker basket on top. There are also thick blankets piled on one side. I'm leaning against the railing, looking at the ocean, fascinated by the rainbow of colors that the imminent sunrise is creating. He takes one of the large blankets, and he stands behind me, with my back against his chest. Then using the blanket, he wraps us both in, forming a cozy cocoon.

It feels so comfortable, warm ... secure. And the lapping of the ocean waves adds to the element of serenity.

"You're probably wondering why I dragged you out of the bed, all the way here in the cold," Magnus says, his cheek leaning against the side of my head.

Smiling back at him, I answer, "Yes, and I'm also wondering what the candles and rose petals are for." Looking up to him, I continue, "But it's very lovely, so thanks to you and your mystery helper."

He gives me a lopsided smile, before looking ahead at the horizon.

"Regan helped out. I asked for her assistance last night."

Last night. *This* is what they were arguing about?

Now I'm getting more curious by the minute.

"I brought you here today to tell you that I made a mistake the other day, and I want to make it right."

Suddenly feeling nervous, yet curious at the same time, I ask, "What mistake are you talking about?"

"The other night, I didn't ask you a question properly. It wasn't fair to you, knowing how much love I have for you, to blurt out that question like it's some kind of a business transaction."

Oh.

Oh.

"We don't have to talk about that anymore, Magnus." I turn around, so I can face him. "Didn't you say we should drop that subject altogether?"

He looks me deeply in the eyes, his hand gently cupping my cheek. "I did say that because that wasn't the right way to ask someone whom I want to spend every waking day of my life with."

319

I stare back at him, puzzled, and unable to speak. He used the same words I've spoken that day I rejected his pseudo marriage proposal.

He continues, "I want to do this right, Isabelle. I've wanted to do this since the first time I realized there was no one else I want to share my life with."

He lets the blanket fall on the floor.

Then he proceeds to bend on one knee.

Oh my God.

"I promise to be that person who you can always run to, the one you can count on to make you laugh, and to remind you every day that you are beautiful, inside and out. But most of all, I want to be the man who will show you that you are loved, fully, and unconditionally." He takes a small box from his pocket, and I suck in my breath, stunned, my whole body beginning to shake.

"Autumn Isabelle Morrison Bridges, will you do me the honor of being my wife?" He opens the box and inside sits the most beautiful ring I've ever seen. And it is not just because of the large, oval diamond, or the emeralds on both sides of it.

The ring symbolizes the love given by this man who, without a doubt, has changed my life forever.

In a good way.

In the best way.

"Yes ..." I whisper, nodding, tears welling in my eyes. "A million times yes!"

He stands back up, his smile ... *oh my* ... it eclipses the brightness of the rising sun. He places the ring on my finger, then, he kisses that spot, before finally taking me in his arms.

"Thank you," he says, his head tucked in the curve of my neck, "I'm going to make you so happy, Isabelle."

Closing my eyes, I answer back, "I know you will. And I hope I can do the same. But are you really sure about this? It's going to be hard in the months to come. I just don't want you to get dragged down by—"

He cuts me off with a kiss, the kind of kiss that blows away all the doubts in my mind. By the time he pulls away, I'm already too giddy to finish my sentence.

"I never thought I'd ever feel this sort of love for anyone. And as pompous as it may sound, no woman has ever managed to bring that out of me. *You* brought that out, Isabelle. My love for you holds no bounds, so it means that whatever happens, good or bad, I will be here not just for you ... but also for Ethan. I will love you the way you deserved to be loved. Do you understand me?"

My head is now buried in his chest, overcome by the happiness I'm feeling this very moment, that I'm unable to form my feelings into words.

"Please nod if you understand, baby," he whispers.

I nod eagerly, raising my head up to meet the eyes I look forward to getting lost in, for the rest of my life.

Is this man for real? Is this really happening to me right now?

He sweeps the tears with his thumbs. "From now on, the only tears you'll shed will be happy ones. I'll make damn sure of it."

Still unable to speak, all I can do is nod once again.

Still holding me close, he turns me around so we can watch the sun make an appearance, welcoming the new day with its bright radiance.

Magnus doesn't have to explain why he chose this time of the day to propose to me, because I understand it completely.

It's the start of a new day ... a new beginning for both of us.

Our clean slate.

CHAPTER 25

Two Months Later

"Are you sure about this, Billie?" Michelle asks, holding my hand tightly.

"For the nth time, yes," I answer back at my obviously concerned friend.

"But you haven't been feeling well lately. Why don't you wait until you're feeling a little better before doing this?"

As much as it pains me to admit it, she's right. These past days, I've been feeling more lethargic than usual, and all the trips I had to and from the bathroom isn't helping either. I can't keep my food in, and even the tiniest morsel I eat comes back up in a bad way.

"You know I can't give up now, not when I'm feeling brave enough to go through with it. This is something I should have done years ago. And it's not just me anymore. Grace needs me, as much as I need her to back me up. And who knows how many other women Cooper had victimized? It needs to stop."

I hold her hands in mine, squeezing them gently. "Magnus is picking me up. He didn't really have to be there, but he insists on coming with me. Actually, I'm grateful that he is. My advocate's going to be at the station as well, but with Magnus there, I just feel a lot more secure."

"Okay, but just remember that after you make your statement, you need to see a doctor, okay? And will you please drink this ginger and mint tea I got for you? It'll help with the nausea."

"Yes, Mom," I answer back rolling my eyes, before continuing, "It could just be nerves. I have to make a statement on a rape that happened years ago, which means I have to relive the whole damn thing. Then there are those reporters and their cameras." I feel my hands go clammy as another onset of nausea is building up.

Clamping my mouth, I rush to the bathroom so I can dry heave on the toilet. I haven't eaten anything since yesterday. Then there's the constant urge to sleep, the mood swings, and the missed period. They all factor into something I'm just in too much denial to admit.

This is why I've been trying to avoid seeing Magnus for over a week now, citing a bad case of stomach flu as an excuse. It sounds unsexy enough to turn him off, but it doesn't seem to deter him one bit. I'm just glad that he's sticking around.

I also made the decision to quit my job. I need to focus on this case, and it's not fair for Helen and Chris if the shop gets any negative attention. I had to explain everything to Helen before I handed in my resignation. But what surprised me was that there wasn't even an iota of judgment in her. She even told me that once the asshole gets jail time, I'll always have a place to work for if I want to return.

And yes, she declined RCT Group's offer, and not after saying a few choice words to the representative of the company.

What can I say, Helen's a bad ass.

Michelle stoops down and massages my back, pulling the hair away from my face. "You still have time before Magnus arrives. Would you like me to get the box?"

Wiping my mouth with the back of my hand, I shake my head from side to side, "No. It's just gonna add to my anxiety. I might do it tomorrow, when he's not around. I want to do the test without added pressure."

I stand up to wash my mouth off over the basin. "He just came back from Japan. Then he's flying tomorrow afternoon for Texas." I turn to her with a wary smile. "My dad finally sold the company to Grant Corp."

Michelle's eyes widen in surprise. "Holy shit, it happened! Did the engagement clinch it?"

"Magnus said it played a part, and my father's desperate not to get the company in any deeper with the Thorntons. I also know it's my father's last attempt to connect with me. He's dying, Michelle." My voice cracks, as I try to maintain some composure.

Daddy's cancer has gotten worse, and there's nothing the doctors can do. I know that his sickness won't wait until this whole rape case is over.

But for some reason, I still can't bring myself to catch that plane and see him.

Until recently.

"Magnus is flying back there again, after the end of the week. I plan to take Ethan and fly back to Texas with him. After all that's happened, I want my father to meet his grandchild. I need to at least give that moment to him before he passes."

"He's going to be so happy, Billie."

"I hope so. When my parents turned their backs on me, I never thought for one second that maybe they were in over their heads too. I think they have realized their shortcomings. I was just so focused on my resentment towards them to see that they're as stuck in quicksand as I was."

Michelle doesn't say anything, only hearing me out.

"I promised myself that before I marry Magnus, I want to be able to wipe the slate clean and start my new life with my past where it belongs … in my past. I don't want to look back there anymore."

"You won't have to, once Cooper's thrown in jail," she muses.

"I know. But it's not gonna be easy."

"Nothing good ever is, baby girl. But I'm proud of you. I really am."

"Thanks, babe. I'm pretty damn proud of myself too," I beam, making us both giggle. "I think I'm going to need that tea now."

My nerves start building up on the drive to the police station. I didn't even notice that my leg was jerking up and down, until I feel Magnus's hand on my thigh.

"Sorry. I'm doing that thing again with my leg, huh? This whole thing's just too nerve-wracking."

"You don't have to do this if you don't want to," he tells me earnestly.

"I know I don't have to. But I need to. Thanks for being here with me, though. I know you left a conference in Tokyo early so you can accompany me today." I lace my fingers with his, loving how large his hand is, compared with mine.

"This is more important than a bunch of suits showing me charts and numbers." Magnus tips my chin up. "I'm going to decrease the number of business trips I'm making from now on. I'm so used to being hands-on, but that's going to change. I want to be here for you."

"You don't have to do that. I understand the nature of your job. To some extent, my father was the same, except you're running a bigger empire than his."

He chuckles, before kissing my temple. "*I* want to make the changes, not because I have to, but because I love you."

"Babe ..." I sigh out, extremely touched by what he said.

He smiles back, but as soon as he looks past me and out the car window, his smile disappears. There is a large group of reporters, congregating outside the station.

Since the news broke out nationwide that Magnus Grant's fiancée—the daughter of a Texas construction tycoon—came out accusing rape against her former childhood sweetheart who's a Texas senator's son, Cooper Thornton Jr., the media latched on it like a pack of rabid dogs. They've started swarming outside the precinct, the Grant Corp building, even camping outside Magnus's abode.

And why won't they, when my story sounds like a real-life soap opera?

It's crazy, and they can be very demanding with their questions. I know this is to be expected because this has blown to a high-profile case. But I didn't ask for this part. All I want, like his other victim, Grace, is for Cooper to go to jail and pay for the crimes that he committed against us.

Alex parks the car in front of the station. Then Magnus instructs him to help with the crowd control. Magnus gets out first, leaving the door open for me to step out. He's blocking the reporters from coming too close to me, while Alex urges them to step back to give us room. And all the while, Magnus's eyes are locked on mine, offering me his hand to take. We make it through the throng of media without saying a word, with Magnus's arm wrapped protectively around me, and Alex, along with a couple of police officers, paving our way. The district attorney is at the door, with my advocate standing next to him. We head inside the precinct where the chief detective who's investigating the case is already waiting.

"Thank you for coming in, Miss Morrison. Are you ready to make your statement today?"

I look up at Magnus, who gives me an encouraging smile. I turn back to the detective, nodding firmly, "Yes. Yes, I'm ready."

I never imagined that narrating and reliving every single excruciating detail I can remember from my whole ordeal eight years ago can be such a horrible, yet a liberating experience in the end.

The DA reassures me that I have a strong case. This and the

fact that Grace Peterson is making her own statement back in Texas are enough to build a case on a solid ground, even against someone as influential as Cooper Thornton Jr.

I told Grace, during one of our recent Skype sessions, that I'll be coming over to Dallas to finally meet her in the flesh. Without her, I'd probably never go through with this. Her courage gave me courage, and I hope that what we're both doing will give Cooper's other victims, if there are anymore, to stand up to him and refuse to be afraid any longer.

After giving my statement, Magnus finally takes me back home, but he tells me he has some issues to attend to, which he has to do from his place. So after he drops me off at home, he promises to see me first thing in the morning. Looking out of the window, I notice that Jacob is already waiting for me outside.

After Magnus told him about our engagement, Jacob must have realized that there's definitely a clear line drawn between us that he can no longer cross. And although Jacob kept the friendly banter, the flirting has come to a halt.

There was a time when I wondered what it would be like if Jacob and I did something about the chemistry between us. But that was only once and it was fleeting. I just hope that he eventually finds the right person for him.

But if that person has those stupid *rules* like he does, maybe he's not really looking for a serious relationship.

Or maybe he hasn't met that woman yet.

Magnus gives me a kiss that I know I'll remember for the rest of the day, before handing me over to Jacob. Both men talk about catching up on the weekend, then after leaving me another kiss, Magnus heads back to the city.

That leaves Jacob and me, standing awkwardly next to each other.

"How'd it go?" Jacob asks.

"Harrowing, but I feel so much better after."

As I walk towards the brownstone, Jacob places a hand on my arm. "Hey, have you had lunch yet? Had to ask, since you came straight from the precinct."

My stomach rumbles at his suggestion, and yet, I'd be stupid to eat anything since I'd probably throw it up anyway. I even had to tell Magnus I was too tired to eat on the way here so he won't suspect anything unconfirmed.

326

"Nah, I've got some food in the fridge if I get hungry."

"You better get inside," he advises, nodding over a couple of vans parked close by, with their network insignia on the sides. "Looks like the press found you."

"But I need to pick up Ethan and Tasha soon."

"I'll pick them up. You need to go inside. Now." With a hand on my back, he leads me inside the building, checking outside, before closing the door behind him.

Once inside the safety of my apartment, I walk towards the windows with a view of the street. "How the hell did they find me?"

"Quite easy. Your address is a public domain, so unfortunately, all they need is Google, then, boom!" Jacob sits on the couch, propping his legs on the coffee table.

"Coffee?" I call out as I approach the kitchen.

"No, thanks. You said you had something to eat, right?" He comes to the kitchen and opens the fridge, takes a bowl of leftover pasta, and places it inside the microwave.

He doesn't need to be around as much nowadays since Nathan agreed to the security system being installed all over his building. This house is a fortress now, thanks to Jacob and Magnus.

But I also like that, whenever Jacob's in my house, he feels comfortable enough to make himself at home. And I welcome any chance to have his company.

Without thinking, I start fiddling with my engagement ring, staring into space as I recall that day Magnus proposed. Then I hear the *ding* of the microwave, breaking me out of my reverie. That's when I notice Jacob staring at the ring, then at me. I let my hands fall to my sides, and he smiles back sheepishly.

"You got yourself a good man, Billie," Jacob says, as he takes the bowl out of the microwave.

"Thanks ... how was he, you know, when he was married to Martine?"

Jacob shakes his head. "Trust me, you don't want to know."

"Why not? All he basically told me was that he worked too hard, so the marriage eventually fell apart. But they've been together for so long before they got married."

"I only met them while we were at the uni. Back then, Magnus wasn't the romantic type, so I can only assume he was the same in high school here in America. I don't even recall him proposing. It was just like a natural progression for them, sort of like the next step for them as a couple." He offers me some of the pasta, and I lightly wave him off so he can finish the whole thing.

"But I've got to hand it to him. He was a loyal husband. His only mistress was his work. But look where that hard work brought him."

I nod back, fully agreeing with him. He does work hard, but I admire that in him. In fact, I find his drive quite sexy.

"What about Martine?"

"She's a bitch."

"No shit, Sherlock," I answer, laughing. "I got to experience that firsthand."

"Well, she broke Magnus when she kept that baby a secret. Who knew how things would've turned out if she had told him about the child? To this day, he's blaming himself over losing the baby."

Oh ... no.

How did I not see that? Of course, Magnus finds it hard to let go of Martine for good because of the guilt he feels when they lost the baby. But that's not his fault. None of that is his fault.

What if the redemption he seeks lies inside of me?

I need to find out as soon as possible.

"You should probably pick up Ethan now, Jacob," I tell him, trying to be as casual as possible without appearing suspicious.

Jacob nods, saying, "Will do," as he finishes off the last forkfuls of pasta.

As soon as Jacob is out the door, I hurry to my room to take the box out of my underwear drawer. One box has three pregnancy test sticks inside. I pee on each stick, grateful that I drank enough water to provide for all three tests.

There's a ten minute wait for the results, so I'm pacing back and forth, checking the same watch that Jacob gave me. On one hand, I'm wishing Michelle's here with me right now to help me through this, but on the other hand, I'm also grateful that no one else knows about this, at least for now.

This is the longest ten minutes of my life.

When the time finally comes, I rush back to the bathroom where I left the test sticks near the sink. I pick up all three, checking, and cross-checking the results several times, as the pounding of my heart increases in strength by the second. The results on all three sticks are the same.

Holy. Shit.

As if on autopilot, I hide the test sticks where no one will see. I make myself a mug of hot chocolate because this is definitely one of those moments when I need one mug, or three.

Maybe I should call Magnus and tell him over the phone.

No. This kind of news needs to be told face-to-face.

Tomorrow. I'll tell him tomorrow morning. Yes. I'll think of a creative way to tell him the news. And he needs to know first, before I announce it to anyone else.

Or maybe, I should confirm with a doctor first?

No, we can confirm with the doctor together.

But maybe it's better if I go first, in case it's a bad news.

Stop. Overthinking. This.

I sit on the couch, switching the TV on to the news channel. I need this diversion. Maybe it will help me from pushing my mind into overload.

My thoughts run to a complete halt when I catch a glimpse of myself on the TV screen with Magnus, our hands held together, as we were about to get inside the police precinct this morning to give my official statement. Since the time when the news about the rape started to circulate, I avoided watching the news whenever Ethan was around. Fortunately, this one comes out while Ethan is still in school. The last thing I want is my son asking questions and knowing the truth about my past and his father, at such a tender age. I just hope that when I do tell him, he'll be able to understand my reasons ... that all I wanted was to protect him from the ugliness of the actual truth.

A short while after, the newsreader decides to divert back to the reporter who is doing a live feed in front of Magnus's apartment building. I roll my eyes at the TV, completely annoyed at the circus they're bringing to Magnus's part of the neighborhood.

But what I see next on the screen leaves me cold. Magnus comes out of his building, his expression brooding as always. And right behind him, Martine saunters out, looking like a million bucks, with a smile on her face to rival that of a Cheshire cat. They head straight to a black Mercedes sedan, where Magnus opens the door for her. But then, Martine throws her arms around Magnus, then Magnus starts whispering something to her, with his lips so close to her ear that he's practically kissing her cheek. The reporter decides to amp up the controversy, implying that with all the chaos, courtesy of his fiancée's rape case, Magnus must have taken solace in the arms of his ex-wife. The segment ends with the reporter stating that this is breaking news, that there might already be trouble brewing in paradise between us.

I think I'm going to be sick.

No, I'm *literally* going to be sick.

I run to the bathroom, ignoring the sudden ringing of the phone, and I throw up. I throw up the only contents of my stomach—the hot chocolate I just drank.

Once I'm done, I wash my face, rinsing the gross aftertaste from my mouth. Then with fire inside of me, I grab my purse, my beanie, and sunglasses. As I'm heading out the door, before I can even change my mind, I send Jacob and Michelle a text message telling them I left to go to Magnus's and will be back. Whether or not I'll be back as Magnus's fiancée is something I'm not sure of.

All I know is I need to see him today.

And based on how my hormones are going on overdrive right now, someone's going to get hurt, and it, sure as hell, won't be me.

There's a missed call and a text message from Magnus: *Jacob told me you're at home. Please answer your phone, or I'll drive over there right now.*

How is he going to lie his way out of this one now?

Not bothering to reply, I toss my phone inside my purse.

There are no cabs in sight, and I'm not going to hang around waiting for a cab, especially since there are media vans parked nearby. The subway is not that far, and it's probably a better idea to stay underground so I can avoid a punch-up with any nosy reporter who comes close.

The café a couple of doors down from where I live, has a back door that leads to another street. Since we're friends with the owner, Tyler, and since news broke out about my rape case, he probably has seen how the media are hounding us. So I head straight to the café, and when I ask Tyler's permission to allow me to exit through the back door, he just lets me go through without any hesitation.

I check around the next street, relieved that my escape plan is working. I start making my way in the direction of the subway, determined to get to the city as quickly as possible, but trying not to get too anxious since that's not wise in my condition. I'm not even considering that Magnus might be making his way to my place. I refuse to just sit around and wait for him.

If this were months ago, I'd probably do what I did before. I would have broken it off and ran away with Ethan in tow. But I'm not running anymore, at least not away from him. I'm running straight to him, and I will confront him and make him choose, once and for all.

It's either lose Martine, or lose me.

My hand instinctively covers my belly.

This isn't just about me and him, anymore.

From now on, I'm choosing fight over flight.

I'm so lost in my thoughts that I don't even notice a van following me. I briefly turn my head, and I let out a curse when I notice the van has an insignia of some obscure TV network on its sides.

Damn it, these people can't be outsmarted!

I turn the corner, and the van does the same.

This is the last thing I need right now. Thank goodness, the subway's entry is just on the other side of the road. I attempt to cross the road, but in an instant, the van accelerates and blocks my path, practically inches from running me over.

Oh, this has gone far enough!

My blood is boiling as I slam my hand on the side door. "You almost ran me over, you asshole!"

I'm sure if this street has more people outside, they'd hear me and think I'm some kind of a nutjob.

The sliding door of the van opens, and I find the inside of it empty, except for two men … and they're both wearing masks.

Oh shit!

I try to step back, to scream, but one of them drags me in and puts a damp cloth in my mouth, shoving a sack over my head, and throwing me on the floor of the van. I can't see a thing, and now I'm in panic. I try kicking them, throwing punches in the air, hoping I'd make contact somehow. But one of them sits on my legs, crushing me against his weight so I can barely move. The other person ties my wrists together, and it's so tight that it feels like my skin is being ripped apart. I try to scream once again, but my voice is now muffled, and with every breath I take in, my whole body becomes increasingly numb.

I can hear them talking with each other, then one of them picks my head up and holds it close to his mouth. It terrifies me, but my body's starting to feel like lead that struggling seems impossible.

"You let my boss down, bitch. You shouldn't have started something that you know ain't gonna end well." Then he flings my head back on the floor.

No ... no.

Oh God, not again!

The same words echo over and over in my head. I try to fight them off with every ounce of strength I have left. The last thing I remember is a sharp sting on the side of my head, then, everything goes black.

I never thought I'd come to that point where I'm wishing that I'm just in the middle of another nightmare, that I'll wake up very soon, and that everything will be back to normal.

As I start to come to, it becomes clearer that I'm not in my own bed, that my head is still covered with a sack, and all I can see through the tiny holes of the sack are vague silhouettes of inanimate objects. My hands and my feet are tied so closely together that my legs are bending backwards, like an animal about to be slaughtered. And judging from the cold air on my skin, I've been stripped of my clothing and left with just my underwear on.

But I'm not waking up from my old nightmare. I'm waking up to this reality.

The tape on my mouth is a little loose, so with every strength that I can muster, I blow the hell out of it until the tape partly comes off. With tears in my eyes, I start screaming, ignoring the way it's making my throat raw. I just hope that someone can hear me from the outside, and I can get help.

But after what feels like an eternity, I hear no one calling back at me. Who the hell am I kidding? I'm obviously someplace where no one can hear my cries.

I shouldn't have let my emotions overrun me. I shouldn't have left without Jacob. I shouldn't have been this stupid.

My baby. What if they hurt my baby?

I hear the door open, and I hold my breath, as if keeping motionless will stop whoever it is from coming near me. Through the sack, I can see a tall figure walking purposely towards me.

"Who's there?" I croak out.

"Well, I'm offended. I mean after all, I am the father of your son, right?"

I knew it.

That motherfucker.

"He is not your son, Cooper. He will *never* be your son!" I feel my anger rising, my blood pumping in my ears. "Do you hear me? He will never be your so—"

My words are cut off when his hand wraps around my neck, his grip tightening, making me choke. And just like that, he lets me go, and as I try to gasp for air, the sack keeps getting sucked in my mouth, choking me even further.

He sits at the edge of the mattress. "You should have just kept your pretty little mouth shut, shug."

"How ... how many were we?" I sputter out, trying a different tactic.

"How many what? You know a gentleman never tells, Autumn."

"I'm not Autumn anymore. And take this sack off. I know it's you, Cooper!"

"You *think* you know who I am. I've been wanting to do this since your asshole boyfriend ... oh, sorry, *fiancé*, threw a couple of lucky punches at me."

"He beat the shit out of you, and you deserved that, and more ... ow!" His hand makes contact on the side of my head, the same side that still hurts when I was taken by his cohorts.

"Shut up!" he yells, moving away. "He's taken everything that supposed to be mine! He's taken your father's company, he's taken you, and now he wants to take my son. Deny it all you want, baby, but he has the Thornton blood in him. Why'd you even report me, huh? You have nothing on me. Not. A. Thing. And now my father's threatening to disown me if I don't take care of your shit!"

"Your father is as much of a criminal as you are."

I hear him laugh harshly. "Maybe it's part of our genes. You know, a legacy I can pass on to Ethan."

That's when my anger rises again. "You leave my son out of this, you hear me? You leave him out, or I'll—"

"Or you'll what, *Autumn*? That's right, you'll always be my *Autumn*." He comes back and places his hand in-between my legs. I try to clamp my legs shut, but he forces them open, hurting me more in the process.

"And just so you know, you're my favorite among all of them." I scream out aloud when I feel his fingers invade me. And when he's done, he shuts my legs closed and flings them aside, turning me onto the other side. "Mmm, oh yes, still the sweetest one of them all."

My stomach turns, an onset of nausea threatening to come out from his sick act.

"I'm gonna kill you, you motherfucker," I sob, "so help me God, I'm going to kill you."

Just then, I hear a commotion coming from outside. Where exactly, I'm not sure. But there are lots of men screaming, and then … oh shit, gunfire! I try to scream out, but he takes the sack off my face and sticks duct tape over my mouth, but not before I catch a glimpse of his face.

Even in that second, I can see that Cooper looks awful, stressed, and a lot older-looking than I remember … just like the recent footages of him on TV.

Good.

If I die now, at least I know that I made him suffer somehow.

I continue to scream out with all my might, even after he puts the sack back over my head, even with my taped mouth. The noise outside is getting closer. That's when I notice Cooper's form take something from a table near the door, and judging from the shape, it appears to be a gun.

Oh shit, he's got a gun, and he's aiming it at the door.

He's owned guns since he was thirteen. He even showed me his collection a few times before, so I know exactly what he's holding … his favorite revolver, and it's a big one. Whoever comes through that door has little to no chance of surviving because Cooper will shoot without hesitation.

If you're listening right now, God, please don't let Cooper win.

Please, God. Don't let this spawn of Satan win.

For a moment, there's only silence. It's so quiet that I can actually hear my own breathing. Then I hear the doorknob turning, but it's followed by some gunshots, and judging from the flashes of light coming from Cooper's firearm, he's doing the shooting. The shots are so loud that my own screams are muted.

Cooper runs out of bullets, and his silhouette appears to be reloading a gun. And just as he's about to aim at the door, someone bursts through, practically breaking it off its hinges. Then he knocks

Cooper on the floor, and all I can see are two large figures fighting, their silhouettes muddled by the faint light. I can hear two men grunting, and the sounds of punches making contact on muscles, and of bones possibly cracking.

I struggle to try to get rid of my binds, but they seem to tighten even further, hurting my wrists further in the process. So I scream once again, not stopping even when my voice is getting too raspy.

Is this a rescue? This has to be a rescue. Maybe there were witnesses who saw me being kidnapped, and they called the cops.

Or maybe this is Jacob.

Oh shit. Jacob. What if this is Jacob?

"You will never hurt her again … ever!" I hear one of them roar out.

And then I hear one gunshot.

Then another.

Then I hear a thud.

And then, silence.

But it's that voice.

It's not Cooper's, or Jacob's.

"Magnus? Magnus! Magnus, I'm here," I scream out, over and over.

Nothing. There's no movement coming from both of them.

I don't see Magnus's silhouette coming for me.

No. No. No. No.

Please answer me, Magnus. *Please. Please. Please!*

"Magnus! I'm right here. Please come and get me. Please! Magnus! Magnus!"

Nothing.

The only sound I hear is the constant swishing of blood in my ears.

With one last deep breath, I bellow out, and all the anger, the anguish, and the complete and utter helplessness I'm feeling inside, emanates from my very core.

I lost him … I can't lose him …

You can't leave me, Magnus. Please.

I'm right here.

CHAPTER 26

Beep ... Beep ...

Why am I hearing beeps?

The inaudible sounds of people talking in the background and the public address system announcing doctors' names confirm my suspicions.

Surely, I must have died.

If not, then I surely deserve to.

I did this.

Because of me, he's gone.

I was too stubborn, too caught up with distrust, jealousy, and anger, that I broke protocol and made myself vulnerable to Cooper and his goons.

And now, Magnus is dead.

I must have whimpered out aloud, because I hear Michelle's voice speak, "She's awake. Quick, call the doctor!" she instructs someone else in the room.

It hurts to even open my eyes, but my tears are breaking through, flowing down my cheeks. Then my mouth cracks open as I call out Magnus's name.

Oh God, it hurts so much.

I lost the love of my life ... the father of this child inside of me.

And what if I lost this baby too?

What did I ever do to lose so much in my life?

"Magnus ..." I rasp out once again.

The relief on Michelle's blurry face is replaced with concern, as she holds my hand. "Baby girl, please, just take it easy. You need to rest. Try not to talk yet. The doctor will be here very soon."

"I killed him, didn't I? It's my fault, he's dead," I sob, fresh tears falling.

"What are you talking about, baby girl?" Michelle asks softly.

"Miss Morrison, you're awake."

I struggle to turn towards the direction of the voice. I see a doctor with a clipboard, approaching my bed. Walking behind him is an equally relieved Nathan, and beside him is my son.

My boy. He's okay.

At least he's okay.

"Ethan," I whisper out, and he runs to me, hugging me tightly with a smile on his face and tears in his eyes.

"I love you, Mommy," Ethan says in a muffled voice, as his face is tucked against the crook of my arm.

I still have Ethan. And I survived, given another chance to live, for my son.

I know that no matter how much I'm hurting, I *have* to stay strong for my son.

Michelle gently takes Ethan aside, with Nathan holding his hand so the doctor can check me. I look on, as Ethan is now hugging Michelle tightly, his shoulders shaking as he continues to cry, breaking my already withered heart at the sight.

"I'm Dr. Howard. So … how are you feeling right now?" the doctor asks kindly. I look up at him incredulously.

"Because of me, my fiancé was killed. How do you think I feel?"

The doctor looks puzzled at my reply. "Your fiancé is Mr. Magnus Grant, isn't that right?"

"Yes. Was," I sob out my answer, overwhelmed with debilitating grief.

"Miss Morrison, Mr. Grant isn't dead. He just came out of surgery. He's going to be alright."

I jerk my head up.

"Where is he? I need to see him." I sit up way too quickly that my head spins, and a feeling of nausea sets in.

That's when I'm reminded that this isn't just about me, or Magnus.

I place a protective hand over my belly. "I'm pregnant. I only found out."

The doctor nods, "Yes. We had to do a series of blood tests, and had to check if you were sexually assaulted as well. Thank goodness you weren't, and I hope that information helps. But I do want to talk to you about the baby."

My chest tightens, as I look up at him.

"You and your baby are fine. It appears you're eight weeks into the pregnancy, so I'm sure you know that the sooner you take folic acid, the better."

I'm nodding back, shocked, then too ecstatic to respond.

Two months.

My baby is two months old.

And the father of my baby is alive.

It's almost funny how I come from being at my lowest, to being ecstatic in just a matter of minutes.

"Please, doctor, I need to see Magnus. He doesn't know about the baby yet. I need to tell him," I plead.

He stares back, hopefully considering my plea. "Okay. I understand. But you need to rest first."

"Do I have any serious injuries? A head trauma?" I ask in panic.

"Thankfully, no, but you—"

"Then let me see my fiancé. Please, doctor, I need to see him."

He regards me thoughtfully. "I suppose if you let me get one of the nurses to assist you. Stay here."

"Thank you … thank you," I bubble over, my heart thumping so hard it feels like it's about to explode. He nods back, before walking out of the room.

As soon as the doctor is gone, Ethan, Michelle, and Nathan all walk back inside. Ethan runs straight to me, unwilling to let go, until a nurse walks in with a wheelchair. I tell Ethan that I'm going to see Magnus, and that it's important that he waits for me in my room, with Nathan and Michelle. My son has been through a big scare of losing her mother, not once, but twice. He shouldn't have to go through another scare with Magnus. Thankfully, he agrees, even trying to help me into the seat. I give my son a hug and a kiss on the forehead before the nurse wheels me out.

We ride the elevator two floors up, and my anticipation to see the love of my life leaves me growing impatient by the second. We finally make it to Magnus's room, and the first people I see is Carlton standing outside with Gerald. They're hesitant at first, but they slowly make their approach towards me.

Carlton speaks first, sounding contrite, "Magnus is going to be okay. He's been asking for you as soon as he starts coming to from his anesthesia."

I nod back, "I'd like to see him now, please."

They let me through, and the nurse wheels me in his room.

As soon as I lay my eyes on him, my heart sinks, and fresh tears start to well up in my eyes.

From afar, Magnus is lying still on the hospital bed, his eyes closed, looking tranquil in his sleep. Yet I know that the tranquillity is deceiving, because as the nurse wheels me closer to him, all I can see is my rock, attached to a machine through a mass of tubes, his stomach heavily bandaged, looking utterly helpless.

It just shatters me inside.

I'm so focused on Magnus that I didn't notice Miranda standing next to him, nor Regan sitting at the far end of the room, nor Jacob who's standing at the foot of the bed with a sling on his left arm.

They are all staring at me, unspeaking, waiting for my next move. With still-wobbly legs, I push myself to stand up so I can take Magnus's hand on mine. His skin feels warm, and I can't help but smile because the warmth on his skin means his heart is beating, helping filter and cleanse the blood coursing through his veins. And even with the tubes attached to him, with one eye swollen black and blue, all I see is his beauty, both inside and out.

My beautiful man.

My hero.

All I want is to be alone with him, to lie down by his side and not leave him until we're ready to go home.

Miranda gives me a hug, and Regan soon follows, both telling me that he's going to be okay, and that they're relieved that I was rescued before anything unimaginable happened to me. I nod in autopilot, my thoughts and my eyes focused only on Magnus. Eventually, both women, including my nurse, excuse themselves and leave the room. Jacob stays, approaching me so we are standing side-by-side in silence.

"I'm so sorry," I finally whisper, tears rolling down my face. "This wouldn't have happened if I wasn't so stubborn. This is all my fault."

"Don't work yourself up about it, Billie. This is no one's fault but Cooper's."

"What happened in there, Jacob?" My hands begin to shake, my voice faltering, as I recall the sounds, the violent silhouettes, not to mention the way I was degraded by Cooper.

He sighs, holding me upright. "Remember that watch I gave you? When you ran off, I managed to trace your location using GPS. They may have broken your phones, but they never thought about the watch. Cooper's men were playing poker for fuck's sake when we got there, and your watch was right on the table, probably as part of a wager for all I know. But anyway, Magnus knew you were going to see him, but when you didn't answer back his calls, we got worried. I wanted to call the police, but Magnus adamantly refused. He couldn't afford to take any chances. He needed to do this for you, and I had to respect that. He met me with Alex, a block away from your location. It was an empty house, an hour or so upstate. They soundproofed your room so that nobody could hear your screams. They had this planned for a while, I'd say. Even before the news came out about the rape charge."

Jacob stops for a moment, before continuing, "When we got in the house, I took care of Cooper's men. They shot first, so I merely retaliated. I didn't kill any of them either. I don't kill unless it's absolutely necessary. One of the injured men pointed us to where you were kept. Alex kept watch of Cooper's men while Magnus went straight for you, against my instructions. I followed him, but that's when I heard the shots coming from the room. I didn't want Magnus armed because I didn't want to expose him to more troubles, so I knew it wasn't him doing the shooting. Magnus got lucky because he has quick reflexes, so he managed to avoid the bullets … all except for one. But by then his adrenalin was so high, he didn't even notice. Magnus is a strong man, trust me, I know what he's capable of. When there was a short break of silence, he tore through that door, and he knocked Cooper down. I don't know what happened after that, maybe they struggled with the gun, but Magnus somehow managed to aim that gun at Cooper, and he pressed the trigger. The first bullet hit Cooper's shoulder, the second one hit a main artery, and he was instantly killed. I discovered Magnus slumped beside Cooper. He must have realized his injury as soon as the adrenalin began to dissipate. The bullet hit his stomach, and it wasn't a through-and-through, that's why he needed to go to surgery. I managed to stem the bleeding before calling 911."

My hand clamps over my mouth, shocked at the lengths Magnus went through to rescue me. It could have gone differently.

A cold chill runs through my spine at the thought of what could have been.

I turn to Jacob, giving him a hug. "Thanks to you and Alex for helping to rescue me, and for saving Magnus's life. But what

---

340

happens now that Cooper's dead? Surely no one is going to jail, right?"

"I was hired to be your bodyguard, and so was Alex. We were just doing our job and our guns are registered. Magnus wasn't armed, and in hindsight, maybe I should've given him one. But it is self-defense on Magnus's part. There's no case to build against neither of us, but we still need to give our statements to the police."

As I listen to Jacob's retelling of Cooper's death, I know that it's probably human nature to feel some sort of grief for any kind of loss of another human being.

But right now, I feel nothing but relief.

His death meant I'm finally free.

And so is Grace and the other nameless and faceless victims of Cooper's viciousness. Justice has been served. And I know if his victims are to be given a chance, they will thank both Jacob and Magnus because they did not only save me, but all these other women as well.

I turn back to Magnus, and I'm suddenly overcome with extreme love and gratitude. I bend down, whispering, "I'm right here Magnus. I'm right here because of you. Thank you, my love. Thank you."

I sweep a few strands of hair that fell from his forehead. As soon as I do, Magnus begins to stir sluggishly, making my heart leap from my chest. When he finally opens his eyes, those beautiful blue eyes of his focus straight at me.

Jacob uses this as his cue to leave the room, so we can have some privacy.

"Isabelle, he's gone," Magnus's voice is coarse, as he struggles to get the words out. "I killed Cooper."

I nod my head, "Shhh, I know, baby. And I have to thank you for that," I tell him softly, cupping his cheek with my hand. "He needed to be stopped, and *you* stopped him. I'm just sorry that it had to happen in your hands." My voice breaks, suddenly feeling intense guilt, feeling responsible for placing him in that position.

He shakes his head sluggishly, "Don't be. I would do it again for you."

"Jacob said you won't be charged. I hope that's true."

He sniffs, "Even if I did, I won't accept the charges without a fight. And the Thorntons will keep this as quiet as possible. I have a feeling that their family's reputation is more important than their son's life."

My eyes drift down on his bandages. "I thought I lost you," I choke out, trying to keep my composure, but failing miserably. "Imagine my relief when I found out you're alive. I just want you to know how grateful I am that you came for me. You protected me the way you promised you would … you even took a bullet to save me."

I brush my thumb on his cheek, my tears blurring my view of his face.

He needs to know right now.

This man *deserves* to know.

"It's not just me you saved, Magnus. You saved … you saved our baby."

"Our … baby?" Magnus's eyes widen at the realization, and the corner of his mouth slowly lifts into a smile. "You're pregnant?" he asks.

I nod back, slowly starting to smile myself. "We must've conceived as soon as we got back together. But just so we're clear, I was on the pill, so this isn't some scheme to pin you down."

He chuckles softly, "I know, my temptress. But I pinned you down, long before our baby was conceived."

Our baby.

Those two words give me the push to continue, "Well, I'm eight weeks along. The doctor just told me, right before I came here to see you. But I knew. I found out about my pregnancy, and that's why, when I saw you and Martine, I knew you had to know, so you can make a choice. But on the way I was …" my voice trails off, unwilling to revisit that horrific moment of my abduction.

That's when I feel Magnus try to squeeze my hand. "Isabelle, I'm so sorry you had to witness Martine and me on TV. I knew you'd be at home so I tried to call you so I can explain. But you were already too upset to the point that you left on your own. I can't take that moment back, but I'll do my best to dispute what you saw. And I'll start by telling you that what you witnessed on TV was just Martine saying good-bye. She's flying back to London, and this time it'll be for good."

"I was ready to fight for you, Magnus. I was ready to fight for us."

He smiles, and it's the kind of smile that I know is solely meant for me. "Fight for me? You didn't have to fight for something that's already yours."

Even recovering from a gunshot wound, he can still manage to make me blush. "I'm happy you said that. *Our* baby's happy you said that."

He tries to reach for my belly, but he's still too weak to do it. So I lean closer, guiding his hand until it's resting over my still-flat belly.

"Wow, I'm going to be a father. It's amazing." Magnus looks up to me. "You're amazing, Isabelle. Does this mean you're really staying put? No more running away when you get upset?"

My lips begin to tremble as fresh tears dribble down. "I'm never running away, Magnus. I promise, in the name of this family … *our* family." Bending down, I plant my lips on his knuckles and leave a tearful kiss. "Well, it's kind of impossible now, anyway, since I'll get larger every month," I chuckle shakily.

He laughs back, "I might need that in writing, you promising not to run. You know, just in case you forget? I hear pregnancy gives women amnesia," Magnus adds, winking slightly in an attempt to be playful, his voice no longer croaky but low and oh-so-smooth. "But if you do forget and you start running, I'll chase after your sexy, pregnant ass, and I'll tie you in our bed if I have to, and I'll remind you what you'll miss if you run again."

Oh. Okay, then.

It tightens my insides, just imagining what he just said.

I can't believe that my injured man can still manage to turn me on the way he just did right now.

I'm blaming this rush of desire for Magnus on the out-of-control hormones, my tremendous relief that he's alive, and my passionate, unequivocal love for him.

"Oh, you *will* get it in writing, you arrogant jerk," I retort, dipping my head until I'm grazing his lips. "It's called a marriage certificate. Hell, I'll even get the words tattooed on myself if I have to."

He kisses me, before he asks, "And where will your tattoo be?"

"Well, Mr. Grant, you better recover real quickly, so you can personally help choose the prime real estate on my body."

He smirks against my lips, letting out a soft growl.

"Challenge accepted."

EPILOGUE

Magnus

"Shit! I'm going to be late," I mutter to myself while adjusting my tie, furious that I can't seem to get the fucking thing done right when I do wear one of these, practically every single day.

"Mate, let me help you out with that," Jacob says, with humor in his voice.

"I can handle it," I quip, playfully slapping his hand away. "What you need to worry about is to make sure the rings are in your damn pocket."

Jacob shows them to me. "See? I told you, I'm the best bloody best man that ever lived," he scoffs, before placing them back in the inside of his suit pocket. "And apparently, according to my girl, I'm the best bloody boyfriend that ever lived!"

"Right, if you say so." I scoff at Jacob. But deep inside I'm happy for him. I knew he felt an attraction with Isabelle. I wasn't blind. But he was wise enough to back off. And now, he found someone … and…well, their story is way too complicated to go into right now.

I'm just glad that my best friend — or as he says, *my good mate*, has finally found his match.

"Just relax. You're *only* getting married, no big deal," he jokes, trying to get a rise out of me.

That British fucker knows this is a *big* deal.

Today is the day that I'm marrying the love of my life.

My beautiful temptress.

It was eight amazing months in the making to finally get to this day.

We chose to wait until Isabelle had given birth to our perfect little girl, Reign Elizabeth Grant, because we want her physically with us when Isabelle and I finally say our wedding vows.

Reign has her mother's hair, just like Ethan's—a beautiful shade of amber, like the color of the leaves in the fall. Her eyes are blue, just like mine, and although it's still too early to see her personality, when she looks at me, there is no doubt whatsoever that she'll get whatever she wants. She has her father in the palm of her teeny tiny hand.

She's a princess. *My* princess.

And I'll make damn sure that everyone around her knows it.

I smile back at my reflection, unable to hide my happiness.

Isabelle and Ethan moved in with me as soon as I was ready to go home from the hospital, that many months ago. She took care of me ... nursed me to good health.

And as Isabelle's belly grew, I just fell even more in love with her.

In lust too. Definitely in lust.

We fucked every single day, then made love straight after.

And it was amazing every single time.

I didn't even need to take painkillers often. She was my drug, and I'm completely addicted. No rehab can cure this kind of addiction, and if I can shoot Isabelle up in my veins, I would.

Like a junkie in heat.

She doesn't know it yet, but after we're officially married, I'll be taking her home, and I'll carry her over the threshold.

Except the threshold is over an hour away, at the East Hamptons, where I bought our first family home.

But there's no way we're getting to our new home by car, not tonight. The helicopter is already waiting on the rooftop of our wedding venue.

Nothing but the best for my wife-to-be.

She'll probably give me shit for it, but on the inside, I know she'd love it.

She always seems more at peace whenever we're upstate, and we'll be a little closer to Michelle and Nathan, so I have no doubt that she'll be happy to make the house I bought, our home base. After all, it also fronts a private beach, it has a heated pool that Ethan and my little princess can swim in every season. I'm also getting a custom playground and basketball court built. There are great schools in the area, and it's not that far from the city. The house has enough rooms for when Isabelle's mother or her girlfriends want to pay us a visit.

Michael Bridges passed away after a long and painful battle with cancer, just three months after he reconciled with Isabelle. I think he was just waiting for that moment when Isabelle forgave him. It was hard on her for quite a while, but she's slowly learning to live her life with no regrets, which is no easy feat, with everything that's happened to her.

Isabelle and her mother are still rebuilding that bridge. Her mother stopped drinking excessively, and it may have a lot to do with her need to have a relationship with her grandkids. Isabelle doesn't know it yet, but I've flown her mother to New York to surprise her on our wedding. She did ask her mother to come, but she was initially hesitant, too ashamed at first because she treated her daughter too harshly back then. But after speaking with her myself, she finally came to realize that her shame was nothing compared to the joy she'd bring her daughter if she attends this special day.

As for me, well, life couldn't get any better. After I was dispatched from the hospital, I saw the change in the way Gerald and my father treated me. Despite all of my success, I know that my decision to branch out and not stay in the family business never sat well with my father. I suppose he saw his failure in my success. His jealousy reared its ugly head for so many years and even influenced my brother against me. But when the shooting happened and they thought they were going to lose me, everything changed. Now we can have conversations without ending up in arguments. Seeing me with Isabelle and her son must have brought back memories of how he was with my mother. Now, my father is off the booze as well, and he even makes time with his kids, with his family. He adores Isabelle and Ethan, like only a grandfather could. And he's already beginning to spoil Reign.

"Ready, mate?" Jacob calls out.

I nod back, smiling, my heart racing a thousand beats a minute with excitement and an ounce of impatience.

I'm ready, alright. Ready to finally make Isabelle my bride.

I just can't imagine living the rest of my life without her.

She doesn't know how much she saved me in so many ways, how grateful I am that she's in my life.

Yes, my life is almost perfect and all because Isabelle is in it.

And now with Ethan and Reign, my life is complete.

I finally feel complete.

What was that again? Oh yeah, that's right.

I've come full circle.

Full. Fucking. Circle.

**********THE END**********

AUTUMN REIGNS PLAYLIST

Music is a major player in my writing process, and for *Autumn Reigns*, I wanted to capture the angst and the pain felt by Magnus and Isabelle when they broke up, their tumultuous reunion, and the joy of finally having their happily ever after. I hope you'll enjoy listening to these songs as much as I did.

"Winter" ~ Daughter
"The City Never Sleeps" ~ Jason Walker
"It Must Have Been Love" ~ Kathleen Edwards
"1000 Times" ~ Sara Bareilles
"Rewind" ~ Diane Birch
"Breathe Again" ~ Sara Bareilles
"Sober" ~ Kelly Clarkson
"All I Wanted" ~ Paramore
"In My Veins" ~ Andrew Belle feat. Erin McCarley
"Not Over You" ~ Gavin McGraw
"Wherever You Go" ~ Ron Pope
"I Never Told You" ~ Colbie Caillat
"Make You Feel My Love" ~ Adele
"Mine" ~ Michael Shulte
"Human" ~ Christina Perri
"Run Every Time" ~ Gavin McGraw
"Before I Ever Met You" ~ Banks
"Only Love Can Hurt Like This" ~ Paloma Faith
"Safe and Sound" ~ Julia Sheer
"Salvation" ~ Gabrielle Aplin
"Arms" ~ Christina Perri
"Capri"~ Colbie Caillat
"Can't Help Falling in Love" ~ Ingrid Michaelson
"You Make It Real" ~ James Morrison
"Shake It Out" ~ Florence and the Machine

ACKNOWLEDGMENTS

Second book ... wow. To this day, I still can't believe I've written one novel, so it blows my mind that I've finished writing my second one, considering I've had a lot more obstacles, both personal and professional ones, to overcome this time around.

I know I wouldn't have even made it this far, if it were not for the support of my family and friends. To my husband and hot PA, who had taken on more responsibilities in the household, on top of his full-time work just to make it easier for me when I needed to write. And whenever I hit a wall and I'm pulling my hair out in frustration, he's the first to offer encouragement, positive energy ... and sushi. He knows that nothing eases my pain, more than a good hug and a good serving of sushi.

To my kids, thank you for continuing to understand that when Mum needs quiet time to write, that means hanging out with Daddy, or going outside of the house to play. You guys believe in me so much that I hope I'll be able to live up to it sooner, rather than later.

To the ladies of A.K.A Book Harlots, especially Kellie, who is probably my one and only fangirl, as well as someone I'm happy to call my friend, thank you for your continued support of my work and for your words of encouragement. I will always be grateful for bloggers and fans like you who are fearless enough to promote authors like me because we're still trying to find our place in the literary world ... and it can be a scary world out there.

To my parents, who have supported me from day one, thank you for the unconditional love and support. Mum, you are an amazing editor. Thank you for continuing to make this whole process of editing my work, less awkward as possible. I'm still learning as a writer, and your feedback will always be helpful to me.

To my beta readers, Tonette and Kitch, love you both. Thank you, thank you, thank you. You ladies are awesome and I truly appreciate your honesty.

Lastly, I'd like to give my thanks to the readers who took that chance to read my first book, *Autumn Falls*, and have waited patiently for *Autumn Reigns*. Thank you for your support and for spreading the love by recommending my work to others.

This isn't the last you'll hear from me.

Until next time!

ABOUT THE AUTHOR

I am a purveyor of romance, of tragedy, of laughter, of sassy women and swoon-worthy men. My goal from this day forward is to make my reader's heart skip a beat or two. Actual skipping is optional, but most welcome.

I am married to a wonderful man, and a mother to two gregarious children. I love to cook, read, bake, and run when I have any spare time, the latter of which, in- between my full-time job, house chores, and writing, is well, almost nonexistent. Yes, my life is busy, but I wouldn't have it any other way. And once they invent a pill that can make people function relatively well without sleep, then my life will be absolutely perfect!

If you would like to know more about me and my upcoming novels, please check out the links below. Your feedback and comments are more than welcome. It would be lovely to hear from all of you!

Website: esmariawrites.wordpress.com
Facebook: https://www.facebook.com/ESMariaAuthor
Email: author@esmaria.com

www.ingramcontent.com/pod-product-compliance
Lightning Source LLC
Chambersburg PA
CBHW020243200626
46816CB00001BA/103